The
Saddlemaker's
Wife

The
Saddlemaker's
Wife

EARLENE FOWLER

BERKLEY PRIME CRIME, NEW YORK

THE BERKLEY PUBLISHING GROUP
Published by the Penguin Group
Penguin Group (USA) Inc.
375 Hudson Street, New York, New York 10014, USA
Penguin Group (Canada), 90 Eglinton Avenue East, Suite 700, Toronto, Ontario M4P 2Y3, Canada
(a division of Pearson Penguin Canada Inc.)
Penguin Books Ltd., 80 Strand, London WC2R 0RL, England
Penguin Group Ireland, 25 St. Stephen's Green, Dublin 2, Ireland (a division of Penguin Books Ltd.)
Penguin Group (Australia), 250 Camberwell Road, Camberwell, Victoria 3124, Australia
(a division of Pearson Australia Group Pty. Ltd.)
Penguin Books India Pvt. Ltd., 11 Community Centre, Panchsheel Park, New Delhi—110 017, India
Penguin Group (NZ), cnr. Airborne and Rosedale Roads, Albany, Auckland 1310, New Zealand
(a division of Pearson New Zealand Ltd.)
Penguin Books (South Africa) (Pty.) Ltd., 24 Sturdee Avenue, Rosebank, Johannesburg 2196, South Africa

Penguin Books Ltd., Registered Offices: 80 Strand, London WC2R 0RL, England

This is an original publication of The Berkley Publishing Group.

This is a work of fiction. Names, characters, places, and incidents either are the product of the author's imagination or are used fictitiously, and any resemblance to actual persons, living or dead, business establishments, events, or locales is entirely coincidental. The publisher does not have any control over and does not assume any responsibility for author or third-party websites or their content.

First edition: May 2006

Library of Congress Cataloging-in-Publication Data

Fowler, Earlene.
    The saddlemaker's wife / by Earlene Fowler.—1st ed.
        p. cm.
    ISBN 0-425-20778-1
        1. Widows—Fiction. 2. Inheritance and succession—Fiction. 3. Ranch life—California—Fiction.
I. Title.

PS3556.O828S23 2006
813'.54—dc22   2005055347

PRINTED IN THE UNITED STATES OF AMERICA

10   9   8   7   6   5   4   3   2   1

*For Allen,
with all my love*

ACKNOWLEDGMENTS

"The entire law is summed up in a single command:
Love your neighbor as yourself."
—Galatians 5:14

My sincere gratitude to:

Father, Son and Holy Spirit

Gail Albutt, Lynne Almeida, Kathy Springer, Ginnie Traver, Nancy and Dick Wood—for your helpful insights about life in the beautiful Owens Valley

Ellen Geiger, agent and friend—for reading way too many versions of this novel and never crying "uncle."

Christine Zika, the best editor in the world—your insights are wise and sensitive and always help me see my stories more clearly

Richard and Trajan Vieira, my two favorite saddlemakers—your artistry inspires and delights me

Kathy Vieira—a dynamite writer, a wonderful friend and the real saddle-maker's wife. That day we met in Paso Robles was meant to be

My friend and fellow dog-lover, Karen Gray, Deputy District Attorney, San Luis Obispo—for technical help on legal issues

My much-loved, incredibly supportive friends and family—Clare Bazley, Tina and Tom Davis, Janice Dischner, Jo Ellen Heil, Christine Hill, Debra Jackson, Jo-Ann Mapson, Carolyn Miller, Karen Olson, Laura Ross-Wingfield and Lela Satterfield

Boudin "Boo" Fowler—for making me get up off the sofa and take a walk even when I didn't want to

Like a horse in open country,
they did not stumble;
like cattle that go down to the plain,
they were given rest by the
Spirit of the Lord.

—Isaiah 63:13–14

PROLOGUE

RUBY

Years later Ruby would drive up to the pasture where the rescued horses still lived. The bright early-morning sun caused her eyes to narrow, and in the lavender shadows painting the craggy Sierra Nevada mountains she sometimes imagined she saw Cole's face. The sorrel mare, white-muzzled and calm now, watched for Ruby, then slowly ambled over to her, waiting patiently for carrot chunks and sweet apple slices. It became a weekly ritual they both anticipated.

Ruby would lean against the old cottonwood tree and sift through every little detail of that year and eventually, in the cool, sage-scented mist that dampened her thick hair and seeped into her pores, it began to feel like it was someone else's story, an improbable tale overheard at a restaurant or in a noisy airport terminal. She made her peace with the path Cole chose, grew to love him again, an authentic love this time, one with full knowledge of who he was, the entire man, the man who gave her hope, took it away, then gave it back again.

Cole McGavin claimed he fell in love first with Ruby's French toast.

"That was the cheesiest line I'd ever heard," Ruby would tease him after they were married, though she suspected his statement was close to being true. Her cream-cheese-and-bacon-stuffed French toast was fa-

mous. It had earned the Oakglen Cafe in San Juan Capistrano the
"Most Decadent Breakfast" award from the *Orange County Register*
three years in a row.

When they met, she was thirty-five years old and had experienced
her fair share of lame pickup lines. It was as much a part of the food
service industry as stingy tippers and aching heels. Fifteen of those
years she worked as a waitress, the last three years as a cook. Though
she hadn't minded waitressing, she preferred working in the kitchen,
where no one saw her, where people's peculiar demands were merely
flimsy squares of paper and sarcastic remarks from a weary server's
lips.

Like most people in this industry, she was more used to complaints
than compliments, so she couldn't help peeking at the man who told
Wanda, the cashier, that he wanted to marry the person who made that
incredible French toast. Wanda, still a romantic, convinced a reluctant
Ruby to come out from the kitchen so he could tell her himself. His obvious embarrassment when he realized that Wanda had actually told
Ruby what he said, caused a flutter of possibility to tickle her stomach.

"I could have been an ex-boxer named Bruno," she said on their
first date. He'd taken her to a seafood restaurant overlooking Balboa
Bay where the rich of Orange County kept their sailboats and million
dollar cottages. After dinner they walked to the end of the pier and
tossed oyster crackers to the raggedy brown and gray gulls.

He smiled and said, "But you weren't."

She fell in love with his steady hazel eyes, his tanned, muscled forearms and how he never failed to do anything he told her he would do.
After years of dating flaky, long-fingered musicians and street-weary
cops, the consequence of working too many swing shifts, Cole and his
work-scarred, dependable hands and easygoing personality were a nice
change. He rose at five a.m. every day and framed new houses, a seem-
ingly never-ending job in Southern California, where people moved
from the Midwest and the East Coast to exchange unpredictable
weather for an unpredictable housing market. She now took quiet comfort in knowing that hundreds of families lived in homes held solidly
together by the nails he'd driven. It seemed a sort of immortality.

"Who do you dream about?" she'd whisper to the mare whose life before the pasture was a mystery. The mare would shake her head and not comment. But Ruby knew she understood. Horses, Lucas told her, knew about loss, about being torn from their familiar first love and thrust into a world where they had to adapt to survive. They learned to forgive. They learned to love again.

"I miss you," she said to the mountains tinted the color of bruised plums, where a handful of Cole's gray-white ashes she had saved to return to this place he had loved, had long ago blended with the soil, their minerals absorbed and renewed every year in emerald spring grasses and crimson columbine. "I always will."

RUBY

Ruby McGavin stopped at the newly restored Manzanar National Historic Site more to delay the inevitable than out of intellectual curiosity. No one was expecting her in Cardinal. What were a few more hours?

The new scrub brush–colored Interpretive Center was once an auditorium and gymnasium for the eleven thousand Japanese-Americans relocated here in 1944, sequestered away from a terrified America. Looking across the barren high desert, she couldn't imagine what a shock it must have been for people accustomed to green fields and cool Pacific ocean breezes.

The museum was both fascinating and sad. She paused before an exhibit of evacuation tags. It listed the person's name, a five digit number and where they were supposed to report so they could be transferred to a camp. They reminded her of the cheap luggage tags that airlines give to unprepared travelers.

She darted out of the auditorium's theater in the middle of the emotional twenty-two minute film narrated by former internees, her stomach threatening to reject the cheese and crackers she'd gulped down at a gas station–mini-mart outside of Victorville. It was the only food she'd eaten today. She should have stuck to straight Coca-Cola. Caffeine and sugar, when taken in carefully measured doses, had kept her going through many sixteen-hour double shifts at the cafe. She hadn't been able to eat a full meal in two months, not since the night an assistant coroner called, a woman who introduced herself as Ginger, and apologized before giving Ruby the news about Cole's fatal car accident. Ruby remembered thinking at the time Ginger seemed an unlikely name for someone who held that job.

She carefully drove the self-guided auto tour around the square mile of the land named Manzanar long before it became an internment camp. Her fifteen-year-old Honda was the only vehicle on the gravel road this Wednesday morning three days before Christmas. The Eastern Sierra Nevada mountains were blanketed with snow, the peaks obscured by a silvery gray fog.

She let the car idle at each numbered stop, places where only wild gray-green sagebrush and chunks of weathered cement foundation remained, most of the buildings, according to the glossy brochure, sold as scrap lumber after the war ended. The only place she felt compelled to stop and get out was the cemetery. Around the cemetery's natural wood fence hung long strands of tiny, colorful origami birds, some type of swan or crane. The center of the dusty cemetery grounds was dominated by a stark, white obelisk with black Japanese writing. The inscription, according to her brochure, translated to "soul consoling tower." She walked over to the monument and circled it, amazed and curious at the objects people left: a faded Batman doll, more strings of wind-wrinkled paper birds, empty bottles of Japanese beer, a bubble wand shaped like a star, unsmoked cigarettes, a red plastic bracelet, candles, pocket change and shards of dirt-encrusted pottery.

She placed her palm on the cold white stone and pressed down, not feeling a bit consoled. But then, the tragedy she'd experienced didn't come close to what those buried here had suffered. She dug into her purse and left a handful of coins, all she had to offer. A new penny shined among her pile of coins, the brightest object on the ledge. She wondered how long it would take until it tarnished as dark as the mountains that loomed over this sacred ground.

Two hours later she was sitting in the Lone Pine Cafe in Cardinal, California, reminded of something she'd read, that all stories began one of two ways—someone goes on a trip or a stranger comes to town. Right at that moment, both scenarios applied to her. She wondered how her husband's family would react to her once they knew she existed. His family, according to the papers found in his safety deposit box, owned one of the last big ranches in Tokopah County and were, contrary to what he had told her, alive and thriving.

She picked up the plastic water glass her teenage waitress had placed in front of her and took a sip. The water tasted bitter and slightly soapy. Years of experience told Ruby that they needed to run them through the rinse cycle one more time.

She looked back down at her book, a new novel by one of her favorite authors, Lee Smith. The author's characters always felt as familiar to Ruby as her own crazy family. Ruby's mother, Loretta, had been born in east Tennessee and Ruby still had aunts and uncles there whom she had never met. Though a native Californian, she felt a strange affinity for the South, a ghostly recognition that she had roots somewhere in that kudzu-covered soil.

An open book was the best way to discourage casual conversation. Customers who had books usually wanted to be left alone. When she'd worked as a waitress, she'd prided herself on being able to read a customer, discern what kind of service they needed. The job had taught her to be a good listener. It wasn't hard. She didn't mind hearing about other people's lives. They often felt like short stories. Of course, with some folks she wished for the ending quicker than others. What she didn't like was sharing her own story. Early on she had learned how to tell just enough about herself to make a customer happy, but not so much she felt robbed of her soul.

The young waitress came back with Ruby's cup of coffee and an order pad. The boot-shaped nametag on her red-and-white gingham shirt read *Cassie*. She appeared to be in her middle teens. Her dark brown hair was cut in a choppy, eighties-rock-star shag, the tips tinted the shade of blue most often seen in gas station toilet bowls. In a funky, Laguna Beach salon, her messy, looks-like-I-did-it-stoned haircut would have cost a hundred bucks plus tip. But here in the foothill town of Cardinal, population 3,259, a burp-in-the-road on the way to Mammoth Mountain's crowded ski slopes, Ruby guessed it was the result of a bored Saturday night with her girlfriends.

"What'll you have?" the girl asked. Her chirpy voice belied her faux hard-edge look.

Ruby wasn't hungry. Like her stop at Manzanar, she was using this place to delay making a decision about what to do now that she'd actually arrived in Cole's hometown.

"Grilled cheese on sourdough," she replied, handing the girl the plastic menu.

"No problem." Cassie pulled a cellophane-wrapped fortune cookie out of her apron pocket and tossed it next to Ruby's coffee. She bounced away before Ruby could ask why.

She stared out the frosty window where black winter storm clouds loomed like Japanese movie monsters. They'd dogged her from the perennially sunny town of San Juan Capistrano where she'd lived five years, longer than anywhere in her life. Her Honda was parked down the street. In the backseat, nestled in a square oak box and wrapped in his favorite brown-and-orange flamestitched afghan, lay the ashes of her husband, Cole McGavin. He was home, though his family didn't know it yet. The same family he'd told her had perished in one single, tragic moment.

"Car accident," he'd said during their third date. They were at the San Diego Zoo, in front of the zebra exhibit. His deeply tanned face had been stoic, his eyes emotionless. "Tule fog," he'd blatantly lied. "Outside of Bakersfield. My parents and two younger brothers."

At the time, the sadness of it had overwhelmed her and she couldn't think of what to say except she was sorry. He never offered details and she'd never asked him about it again. It wasn't difficult not knowing much about his family considering her own, and their peculiarities were not something she liked discussing. Cole had never met her father, Joe, or her brother, Nash. Get-togethers were not a Stoddard family tradition. But Cole never commented on her family's itinerant or disconnected nature. When Ruby had told him she was thirteen when her mother left the family and they never heard from her again, he'd simply commented, "That's tough on a kid." His deep voice was sympathetic, but without pity. She liked that.

By the time she met Cole, Ruby had been on too many dates where her life story had been offered up like a plate of hash browns to be tasted and either rejected as odd or topped by her date's even more bizarre childhood. A few months earlier she'd decided to stop dating altogether. It was too exhausting and her dates' stories started taking on a sort of colorless monotony that exhausted her more than a double shift. She'd come to prefer spending Saturday nights soaking her feet in warm lavender water and reading novels about places she wished she could visit—Haines, Alaska; New York City or Madison, Georgia. After one date, Cole changed her mind. Three months later they had been married at the Love-Me-Tender wedding chapel in Las Vegas.

She picked up the fortune cookie, unwrapped the cellophane and cracked it open. Two small slips of paper stuck together with gluey, fortune cookie dust.

Any rough times are behind you now. A resort area will be part of your next holiday plans.

There was no chance of the first one happening anytime soon, but the second one was close enough to the truth to send an icy shiver down her already chilled spine. She wondered if she should turn tail and barrel back down the water-starved Mojave Desert road that brought her to this small town.

"Double fortunes?" her waitress said fifteen minutes later, slipping the steaming grilled cheese sandwich in front of her. "My mom would die if that happened to her. She's *nuclear* over fortune cookies. Has been ever since I can remember. She thinks they'll all come true or something." The girl rolled her black-lined, pale blue eyes. A shiny silver rod pierced one of her thick, unplucked eyebrows. Her lips turned down in a teenager's condescending grimace. "Is that totally lame or what?"

Ruby didn't answer. Heaven knows, she wasn't about to comment on someone else's method of coping with whatever poker hand life dealt them. These days, believing the vague predictions inside fortune cookies seemed as reasonable to her as believing anything else.

The Lone Pine Cafe advertised hunter's breakfasts (16 oz. T-bone steak, five eggs, hash browns, toast and coffee), biscuits and gravy, barbecued chicken and beef and ten rotating flavors of pie. The decor consisted of brown tuck-and-roll leatherette booths, a bunch of corner-chipped, four-person tables, a wagon-wheel chandelier and some fly-spotted photos of Roy Rogers and Gene Autry. Rusty horseshoes, branding irons, a surprised-looking stuffed trout and dangerous-looking spurs rounded out the wall decor. They were items that would have cost a bundle in a Southern California antique store, but here were probably from someone's old barn.

She turned the cellophane-wrapped cookie over in her hand. Home-made peach cobbler was believable, but fortune cookies? They seemed as out of place as Ruby did.

"Why do you give out fortune cookies?" Ruby asked.

"I dunno," Cassie said, plucking at the collapsed puffed sleeve of her red gingham blouse. "We've always given them out on Wednes-days." Her western top and denim skirt were obviously the diner's uni-form. "My mom's been collecting fortunes for years. Not just ours either. People bring fortune cookies to her from all over. She's making a what-you-call-it with them. You know, pasting them all together on a board with stuff like crows' feathers she finds and old pictures and movie tickets, crap like that." She clamped a nail-bitten hand over her mouth. "Sorry. Mom says I shouldn't use a word like that in front of customers."

Ruby smiled, intrigued by the girl's unwitting wholesome honesty. No teenager she'd served in Orange County would ever think to apol-ogize for that word. "Your mom's making a collage."

"I guess. She even has some Spanish ones. Those are kinda cool."

Ruby fingered the gritty slips of paper. "Do you suppose anyone's fortunes ever come true?"

Cassie snorted. "In Cardinal? Not a chance."

Though she wasn't particularly interested in anybody's future but her own, Ruby liked talking to this girl. She realized when Cassie spoke to her that she was the first person Ruby had carried on a real conver-sation with since she'd quit her job at the cafe two weeks ago. These days, what with drive-thru fast food and automated, swipe-your-credit-card gas station pumps, it was possible, if you had the inclination, to go for weeks without actually conversing with anyone beyond "thank you" and "two ketchups, please." Her longest conversation lately had been about the ominous weather with the desk clerk of the budget motel she'd stayed at in Ridgecrest last night.

There was no reason to stay in that motel last night, taking two days to drive what could have easily been accomplished in six hours, but she'd been in no hurry to reach Cardinal. Though she'd found the will in Cole's safety deposit box right after he'd died in October, she'd put off doing anything about it. The fact that she owned one-quarter of his family's ranch was still unbelievable to her. She might have delayed this trip indefinitely if she hadn't been asked to leave the house Cole and she had rented since they were married. His boss, one of Orange County's biggest developers, had decided to bulldoze his great-grandfather's hundred-year-old farmhouse on the fringe of San Juan Capistrano's city limits and build upscale condos for seniors.

"I'm sorry, Mrs. McGavin," the property management person had said when she'd called to tell Ruby she needed to be out by December thirty-first. "Thank you for being so prompt with your rental payments. There'll be no problem with you getting your thousand-dollar deposit back. I'll stick it in the mail today." The woman paused. "I'm sorry about your husband."

"Thank you," Ruby said automatically. "It's a . . ." She wanted to say it was a shame that Cole's boss cared so little for his own history that he was willing to sell it for money he probably didn't need.

"Yes?" the woman said.

"I'll be out before Christmas."

"Thank you," the woman replied, her voice relieved. Had she been afraid that Ruby would put up a fuss? In a strange way, Ruby was almost glad that the decision to move had been made for her and that Cole never had to know their house was demolished. In the short six months they'd been married they'd painted rooms, planted rose bushes, even refinished the wooden floor in their bedroom. He'd talked about going to his boss and arranging to buy the house and a small part of the five still-wild acres. Ruby realized now what an unrealistic dream that had been.

"There's no fortune of any kind around here," Cassie continued, apparently happy to denigrate her hometown to anyone who cared to listen. She grinned at Ruby and pointed to a bulletin board next to the ancient push key cash register. "The regulars put the craziest fortunes on the board. They have contests to see who gets the most fun fortune, like ones that promise money or a trip. When somebody gets two fortunes in one cookie like you did, it's like they won the lottery or something. They're insane." The girl pulled at a strand of her stiff hair and gave a deep, put-upon sigh. She nodded at the counter where a trim, wiry woman in her early thirties with two waist-long, strawberry-blond braids was making a fresh pot of coffee in the silver Bunn coffeemaker. She didn't appear much older than Cassie. "Mom's just mental to get two fortunes. I guess it's, like, really good luck."

Or maybe longing for something to tell her which way to go, Ruby thought, a desire she completely understood. "What's your favorite one so far?" she asked the girl.

Cassie's maroon-painted lips turned up in a crooked smile. "The one that said *Fight illiteracy. Buy more fortune cookies.* It cracked me up."

Ruby couldn't help smiling back, though her lips felt stiff, like the gesture was something they'd forgotten how to perform.

"Yep," Cassie said. "If you want any kind of fortune, you'd better get out of Cardinal to find it. Which is exactly what me and my boyfriend, Hunter, are going to do as soon as I graduate in June. He's almost twenty-one. My mom thinks he's too old for me, but she was only sixteen when she married my dad and he was twenty. That's 'cause they were expecting me. Isn't that so hypocritical?"

"Where are you and Hunter planning to go?" Ruby asked.

Cassie shrugged. "Anywhere is better than here. Hunter's a musician. He plays lead guitar and sings and writes awesome songs. We could live anywhere because no matter where you go, there are bars, and people want to hear music."

"Order up, Cassie!" Her mother's sharp voice carried across the lunch hour buzz with the authority of a police whistle. With the efficiency of a longtime waitress and using a minimum amount of movement, she also filled the coffee cups of three old guys sitting at the counter. Her freckled arms were wiry and strong, like those of the affluent horsewomen who had frequented the cafe where Ruby worked.

"Better get those spurs a'jingle-jangle-jingling, Cass," called a man from one of the booths. His plaid flannel shirt was faded to the color of lint. "Your mama's on the warpath today." The two men with him laughed.

"So what else is new?" Cassie shot back, not a bit perturbed. She turned back to Ruby and giggled. "If you need anything else, just yell at me. I'm used to it."

She watched the girl weave her way through the crowded room, calling out a greeting to this person, answering a teasing question from another. It was apparent, even with her attempt to look dangerous, this was a girl who was known, tolerated and, most likely, loved by practically everyone in the cafe. Ruby envied that history, considering how her own meager family was sprinkled around the country like grain flung across a field.

She opened her purse and found the last postcard she'd received from her thirty-year-old brother, Nash. It was postmarked a month ago and showed the Bluebird Cafe in Nashville, Tennessee, the city their mother, Loretta, had named him for because she'd always dreamed of being a country-western music star. He played bass guitar for whoever would hire him, and had never lived in one place longer than three months since he was eighteen. She could have told Cassie that finding work as a musician wasn't as easy as just walking into a bar, but who was she to throw gravel at someone else's dreams?

Hey, Ruby Tuesday, Nash's postcard read. *Got a line on a possible studio gig. May be here thru the winter. Will let you know my address when I find a place to crash. Hope you're doing okay. Love, Nash.* There was no return address and he'd never contacted her about where he lived so she couldn't even let him know she'd left Southern California or the number of her new cell phone.

She'd called her father's cell phone last week to tell him she was moving and ask if he knew where Nash was living.

"Haven't heard from the boy since you have," Joe said. Right now, he and his fourth wife, Prissy, were in Oklahoma City. They swung through California once every couple of months in the bright green Peterbilt truck that both housed and supported them. Prissy had inherited the truck when her second husband was killed in a motorcycle accident. "Nash will pop up sooner or later. Priss says to hang in there." In the background, Ruby could hear the thundering rumble of diesel engines.

"Tell her thanks," she'd replied. "I have to leave our house. Cole's boss finally sold out." Her voice caught, though not enough for her father to notice. Having to leave the rickety old clapboard house with its red and white geraniums was almost like losing Cole a second time. She gave her father her cell phone number, the kind you could purchase bulk minutes for like script for a slot machine. Right now, it was the most permanent thing about her. "I'll let you know where I finally land."

That could be our family motto, she thought. She'd always prided herself in being the one person in her fractured family who, throughout the years, had managed to maintain a permanent address, a place where messages could be left and passed on. Now she was a homeless drifter like her father, her brother and, for all she knew, her mother. Maybe you never really do escape your roots.

"Okay," her father replied, not offering any advice or help. It would never occur to him that she would need either.

"Look, kids, let's just keep things loose and uncomplicated," he'd said years ago, right after Loretta left. Ruby had turned thirteen four days before, and Nash was seven. "You're smart kids. Unless there's blood involved, just handle it, okay?" Then he'd given them each a twenty dollar bill for a week's worth of dinners at McDonald's or Taco Bell and stayed out until two a.m. with his latest girlfriend. It was from her young neighbor, Juana, that Ruby learned how to cook, do laundry, pay the utility bills and forge her father's name on both her and Nash's report cards.

So it felt natural for her to not tell her father the truth about Cole's death or about the will she'd found in his safety deposit box. The document that left her one-fourth of the Circle MG ranch in Tokopah

County, California. Written in Cole's own handwriting on the document, right under his signature, were the words *I love you. I'm sorry.* How long ago had he written them? What was he sorry about? Leaving her the ranch? Lying to her? How he died? She would have given every last thing she owned to know what he meant.

The Lone Pine Cafe, situated right in the center of Cardinal, was almost filled to peak capacity now, about forty to fifty customers by Ruby's guess. It appeared to be a favorite local lunch spot. Almost every person who walked in the door was greeted by name. The six-person booths were crowded with men and women dressed in everything from neat, conservative office attire to knife-pressed Wranglers and clean Stetsons to dusty overalls and stained bill caps advertising Walt's Feed and Seed, Cardinal Valley Bank or Eastern Sierra's Wild Mustang Days.

Someone dropped a quarter in the jukebox and out came Patsy Cline, falling to pieces. Until she'd met Cole, Ruby had never listened to country music. It reminded her too much of her mother and her hopeless dreams. One of Ruby's strongest childhood memories was of coming home from school to find her mother sitting in their bare-walled apartment silently listening to a country music station, staring out the front window. Without looking at her, Loretta would tell Ruby there were cookies in the cupboard, and light up another menthol cigarette, her lipstick like bloody fingerprints on the smooth, white filter. Loretta always worked the evening shift at one restaurant or another, looking for ones who would let her sing a couple of songs with the bar band if there weren't too many patrons craving late-night bacon and eggs. Loretta was the only one, Joe used to tell Ruby, who didn't realize her thin, soprano voice would never be good enough for anything except small town honky-tonks.

The mournful lyrics snaked through the warm buzz of conversations, Patsy's words fading in and out. Cole had played the old country singers so often that Ruby had teased him claiming she was a victim of the Stockholm syndrome, and that he had won her over by sheer saturation. That always made him laugh. After a while, she began to enjoy those nasal-sweet singers and their love-done-me-wrong songs. Easier to do when you actually felt you had won at love. Now they only served as a reminder of Cole, how much she missed him and the volcano of panic, anger and guilt she felt when she thought about how he died.

Outside, people looked like walking Christmas packages, their necks tied with colorful scarf-ribbons. They stepped carefully along the snow-covered sidewalk, glancing tentatively at the sky. The storm clouds had turned an eerie shade of metallic lavender-gray, making the sky look like burnished steel. Coming into town she had heard the forecaster on the radio predict a 100 percent chance of rain or snow throughout most of eastern California. The storm was due around seven p.m. Snow levels were expected to drop to two thousand feet. Cardinal's elevation was 4,300 feet.

When was the last time she changed the blades on her windshield wipers? They were as brittle as seashells and would probably dissolve into black mush the first time something damp hit them. In the six months they'd been married, things like that had become Cole's job, his part of their relationship, like grocery shopping and paying the car insurance had become hers. No matter how unfeminist it sounded, car maintenance was a job she'd happily relinquished. After so many years of solitary worry, she was relieved to let Cole deal with balding tires, corroded batteries and crooked car mechanics.

She'd have to find a place to stay for a few days. On Cardinal's mile-long Main Street, which she'd cruised before coming back to the Lone Pine Cafe, she'd seen a number of possibilities. Cardinal was a tourist town now, despite its ranching and mining history. Once, according to the information Ruby had looked up at the library, before the budding city of Los Angeles acquired most of the county's water rights back in the early twentieth century, Tokopah County boasted green pastures, fertile almond and olive orchards and a lake deep enough to float a paddlewheel steam ship. Now, the town was supported primarily by affluent skiers, trout fishermen, hunters, RV enthusiasts and European tourists seeking the back road to Yosemite or Death Valley.

Not really hungry, Ruby nibbled at her grilled cheese, trying to overhear the conversations around her, straining to hear the name Mc-Gavin. The only group close enough for her to make out their conversation was a table of five men a few feet away. They appeared to be in their sixties and wore a rainbow assortment of starched, snap-button western shirts, branding them as locals. They loudly discussed the weather, the Christmas celebrations coming up this last week before the holiday and the latest stupid tourist antic.

"Take one of these and shut up, you old fools," Cassie's mom said, tossing a handful of fortune cookies in the center of their table. "Anybody here going to have anything different or is it the same dang lunch you all have been eating for the last fifty years?"

"Marry me, Sueann," one of the men said, tapping his coffee cup for a refill. He looked to be the leader of the group, wearing an expensive-looking white western shirt and a large, turquoise bolo tie. "Make me an honest man."

"Walt Creston," she said, filling his cup, "it would take a combined act of congress and the pope to make you an honest man." She called over the restaurant's noisy chatter to the cook. "Carlos, the over-the-hill gang wants their usual. Do me a favor and use that old, green-looking ground meat we were going to throw to the crows." Ignoring their spirited hoots and laugher, she came over to Ruby. "Warm that up?"

"Thanks." Ruby watched Sueann top off her coffee, the strong, rich scent of it a comfort. The mug was still three-fourths full so the offer was more psychological than physical. But Ruby knew little gestures like that often made the difference between a 10 percent and a 15 or 20 percent tip.

"My girl take your order okay?" Sueann asked.

"Yes, she was great."

"I try like heck to talk her into looking like a normal human being, but what can you do? That little girl has always had a mind of her own." Her pale green eyes were as transparent as creek water. "Guess that's not always a bad thing."

"Not always," Ruby agreed.

"You have kids?"

"No, I don't." She looked down at her half-eaten sandwich. Ruby always dreaded that inevitable question. It immediately categorized you into a have or have not, someone who understood or didn't. Like it was some kind of sorority that she'd never be asked to join. Especially now. Thirty-six and widowed. What were the chances of her finding love again? Especially before her insides dried up like a bowl of old fruit?

"They're sweet as coconut cake when they're babies," Sueann said, "but as far as I'm concerned you can have teenagers, every last one of them. Hope she didn't talk your ear off. She's a good girl, but has trouble staying focused. And do I despise her boyfriend? He is a train wreck waiting to happen. But that's a whole other story." She gave Ruby a tired smile.

Ruby felt herself smiling back. She reminded Ruby of Gaynelle, a woman she'd worked with on her first full-time waitressing job right after she'd graduated high school and aged out of the foster care system. Gaynelle had raised five daughters alone on a waitress's salary, putting three of them through community college. When Ruby moved out on her own, Gaynelle bought her an iron skillet as a housewarming gift.

"You'll need it, honey," she'd said, giving a great, bellowing laugh. "To cook for and control the men in your life."

Gaynelle had taught Ruby how to use memory tricks to keep the customers' constant demands straight and warned her to never short her busboy's share of the tips so her tables would always be cleaned promptly. Even after they no longer worked together, they'd remained friends. She was, Ruby thought, her only real friend.

Five years ago Gaynelle and two of her daughters had moved to Coos Bay, Oregon, to care for Gaynelle's aging mother. They still sent birthday and Christmas cards to each other. Maybe I should head west after leaving Cardinal, she thought. It would be nice to hear Gaynelle's laugh again.

"Are you on your way to Mammoth?" Sueann's voice brought Ruby back to the present.

Ruby hesitated before answering, her natural inclination to keep her business private grappling with the need to find out as much as she could about this town. She knew this Sueann could be a valuable source of information. In small towns, Ruby had read somewhere, the local waitress, hairdresser, bank teller and minister, priest or rabbi were almost equal in their insight and knowledge of people's personal lives. It made sense when you thought about it. What was more important in your life than your food, your hair, your money and your soul?

"I'm thinking about spending a few days in Cardinal," Ruby said. "I'm on vacation." The lie slipped out as easily as pouring coffee.

Sueann glanced down at Ruby's left hand. "Your husband joining you?"

Ruby instinctively touched her gold wedding band. She'd meant to take it off before driving into Cardinal. "No," she replied, looking directly into Sueann's sympathetic face.

Sueann studied Ruby gravely. "Have a place to stay yet?"

She shook her head.

"Try the Tokopah Lodge next to Maxie's Bavarian Bakery. It's three blocks north on Main Street. They have weekly rates. Might be cheaper in the long run than the Holiday Inn Express or Best Western. A continental breakfast is included with your room. Tell them Sueann from the Lone Pine sent you over." She reached into her denim skirt's deep pocket, pulled out a fortune cookie and placed it next to Ruby's plate.

"Thanks, but your daughter already gave me one."

"Honey, everyone can use a little extra fortune." She started back through the crowd carrying her empty coffeepot. "Good luck to you," she called over her shoulder.

"Thank you," Ruby said. The woman's unexpected kindness caused her eyes to burn as if someone had blown a mouthful of smoke into them. She threw ten dollars on the table, grabbed the extra fortune cookie and hurried out of the cafe. She wouldn't let herself break down in such a public place.

Outside, the dry cold shocked her back into control. The temperature on the bank sign next door blinked thirty-one degrees. The looming clouds looked ready to burst. Pulling Cole's brown leather jacket close, she walked down the street to her car, parked in front of a Napa Auto Parts store. The well-worn, aviator-style jacket was the only thing of his she'd not put into the twelve-by-twelve-foot storage unit in Orange County. Their possessions had barely filled the small space.

She opened the Honda's door and glanced into the backseat. The red Macy's shopping bag was still there. It was stupid of her to leave the bag containing the afghan-wrapped box where it could be seen. What if someone broke into her car and stole the bag thinking it was some expensive Christmas present? Her heart fluttered in her chest. She'd have to be more careful with it . . . *him* . . . until she decided what to do.

She turned the key in the ignition, heard an empty-sounding click, then nothing. She tried again. Another click. Still no engine growl. She sat there for a moment, stunned and disbelieving. This could not be happening. She cranked the ignition again. With each turn she commanded out loud, "Start, you lousy piece of junk. *Start.*"

After the sixth time, she hit the steering wheel with her palm. Then she hit it again and again, enjoying the stinging sensation in that weird, unexplainable way a person sometimes derives a sick pleasure from the pain of an aching tooth.

She jerked open the door, slammed it shut and stood on the slick sidewalk, breathing hard. How much would this cost to fix? How long would it take? Why did this have to happen *now*? The last question was exactly what she'd been asking herself over and over since Cole died.

In frustration, she kicked the Honda's faded green door panel. Her leather loafer left a little pebble in the smooth metal. She kicked again, feeling an even greater satisfaction at the second dent. When she kicked it a third time, she knew she was a goner. Like eating chocolate-covered raisins at the movies, she couldn't stop. She kicked the door over and over, experiencing the most intense, yet peaceful pleasure she'd felt in months. She knew it wouldn't do a bit of good, knew it would never change what Cole had done, suspected she'd probably end up with a broken toe. Still, she kicked the door and silently repeated his name— *Cole, Cole, Cole*—not entirely sure if the word was a curse or a prayer.

LUCAS

Lucas McGavin peered through the window of his saddlemaking shop and watched the tall, dark-haired woman wearing a man's worn leather jacket kick the snot out of her little green car. She swung her long leg with the agility of a Brazilian soccer player, her mouth moving as fast as her foot. He tried to imagine the words she uttered while she went to town on that defenseless door.

With his dye-stained thumb, he rubbed a clear circle on the filmy window. She looked to be in her midthirties, had wavy chestnut brown hair to her shoulders and was attractive enough to cause most men's eyes to linger a minute. She was also distraught in that last-straw, teeth-gnashing, door-kicking sort of way he completely understood.

She momentarily lost her balance on the icy sidewalk, caught herself with a desperate grab at the side mirror and bent it to an odd angle. She wore faded jeans and a tan sweater. The leather jacket looked at least two sizes too big for her. Was it her boyfriend's? At any rate, ten minutes in a good Eastern Sierra rainstorm would soak right through that sky jockey jacket and wouldn't keep her warm, much less dry.

She paused a moment, her chest heaving up and down with the exertion. He felt a stirring in his groin, then mentally cuffed himself. Was he honestly so lonely for a woman that the sight of one kicking a car door excited him? He thought about the letter his ex-wife had sent last week that he'd still not answered. That cooled his ardor real quick. She wanted to buy out his share of their condo in San Francisco, the only thing they'd jointly owned, but she wanted to make payments. That's all he needed to feel like a complete failure, a check every month from an account printed with the names of his ex-wife and her lover.

He waited to see what the car-assaulting woman would do next. She'd finally lost steam and was looking up one side of Cardinal's mile-long main drag, then the other, as if trying to decide which way to start walking. Then she gave the door one more halfhearted kick. Lucas thought about offering help, then decided against it. Cars and their inner workings were as much a mystery to him as the female sex. He drove a rust-speckled 1972 Ford pickup that was jerry-rigged and kept running by his friend Ely Grey, who, Lucas swore, could turn a May-tag washing machine into a Trans Am.

"Speak of the devil," Lucas murmured.

Just as the woman appeared to be ready to stomp north up the street, Ely Grey walked out of the Napa Auto Parts directly across the street from Lucas's shop. Lucas guessed that Ely, as well as Bert and Ed, the two old farts who worked the weekday shift, had also been ob-serving the woman's impressive hissy fit.

Ely ambled over to her in that slow, kiss-my-ass walk that used to drive the male and female teachers nuts at Cardinal Union High School for completely different reasons. Lanky, copper-skinned and sinewy, he was six years older than Lucas. He'd been a classmate of Lucas's older brother, Cole, though they hadn't been friends. Cole was the oldest son of one of the county's respected ranching families; Ely Grey was the son of a woman who sporadically tended bar at the Red Coyote until she'd died of cirrhosis, and a father who, according to town gossip, was ei-ther Paiute-Shoshone or one of the area's itinerant Mexican cowboys.

When Lucas returned to Cardinal a year and a half ago, he started going to the Red Coyote Saloon. Ely seemed to be there every time Lucas was. Through casual conversation, Lucas found out that Ely had just come back to town himself, about two months after Lucas. They'd struck up an easygoing friendship that would have never happened when they were kids, at least not past the fourth grade, a sort of unwritten rule between Cardinal's Pauite-Shoshone and white population. Now they had something in common. Both were an odd mixture of hometown boy and newcomer.

Ely bent toward the woman, cocked his head and listened to her explanation. Then he popped the hood of the car.

Lucas turned away from the window. Ely'd have the car running in no time. There weren't many engines Ely couldn't tinker into working, which was why the Chevron station where he was manager and head mechanic was the place where locals went to get their own cars fixed. He was constantly bombarded with automotive questions whenever he and Lucas grabbed a meal at the Lone Pine Cafe, which was next door to Lucas's custom saddle shop.

He went back around the glass-topped front counter to his pockmarked worktable and contemplated the saddle fender he was working on, a piece carved Sheridan-style with twisting vines and flowers in connecting circles. The best carving showed no beginning and no end. He saw a tiny place where he knew another carver would see where Lucas had stopped.

He sighed in disappointment, took a strip of heavy muslin and started rubbing the fender's edges. The sharp, comforting medicinal smell of the clear gum sealer rose up in waves around him. Rubbing edges was work despised by most saddlemakers, but Jake Seligman had taught him it was the sign of a well-made custom saddle. Raw-cut edges show a lazy man, Jake liked to say, usually around a huge wad of Red Man snuff. This particular task in saddlemaking could be done by a moron, but Lucas took pleasure in it simply because he could turn off his brain and just immerse himself in the sugary-sad voice of Norah Jones floating out of his CD player. Hard to believe her dad was that weird sitar-player from the sixties who hung out with the Beatles. Then again, a person doesn't get to pick his parents or his start in life. As his aunt Birch used to tell him when he was a boy and complained that he didn't like what she was having for dinner—"Lucas, most of the time in this life you have to make do with what's on the pantry shelf."

In fifteen minutes he had customers due for a saddle fitting, customers he dreaded, but whose work he needed if he wanted his shop to show any kind of decent profit. Though in the last year and a half he'd never regretted giving up the law, he'd often regretted taking over Jake's saddlemaking and leather repair business. It wasn't the work itself he hated, but dealing with customers. Truth be told, if there were a way he could never speak to a member of the general public again, he'd give his right foot for it. Well, maybe a toe or two, his trained lawyer's mind automatically counteroffered.

The cowbell on the front door rattled. His stomach tightened, then relaxed when he saw it wasn't Bernie Gorman of Bel Air.

"Hey, Lucas," said Ely, coming over to lean on the filmy glass counter. The sleeves of his plaid flannel shirt were folded to the elbow, revealing corded forearms. "Want to grab some lunch at the Lone Pine? Today's fortune cookie day. You might just find out you're going to be rich and famous."

"Rich sounds okay," Lucas said, his tone light. "Not interested in famous." He pushed the unfinished saddle fender aside. "What's with the car beater? You get her up and on her way to the ski slopes?" That was where most young women passing through Cardinal were headed, the bachelor-rich ski slopes and fancy clothing shops of Mammoth Mountain.

Ely's wide-set black eyes crinkled, the smile never working its way farther down. "That was something, watching her whale on that door, wasn't it? You should have seen it from our angle. Bert and Ed won't be needing their Viagra for a month." He moved the wooden toothpick in his mouth from one side to the other. "Thing is, that bucket of bolts needs more work than my grandpa's arteries."

"You tell her that?"

He nodded. "She gave that poor old door one more kick. I don't know, it was that last kick that did me in."

"Don't tell me you offered to fix it yourself," Lucas said, a little jealous that he hadn't been the one to rescue her. "With your schedule?"

"Having it towed over to the station. Told her I might be able to get her up and running again, but if it needs any electronic gizmos, we didn't have a Honda dealer in town and what with the holidays, it might take a few days to get parts."

"Sucker," Lucas said. "She doesn't look like she has much money."

"The kick had spirit," Ely said, taking the toothpick from his mouth and flicking it at Lucas. "Looks like it's attached to some pretty fine legs too."

"I doubt that one will dance right into your arms."

Ely just laughed. "No doubt you're right on both counts. Consider it my good deed for the year."

"Year's almost over."

"Then I was just in time, wasn't I? Got some new Justins in at the feed store. Want me to put you aside a pair?" Ely sometimes worked weekends at Walt's Feed and Seed, the same Walt who owned the Chevron station Ely managed. Walt Creston owned half the profitable businesses in town.

"Maybe. I guess."

"That answer's about as clear as Sueann's coffee, counselor," Ely said in a lazy voice.

"Brown ropers. Size eleven."

"More like it. I'm proud of you, son, making up your mind so decisively like that. Just like a real grown-up."

"Up yours, " Lucas replied, tossing a stained piece of practice leather over the counter at him. He glanced up at the yellow plastic Bowden Saddle Tree Company clock hanging over the door. The Gormans were twenty minutes' late. Should he make coffee for them? Before he could decide, the cowbell rattled again and Mr. Bernie C. Gorman entered the shop. Ely moved from the counter to the far side of the nubby love seat under the front window.

"It's colder than a whore's heart out there," Bernie Gorman bellowed. He was a large-chested man with a thick head of gray-blond hair and a windburned face. His black leather jacket probably cost more than Lucas paid for his pickup.

"It's not any better in here," his wife said, shivering in her fashionable, teal-colored ski jacket. She was one of those sapling-thin, Southern California women whose beautiful face looked as if it had been shaved too many times with a wood plane. Behind her stood a sullen-looking girl of about fifteen or so with frizzy, chocolate-colored hair.

"Sorry, ma'am," he said, not realizing how cold the room had become.

"Are you sure this man knows anything about saddles?" Mrs. Gorman said, ignoring Lucas.

Lucas glanced over at Ely, who raised one eyebrow.

"Shut up, Marian," Mr. Gorman said.

"I've been having some trouble with my heating system," Lucas said. Heating system was a slight exaggeration. Most of the time he didn't even bother with the antique wall heater and used an electric plug-in he set up right next to where he was building a saddle, moving it to his workbench when necessary. Or he just wore thermal underwear.

"We'll survive," Mr. Gorman said.

"Maybe *you* will," his wife answered. Her piercing voice scraped across Lucas's ears like shards of glass. "Tiffany's going to get bronchitis again."

Tiffany, a round-rumped Lolita in a stomach-revealing black sweater, took that opportunity to flop down on the love seat next to Ely and flash him a smile that was way too lascivious for someone her age. Ely stared her down with unamused black eyes until she finally blushed and looked down at the tips of her sharp-toed red boots.

"Would you like some coffee?" Lucas asked Mrs. Gorman.

Mrs. Gorman scowled at her husband. "I don't see why we have to do this *now*."

"Do we have to go over this again?" Bernie said. "We were already in Mammoth, which was *your* idea, in case we're keeping track. This is on our way home. I need Mr. McGavin to start on these saddles because they are handmade saddles. You don't order them two weeks before you want them."

"For crying out loud, Bernie. How good can he be?" She gestured around at the cramped, dust-caked shop. "Why don't you just have that funny little man in the Valley make them like Roy does?"

"This guy is better," Mr. Gorman said. "He was trained by Jake Seligman."

"Who?" she answered.

Ely stood up, the disgust on his face announcing he couldn't stand the company of these people any longer. "Meet me at the Lone Pine when you're through," he called over his shoulder.

"Okay," Lucas called back, wishing he could walk out of the shop with Ely.

"Can we get this over with some time this century?" Mrs. Gorman asked.

Lucas smiled stiffly, glancing over at the razor-sharp, crescent-shaped head knife on his workbench, the one he called his moose-skinner. He silently sentenced himself to second-degree murder, malice aforethought, but no premeditation. Of course, a really good prosecutor like some of the pit bulls he'd tried cases against as a public defender in San Francisco might have pried out of him that, even in this short period of time, he, the defendant, had maturely and meaningfully reflected upon the gravity of his act and thereupon acted anyway. That would make first-degree murder a possibility. Still, second degree would be the most likely verdict. At most he would receive a fifteen-to-life sentence with the possibility of parole. With good behavior, he would only serve 85 percent of his time.

"Hello?" the woman called. "Could you just get on with measuring my husband's ass so we can get back to Bel Air sometime before Christmas?"

"Cowboy," the daughter purred from over on the love seat, "you can measure my ass anytime you want." She ran a French-manicured hand chubby with baby fat down one thigh of her skintight blue jeans.

"Tiffany Brianne, shut that trashy mouth of yours," her mother said.

Tiffany ignored her mother and seductively licked her maroon lips. Under his flannel shirt, Lucas felt sweat pool at the small of his back. At thirty-four, he was young enough to be flattered and old enough to be appalled. Lordy Mama, there had to be an easier way to make a living.

Ever since his aunt Birch had talked him into putting up that website three months ago, business had definitely picked up. Unfortunately, it was only rich, spoiled city folk who had the money for handmade saddles. Despite Birch's protests, Lucas stated on his website that he did not travel to customers, they had to come to him.

"You're going to discourage customers," she'd fretted.

"Hopefully, only the irritating ones," he'd replied. Cardinal was a good six-hour drive from both Los Angeles and San Francisco, surely too daunting a trip for most people.

He was wrong. Much to his aunt's delight, it appeared that wealthy people liked it when someone of the working class was temperamental and hard to reach. Somehow it made his saddles more desirable. Rich people, Lucas learned, loved to acquire what seemed impossible just so they could brag about it to their friends. Over e-mail Lucas had learned that Bernie owned a plumbing supply business, a stable of twenty-two horses and wanted two custom-made saddles with the possibility of more orders in the future.

Lucas's mentor, Jake Seligman, a seventy-nine-year-old retired saddlemaker up the road in Bridgeport, had recommended Lucas to Bernie. Jake was the same man who'd taught Lucas's brother Cole everything he knew about saddlemaking. Every tool Lucas used was stained with his older brother's sweat. Lucas read somewhere that DNA could last hundreds of years. Weird to think his and Cole's DNA were mixing when he used the leatherworking tools.

Jake didn't do work for hire any longer, but had built twenty-seven saddles for Bernie in the last fifteen years. Bernie Gorman had the potential to be a very good customer. Price was no object, Bernie had written in his e-mail to Lucas. Lucas's four favorite words.

No, Mr. Gorman was not a person he wanted to run off. Lucas needed this saddlemaking business to survive. He was never, if he had a choice in the matter, going to practice law again, and he wasn't about to work for his mother on the ranch. Unlike his brother Derek, he didn't have the fortitude for that. Next to saddlemaking, law and cattle were the only skills he possessed.

Mrs. Gorman pulled out a silver cigarette case and glanced at her diamond-studded watch. "We're supposed to be at the Andersons' in Huntington Harbour by six o'clock to watch the Christmas boat parade."

Lucas deliberately waited until Mrs. Gorman stuck the cigarette in her painted mouth, then cleared his throat and flicked his hazel eyes over at the leather sign he remembered Cole carving—NO SMOKING . . . PLEASE. The "please" had been added after their aunt Birch had wryly suggested it. When Aunt Birch had turned her back and Cole rolled his eyes at Lucas, she'd said, without turning around, "Don't you be making funny faces at me, Mr. Cole McGavin." He and Cole had gawked at each other in surprise. Then again, Aunt Birch had taught fourth grade for thirty-five years. The memory caused Lucas to smile.

Mrs. Gorman gave a theatrical sigh and shoved the cigarette inside her gray leather purse. "Why can't you just buy that saddle over there, Bernie?" She gestured at the elaborately carved saddle sitting on a wooden tree behind the counter. "It's already finished."

Bernie looked up from the photo album Lucas had given him showing the detailed photographs of saddles Lucas had built. "What size is it?" he said.

"Not for sale," Lucas said bluntly.

His statement caused Bernie's eyes to gleam. "Everything's for sale, son."

"It's not for sale," he repeated.

Without asking, Bernie walked around the counter to inspect the saddle, running his hand over the carved seat. "I like it. What's this kind of carving called?"

"It's done in a Sheridan-style," Lucas said. "I can make you a similar one."

"Will it be as good as this?" Bernie asked.

The question pained Lucas. "I'll do my best," he said.

Bernie bent closer to the saddle, inspecting it from all angles. His face lit up at what he saw under the cantle. "Hey, what's this?"

"A pineapple," Lucas said.

"Well, I'll be," Bernie replied. "Why's it hidden like that? Can you do that on mine?"

"Pineapples are a symbol of friendship," his wife said. "Remember, we decorated the last Save the Whales ball in a pineapple theme."

Bernie grunted in reply.

"I'm hungry," Tiffany whined.

Bernie turned back to Lucas, ignoring his daughter. "I'll give you four thousand cash. Right now."

Lucas felt a twist in his gut. Four *thousand* dollars. That would buy a lot of horse feed. "I'm sorry, Mr. Gorman. But it's not mine to sell."

"Put me in touch with the owner," he said.

"He's . . . away."

"When will he be back?"

"Don't know." Lucas turned back to his sample album. "I'd be glad to make one similar for you. How about a four-leaf clover under your cantle instead of a pineapple? In honor of your business." Mr. Gorman's plumbing business was called Lucky Plumbing Supplies.

Bernie thought about it for a moment, then said, "Okay. What kind of tree do you suggest? Can we put more silver on it? I want lots of silver."

Lucas thought for a moment. "I'd say a 3-B Visalia with a Number 2R Mex horn." He dug through his desk and found a tattered catalog to show Bernie what he meant. "More silver is no problem if your horse can handle it."

"Mine can," Bernie said. "Or they're gone."

For the first time, Lucas felt a stab of sympathy for both Mrs. Gorman and her daughter. Living with Bernie couldn't be easy.

Silver was 100 percent markup. His silver guy in Santa Fe would jump at the work. He started tallying up the cost in his head, his stomach tightening in excitement. This was probably close to a ten-thousand-dollar saddle. He really needed that deposit money.

"I need it by March for a Saint Patrick's Day parade. Think you can get it done by then?"

It was a statement more than a question. Bernie was obviously used to getting what he wanted, when he wanted it.

"No problem." Lucas pulled out one of his order forms.

"Where's a decent restaurant?" Mrs. Gorman asked.

"What're you hungry for?" Lucas started searching the countertop and the workbench behind him for a pen. Bernie pulled a gold Montblanc out of his leather jacket and handed it to Lucas. "Thanks," Lucas said, embarrassed that he didn't even have a decent pen handy.

"Some place close so we don't turn into Popsicles before we get there," she said.

"The Lone Pine Cafe next door has a good menu," he said, keeping his voice even.

"Do they have French toast?" Tiffany asked. "If they don't have French toast then I'm not going to eat."

"Is there an edible Caesar salad in this town?" the mother asked.

"He isn't the friggin' Chamber of Commerce," Bernie snapped. "Just go find yourselves some lunch and let the man do his job."

Bless you, Lucas said silently, as he watched the women flounce out the door and head for the Wagon Wheel. Sueann, owner of the cafe, and his older brother Derek's ex-wife, would burn Lucas's toast for sure if she found out he'd sent the Gorman women over. He'd have to double tip her for a month.

Once the women were gone, it didn't take long for Lucas to fill out the order form, write in the measurements of the horse and measure Bernie himself without once touching his ass.

After Bernie wrote out a check for the five-thousand-dollar deposit and left to join his family, Lucas put the check in his wallet, turned the wooden sign around to CLOSED and locked the front door. It was past one o'clock and he was starving.

Standing on the top step of his shop he noticed the little green car was gone. The tow truck had apparently already taken it to the Chevron station. Lucas briefly wondered where the woman went.

Snow, left over from yesterday's storm, crunched like fish bones under his flat-heeled boots when he walked to the cafe. The air was crisp and cold, his breath a powdery cloud. He shoved his hands deep into the pockets of his worn Carhartt jacket. The last few days the daytime temps had been in the thirties with evening lows in the teens, warm for those tough souls who made their homes in Montana and Maine, but downright chilly for Californians. The ski resorts fifty miles up the road would be drunk with joy over this early and generous snowfall.

He looked up at the white-topped Sierra Nevada, the grandfather mountains that both loomed over and protected his hometown. The shadowed, mysterious peaks had always frightened him as a child, especially when Aunt Birch's husband, Bobby, part Mexican and part Paiute-Shoshone, scared his nieces and nephews into giggly hysterics with late-night stories he made up about vengeful mountain lions the color of new snow.

"They stalk the foothills looking for boys and girls who shoot at the lion's fellow creatures," Uncle Bobby would whisper in his impressive bass voice while they sat around a blazing campfire in his large backyard, the yard Lucas now saw every morning from the kitchen window of his apartment over the garage. "Boys and girls who killed his forest friends for no good reason except to hear the blast of the gunshot and watch a blood blossom spread across a fur-covered rib cage."

Uncle Bobby's normally round and genial face always seemed to take on a frightening array of dark planes and mysterious edges in the flicker of the orange campfire. Before the story's end, the youngest ones inevitably ran for Aunt Birch's comforting arms, always open and ready for a terrified child.

Finally, when they'd all been worked up to a feverish pitch, she'd announce in her no-nonsense, teacher's voice, "That's enough, Bobby. The children have to sleep sometime this month." She always softened her admonishment with a smile and a wink. Even today Birch's smile had the power to cause Lucas's often tight stomach to relax.

But because of his uncle Bobby's stories, ones Bobby admitted weren't exactly of Paiute-Shoshone origin, but more of his own making and philosophy, Lucas never took to hunting like his older brothers, Cole and Derek. Like so many things Lucas did, it had angered his father, Carson, and worse, it widened the already canyon-sized rift between Bobby Hernandez and his brother-in-law. Carson McGavin had been Kitteridge McGavin's son through and through and agreed with his father that Birch marrying an Indian was a slap in the face to the whole McGavin clan. Though, unlike his father, Carson never stopped speaking to Birch and Bobby, the relationship was never a comfortable one.

Lucas thought about his father and the influence he still held in this town. Even today, seventeen years after his death, people still quoted him and told stories about him as if he'd died only last week. Like Lucas's grandpa Kitt, Carson had been powerful and feared, but he had also been adored. Women of all ages would follow his imposing figure wherever he'd gone and men plotted and maneuvered to be his friend. The only person Lucas had ever known who had come close to having that sort of charisma was Cole.

Lucas walked into the Lone Pine and glanced around the room for Ely. He spotted him at the end of the counter reading a paperback.

Over in a corner booth, the Gorman women were talking a mile a minute, obviously giving Sueann a bucketful of grief. Sueann stood in front of their booth, her long strawberry-blond braids tied with leather strips, her pencil poised patiently over her order pad. Bernie was safely hidden behind a copy of the *Cardinal Valley Gazette*. When one of the men at a nearby table called out Lucas's name, Sueann turned to look at him. He touched the brim of his wool baseball cap and grinned an apology. She shot him with a finger pistol, letting him know he was busted.

He slipped onto the stool next to Ely, who finished the page he was reading before looking up. A cooling plate of huevos rancheros sat in front of him.

"What're you reading?" Lucas asked.

Ely saved his place with a paper napkin and held up the book so Lucas could read the cover. *One Flew over the Cuckoo's Nest.*

"Story of my life," Lucas said. "Good movie, but Jack Nicholson hasn't had a decent role since."

"Book is better," Ely said, taking a sip of his coffee. "Surprised to see you here. Thought you'd be trying to hide from the Addams family."

"Bernie wrote me a five-thousand-dollar deposit check," Lucas said. "I'm feeling kind of warm and fuzzy about the Gormans right now."

"Enough to buy their lunch?" Ely asked.

"No," Lucas replied, grinning. "But enough to buy yours."

"If I'd have known that, I'd have asked for sour cream on the side," Ely said.

Cassie planted herself directly in front of Lucas, setting a large Coke, extra ice, in front of him. "Hey, Uncle Lucas, when can I ride that new mare of yours?"

Lucas smiled affectionately at his blue-haired niece. "Don't know, sweetheart. She's still pretty goosey." The sorrel mare was a new addition to the misfit band of horses he kept out on a section of his family's ranch called Clear Creek. The Circle MG ranch was one-fourth his, an inheritance from his grandfather. Like many ranchers these days, it made him affluent on paper, but piss-poor in terms of actual cash.

"Haven't you even named her yet?" Cassie asked, placing a paper napkin, knife, fork and spoon in front of him. "You sure you want a cheeseburger? Aren't you getting too old for cheese? What's your cholesterol anyway? Did you know that when they suck out the fat in your blood it's, like, this gross yellow? We saw a film in health class. Our teacher's trying to make us stop eating fast food." She tugged at her short denim skirt and giggled. "Like that's ever going to happen."

"Yes, I want a cheeseburger. With extra cheese and a large order of fries." He had no idea what his cholesterol was and until someone forced him into it, he wasn't going to find out. His daily burger was a ritual he was not ready to surrender. "Speaking of school . . ."

"Winter break," she reminded him. "You need to name her. Bet she'd quit being so goosey if she had a name."

"It'll take more than that," Lucas said indulgently. This mare was a sad-eyed little Mustang left to die at an abandoned shanty-ranch in south county. He guessed she'd been an inexpensive Bureau of Land Management purchase. When no one else would take her, the local vet called Lucas, a sucker every time, as his mother would say. "But I'll think about it."

"I could name her for you," Cassie said, turning around and sticking his order on the metal rack for Carlos. "Mom has a baby name book that has, like, the meanings of names and stuff."

"Be my guest, but I retain rights to final approval."

"Just what color is that you dipped your head in?" Ely asked Cassie.

She stuck her tongue out at him. The silver ball on her tongue glistened in the restaurant's florescent lighting. "Not that it's any of your business, but it's called blue sapphire."

"Why in the world your mama let you mutilate your tongue like that is beyond me," Lucas said. He took a long drag of his Coke, enjoying the burn down his scratchy throat.

"Because unlike some people in this pathetic town, she has at least a vestige of being cool." Carlos rang the bell for a pickup. Cassie turned around, picked up the plate of tri-tip steak and eggs and started around the counter toward the dining room.

"Vestige?" Ely repeated. "What's our little Cassie doing when not busy dipping her head in dye pots, actually reading a book?"

"It means a small amount of something," she said. "Kind of like your brain." She grinned at him. "Ha, two points, Professor Dumbo."

Ely winked at her. "That was an obvious one, grasshopper. Get back to work."

She reached into the pocket of her denim skirt and tossed both of them a fortune cookie. "Knock yourself out, boys," she said, sounding more like forty-five than seventeen.

"She's been watching Barbara Stanwyck movies," commented Ely, snapping the cookie's cellophane wrapper open with one hand.

Fortune cookie Wednesday at the Lone Pine Cafe was a tradition as old as the building itself. When the original structure was built back in the twenties, it was a Chinese restaurant and the owner predictably gave out fortune cookies with each meal. Throughout the sale and resale of the restaurant and all its cuisine mutations from Chinese to Basque to Italian to its present-day diner fare, the tradition of fortune cookies, at some point relegated to just being given out on Wednesdays, was the only enduring factor. When Sueann bought the diner thirteen years before with her divorce settlement from Lucas's brother Derek she'd seen no reason to stop the tradition.

Ely read his fortune out loud. "You will be invited to a small gathering with lots of spicy conversation." He tossed the tiny slip of paper onto his half-eaten eggs. "Guess that means Gordon will be bringing his sausage to the wassail party tonight." Gordon Vieira, famous for his homemade Portuguese linguica sausage, was a local sheriff's deputy. "What does yours say?"

Lucas opened his package and broke the cookie in half. "You will attend a party where strange customs prevail." Lucas crumpled the fortune in his hand. "Looks like we're going to the same party."

"Can't wait," Ely said. "Hear from Cole lately?"

Lucas shook his head no. "It's been a while, but that's Cole. Pisses me off because it worries Birch so much. She really misses him." It still annoyed Lucas that Cole refused, even after all these years, to let anyone know where he lived or how to get in touch with him.

"What if something happened to Aunt Birch or Mom or Uncle Bobby?" he'd ask his oldest brother when they'd meet once a year at some burnt-meat-smelling coffee shop in Las Vegas, a town Cole could fly into from anywhere.

"I'll know if something happens to one of you," Cole said, his voice so laid-back and certain, sounding so much like their father's, that Lucas often felt like reaching across the table and punching him. Before Lucas could pursue it further, Cole always changed the subject. "How's things out on the ranch? Derek still trying to be big man in town? How's Cassie doing? Mom still queen bee of the city council? She still making all the men paw at the ground like randy old bulls? Feel like shooting a game of pool?"

Lucas had even thought of hiring someone to search for his brother, find out where he lived. He knew people in San Francisco who would do it for him. But loyalty to his favorite brother's wishes kept him from it. After all that Cole had gone through, what he had suffered, if he wanted to keep his life private, what right did Lucas have to interfere?

"Your mom ever mention him?" Ely asked.

"No, but that's not new."

Ely stood up, stuck his book under his arm and threw a five dollar bill and two ones down on the counter.

Lucas pushed his money back toward him. "I said I'd buy your lunch."

"Leave it for Cassie then."

"You're leaving her a seven-dollar tip?"

Ely slapped Lucas on the back. "Tell her to buy some more hair dye. Maybe magenta would be good. See you round the wassail bowl."

"If I go," Lucas said. Truth was, he would prefer to stay home than attend the Tokopah Lodge's annual wassail party.

"Birch ain't likely to allow you to miss it. You know all these Christmas doings are the highlight of her year. She'll come get you and carry you there on her back."

"You're probably right," Lucas agreed.

A few minutes after Ely left, Cassie slid Lucas's lunch in front of him. He inhaled the meaty odor, relishing the heat on his face. There was nothing better on a cold afternoon than a hot cheeseburger and fries.

Halfway through his lunch, a headache started tapping at the inside of his skull. Though he knew he should get back to the shop and work on Bob Kesey's favorite roping saddle—he'd promised the repairs would be done before Christmas—the now-familiar pain that had struck the first month he'd come back to Cardinal informed him that wasn't likely. The agonizing aurora borealis started to waver behind his eye sockets. It was something he still hadn't learned to expect.

Migraines, Doc Winters had pronounced with the same certainty he'd said "It's a boy" when he'd brought Lucas into this world thirty-four years ago.

"That's nuts," Lucas replied. "I lived an incredibly stressful life in San Francisco and never even had to take an aspirin. How could living in a town like Cardinal give me migraines?"

Doc shrugged and prescribed some pills that dulled the pain, but didn't stop it permanently.

Like the circumstances of his life, there was no rhyme or reason to their attacks, and Lucas was trying to learn to just flow with them when they happened. It helped to get away from people, to tune down the clanging bell clapper of human voices. Last summer, he often drove out to the pasture where he kept his damaged horses and threw down an old camp blanket under the cottonwood tree that dominated the pasture. He'd stretch out with his eyes closed, listening to the horses snuffle and snort, waiting for the pain to subside.

But it was too cold to go out to the pasture today so he left the cafe and slowly walked the three blocks to his garage apartment. He took the stairs like an old man, placing one foot carefully in front of the other, trying not to move his head too quickly.

Pain totally enveloped his body when he eased down on the double bed without removing his boots. He didn't fight it now, but let it roll over him like a tank, almost thankful, because when it came, he thought of nothing, not his murdered father or his pushy ex-wife or his runaway brother or his angry mother. He didn't even think about the real reason he'd left San Francisco and the law and run home like the coward he believed himself to be.

He lay in the dark and rode the pain like a bronco, certain each time that this ride would be the one where his foot was caught in the stirrup and he was dragged to his death underneath a trampling set of blade-sharp hooves. Then, if he was lucky, he slept, hoping at times before he slipped off into darkness that he would not wake up if the pain was there waiting for him.

But he always woke, his eyes grainy and tender, in the summer to the milky coo of mourning doves and twittering western meadowlarks outside his window, in the winter to a frigid silence. The sharp scent of wild sage seemed to always cling to his clothes, constantly reminding him that where he lived now there were no cable cars, no martini bars, no walking the streets for hours without having to acknowledge one single person.

On his last day in San Francisco, before running home to Cardinal, he'd sat in the back of a stale-smelling courtroom wearing a faded flannel shirt and jeans and watched his former client, Mitchell Weeks, who'd killed his wife and three children in a moment of uncontrolled rage, be sentenced to life without the possibility of parole. And, Lucas often thought, unable to forget his secret complicity in their deaths, so was he.

3

RUBY

Ruby walked the four blocks to the Chevron station where the Indian-looking man named Ely said he'd tow her car. She was slightly out of breath and a little less agitated when she opened the grimy glass door leading into the office. A lank-haired teenage boy wearing a Dodgers T-shirt sat behind the counter playing a handheld video game.

"Is Mr. . . . ?" She hesitated. Ely had never given her his last name.

"Ely just called," the boy said without looking up. "Said he'd be here in a few minutes."

"Thank you." She glanced around, then sat down on a plastic lawn chair next to a bubble gum machine. Her hand tightened around the handle of the Macy's bag, the only thing she'd grabbed from the car before it was towed.

Ely showed up fifteen minutes later. He walked behind the counter and nudged the boy. "That thing'll rot your brain. Go out and sweep the sidewalk." The boy shrugged away Ely's hand, but set the game on the counter and obeyed. After he was gone, Ely said to Ruby, "Like I said, it might take a few days to get parts." Behind him, "Rudolph, the Red-Nosed Reindeer" played on a grease-stained white radio. "Especially since it's the holidays. Hard to light a fire under folks 'round Christmas."

She struggled not to sound impatient or snotty. She needed this man's help. "Just order the parts, please, and start as soon as you can."

"Where can I reach you?"

She glanced down the street. The hotel the waitress had recommended looked fairly close, the sign visible from here. "I'll try to get a room at the Tokopah Lodge. If I can't, I'll come back and let you know where I'll be staying. But don't worry, I'll be checking every day."

The man gave a throaty chuckle. "I'm not worried. You can check all you want, but it won't get those parts here any quicker."

Ruby frowned and didn't answer. Instead, she turned her back to him, grabbed the red Macy's bag and walked out of the office. She took her green wheeled suitcase from the trunk and started down the slick sidewalk toward the lodge. Within minutes, the frigid air made her hands feel burnt with cold.

The Tokopah Lodge was an odd mixture of architectural motifs. It was a two-story, oyster-white building with a reddish brown Spanish tile roof and a wide front porch held up by four Southern-style plantation columns. The columns were, at present, wrapped with artificial pine boughs and blue and green twinkling lights. A picture window stretched half the length of the porch, highlighting a perfect triangle-shaped Christmas tree in what Ruby assumed was the lobby. The room windows were long and vertical, arched at the top and flat on the bottom with wooden trim painted a deep red-brown. The front of the old hotel was flanked by two huge leafless trees who reached skeleton fingers to the ponderous clouds.

She stood at the bottom of the five concrete steps for a moment, then, despite the fact that she was freezing, turned and walked across the street to the small city park. She sat down on a damp green bench underneath a thirty-foot pine tree decorated with shiny silver bells and multicolored Christmas lights.

She opened her leather shoulder bag to look for the lodge's listing in the used Frommer's travel guide she'd bought at a library book sale. There was no point even walking into the lobby if the rooms were too expensive. She had about three thousand dollars in her checking account and two thousand dollars credit left on her Visa. Who knew how long that had to last her? She'd need it to start over somewhere, rent an apartment and pay for utilities and food until she found another job. On top of that, there were the car repairs that she hadn't counted on. She didn't want to waste her money on a fancy hotel room.

Inside her purse, the fortune cookie Sueann had given her rested on top of the travel guide. She placed it on the bench next to her and thumbed through the guide. The lodge wasn't listed, which meant it was either popular enough not to need the listing or too tacky for this guide to consider. With the building's tidy and well-kept appearance, she doubted that it was the latter.

She tucked the guide back inside her purse, then glanced down at the fortune cookie. She slowly opened it, the crackle of the cellophane loud in the empty park. Anticipation fluttered in her chest, making her feel a little foolish. Was she so desperate for assurance that coming here was the right thing to do that, like the diner waitress, she would actually grant the tiny slip of paper's words credence?

Your misfortunes will arrive on foot and depart on horseback.

She glanced down into the red Macy's bag at the plain wooden box wrapped in the colorful afghan. Bits and pieces of the last year sparkled in front of her eyes. She thought about the last day she saw Cole, tried to remember what they'd talked about, what he'd been like. Had he been sad, angry, depressed? She couldn't remember. That was one of the hardest things she'd had to live with the last three months. She couldn't remember the smallest details of their last day together.

"Well, Cole McGavin," she said out loud, wondering if there was some possible way he could hear what she was saying. "Here I am, smack dab in the bosom of your hometown, looking for the family you obviously felt compelled to keep secret from me. What should I do now?"

The cheerfully lit lodge loomed in front of her, a decision to be made. She could at least go inside and ask about a room. Asking didn't cost a dime. She fingered the tiny slip of paper. "And as long as we're talking, would you please explain to me just exactly what this stupid fortune means?"

BIRCH

Though she wasn't much of a gambler, Birch McGavin Hernandez would have bet her last hundred dollars that the attractive young woman sitting in the park across the street from the lodge was experiencing an emotional crisis of some kind. The woman sat under the huge pine tree Birch's late brother, Carson, gave the city. It was presently decorated with huge, specially designed silver-plated ornaments and twinkling lights also paid for by Carson. Even after all the years he'd been gone, things that Carson McGavin had given this town remained, his generosity to Cardinal a constant legacy.

Birch pretended to rearrange the handpainted postcards on the rack in front of one of the lodge's windows and watched the girl dig through her bulky leather handbag. "She's been out there a long time," she said to her husband, Bobby, who stood behind the knotty-pine counter cracking a roll of quarters. "She's going to catch her death of cold. Is it my imagination or does she look like she's talking to herself?"

"Leave her be, Birch," Bobby said, his deep voice sounding both indulgent and resigned to being ignored.

Birch continued to watch the girl. She seemed to be talking to the red shopping bag at her feet. Was she on some kind of drug? No, she didn't look the type. She was dressed too neatly, even if the leather jacket she wore looked two sizes too big for her. And she looked too healthy, at least from here.

Most likely her agitation had something to do with some man. In her sixty-four years on this earth Birch had learned a few things about women's problems. Most of them had their origin with some man you loved or thought you loved or who thought he loved you or thought he loved someone else.

Maybe she was recently divorced. Or running from an abusive husband. My land, wasn't that an old, sad story? People just didn't raise their boys with an ounce of respect for women anymore. Birch wondered where her family was. Was she too afraid to go home to them? Perhaps ashamed that the dire predictions of her marriage to the bad husband came true? What a shame. Here it was only a few days before Christmas and that pretty young woman was all alone out there in the cold.

She sighed and pulled her blue fleecy jacket closer around her. The weak afternoon sun coming through the windows didn't do much to warm her aching bones. There was a time when she ran around in chilly weather like this with only a thin wool sweater. She switched some postcards around, then turned back to her husband.

He walked across the empty lobby, the slight limp from his arthritic knees barely noticeable, and added three pine logs to the crackling fire. The massive smooth stone fireplace was hung with fifteen handmade Christmas stockings, one for each of her and Bobby's nieces and nephews. She still filled them every Christmas Eve even for the ones who'd long since left Cardinal, though all of them, except for Cole, eventually wandered back here sometime around the holidays. This time of year was when she especially missed her oldest nephew, the one she felt the closest to, who she thought of as *hers*, though she hoped the others didn't notice. After all, she was the one who took care of him for the first year of his life when his own mother couldn't . . . or wouldn't, as some people in this town would say. June had not been thrilled about becoming a mother so young, and she'd made sure everyone, especially Carson, knew that.

She went over to the blue spruce Christmas tree decorated with her collection of western and Indian ornaments and straightened out a hand-beaded Shoshone horseshoe-shaped ornament. Birch loved Christmas, especially here in Cardinal, where most folks weren't overly commercial about it. They couldn't be really. There wasn't all that much money in their pockets to buy fancy computer games and the latest gizmos for their kids. Most of the working people in Cardinal were getting by all right, but didn't have a whole lot left over from their paychecks each week. In her estimation, that made the old-fashioned celebrations, like the Christmas tree lighting in the town park three weeks ago and the caroling the church groups did even more special. Not to mention the Tokopah Lodge's own special Christmas traditions.

This seventy-five-year-old room with its bold-patterned Pendleton wool sofas, photographs of old movie stars who'd stayed here in the thirties and forties, and uneven wooden floors held a truckload of sweet memories. She was proud that she and Bobby had always been able to provide some kind of Christmas for whomever had no place to go during the holidays.

Birch and Bobby's wassail party three days before Christmas as well as their Christmas Eve open house here at the lodge were events the town anticipated. They were the same every year as the year before. Tradition meant something in Cardinal. It meant something to her and Bobby.

"Maybe I should go out there and see if she needs anything," she said.

Bobby smiled at her, his black, almond-shaped eyes amused. "Are we so desperate for guests that we have to drag them in off the streets?"

"Oh, you," she said, brushing away his comment with a flip of her hand. "We're doing fine this year and you know it."

Though they'd supplemented the lodge's income with her salary as an elementary school teacher for most of the forty-one years they'd owned it, now, except for her modest pension, this lodge was how they put beans on the table. This year had been a profitable one so far since snow fell early, bringing the tourists. But the dry years lurked out there, years of them. You had to put money aside in anticipation. That type of life was familiar as an old saddle for Birch and Bobby. Both of them grew up on ranches, both were used to the year-to-year survival that came with jobs that depended on the weather's fickle charity.

"Okay," Bobby said, coming up behind her and giving her a hug around the waist. "Since it's almost Christmas, I'll indulge you. What do you think her sob-sister story is?"

She turned, pulled out of his embrace and poked him gently on the shoulder. "Don't you make fun of me, Roberto Domingo Luis Hernandez."

He lifted his wide hands in protest. "I am not making fun, I swear."

She went around the counter and started rearranging the antique brass call bell, their shiny brochures and the guest book, which was more show than a legal record of who had stayed there. She liked pointing out to guests the signatures of Roy Rogers and Dale Evans, Gene Autry, Clark Gable, Marilyn Monroe and John Wayne. A lot of old Westerns had been filmed in the rugged, semi-arid foothills of Tokopah county, and often the stars had stayed in this very lodge, though long before Birch and Bobby bought it in the early sixties.

She propped her elbows on the counter and rested her chin in her hands. "I'd venture to say she's running from a man, doesn't have much money and is contemplating spending what she does have on a room here." She sighed again and scratched a spot in her short, gray curls with a red Tokopah Lodge pencil. "I can't blame her. If I was alone at Christmas, I'd rather stay here than at the Motel Six or the Holiday Inn."

"What makes you think she's alone?" Bobby asked. "Maybe someone is meeting her."

Birch straightened up and shook her head. "No, she's alone. I can tell." Though she'd not traveled much and had spent most of her life right here in Cardinal, working with kids and the public had taught her one certain thing: If you studied a person long enough, they gave away their whole life story. If you were paying attention, usually within the first half hour. That woman was alone and she was having troubles.

He came around the counter and stood next to her, bumping her shoulder with his. "The Dale Evans room is open."

She smiled up at him. "My thought exactly."

The lodge's rooms were named for the famous Western celebrities who used to stay here. The Dale Evans, an upstairs corner room overlooking Main Street, was Birch's personal favorite. She'd decorated it herself, picking out the bleached lodge pole pine head- and footboards, the chenille bedspread with the picture of Dale Evans and her horse, Buttermilk, the cowgirl knickknacks and black and white photographs of movie cowgirls like Dale, Judy Canova, Barbara Stanwyck, and real cowgirls, like Faye Johnson Blesing, Polly Burson and her favorite, Pee Wee Burge. It also displayed in a place of honor over the bird's eye maple bureau, Bobby's treasured autographed picture of Patsy Cline in her fringed cowgirl outfit.

Though Bobby teased her about using the room for her family, they also tried to keep the room free for any of his extended family, a huge conglomerate of Hispanics and Paiute-Shoshone Indians who lived here in Tokopah county as well as all around the West—Reno, Elko, Flagstaff and Cody. Someone's daughter, son, niece or nephew was always looking for a night's or a week's lodging. Bobby and Birch, never able to have children of their own, took them in, fed them, sheltered them, gave them work if they needed it and love until they were ready to move on.

"I suppose we could make her a deal," he said, rubbing his chin thoughtfully. "Maybe give her the room for half price. It's going to be empty anyway. At least we'll make *some* money."

She shook her red pencil at him. "You are nothing but a big old marshmallow."

He scrunched his coppery face and gave her a mock scowl. "You take that back. I won't have my fierce warrior image tainted."

She laughed and kissed his cheek. Even after all this time married, forty-four years come March, Birch never tired of his soft-as-deer-skin voice, the beautiful angles of his face, his silvery gray braid or, despite his outwardly gruff attitude, his compassionate concern for anyone in trouble. He was born right here in Cardinal, only twenty-nine days before her. He'd been one of her father's ranch hands when they fell in love. They had both been barely twenty-one years old and she had never regretted marrying him, not one moment, even though her father,

Kitteridge McGavin, had told her if she went through with it he would disinherit her and never speak to her again. He'd kept his word. Though she had been open to mending that fence, he wouldn't even see her on the day he died from heart failure twenty years ago.

Heart failure, she thought with the sorrow mixed with anger that she felt whenever her father came to mind. Didn't a person have to possess a heart for it to fail?

She stood on tiptoe and whispered into her husband's ear. "Just for that, chief, there might be a little something special in your stocking this year."

"I feel my image rising again," he said. "No, wait, that's not my image . . ."

"Stop it, you crazy old man," she said, her cheeks turning a soft rose.

He laughed and kissed her forehead. "Can't believe I can still make you blush."

They were still laughing when the woman walked through the lodge's double doors clutching the red shopping bag close to her body and pulling a green wheeled suitcase. A rush of cold air blew in around her. Behind her, a family of six who'd rented three rooms on the first floor, stumbled in, and for a moment, in the confusion of people asking Birch and Bobby questions about restaurants, hiking trails and the menu for the wassail party that night, the young woman froze, then seemed to change her mind and start to leave.

"Excuse me a moment," Birch told the lady wearing a mint green ski sweater who was asking Birch about the food being served at the party. For some reason, Birch felt compelled to speak to this girl.

"I'm allergic to shellfish," the woman said.

"We're only serving beef and chicken," Birch answered, hurrying around the counter. "And green chile and cheese tamales."

"What kind of cheese?" the woman continued. "I can't eat any wheat products. Is there any breading on the chicken?"

Birch held up one finger and gave the woman an apologetic smile. "Please, just one moment. Let me see if this young lady wants a brochure and then we can go over the whole menu."

Birch walked across the lobby and caught the girl just as she had her hand on the doorknob.

"Can I help you, hon?" Birch asked.

The girl jumped at the sound of Birch's strong, clear teacher's voice. She turned, stared at Birch, then said, "No, thanks."

She was older than Birch originally thought, in her early to mid-thirties. And pretty, in a fresh, soap commercial sort of way. A hint of freckles was sprinkled across her nose and pink cheeks.

"Would you like to hear our Christmas special?" Birch asked. They didn't actually have a special, but something compelled her to offer a room to this girl.

The girl continued to study Birch, her eyes a wintry gray with flecks of black. They reminded Birch of granite.

"What sort of discount?" the girl asked, her voice low and wary. "My car is being repaired over at the Chevron station and I might be here for a few days." She hesitated, then added, "Sueann at the cafe down the street told me to try here."

That cinched it for Birch. She trusted Sueann's judgment. Sueann wouldn't have told the girl to use her name unless she thought the girl really needed help. Sueann would recognize desperation. She had stayed at the lodge herself when she finally worked up enough nerve to leave Derek.

"Our normal room rate is seventy dollars, but if you take this room for a week, it'll be . . ." Birch paused, trying to quickly figure out a price that the girl could afford, but wouldn't scream out *charitable gesture*. "One hundred seventy-five dollars. That includes breakfast."

She could see the girl quickly calculate the daily rate in her head. Twenty-five dollars a night was nothing to sneeze at. It was cheaper than the older motels in town and definitely cheaper than any of the chains. The girl gave Birch a guarded look.

"It's not one of our best rooms," Birch lied, realizing she'd probably made the price too low and given away her altruistic intentions. "But it's comfortable and clean."

The girl hesitated again, her eyes sweeping over Tokopah's spacious lobby, resting briefly on the brightly patterned sofas and chairs, the stone fireplace with the beaded Paiute baskets on the mantel, the well-used old grand piano in the corner with Birch's nativity collection displayed on the closed lid, the French doors leading to the dining room. Birch could almost feel her longing to stop and rest here. That made Birch partial to her before they'd even gotten acquainted.

"You can pay by the day, if it's easier," Birch said.

The girl's face stiffened. "Thank you, but I don't take charity."

Birch straightened her spine, taken aback by the girl's bluntness. "Let me know what you decide," she said, clipping off the words like a snip of sharp scissors. Her face flushed with embarrassment, she turned and walked back to the woman who wanted to know about the wassail party menu. She answered every question without once looking at what the girl was doing. She was flipping through the day's junk mail when the girl walked up to the counter

"I'll take the room," the girl blurted out. "But, please, for its real price."

Birch gave her a cool look, not about to let herself be taken in again. "A week would be four hundred fifty dollars. It's a little less than seventy dollars a night." She narrowed her eyes at the girl. "It's the discount we give anyone who stays here a week."

The girl lifted her chin just slightly. "Fine. Thank you."

"Check, credit card or cash?" Birch asked, pushing the registration card toward her. She was guessing the girl wouldn't use a credit card even if she had one. Covering her tracks, no doubt.

"Cash," the girl replied. Her open wallet showed the credit card slots held only one Visa card.

Birch felt a smug satisfaction at calling it right. "Just fill out this card, please."

The girl completed the card with a careful, neat printing. Birch read the information while the girl fiddled with the bills in her wallet. *Ruby Stoddard General Delivery Cardinal, California. Car: 1991 Honda Civic.* The only phone number she gave was her cell phone, obviously a new one, because she had to check its number while filling out the card.

Well, this one sure wasn't going to reveal much. Birch wrote out a receipt and handed her the old-fashioned room key as well as a more modern flat one. She gave her a quick rundown of the next few days' activities, which the girl listened to intently, her silvery eyes solemn.

"Your room is number twelve. Upstairs, turn left, all the way to the end of the hall. We serve a complimentary continental breakfast from seven to ten. The dining room is open for lunch and dinner—noon to three and six to ten. Things are a little different around here this week though, it being Christmas and all. We're having a wassail party here tonight at seven p.m. Just a bunch of locals eating munchies, drinking wassail or homemade eggnog, stronger spirits if you're so inclined, and singing Christmas carols. All the guests at the lodge are invited. Christmas Eve we host an open house with a buffet of turkey and all the fixings to anyone who walks in the door. On Christmas day, you are on your own, though you're welcome to any leftovers in the kitchen and there's always plenty. All that's included in the price of *every* guest's room." She made it clear to this girl that no charity was involved.

"Thank you," Ruby said, her face not changing expression at Birch's litany of holiday activities or her tone.

"There's a parking lot in the back for whenever you get your car back," Birch added. "We lock the front and side hotel doors after eleven o'clock. You'll have to use that flat key to get in if you're out gallivanting past then." She lifted her eyebrows. "Not that there's a lot to gallivant to around here. There's a couple of cowboy bars downtown, the movie theater and the casino out on the reservation, which isn't very far, a half mile north of town. They have a nice buffet there on Saturday nights."

"I'm not much of a night person," Ruby said, tucking the keys inside her purse. "Is there a bookstore in town?"

Birch gave a tart, approving nod, starting to like the girl again despite her prickly attitude. A reader was almost always a good sign of someone who wouldn't be trouble.

"There's two. Leonard's Used Books over in the Wal-Mart plaza north of town. It's right next door to Jocko's Jerky Emporium. Downtown there's The Novel Experience. It's small, but has a good selection.

Man who owns it is named Lincoln Holyoke. He also owns the coffee-house next door called Holy Grounds." Birch gave a wry smile. "He's an odd duck, but nice as a spring rain. And he makes the best snicker-doodles I've ever eaten."

The girl's face remained aloof.

Okay, Miss Ruby Stoddard, Birch thought, be that way. I'll just give you the rest of my tourist spiel and leave you alone to brood. "We have lots of nice shops in town. Walt's Western Toggery down by the movie theater has some real pretty things. Lots of little antique and crafty stores down on the other side of the Mountainview Stop 'n' Shop, our three feed stores each have a small selection of clothes and whatnots, Ben Franklin's Five and Dime and there's always Mr. J.C. Penney."

"Thank you," Ruby said, her voice polite.

After Ruby left for her room, Birch went into the small office behind the counter where Bobby was balancing the lodge's checkbook.

"What'd they say the high would be today?" she asked.

"Thirty-nine, but looks like we won't even make that."

"Heavens, that has to be some kind of record." She perched on the corner of the desk. "Wonder where my long silk underwear is. The girl's name is Ruby Stoddard."

He grunted and kept adding up checks.

"She's a strange one," she said.

He didn't look up from his work. "Heard your little exchange with her. That one's got some pride in her."

"Not always a good thing," Birch said, looking down at his bent head. "She had me irritated there for a minute."

"Could tell."

"But I think it's just a shield. Deep down I think she's hurting." And, despite how off-putting this Ruby Stoddard was, it made Birch want to hug her. She understood that kind of defense. Sometimes being angry at the world was the only thing that kept a person from packing it all in.

Bobby hit the adding machine total button, then looked up at her, his expression thoughtful. "My uncle Tomas once had this nice little buckskin filly. A sweet thing, but she had one bad habit. If you came at her from the wrong side, she would just as soon bite you as look at you. Never could trust her."

Birch laughed, bent down and kissed the top of his silvery head. "Oh, she's just a little jumpy. All I hope is there isn't some shotgun-toting husband or boyfriend two days behind her."

"If there is, I'm not certain I'd put my money on *him*," Bobby said. "When that filly became grown and had her some babies, she turned out to be a real nice little mama, but, you know, she never did stop biting."

5

LUCAS

It was past six o'clock and dark. Lucas, hands shoved deep into the pockets of his old barn jacket, stood in the city park across the street from the Tokopah Lodge and watched the wassail party through the large picture window. He was in no hurry to join the festivities. Among the hundred or so people already there he could see his aunt Birch standing behind the folding tables covered with food, serving her guests, his uncle Bobby adding another log to the fire and his mother, June, dressed to impress in a bright red, embroidered western shirt. Walt Creston, his late father's best friend, rested his arm around June's shoulders in a proprietary way that still caused Lucas's back teeth to clamp down in disgust.

One of the local girls, Andrea, whose mother owned Cardinal's only bakery, had told him about it during a dinner date that had been arranged by his aunt when Lucas first moved back home. Andrea had been three years behind him in school. Head of the high school's debate team for two years, she had an annoying habit of waving her fork at him whenever she wanted to make a point.

"I can't believe you never knew about them," she'd said over broiled halibut at an upscale restaurant in Mammoth. The wait for their tiny, marble-topped table had been forty minutes despite the fact that he'd made reservations. That and the indiscriminate use of the word *fusion* when describing food represented to Lucas everything he hated about this ski town.

Andrea wagged her fork. "They've been going at it since before your dad died." She smiled, cherry-colored lipstick staining one of her front teeth.

He had tried not to appear shocked. After all, he was the one who'd supposedly lived the sophisticated city life. Andrea had lived in this tiny town her whole life. The only job she'd ever held was cashiering at her mother's bakery. Yet she seemed to take his mother's and Walt Creston's long-running affair with a nonchalance befitting the most relationship-soured city girl. Then again, it wasn't her mother's sex life being discussed.

"I'd rather not talk about my mother's personal life," he'd said stiffly.

Had his father known about the affair? Carson McGavin had been such a charismatic man. When Lucas was growing up, he'd watched dozens of women whisper and stare at his father during barbecues and ranch roundups. Why would his mother cheat on his father, the most sought-after man in the county? Besides that, he couldn't imagine his father accepting it. It was a well-known fact that June McGavin was considered lucky to have landed someone like Carson. She was the only girl in a dirt-poor Bakersfield family whose father was overjoyed when his only daughter out of six children "made good" by marrying a rich rancher.

"Whatever," Andrea said, shrugging. "Sorry I had to be the one to burst your bubble about your mom."

He looked down at his half-eaten halibut, not about to confide in her the bubble concerning his mother's character had exploded long before he left for UC Berkeley. Her unemotional nature had never been a secret, at least within the family. Family to her meant Carson and her three sons. Long before Lucas was born she broke ties with her family of birth. Her devotion had always been for the ranch, her position in Cardinal's society and the memory of his father. He was never sure which was more important.

Lucas saw his maternal grandfather only one time before he died of emphysema at fifty-seven. It was Birch who drove him by the sun-baked, one-bedroom apartment in Oildale. He'd been ten years old and on his way to Boy Scout camp. It shamed him now to recall that all he could think about at the time was escaping the smoke-stained, sweet-hot, beer scented room as fast as possible. Looking back at it now, a part of him understood why his mother wanted so desperately to leave her past behind.

Had June really been involved with Walt Creston that long? Had that somehow been a part of what happened that dry September night seventeen years ago? Lucas was sixteen when his father was killed. He had stayed in town with his aunt and uncle that night to attend a friend's birthday party. After Cole shot their father, an impenetrable cloud of family secrecy surrounded the event, despite its publicity. Only Mom, Cole and Derek really knew what happened. Despite his persistence and angry accusations of being left out of the family, Lucas could never persuade any of them to talk about it. He thought about it every September twenty-fifth. He always wondered what Cole did on that day.

He blew out a breath, a fist-sized white cloud of freezing air. It looked warm and welcoming inside the lodge. Though his head still ached slightly from his migraine, he was feeling a little hungry. Birch's green chile tamales would taste good.

He was halfway up the lodge's stone steps when the front door opened.

Ely stepped out onto the wide porch, a red plastic cup dangling from his fingers. "Birch sent me out to drag you inside." He wore a dark blue sweater and clean pressed Wranglers.

Lucas glanced down at the clothes he hadn't changed from this afternoon. They were even more rumpled now that he'd slept in them. Birch would have his head on a platter. "Guess I should have at least changed my shirt."

"Don't worry, Birch'll just be glad you're here." Ely held out the plastic cup. "Take a swig of this. It'll get you through the first five minutes. The eggnog in the red punch bowl has the rum, but Birch is guarding it like a mother sow. I'm guessing she doesn't plan on having a re-peat of last year."

"Derek here yet?"

"No, but Birch says he's coming. Took his latest girlfriend up to the Mammoth shopping outlets. Sueann's supposed to be dropping by, too."

"Oh, great," Lucas said. "Hope they miss each other."

Last year, after Derek had chased too many spiked eggnogs with straight shots of Captain Hook's 180-proof rum, he took it upon himself to start reliving, very loudly, the five tumultuous years of his and Sueann's marriage. The evening ended with a fistfight out on the front lawn between Derek and Sueann's older brother, John Lynley, the owner and publisher of the *Cardinal Valley Gazette*. It embarrassed and angered Birch, but because both men habitually dressed in western clothing, it actually provided a memorable evening's entertainment for her guests, who speculated among themselves if the fight was real or staged.

"I used to love Birch and Bobby's Christmas get-togethers," Lucas said, tilting his head back and drinking the eggnog in two long gulps. The rum hit his stomach with a sweet warmth that felt both comforting and dangerous. "Now they just make me feel trapped."

Ely gave him a thoughtful look. "You can walk out whenever you want. That's not the definition of trapped."

"I suppose." Lucas turned and looked through the window at his mother again. June was talking with great animation to a middle-aged man in an expensive brown Stetson who'd recently approached Lucas about building him a saddle. He was a retired patent attorney who'd bought a hundred-acre spread next to the Circle MG and was contemplating buying a few head of the MG's award-winning Black Angus. Lucas suspected he was more interested in bedding June. Though he hated admitting it, even at fifty-nine years old his mother was a woman who men still made fools of themselves over.

"Just look at Circe working her magic," Ely commented dryly.

Lucas turned to look at him. "What?"

Ely pointed at June. "Enchantress in the *Odyssey*. She turned men into swine."

Lucas shook his head and laughed. "You are so right." He stomped the snow off his boots and ran a hand through his shaggy hair. "Let's get on with it. After a few more cups of this eggnog, I'm sure we'll be standing around the piano singing about Jack Frost's roasted chestnuts with Derek and Walt."

"Not enough rum on this green earth that'll make that happen, partner," Ely replied.

They turned to open the front door when Lucas was hit in the back of the head with a wet snowball. A second one hit Ely in the left shoulder.

"Ha!" Sueann called from out on the front lawn. "You cowboys are too easy. Like shooting ducks in a pond." By the time they'd spun around, she'd stooped down and was packing another snowball with her mittened hands. She wore a dark brown wool barn jacket and a red and brown patterned knit hat.

"Peace," Lucas said, coming down the steps, Ely right behind him. He held up his hands in surrender. "We come to your planet in peace."

She answered by tossing the loose snowball at his chest. It fell apart a foot short of him, causing him to laugh.

"This snow is worthless," she said, brushing her hands down the sides of her jeans. "Snow was better when we were kids."

"No kidding. Remember the year we all got sleds? When Bobby took us up to Drake's Hill every weekend?"

"*That* was snow," she said, smiling. "I loved my Flexible Flyer."

"Birch would bring us hot chocolate and chili."

"She'd make us stop and eat even though we didn't want to. We'd eat standing up because we wanted to get back on our sleds as soon as possible."

"You had a bright pink snowsuit that year."

She flipped her thick, single braid over her shoulder. "You remember that snowsuit?"

"How could I forget? You looked like a bottle of Pepto-Bismol."

She punched his shoulder, making a soft thump with her snow-crusted glove. "You jerk. I begged my mom for that suit. I thought I looked very stylish."

"We'd all pile into the back of Bobby's truck and come back to the lodge afterward. Our faces were blue by the time we drove into town."

She brushed snow off the palm of her glove. "That was back before the safety gurus stopped all the fun stuff like riding in the beds of pickup trucks and skating without a helmet. Birch would have popcorn balls waiting for us. And more hot chocolate." She adjusted her knit cap, pulling it down over her ears, then rubbed her pink nose. "Even hot chocolate was better when we were kids. Real milk and real cocoa. No one made instant like we do now. Man alive, our generation is a lazy bunch."

"Everything was better when we were kids," Lucas said.

"You two old folks through reminiscing?" Ely asked, standing slightly apart, watching them, his dark eyes blank. "It's getting chilly out here."

Lucas and Sueann looked at him and then at each other, embarrassed. It was easy to forget now that they were adults that Ely had not experienced the same carefree childhood they had. For the first time, Lucas wondered what Ely had been doing those times he and Sueann had been flying carefree down the hills on their sleds and drinking Birch's cinnamon-laced hot chocolate.

"Let's scoot inside before all the tamales are gone," Sueann said, breaking the awkward moment. She hooked one arm through Lucas's and the other through Ely's. "I'll make all the women jealous by walking in with the two most eligible bachelors in Cardinal."

"Which," Ely said, "as your astute daughter would point out, proves what a truly pathetic town this is."

RUBY

aughter in the hallway outside Ruby's room startled her awake. She bolted up in the queen-size bed, unaware for a few seconds where she was. In the dark room, it came back to her in pieces, like a shattered mirror. *Cole. Cardinal. His will. The Circle MG ranch. Her broken car. The Tokopah Lodge.*

She glanced up at the signed photograph of Patsy Cline over the tall bureau. Her dark, perfect lips reminded Ruby of her mother. She sat up in bed and turned on the bedside lamp, flooding the room with golden light. She'd been too exhausted to inspect the room closely when she'd first checked in. She'd immediately crawled under the denim-covered down comforter and fell asleep the minute her head hit the pillow.

Just as she suspected, the silver-haired woman had told a white lie when she tried to rent it to Ruby at that ridiculous rate. It was definitely not one of their cheap rooms. The decor was straight out of one of those fancy western magazines, a room fit for a rodeo queen—lodgepole pine bed, vintage Annie Oakley pillows and a brown overstuffed leather chair etched with cattle brands.

Outside her door, the laughter faded away. The clock-radio next to the bed read seven o'clock. She'd been asleep almost three hours and still felt exhausted. But, to her surprise, hunger gnawed at her ribs, that half-eaten grilled cheese sandwich a distant memory. Though hungry, she really didn't want to leave this room tonight. It felt, if not safe, at least, someplace to *be* until she could decide what to do. Right now, no matter how closely she was watching her money, she would have paid thirty bucks for the privacy of a room service hamburger. But, the Tokopah didn't have room service.

Maybe if she waited long enough, the hunger would go away. A minute later, her stomach rumbled again. There was no disputing it. She'd have to find something to eat or be kept awake the rest of the night. Though she was thankful to have the feeling of hunger return, something she'd experienced rarely since Cole died, why did it have to come back full force tonight?

She burrowed under the comforter, wishing she was back in the little vine-covered house on the edge of one of Orange County's last citrus groves. It lay only a quarter of a mile from the San Diego freeway, but in the backyard, at night, over the hum of the traffic, she and Cole could still hear coyotes howling. They'd lived in the house their whole marriage—exactly six months. By now, it was probably a pile of broken lumber, ready to be hauled to the dump.

She had no idea what the McGavin family would be willing to pay for her share of the Circle MG Ranch, but whatever it was, she'd add it to what she'd already saved to help her begin a new life somewhere far away. Someplace that would help her forget how for six months of this year she'd been happier than she'd ever imagined being. And the last two months and twenty days, the saddest she'd ever been.

Maybe she'd track down her brother, find out if he was still in Nashville. She didn't know anything about Tennessee, but it seemed as good a place as any to start over. It was ironic, really, leaving California to start over. Most people, in stories and in real life, came to this state to start a new life. She'd always wondered where Californians went to start over—Alaska, Brazil, the Yukon?

The bed felt so good she didn't want to move. It felt so good she wanted to thank someone for it. She felt guilty remembering how rude she'd been to the woman who'd checked her in, the one who'd tried to practically give her this room. She had obviously been trying to do something kind for a stranger at Christmas.

Ruby suspected it was the downward cast to her gray eyes that elicited the woman's pity. She was constantly being asked by customers why she looked so sad, even when she wasn't. They would admonish her to be happy, try to make her smile. Though she knew it came with the territory of working with the public, it annoyed her that, just because she served them food, people somehow felt they had the right to comment on her appearance or tell her what she should be feeling.

"You have sad eyes," Cole used to tell her when she complained about people's presumptuous remarks. Then he laughed. "Some people would call them bedroom eyes. They're the first thing I noticed about you."

"That is so sexist I'm not even going to dignify it with an answer," she'd said, but smiled. Somehow, when Cole said things like that, they made her laugh.

"Men have sad eyes, too. Look at Sylvester Stallone, or Nicolas Cage."

"No, thanks. I prefer my men more upbeat."

"Like Steve Martin?"

"No," she said, taking his smiling face in her hands, not realizing how these words would come back to haunt her. "Like you."

The words of the coroner's assistant with the cheerleader name came back to her. "I'm sorry, Mrs. McGavin," Ginger had said. "It appears that there were no skid marks. His truck was found at the bottom of a ravine off Ortega Highway." Cole and she had driven on that highway, one of the few semi-country roads left in Orange County, during one of their early dates. They'd driven it all the way to Lake Elsinore and eaten at a hamburger stand Cole knew about.

"We'll know more after the autopsy," Ginger added.

More, such as, he had been drinking, Ruby realized she was trying to diplomatically say. That, at least, would have made sense, though she had never known him to drink alcohol. But when neither alcohol nor drugs were found in his system, it was listed as an accident. They didn't officially call it suicide, but Ruby knew they suspected he deliberately drove off the highway. She also knew they were probably right. The note in his safety deposit box, which she didn't share with anyone, supported what they suspected.

Ruby felt betrayed, like he'd cheated on her, only worse. She'd known too many times the sting in your heart when a man made it clear he preferred another woman to you. But this was different. It was like he had said, I'd rather be dead than be with you.

She threw the comforter back and climbed out of bed. No more of that. If she started thinking too much about Cole, she'd crawl under the covers and never come out. She had business to take care of with his family and the sooner it was settled, the sooner she could leave.

Opening her suitcase, she took out a pink cotton shirt, a gray sweater and another pair of jeans. The woman had said something about a Penney's store downtown. Maybe she should see if they were still open and buy some gloves. In the bathroom, she ran a brush through her sleep-tangled hair, pulled it back with a silver clip and splashed cold water on her face.

Stepping into the empty hallway, the sound of laugher and talking became louder, increasing as she walked toward the top of the stairs. She paused a moment. The wassail party. She'd forgotten it was tonight. The last thing she wanted to do was mingle with a bunch of strangers pretending she felt any sort of holiday cheer.

Her hungry stomach started to feel sour. The stairs led right into the middle of the lobby. Was there a back way out? Down at the end of the hall she saw a door marked Emergency Exit. Would an alarm sound if she opened it? She wasn't willing to take that chance.

Taking a deep breath she started down the stairs, determined to move through the crowd without a word and escape through the front door.

"Glad you could make it," a copper-skinned, sixtyish man said when she reached the bottom step. He leaned against the dark banister wrapped with pine boughs and red velvet bows, holding a glass cup of pale yellow liquid. "There's plenty of tamales left. The eggnog in the blue bowl is the unleaded kind, if you know what I mean. The wassail is also unleaded." His smile was a brilliant white and genuine. She found herself smiling back.

"I'm Bobby Hernandez," he said, holding out his calloused hand to help her down the last step. "Part owner of this place. Hope the Dale Evans room is to your liking."

"It's wonderful," she said. His gentle eyes instantly calmed her nervous stomach. "Thank you."

"My wife decorated it herself." He pointed over at the woman who'd checked Ruby in. She stood behind a long table of food and was dressed in a bright red sweater sporting a smiling Santa face. Santa, in this case, had dark brown skin and black eyes that were obviously based on her husband's features. "It's actually the room we reserve for family members," he added. "Birch only rents it to special people."

Now she felt like a real jerk. "I'm . . ." Not certain what to say, she lifted her chin and looked directly into the man's curious face. Should she apologize? For what? She hadn't asked for anything except to rent a room like anyone else who walked through the lodge's front door. She hadn't asked for anyone's pity. That had been a sore spot with her since she was a teenager.

She'd had all the pity she could stomach from the one year she spent in foster care. They'd been doing fine, she and Nash, even when their father left for a week at a time driving a truck to the East Coast and back, hauling electronics, batteries, cotton products, whatever the small trucking firm's owner could finagle. A neighbor lady, who objected to Nash's late-night guitar playing, noticed their father's long absences and called Social Services. Their father didn't fight it when she and Nash were placed in separate foster homes.

"Might be best," was all he said, obviously relieved that he didn't have to be responsible for them anymore.

For you, she wanted to scream, but couldn't get the words out.

Nash, to Ruby's relief, had been lucky enough to move in with a friend from school whose parents took in foster children. Ruby ended up thirty miles away and had to change schools at the beginning of her senior year. Though Mr. and Mrs. Pryor, the couple she was placed with, were nice enough, their pity for Ruby, which Mrs. Pryor constantly voiced in a soft, whispery voice to her many friends and relatives, made Ruby feel powerless and weak. She'd left their home soon after she graduated. She worked two waitressing jobs, moved into a rented room and took her brother to dinner every Sunday night. Whenever her father and Prissy swung through town, Ruby dutifully saw them. Every Christmas she sent an expensive Christmas card to the Pryors. She swore to herself she'd never be the object of someone's pity again.

All she wanted from the Tokopah Lodge was an anonymous place to stay until she could take care of the business with Cole's family and have her car repaired. If she had to stay longer than a week, and she was hoping she didn't, maybe she'd be better off going to the Holiday Inn Express where the desk clerk was a corporate employee who couldn't care less about what she could or couldn't afford.

Gaynelle's voice came back to her as loud and clear as if she were standing next to her. "Sweetie, taking help when you need it is not disgraceful. Not if you use it to get on your feet and give another person a hand up. That's what makes the world keep turning. You got to be careful you don't let those prickles you got sticking out all over you stab folks who're just trying to be nice."

"People are never just nice," Ruby would reply. "There's always a catch, Gaynelle. They're always looking for a payoff."

Gaynelle would shake her head and sigh. "Ruby, girl, someday you're going to find out it's a lot less painful to stop trying to free your leg by chewing it off and just let someone open the trap."

Then Ruby met Cole. When she fell in love with him, for the first time she allowed herself to depend on someone else, allowed herself to rest for just a moment and let him drive. And look where that got her.

"She won't bite," the copper-faced man said in a soft voice.

She lowered her eyes, remembering Gayelle's words. This man's wife had only been trying to be kind. It wouldn't kill her to acknowledge that. "It was very nice of her to rent it to me," she said, haltingly. "I don't want her to think I don't appreciate—"

"No matter," Bobby interrupted, smiling. "Just go over and have one of her tamales and tell her they're the best you've ever eaten. That'll smooth things over. You won't have to lie. They are better than my *abuelita's*, God rest her soul." He crossed himself, kissed his thumbnail and looked up. *"Lo siento, 'Lita."* Then he looked back at Ruby. "Wait'll you taste Birch's Indian fry bread. Better than my Indian mama's. Even *she* said so, and she didn't much care for white people."

She didn't answer, though she wanted to ask about his background.

"Let me fill you in," he said. "I'm Mexican on my father's side. My mother was one-half Paiute-Shoshone, one-quarter Navajo and one-quarter Scotch-Irish. Her grandfather was the Scotch-Irish part of the equation. He came here to work in the silver mines and met my great-grandma at a powwow. My mother said we have some Chinese in our background too, a great-grandmother or something. From when they were brought here to build the railroad. When all my backgrounds start to squabbling, I'm a regular United Nations."

Ruby couldn't help smiling.

"So, when I say Birch makes good tamales and fry bread, I know what I'm talking about."

"Maybe I will try a tamale."

"You won't be sorry."

"Birch is your wife's name?"

He nodded and sipped his eggnog. "Named after her grandfather's favorite tree. Fits her, too. You see, the birch tree is very multifaceted. It can be hard enough to use for good furniture, but its bark is also pliable enough to be used for canoes and baskets. Birch trees can produce edible fruit, sugar and vinegar. They can be sweet and tart, just like my wife. You can make tea from its leaves and birch beer from its sap. There's not a bit of waste on a birch tree."

"You love your wife very much," she said softly, envying the woman.

"Yes, ma'am, I do."

"She's a lucky woman."

He toasted her with his glass. "Oh, no, I'm the lucky one."

Over at the food table, she picked up a paper plate decorated with prancing reindeer and moved into the long line. There were at least twenty people ahead of her, probably over a hundred in the lobby and dining room of the lodge. In the background, Alvin and the Chipmunks warbled "White Christmas." When she reached Birch, who stood in front of a five-gallon aluminum stew pot, she held out her plate and met the older woman's direct gaze.

"How many would you like?" Birch asked, her voice cool, but friendly.

"Two, please."

With metal tongs she grabbed two steaming, husk-wrapped tamales and placed them on Ruby's plate. She pointed at a large blue Crock-Pot. "Beans? Rice? How's your room?"

Ruby nodded yes. "It's . . ." She paused, trying to think of the right words, the words that would make this woman see that she wasn't the rude person she seemed when she checked in. "It feels like I'm staying in someone's . . . a friend's . . . home." She hoped her comment sounded sincere. If she was going to be truthful, she would have to say she wasn't even sure what the word *home* meant anymore. Maybe she had never known.

Birch gave a quick nod, adding beans and rice to her plate. "Glad you like it." She reached into the stew pot and took out another tamale. "These are pretty small." She pointed the tongs at the rest of the food-ladened table. "Help yourself. I don't want to have to freeze any of this."

"It looks wonderful," she said, taking a set of wrapped plastic ware and moving down the line.

"Let us know if you need anything," Birch said before turning to the next guest.

Ruby took her tamales and a plastic cup of lemonade and searched for a place to sit. Across the room, through the double French doors that led to the dining room, she spotted a couple leaving a small pine table with two ladder-back chairs. She wove her way through the crowd and claimed it. The tamales tasted as good as they smelled and within fifteen minutes she'd finished all three. She contemplated going for seconds, but the line was even longer now. The clock in the dining room read seven forty-five. It would be a good time to slip out and see if any stores were still open. She stood up, then abruptly sat back down when she heard the name "McGavin."

"You McGavins are all alike," the woman was saying to her

tablemates. "Think the sun rises and sets on what's happening in your lives." Her hearty laugh carried across the crowded room.

Ruby strained to hear the conversation without appearing to be eavesdropping. The voice sounded familiar and when she located it two tables away, she saw it was Cassie's mother from the cafe, Sueann, the one who told her about this lodge. She was sitting with two men. Ruby couldn't see the face of the man she was speaking to, the man who was possibly related to Cole. But the other man looked up and caught her staring. He nodded once in recognition.

She looked down at her plate, embarrassed that she was caught staring. It was the man, Ely, who was fixing her car. She was already finding it disconcerting, how connected people were in Cardinal. She couldn't help wondering how Cole fit into this town. It was bizarre to think he had this whole shadow life that she didn't know about. She'd thought she knew him so well. She'd talked about such personal feelings, opening up about things she'd never told anyone. When they made love . . . her mind flashed back to long mornings in bed, his rough, scratchy hand on her back, the sounds he made when he felt vulnerable, his lips tracing the lines of her body, his tongue tasting of apricots and cinnamon, his blond hair coarse and dry and smelling like fresh grass and Ivory soap.

She stood up, panic rising in her chest like a hand grabbing for her voice box. She left her plate where it sat, something she'd normally never do and headed for the room's French doors. She couldn't face any of them tonight, not tonight. Maybe tomorrow, after a good night's sleep. Maybe something would come to her about how to approach this family. Maybe she'd just leave and never approach them at all. When she started through the double doors, a tall man in a Stetson accidentally bumped into her.

"Excuse me, ma'am," he mumbled in a gravelly, slightly slurred voice.

She glanced up in shock. It was Cole's voice. She only caught a glimpse of the man's face under the hat, but saw enough to bite her lip. There was no doubt that this man wearing a white Stetson and an irritated expression was related to Cole. The resemblance was remarkable. The same wide-set hazel eyes, thick blond eyebrows, skin tanned a deep brown from the sun. He weaved through the crowd and stopped in front of the table where Sueann sat with the possible other McGavin, the one whose face Ruby still couldn't see.

"What's this crap about Cassie getting a tattoo for Christmas?" the man in the white Stetson said.

"Don't get your panties in a bunch, Derek. We're just talking about it," Sueann said, her voice calm, though Ruby could hear the tremor of tension.

"That's not what she says," he replied. "She says it's a done deal."

"Well, it's not," Sueann said. "But she's going to be eighteen soon enough and then we won't be able to stop her. Frankly, if she's set on getting one, I'd rather go with her and make sure it's not some skanky place that will give her a case of hepatitis or worse along with the rose on her ankle."

"She already looks like some kind of street whore with all that metal stuck in her face. You're just encouraging her."

Sueann shifted in her chair, glancing at the other McGavin man. "Derek, lower your voice. This isn't the right place or time for this discussion. Let's not ruin everyone's evening."

Ruby thought she saw the woman's bottom lip tremble. Still Sueann didn't avert her gaze, didn't once look at any of the people who were sitting at nearby tables reveling in this entertaining bit of domestic disharmony. Ruby admired her backbone.

He bent closer, lowering his voice, the tone no less hostile. "Screw everyone's evening."

The other McGavin man stood up and faced Derek. A second electric shock shot through Ruby. This man, wearing a wrinkled blue cowboy shirt and Levi's with a stained knee, also looked like Cole, a younger Cole, one a little less angular, a little less hard. He was taller than both Cole and this man, and lankier. Unhesitating, he moved between Derek and Sueann.

"C'mon, Derek," the younger man said. "Why don't you leave this until tomorrow?"

Derek pushed his brother aside. "Mind your own business, Lucas. This is between me and my wife."

"Ex-wife," Sueann corrected, standing up. "Go home, Derek. You've had too much to drink."

He pointed a finger at her. "We're going talk about our daughter—"

Before he could finish his sentence, Ruby felt someone brush past her. Bobby Hernandez and a shorter, broad-shouldered man with curly black hair moved to both sides of Derek. In minutes they had him pulled aside and through the swinging kitchen doors.

She watched the younger McGavin, Lucas, help a white-faced Sueann sit back down, lean close and start talking softly. The dark-haired mechanic observed the scenario with the dispassionate expression of a person watching a movie he'd seen many times. The disappointed crowd slowly started chattering again, the possibility for a fistfight over.

Another person pushed past her in the dining room doorway. Though she knew she shouldn't stare, she couldn't stop watching these people. The more she knew about them, the better prepared she could be.

"What happened?" demanded the trim, stylish, fiftyish woman wearing a red pearl-button western shirt. Though not tall, she walked with purpose and authority. With hair the color of rich mahogany and trailing a scent of heavy perfume, she was beautiful in a tough, Bette Davis kind of way. Sueann's freckled face visibly stiffened.

"Nothing, Mom," the younger man said. "Derek just had too much to drink. Uncle Bobby and Gordon are talking to him in the kitchen."

"What did you do to upset him?" she shot at Sueann, ignoring her son's explanation.

Sueann answered in a tight, controlled voice, her dislike for the older woman obvious. "I didn't do anything, June."

"It's about Cassie, isn't it?" the older woman said.

"Mom, let it go," Lucas said, taking his mother's arm. "Let's see if Derek is okay."

The woman threw Sueann an angry look, then allowed Lucas to lead her to the kitchen.

Ruby suddenly felt in way over her head. Who were these McGavins? How were they related to Cole? If those two men were his brothers, as Ruby suspected, then that angry woman was his mother.

How in the world was she going to tell them he was dead and even worse, how he died?

She needed time to think. She pushed her way through the crowd toward the front door. Outside, the deep front porch was empty, the steps slick with ice. She carefully picked her way down. In the middle of the sidewalk, she took a deep breath. The cool air was a relief, making her chest feel pleasantly numb. She stared across the street at the city park where a thirty-foot pine tree was lit up with multicolored Christmas lights. During the last hour, it had started snowing. She'd never experienced a snowy Christmas. Once, this weather would have delighted her, a childhood dream come true. Now she just worried about whether it meant a longer stay in Cardinal.

She hugged herself, trying to assimilate what she'd seen. Within minutes, the snow was already melting through her cotton sweater and shirt, making her skin feel clammy. Her fingers tingled with cold. She would go back inside and head directly to her room, avoiding the dining room. She couldn't stand the thought of seeing any of the McGavins again tonight. Back in her room, she could pull on flannel pajamas and crawl under that soft, warm comforter. Like Scarlett O'Hara, she could just deal with all this tomorrow.

"Pretty cold out here," a man's voice said behind her, causing her to jump in surprise.

She turned around to face him, still hugging herself. It was the mechanic, Ely. He stood only a few feet from her, hands shoved deep into the pockets of his worn denim jacket.

"I was just going back in," she replied, dropping her arms and moving past him.

"Wait," he said, his voice low and urgent.

She kept walking. He was obviously somehow connected to the McGavins and she didn't want to take a chance of giving away who she was.

"Wait," he called again, when she reached the porch's bottom step. She didn't even break stride. His voice hardened. "Ruby McGavin."

She froze, fear gripping her chest. She'd only given him her maiden name. The same with the hotel. No one in this town knew who she really was. At least, that's what she thought. She turned slowly around to face him.

He started walking toward her. His black hair glowed like a glossy piece of stone, reflecting the moon-colored porch lights. "I know who you are."

She held herself perfectly still, like a rabbit waiting for the first shot. "What are you talking about?"

He came closer, the crush of snow and ice hissing softly under his black boots. His lean, shadowed face showed no discernible expression. A few loose strands of his long hair were whipped around by the cold wind. "I tried calling today and his phone is disconnected. What's happened to Cole?"

RUBY

"I don't know what you're talking about," she said, trying to buy time. "Did you two break up?" he asked, his voice friendly, but firm, like the dog trainers she'd seen on cable television.

She felt cornered. How much should she reveal to this stranger? A question for a question seemed the safest way to answer. "How do you know Cole?"

He hunched his shoulders against the frigid wind. "We're friends."

She frowned and took a step backward. "That tells me nothing."

He cocked his head. "We were roommates for a while."

"So?"

"In a halfway house."

His words seemed to suck the air out of her lungs. She turned her back to him and started walking down the street. A halfway house? What did he mean? Like in drugs? She knew Cole had a life, a past, before he met her. So did she, for that matter. But a halfway house? That was something he should have told her. She felt like her head was going to explode in a thousand pieces. What else didn't she know about this man she'd married?

The snow seemed to turn liquid under her leather loafers. With every other step, she slipped on small mirrors of ice hidden by the darkness. The third time she almost fell. A hand reached out and caught her elbow, steadying her.

"You're going to break your neck." His voice was calm.

She pulled away and faced him. "I don't know who you are or what kind of connection you might have had with my husband, but I don't want to talk to you. Please, go away."

The streetlight behind him back lit his frame, shadowing his face, making it impossible to see his expression. "I'm sorry, I can't."

She started walking toward the twinkling lights of downtown Cardinal. He fell in beside her, matching his stride to hers. For two blocks she pretended he wasn't there. He didn't say a word.

She stopped abruptly in front of a closed real estate office, pretending to study the photographs. One of the offerings was for a three-hundred-acre ranch with two houses, a barn and corral outside of Cardinal, twenty miles from Mammoth. Three million or best offer, it read. It was hard for her to imagine that amount of money. Was the Circle MG worth this much or more? She had no doubt his family would fight this will with all their probably considerable power. Though she needed the money, she wasn't sure she had the strength for a legal battle. She certainly didn't have the money. She'd have to just walk away.

"He's dead," Ruby said, not turning her head. The real estate window blurred in her eyes. Her rage spun quickly back into despair. It amazed her, how her emotions were still as volatile and unpredictable as a mud slide.

She didn't know what she expected—a gasp, a swear word, some kind of exclamation, something. Even with him standing only six inches away, she didn't hear any reaction. She couldn't even hear him breathe.

"How?" he asked.

"Doesn't matter," she whispered.

"It does."

He couldn't know that this was the first time she'd said the words out loud. Their permanence, their reality seemed to hang in the air like icicles. She wished she could project herself right into the picture in front of her, right into the warm living room where a fire of pine logs burned, a fantasy place where happy people lived and loved, people who didn't lie to each other, people who told each other what they felt, asked for help, didn't just disappear one day with no warning, no explanation. She gave an involuntary shudder.

"We should go somewhere warm and talk." His tone held a stubbornness that told her he would not give up easily. She glanced around, thankful that the street was still crowded with holiday shoppers.

"That's all I have to say," she said.

"If what you say is true, then we need to talk."

"If what I say is true!" She whipped around to face him. "Why would I make anything like that up?" The tamales she'd eaten only an hour ago churned in her stomach.

He studied her face with a serious expression. "What do I really know about you except that Cole told me he loved you and now you claim he's dead?"

She stared directly into the man's black eyes. How in the world did anyone ever read the emotions of someone with such dark eyes? Cole's blue eyes were like weather barometers telling her exactly how he felt every day. At least she'd always thought so. "I wouldn't lie about something so . . ." *Big* didn't seem like enough of a word. Important? Life-shattering?

"The McGavin family and their problems are not easy to walk into without being prepared. Trust me."

Trust him? Trust anyone? That wasn't likely to happen. She'd trusted Cole, the first person in a long time, maybe ever, and look where that had gotten her. But this man was right about one thing: The McGavin family, what she'd seen of them, would not be easy to deal with and the more she knew about them, the better. This man might be irritating, but he apparently knew Cole and his family. Besides, she had no other plan at this point. The bravado that had gotten her this far seemed to have disappeared.

"Okay," she said, defeat making her feel twenty pounds heavier.

"There's a place we can go about a block from here. Doubt you'd last longer than that in this cold."

"I'm fine," she said, determined not to show an ounce of weakness. They ended up at a coffeehouse called Holy Grounds.

"It's not exactly what you think," Ely said, holding the door open for her. "The guy who owns it is named Lincoln Holyoke."

Inside the coffeehouse it was warm, and smelled of ginger, vanilla and roasting coffee beans. The decor was spare and not a bit western like the rest of Cardinal. Large, colorful, primitive paintings featuring quilting bees, bug-eyed angels, barn raisings and animals playing musical instruments hung on the walls. The chairs and tables were a mishmash of fifties-style dinettes. A man wearing a fishing hat glittering with colorful lures played a soft blues guitar on the minuscule stage next to the red and blue tile counter. A middle-aged blond man with wild, Albert Einstein hair mixed coffee drinks in front of the silver and copper espresso machine. He wore an Hawaiian shirt, and a puka shell necklace and looked like he should be working in a Malibu surf shop.

"Hey, Ely," he called out. "The usual?"

"Yep," Ely said, then gave Ruby a questioning look.

"Black coffee," she said, choosing a table near the door.

"That's Lincoln behind the counter," Ely said when he came back a few minutes later with their drinks.

She wrapped her hands around the warm, blue mug. "How do you know Cole? And what's the story behind his family?"

"In a hurry?" he asked, sipping his coffee.

"I just want to take care of my business here as soon as possible." She took a huge gulp of coffee, burning her throat.

"What business would that be?"

"You first," she said, putting down her mug, blinking back tears of pain.

He stared at her a moment. His eyelashes were long and thick, one of those unfair advantages nature often bestowed upon unappreciative men.

"Cole and I are ex-cons," he said, surprising her with his candor. "We shared a room at a halfway house for about six months. We also went to school together as kids, but weren't friends until we met each other again in Los Angeles. How did he die?"

She stared at him, unable to speak for a moment. The owner of the coffeehouse, came over with a couple of muffins.

"Cranberry-cinnamon," he said, slipping the plate between them. "Just baked. In honor of our Lord's birthday."

"They grow cranberries in Bethlehem?" Ely said, giving Lincoln a teasing grin.

"Ever hear of frankincense and myrrh muffins?" he answered, raising his bleached-out eyebrows. "Don't forget the Blue Christmas service tomorrow night. Bring your friend if you want." He smiled at Ruby.

"We'll see," Ely said.

After he left, Ruby asked, "Why was Cole in prison?"

Ely was quiet for a moment, fingering his mug. "He didn't tell you." It was a statement, not a question.

"Obviously not," she said, wanting to hit him, hit the table, hit *something.*

He picked up a muffin and broke it open. The scent of cinnamon rose up, reminding Ruby of the first time she and Cole went to someone's house as a couple. They'd been dating a month and went to his friend Jorge's house. Jorge's wife, Flora, in honor of Valentine's day, served heart-shaped cookies and Mexican hot chocolate laced with cinnamon and cayenne pepper.

"He killed his father." His words were unemotional, matter-of-fact.

She was stunned silent.

He stared at his hands holding the two muffin pieces. "It was in September. Seventeen years ago. There was an argument between Cole and his father." He looked up at her, his eyes hooded. "Cole never told me what about. There was an argument and a struggle with a gun. Carson McGavin died. Cole's mother, June, saw it all. So did his younger brother, Derek. Cole went to prison. Voluntary manslaughter."

Her brain sizzled, like someone had set it on fire. All she could think was—do not open your mouth. Concentrate. Do not open your mouth or a scream will come out and it will never stop. Behind her, the guitarist played a riff from a B.B. King song that reminded Ruby of her brother, Nash. Nash loved B.B. King. How could Cole keep something like that from her?

"He should have told you," Ely said.

Words of defense automatically sprang to her lips. "He had . . ." She stopped, wanting to say, his reasons. *He had his reasons.* The truth was, he *should* have told her. It was bad enough that he held back his family, but this? Who was this man she married? This man she was so in love with that one weekend in Las Vegas she did what she said she'd never do, what she'd managed to avoid for thirty-five years. Marriage was something she'd always believed, always *knew* would end up like this, a deep well of disappointment. Marriage made you vulnerable. It made mothers run away and fathers run into the arms of the nearest woman they could find. After Loretta took off, Joe Stoddard left wives strewn behind him like candy wrappers.

"Yes," she said to this man who knew more about her husband's past than she did. "Apparently he should have told me a lot of things." She stood up to leave. There was no way she'd approach the McGavins now. She had no idea what kind of situation would make a son kill his father and though someday she was certain she'd be curious about the details, her first reaction was to put as much distance as possible between her and this family. As soon as her car was fixed, she'd leave his ashes with a note somewhere safe, maybe with a local minister, and drive straight out of town.

Ely followed her out of the coffeehouse into the still busy Main Street. She felt his hand grab her upper arm.

"No way will you walk away and not tell me what happened to Cole."

She looked directly into his black eyes. How could she tell him and not sound cruel? Just like the word *dead,* she had never said the other word out loud, never put into words what the deputy coroner had intimated when she informed Ruby of Cole's accident. Cole's short, cryptic note was stuck inside her copy of *To Kill a Mockingbird,* a book she knew she'd never give away.

"He was killed in a car accident," she said, her lips unable to form the word *suicide* even now. "His ashes are in my room at the lodge."

BIRCH

I t was past ten p.m. when June found Birch behind the lodge carrying out a trash bag. The temperature had dropped to below freezing and most of the guests had gone back to their rooms or trudged home through the slushy snow.

"Did you see that sorry excuse of a jacket Lucas was wearing?" June said. "*Strings* are hanging from the sleeves! I can't believe he threw away a good-paying job, not to mention all that money I spent on a law degree just so he could look rattier than one of my Mexican ranch hands."

"You could buy him a new one," Birch answered, slamming the lid on the metal trash can and locking it with a padlock. They'd had a family of clever raccoons who had figured out how to open the old can's latch. "Walt's has a new shipment of Carhartts." Actually, Birch had already bought him a wool-lined barn coat for Christmas, safely assuming June wouldn't buy him one.

"I refuse to reward immature behavior," June said, folding her arms across her chest. "It's bad enough you let him live rent-free in your garage apartment."

"He pays utilities," Birch said, wondering why she was going through this with June again. She looked up at the three-quarter moon, a bright Monterey Jack white. Foolish dreams die hard. The two women had disagreed over more things than Birch could remember since June, a welfare kid from Bakersfield, married Birch's only brother, Carson, forty-two years ago. June had been seventeen and Birch twenty-one. Birch had always longed for a sister and had naively hoped she and June would become close, since June only had five brothers. She quickly realized that June was interested in one thing only: leaving behind her poverty-stricken background and getting on the good side of Birch and Carson's wealthy father, Kitteridge. June had always craved the prestige and power of the McGavin name and did what she needed to acquire Kitt McGavin's favor.

When June came into the family, Birch and Bobby were newly married. Kitt McGavin had already kept his word about disowning Birch if she married Bobby. After seeing the lay of the land, June sided firmly with her new father-in-law. Her next attempt was to fill Birch's shoes. It wasn't very hard. Though Kitt McGavin would never admit it, there was a hole left in his life when he shunned his only daughter. He admired June's drive and beauty, but especially enjoyed making sure Birch knew that his paternal favors were now bestowed upon a daughter-in-law who eventually gave him grandsons to carry on the McGavin name.

"Ones with *white* skin," he would remark loudly in Birch's presence when they happened to be in the same place in town, something Birch had tried to avoid as much as possible. Kitt McGavin would have never pulled a stunt like that when his wife was alive, but Emily McGavin had died of emphysema when Birch was sixteen, leaving a painful hollowness Birch felt in her heart every day of her life.

"You need to talk to him, Birch," June said, her lips barely moving.

Birch knew where this conversation was headed. Everything June talked about these days circled around to the selling of the Clear Creek section of the ranch. Developers from Los Angeles wanted to build weekend ski condos for people priced out of Mammoth's outrageous real estate.

That prime bit of private land was even more valuable because of

the county's history. Most of the land in Tokopah county was owned
by the Los Angeles Department of Water and Power, a situation that
transpired at the turn of the twentieth century so the water rights could
be used for the burgeoning city of Los Angeles. But there were a few
ranchers, like Birch's grandfather, who didn't sell out. For the last hundred years the McGavins and a few other longtime ranching families
owned what little private land was left in Tokopah County. The old
land deal had been a mixed blessing, keeping the area rural, the town
almost unchanged in the last century, something rare in California. But
because it made affordable housing hard to find and jobs scarce, not
many children who grew up in Cardinal stayed to raise their own families. It had changed into a town of older folks, the haves and the have
nots. The haves were smart enough to have been born into the right
families, the "lucky sperm club" as Cole used to call it, or were well-
off retirees from the very towns that acquired—some still say stole—
Cardinal's water a hundred years ago. The have-nots were those who
worked for them, or lived on the reservation.

Now the McGavins were being offered an excellent price for one of
their best parcels, but since it was owned equally by all four McGavins,
a legacy of Birch and Carson's father, all four signatures were needed
for any sale of property. The developers especially lusted after the Clear
Creek section, with its unparalleled view of the Sierra Nevada mountain range and year-round creek. It was also only forty miles from
Mammoth's most popular ski slopes. And it was where Lucas kept his
rescue horses. He had steadily refused to agree to a sell. June had been
trying for months to convince Birch to change Lucas's mind. Everyone
knew how much Lucas respected his aunt's opinion.

"If you didn't make it so easy for him, he'd have to go back to being
a lawyer to support his hobby horses," June said, following Birch into
the kitchen where Sueann was filling plastic bags with leftover peanut
butter–chocolate chip cookies. June pointedly ignored her former
daughter-in-law. Behind June's back, Sueann mimicked her ex–mother-
in-law's pursed lips.

Birch tried to hide her smile. "June, I wish it were that easy. You
know I agree with you that Lucas should be practicing law. He was—

is—a wonderful lawyer. But you can't make a child . . ." She corrected herself. "A grown man do what he doesn't want to do."

"You also don't have to make it easy for him to keep being irresponsible. That's what too many parents do, make it easy for their kids to do whatever they please, ignoring the fact that it isn't good for them. People like that shouldn't even have children." Her sculpted eyebrows rose dramatically, her red lips a straight line.

Birch stared at June, too angry to speak. This time she knew June was poking at Sueann, who looked ready to spit nails, but her words also cut Birch to the core. It had always hurt and perplexed Birch that God would allow a woman as mean and uncaring as June to produce three healthy sons and Birch to lose the only child she would ever conceive one month before the baby was born. Emily Robertina Hernandez. Every February first Birch laid white roses on her tiny grave in Cardinal's dry, windblown cemetery. Was it because she conceived the child before she and Bobby were married? Was God that vengeful? She was positive that back then, there were those in this town who made that judgment. She'd never had nerve enough to ask any of the three ministers who'd pastored the Methodist church she attended if that was a possibility. Nor did she ever ask Father Domingo, the priest at St. Mary's where Bobby went to Mass. She and Bobby never spoke of it, but every February first, he disappeared for the day and she was left to go to the cemetery alone.

"We need the money that land will bring," June said. "Lucas knows how much money it takes to run the ranch."

You don't *need* the money, Birch thought, you want it so you don't have to give up your fancy lifestyle. She wanted to say, why don't you just marry nasty old Walt Creston, let him pay for your silver belt buckles and rhinestone western shirts and leave Lucas be?

When Birch didn't answer, June asked, "Have you heard from Cole?" His was another signature June needed, but she'd not spent time looking for her oldest son since she hadn't been able to convince Lucas yet. She knew once Lucas signed, Cole would also.

"No," Birch said, her chest heavy with sadness. "I wish I had." She looked at her sister-in-law's face, searching it for any sign of sorrow or regret. Was that a flicker of longing in June's face? Birch wanted to believe it was.

"You don't know how lucky you are," June said. "You have no idea the heartbreak kids bring." She turned and marched out of the kitchen without even acknowledging the stricken look on Birch's face.

"That woman is so full of crap," Sueann said, putting an arm around Birch's shoulders. "If God is just, she will be struck with a hemorrhoid the size of a grapefruit. And then a case of Montezuma's revenge. Don't you listen to her for one minute."

Birch didn't answer, afraid if she said a word, she'd burst into tears. And she didn't have time to cry tonight.

An hour later, while putting away the rest of the Tokopah's serving dishes, Birch replayed June's remarks to Bobby, even managing to smile at Sueann's wisecrack. No one was left in the kitchen except the two of them.

"Sueann's right," he said. "You shouldn't take what June says seriously. Dollar signs have squeezed out any compassion that woman might have ever had."

"I suppose," Birch said, wondering again why in the world someone like that would be blessed with three children. "Oh, I forgot to tell you. I think something's happened with our newest guest, Miss Stoddard."

"What's that?"

"Around nine-thirty, right before I went to empty the trash, I saw her run up the stairs to her room looking like she was ready to burst into tears." Birch rinsed out a stray glass sitting on the counter and placed it inside the commercial dishwasher. "Something really upset that girl. Do you think the crazy husband found her?"

Bobby leaned against the old wooden chopping block sitting in the middle of the kitchen. Small bags under his tired eyes made Birch's heart contract. It was hard watching someone you love age. It struck her with small things like this puffiness that time was like a runaway horse, one of those wild mustangs the county was so famous for, charging forward, head up, to heck with whatever stood in its way. It made her want to grab all the people she loved and hold them close, stopping time for just that moment.

"Birch, honey, what is it about this girl that has you so riled?" He shook his head. "She's nice and all, but she'll be moving on in a week. You need to let go."

She wiped her damp hands down the sides of her red sweater. "I know, I know. It's just that she reminds me of . . ." Her hands fluttered in front of her, nervous, craving something to do.

"You?" Bobby said, pulling her into his arms.

"No," she said, her voice muffled against his chest. "Maybe."

"Don't you have enough to worry about with people who are actually related to you? I think you're focusing on this stranger because it's easier than dealing with real family. What's going on with Lucas? And what about Derek and Sueann? I don't think we've seen the last of the arguments about Cassie's tattoo or that weird boyfriend of hers."

She pulled out of his arms, glad to dwell on something other than that troubling young woman. Bobby was right. There was enough to worry about with their own family. Why hadn't she heard from Cole? He always called by this time each year. "Truth is, I agree with Derek on this one. Cassie's too young to get a tattoo. I'm still surprised Sueann let her get those piercings. And that boy." Birch made a sour-looking face.

"Sueann's got a point; if she insists on doing it, she may as well go someplace safe. Cassie's a good girl, never been a bit of trouble. Why should Sueann say no?" He gave a small chuckle. "As for her boyfriend. Well, I'll admit, he gives me pause, but we might try showing him some grace. Remember what people said about me when we got married."

She took a deep breath, knowing he was right. As weird as that boy was to her with his black, baggy clothes and snippy attitude, Cassie cared about him just as Birch had fallen in love so immediately and completely with Bobby's sharp, vulnerable cheekbones and melodious voice. "I suppose you're right. I'm sure he'll grow out of that attitude. As for Lucas, I've about given up on him. He's barely making ends meet building saddles."

"Aren't things looking up since he got the website?"

"Yes, but he'll never make enough to support a family."

Bobby laughed. "You know something I don't?"

Birch frowned at him. "He's thirty-four. He needs to get married and start a family. But what woman would want a man who lives in his aunt and uncle's garage apartment and hardly makes enough to heat his shop?"

"One who loves him?" Bobby suggested.

She gave a reluctant smile. "Okay, you have me there. Still, I do think he misses being a lawyer. I don't understand why he won't tell us why he left San Francisco. It was a long time after he and Lisa broke up, so that couldn't be it."

"He'll talk about it when he's ready," Bobby said, leading her out of the kitchen, turning the light off after them. The fire in the stone fireplace was glowing embers. Through the lodge's front windows, the bright December moon shined from behind smoky-colored clouds, turning the silhouetted Christmas tree a soft blue-green.

He turned and locked the lodge's double doors behind them. Birch watched him say a quick prayer for all those sleeping in the lodge, crossing himself as he did. It was a ritual he began when they put the down payment on the lodge with the money left to her by her mother. Throughout the years he must have prayed for thousands of strangers. Did it make any difference? Birch often wondered. She knew he'd say a special prayer for the troubled girl in the Dale Evans room. Ruby. Such an old-fashioned name. Was she named for her grandmother, a favorite old aunt? What was her story?

"Lucas will tell us what's bothering him when he's ready," Bobby repeated, slipping his arm around her shoulders. "He must have had a good reason. He doesn't do things lightly."

"No," she agreed. "He doesn't."

Holding hands, they walked the two blocks to their house, entering through the kitchen door. She glanced up at Lucas's apartment where a light still burned in the living room. What did he do all alone up there night after night? The winter months were silent, the storm windows hiding whatever sounds he made. Last summer she had heard music float through the trees through her open kitchen window. She never recognized any of the singers, but they were always gentle, sad songs and she hoped they soothed her nephew, gave him some comfort for whatever it was that haunted him, that caused his young face to sink every so often, as if it were trying to hide from itself. Something had happened to Lucas in San Francisco, something more than his wife cheating on him, something that made him run home and endure the stares and whispers of the town, endure his mother's carping, endure the uncertain economics that accompanied his new career.

Did Cole know what it was? She knew they sometimes met in Las Vegas. Four years ago she convinced Lucas to take her with him to see Cole in Las Vegas. She sobbed when Cole hugged her good-bye in the Denny's parking lot on Las Vegas Boulevard. Cole had asked her through Lucas not to come again. It was too hard seeing her, he'd said. It made him too homesick.

Then come home, she wanted to cry. Just come home. But she knew he couldn't. There was nothing for him anymore in Cardinal. He would never come home. It shattered her heart like a bullet. Like the bullet that killed her brother, Carson, so many years ago.

LUCAS

The next morning at a little past eight, Ely leaned against the wall of the saddle shop, waiting for Lucas.

"What's up?" Lucas asked, fumbling through his keys.

"We gotta talk," Ely said.

Lucas laughed at Ely's serious expression. "You look like you robbed a bank. We can talk while I fill out the order for Bernie Gorman's saddle tree."

"Forget his saddle," Ely said, pacing in the small foyer. "Let's take a ride."

Lucas's gut seized up, sensing Ely's agitation. In the short time he and Ely had been acquaintances—friends, he liked to think—he'd never seen him this jumpy. He looked at his watch and said, "Okay, how about we take a drive out to Clear Creek? I can feed the horses early."

Lucas swung by the feed store to pick up some hay and sweet grain. Once they were on the road, Lucas probed his friend. "C'mon, Ely, you show up at my shop before I've had my second cup of coffee and tell me we have to talk and now you won't say a word. What's going on?"

"We'll talk at Clear Creek," Ely said, turning his head toward the window.

Lucas knew better than to force the issue. Ely was playing his silent Indian routine. Nothing would make him talk when he didn't want to.

Lucas concentrated on the slick, newly plowed highway. Snow had fallen again last night and Main Street looked like an idyllic Christmas card of Wyoming or Montana. The Valley Bank clock showed seven fifty-four a.m. Temperature was thirty-one degrees. Inside the cab of Lucas's old pickup cold air leaked around the edges of the windows where the weatherstripping had long deteriorated. He turned the heater on high, cursing under his breath at its weak wheezing.

Ely, who would normally wisecrack about Lucas's truck being held together with baling wire and Birch's prayers, didn't say a word. Ely's mood reminded Lucas of Cole and his ability to shut down, show no emotion, maybe, for all Lucas knew, feel no emotion. A means of not getting hurt, Lucas assumed, or wanted to believe, anyway. It was something he was sure Cole learned in prison, or before, during the trial, to cope with the public humiliation of his life and his crime and their family's private sins being dissected in front of all of Tokopah county.

When they reached the gate that led to Clear Creek, Ely opened the passenger door before Lucas completely stopped the truck. He had the aluminum gate unlocked in ten seconds.

After closing the gate behind them, within minutes they were parked up on the rise, near the century-old cottonwood tree where Lucas sometimes slept off his headaches. In the distance, four of his five rescued horses heard the rumble of his truck's engine and started meandering toward them, knowing that he was the bearer of timothy hay and sometimes, when he was flush, buckets of sweet grain and fresh carrots. It being the Christmas holiday, today he had all three. They'd be happy little campers this morning. Only the new mare, the unnamed mustang, hung back, skittish and wary.

The horses crowded up to Lucas and Ely, nosing them like new puppies. Lucas, forgetting about Ely's problem for a moment, counted heads—Muddy Waters, Beau, Eddie and Spike. He quickly scanned their bodies, making sure each was surviving the cold weather all right. There was a ramshackle, but adequate, barn at the corner of the prop-

erty. None had a dusting of snow on their haunches, so he knew they'd
spent the night inside. He glanced over at the mare who stood off a
good hundred yards. She eyed him suspiciously and pawed the ground.
He was stymied by this animal. Even Ely couldn't seduce this one to let
him near her. She appeared healthy, so she was eating, apparently after
they left.

"I've got an idea," Lucas said, nodding over at her. "I should name
her Greta. As in Garbo. 'I vant to be alone.' " He grinned at Ely.

"Suits her," Ely said, unsmiling.

"Cassie will kill me. She wanted to name her."

Ely shrugged, pulled down the tailgate and jumped up into the
truck bed. He took out his knife, cut the twine on the top hay bale and
started separating flakes of hay, tossing them over the side of the truck,
far enough apart that the horses wouldn't squabble.

Lucas surveyed the thirty-acre pasture, some of the best land in the
county. Though it was quality land that his mother would have liked to
use for her cattle, this part was, emotionally, anyway, his. Like his
brothers, he legally owned one-fourth of the ranch, inherited directly
from their grandfather, Kitt. June now owned his father's fourth. Because Lucas never interfered in any other way with her and Derek's
ranch operations, she only occasionally nagged him about using this
section for such a nonprofitable purpose. That was before the develop-
ment offer six months ago. Now her halfhearted complaining had
turned into belligerent badgering. He dreaded seeing her or Derek even
more than usual.

He cut the twine from a second bale, stripping it from the hay. He
could feel his blood pressure decrease, his mind ease, as it always did
when he came out here. Out here with the horses was the only time he
ever felt completely sane. According to Bill, his tax guy, it was technically a horse boarding business, even if it didn't make him any money.
Kind of like the saddle shop.

"Are you sure you want to keep up two . . . uh . . . unprofitable
businesses?" Bill tried to diplomatically point out a few months ago.

"Yep," Lucas had said, wondering if Bill had been bought off by his
mother. He'd mentioned it few days later to Sueann.

"He probably was," she said. "You can always tell June that your horses are much cheaper than going to a psychiatrist three times a week."

He laughed at her observation. Sueann understood the McGavin family better than anyone.

This side business, if it could be called that, had begun accidentally. He never started out to be a keeper of horses, but there you go, sometimes you're just minding your own business and fate had her way with you. It started with Mr. Ed, a predictable name for the horse since his owner wrote comedy scripts for television. Eddie, as Lucas renamed him, was a nine-year-old Thoroughbred bay gelding off the track at Santa Anita. He'd been bought for pennies on the dollar when he wasn't winning enough races and retrained for pleasure riding for the writer's daughter. She promptly lamed him by galloping down the streets of Beverly Hills. After that, the sound of anything resembling a car horn or an engine made the horse rear up, his ears laid flat in fear. After Eddie destroyed two stalls at a local stable, the girl's father had enough shame to ask around and see if there was someplace to board the horse permanently where it would get quality care and thus relieve his guilty, politically correct conscience. A trainer at the stable, the husband of a public defender Lucas had worked with in San Francisco, remembered Lucas had moved to Cardinal and called him. It took Lucas six months before he was able to drive his truck closer than a quarter mile to Eddie.

Word spread, and Lucas ended up boarding troubled horses. None of them were currently rideable; all had some kind of emotional or physical problem. A sympathetic local vet, Sean O'Brien, worked on the physical problems, and sent the bills directly to the owners. The emotional problems, Lucas figured, would either work themselves out or not. He fed them and talked to them, occasionally scratching a withers or a neck, checking their feet for stones or disease. Mostly, he left them alone to heal underneath the venerable shadow of the Sierra Nevada, drinking in the clean, high plains air, their only company the cottonwood tree, some scrub brush, a stand of quaking aspens, a few rabbits and the occasional red-tailed hawk.

There was only one problem. After a few years, all but one of the owners quit sending checks. No explanation, no forwarding addresses. What could Lucas do? He couldn't sell them, because they weren't legally his. So he kept feeding them, carried a ridiculous tab with Sean, knowing they would never be claimed. He hoped they never sensed that they'd been abandoned, but he knew horses had long memories. He remembered his first horse, Maggie, a paint whose eyes reminded him of Greta's. He was twelve when he rode Maggie in a Fourth of July parade down in the town of Big Pine. During the parade, she recognized a horse she'd been pastured with five years earlier, a white-faced quarter horse name Ralph. They'd whinnied, greeting each other like long-lost siblings. He wondered what Greta remembered, what relationships she lost and mourned.

His mother would have laughed at his musings. June believed animals were to use and discard when they could no longer adequately perform their appointed function. Maybe it was the same way with sons. Was that the reason she could let go of her oldest son and so easily slip the next son into his place?

Across the pasture, the mare whinnied, the sound carrying across the clear, sweet-smelling air. She had only been here three months. Her mysterious owner, was long gone, so it looked like Lucas was all she had. She just didn't know it yet.

After they'd spread out the hay, taking some of it inside the barn, driving the truck to the far end of the pasture and leaving some there as well, they climbed back into the cab. Lucas turned to Ely. "Okay, my friend, I've just about had it. What did you do?"

Ely wouldn't look at him, which gave Lucas an odd, panicked feeling. It was something bad. He knew Ely had been in prison, though he'd never known why. That wasn't a question you flat-out asked a man. If Ely had wanted Lucas to know, he would have told him. Even as small as Cardinal was, Lucas was pretty sure he was the only one who knew about Ely's past. That was only because one night when they'd been drinking Lucas was complaining about Derek getting on his back about helping out more at the ranch.

Ely had peered at Lucas over his beer and said, "You gotta feel sorry for the guy. He's trying like crazy to earn his good time, but your mama just ain't gonna cut him any slack."

Lucas stared at Ely. "Good time" was credit that prisoners could earn toward their sentence, one day for two served. It was not a term most people used in casual conversation.

Ely had seen Lucas's surprised face and curtly verified that yes, he'd spent a some time in prison and left it at that.

A sharp wind came up over the foothills the Clear Creek pasture butted up against. Lucas shivered inside his jacket. He should have put on his thermals.

Ely's face looked as if it were carved from ironwood. "There's no easy way to tell you this, Lucas. Cole's dead."

BIRCH

From behind the lodge's front counter, Birch watched Ruby Stoddard eat breakfast and read. The girl read her book as carefully as she ate, allotting a tiny piece of the lodge's signature cinnamon-peach bread for each page. Birch once again wondered what had caused the girl to rush up the stairs last night, her dark head down. For some reason, she wanted to both hug and shake her. Her emotional reaction to this virtual stranger was starting to get obsessive, as Bobby had already pointed out.

She knew better. She'd learned how to disengage emotionally when she was a teacher. One had to if one were going to last at teaching for any length of time. Oh, she cared, more than she wanted sometimes, but she learned early that she couldn't become personally invested in the outcome of her students. They all had free will. At most, she was only an influence, not the deciding factor of how they would turn out or what would happen to their lives. So this sudden emotional responsibility she felt toward this girl was as perplexing to her as it was to her husband.

"Hey, Aunt Birch! It's raspberry muffin day!" Cassie burst into the lobby, bringing a gust of cold air with her. She was dressed in black jeans, black sweater, black jacket and black snow boots. The only bit of color on her was a bright purple knit hat. She carried a large plastic container that Birch knew held three dozen of Sueann's crumb-topped raspberry muffins. Behind her lurked her boyfriend, Hunter, in his baggy, funeral-colored clothes, looking shifty and unpredictable.

Show some grace, Birch, she heard Bobby's voice scold inside her head.

"Hi, sweetie," she replied, smiling at her great-niece. "Good morning, Hunter."

Hunter jerked his head at her, then flopped down on one of the lodge's sofas; his unshaven face appeared bored and, *forgive me, Bobby*, she couldn't help thinking it, *shifty*.

"There's only thirty-five," Cassie confessed. "Hunter and me ate one on the way over. Don't tell Mom."

"Hunter and I," she automatically corrected. "I'll add it to the list of things I can blackmail you with."

"Hey, isn't that like a dangling something or other?" Cassie grinned at her. "As for blackmailing me for money, that ain't . . . isn't . . . going to do you any good this year, for sure." She carried the box through the dining room into the kitchen. "I'm so broke I'm having to borrow money from Mom for Christmas presents."

Birch followed her, glancing down at Ruby as they passed. She didn't even look up. "Do you want to go in with me on Lucas's present?" she asked Cassie while they stacked the muffins in the pantry.

"Sure, what're we getting him?"

"A new barn jacket."

"Why? He's got a jacket." Cassie picked up another muffin and peeled off the paper baking wrapper.

"Put that down. These are for the guests. It's as ragged as one of his rescue horses. Besides, it'll get your grandma off his back."

Cassie rolled her black-lined eyes. "Grandma June is so weird. You know what she's buying me for Christmas? A savings bond for a hundred bucks. I think I can't cash it in until I'm really old, like, fifty or something." She took a large bite of the muffin. "I don't know why she couldn't put that money toward my tattoo. The one I want is so cool, Aunt Birch. A blue swallow holding a red heart in its beak."

Birch tried not to grimace. "Where are you getting it?"

"At a place in L.A. where they are, like, super careful about needles and stuff. I found it on the Internet. Don't worry, Mom's going with me."

Birch picked up a sponge and wiped off an already clean counter. Their breakfast cook, Eva, was as meticulous as a surgeon. "I meant where on your body."

Cassie set down the half-eaten muffin. "Maybe on my hip. Or my lower back. I'm still thinking about it."

Birch was tempted to say, think about not doing it, but refrained. Her years working with children had taught her one dependable lesson: Tell them not to do something and the genetic code wired into every child will cause them to do just the opposite. And don't try any of that reverse psychology malarkey. Even the dimmest of them saw right through that.

"Just make sure you watch them take the needle out of the package," she couldn't help saying, even though she knew Sueann would be standing over the tattoo artist . . . engraver . . . technician—whatever they called themselves—like a mother grizzly. "Make sure he washes his hands really good first and with antibacterial soap." That part she couldn't help. Birch firmly believed nobody washed their hands enough these days. "And make sure he wears gloves."

"It could be a she," Cassie said, looking at her slightly greasy hand, then wiping it down the side of her black jeans.

There's a good reason for kids to wear black, Birch thought.

"Maybe I'll become a tattoo artist," Cassie said. "Set up shop right here on Main Street. What do you think? Wouldn't Grandma June have a heifer?"

Birch smiled. It might almost be worth ruining downtown to see June's reaction "The city council would never approve your business license."

Cassie sighed. "I know. That's why I'm blowing this place as soon as I graduate. It is so twentieth century here."

Birch's chest constricted at the thought of Cassie moving away. Her family was fluttering away, like a bunch of nervous sparrows in the shadow of a hawk. "You know you always have a home here at the lodge."

Cassie threw her arms around her great-aunt, burying her head in Birch's neck, like she used to when she was eleven and gangly as a colt.

"I know, Aunt Birchie. I'll come back lots to visit. Even at Christmas. I know you miss Uncle Cole. Has he called yet?"

"No, not yet." Birch felt her insides grow cold.

They walked back into the dining room, which had emptied of everyone except Manny, the busboy and the Stoddard girl.

Cassie went right over to Ruby and said, "Hey, remember me from the cafe? I waited on you. Grilled cheese on sourdough. Are you staying here?"

For the first time, Birch saw the girl smile. It totally changed her face, softening it, making her appear friendly and approachable.

"Yes, I remember," Ruby said. "I'm staying in the Dale Evans room."

"Awesome," Cassie said. "I've stayed there lots of times. Usually when my mom and I have had a fight and she needs space. The second drawer of the chest sticks. Lift it up a little when you pull it out."

Ruby nodded. "Thanks."

"Are you here through Christmas?" Cassie asked. "In case you don't remember, I'm Cassie."

She looked back down at her open book. "I'm Ruby. It looks like I'll be here until after the holidays. My car broke down. It's over at the Chevron station."

"Is Ely fixing your car?"

"Yes, he is. At least, I hope he can fix it."

"Don't worry, Professor Ely can fix any machine."

"Professor?" The woman looked confused. Birch watched, listening to the exchange between Ruby and Cassie, hoping to observe something that would tell her more about the woman.

"He's not really a professor," Cassie said. "I just call him that because he reads all these weird kinda books and he, like, remembers *everything* he reads. He is a genius with motors. Everyone says so." She turned to Birch. "Gotta go. I told Mom I'd only be a minute. The cafe's full this morning. A busload of skiers from the OC." She wrinkled her nose. "See you later."

"Okay," Birch said, patting her niece on the back. "Be careful." She stayed where she was, hoping to use this opening to start a conversation with Miss Ruby Stoddard.

Just as Cassie and Hunter reached the lodge's front door, June threw it open, her purposeful expression like one of the bow hunters who stayed at the lodge during deer season.

"Cassie," June called, her voice carrying across the almost empty room. "I need to speak to you."

Birch could see Cassie's posture turned rigid. "No time, Grandma. Mom needs me back at the cafe."

"She can wait just two minutes while I give my only grandchild some advice, can't she?" June's tough, ranch manager voice wasn't asking.

Cassie shrugged, her expression turning sullen. Birch walked up beside Cassie, tempted to put an arm around her, but knew it would only further antagonize June.

"This tattoo business is unacceptable," June said. "I won't allow it."

Cassie glanced over at Birch, then back at June. "Mom said I could. She has custody."

"Shared custody," her grandmother reminded. "And we can go back to court and change that if we have to."

Cassie's mouth opened in surprise. Birch could see her great-niece's bottom lip give an almost imperceptible tremble.

"That's enough, June," Birch said, stepping in, knowing good and well she'd pay for interfering. "Why don't we let Sueann, Cassie and Derek work this out?" If nothing else, she could deflect June's anger.

June gave her sister-in-law a furious look.

"Bye," Cassie said, grabbing the chance to flee the scene, but not before flashing Birch a grateful smile.

"You should mind your own business," June said, walking over to Birch.

"Cassie's my blood, too," Birch said, keeping her voice neutral.

"You are not an immediate relative. Please stay out of our personal family decisions." She turned and walked toward the lodge's front doors. "Tell Lucas I'm looking for him. He's not in his shop."

Birch silently watched her brother's wife stride as confidently out the door as one of the Western female movie stars who'd stayed here during the forties and fifties, certain this B picture role would rocket her to Hollywood stardom. Birch went back behind the front desk. There were guests due today, no time to worry about June. She glanced at the Stoddard woman, who had observed the ruckus between June, Cassie and Birch with more than a passing interest. Did it remind her of conflict in her own family? The woman was no longer smiling and she appeared to be deep in thought. The desk phone rang, causing the woman to look over at Birch. Their eyes met briefly, then Ruby broke the exchange before Birch could learn another thing about her.

LUCAS

"What happened?" Lucas demanded. "I want to know details. Where was he? When did it happen? Was anyone with him? Where's he buried?" The horses calmly chewed their hay while Lucas felt himself shatter inside like a beer bottle thrown against a brick wall.

"I only know what Ruby told me," Ely said, leaning against the side of the truck. "Cole died in a car accident on the way to work one morning. Someone from the coroner's office called her with the news."

"Who's Ruby?"

"That girl we watched kick in her car door yesterday. Ruby is Cole's wife."

Lucas's face looked stricken again. "Wife? Cole was married? When did that happen? How do you know all of this?"

"They've been married for six months."

Lucas stared at Ely for a few moments, his mouth slightly open. "The last time I saw Cole was in August. We met in Las Vegas like always. He never said anything about a wife."

Ely shrugged, obviously unable or unwilling to explain Cole's actions.

Lucas felt his jaw tighten. "How do *you* know all this?"

"I knew Cole."

Lucas looked at him like he was crazy. "Of course you did. You went to school together since kindergarten."

"After he left here. We were in the same halfway house in L.A."

Lucas stared at Ely, slowly comprehending what his friend was saying.

"When I decided to move back to Cardinal, he asked me to keep an eye on you and Birch and Cassie."

Lucas continued staring at the man he thought of as his only friend in Cardinal, next to Sueann. "You've been spying on us for Cole?"

"No," Ely said, shaking his head. His stiff black braid, tied with a strip of leather and two handmade beads, barely moved. His voice held no emotion that Lucas could discern. "He was my friend, and when he heard I was coming back to Cardinal, he asked me to keep him up on how you all were doing. He missed you, Lucas, and he cared about you. All of you. You and Birch and Bobby and Cassie. He even cared about your mom and Derek."

"Right," Lucas said bitterly. "That's why he kept his whole life a secret. Because he cared so much."

Ely stared silently over Lucas's shoulder.

Lucas squeezed his hands into fists, trying to keep his mind off the numbing fact that his favorite brother was gone. Shouldn't he have known? Felt something the moment it happened? Were he and Cole so lightly connected that Cole could die so quickly, so violently, and Lucas never even felt a shudder? Above him, a hawk swooped down onto some unsuspecting rodent in the grass, death in an instant. Like Mrs. Weeks and her children. He clenched his fists harder. Don't think about them, not right now. It was something he'd intended to tell Cole, to confess, really. Cole was the only person he didn't think would find him completely despicable. Someone who would understand, but would also agree that he never deserved to be someone's attorney again. He'd tried to tell Cole in August, but hadn't been able to find the words. Now, it was too late.

"I need to know more," Lucas said.

"Ruby wouldn't tell me much," Ely said. "You should talk to her."

"Don't worry, I will." He looked directly into Ely's black, fathomless eyes. "Why didn't you tell me about Cole and you?"

Ely held his gaze. "He asked me not to. He was my friend. I honored his request."

What about me, Lucas wanted to ask, but didn't. The words would sound pathetic, like some jealous teenager. He should have known better than to trust Ely, a man who had no reason to be loyal to anyone except himself. Could Lucas really blame him?

Then it occurred to Lucas. The ranch. "Did she inherit Cole's share of the ranch?"

"I didn't ask."

"That explains why she's here. She wants money."

Ely opened the truck's passenger door. "We'd better get back to town. You need to talk to her yourself."

It hit Lucas then. He'd have to tell Birch. Birch and Bobby and June and Derek. And Cassie, who had never met Cole. To her, he was only a voice on the phone, a picture on Birch's bureau, on the back wall of Lucas's saddle shop, on the grand piano out at the ranch, the one only played on Christmas Day, when Cassie picked out "Silver Bells" and "Frosty, the Snowman."

"I can't do it," he murmured. It would break Birch's heart right in two. Though she'd deny it to her death, Lucas always knew that Cole was special to her in a way he and Derek never were.

He gave the horses one last look, spending a few seconds longer on the skittish mare. She watched them from the far corner of the pasture, waiting for them to leave so she could eat.

"Enjoy it while you can, Greta," he said softly. "By next winter, this could all be condos."

12

RUBY

Ruby watched the confrontation between Cole's mother and her granddaughter, Cassie. The woman named Birch jumped right in without hesitation, like a family member or close friend. Cassie called her Aunt Birch so somehow this Birch must also be related to Cole. When Cole's mother came in, the heated discussion between the three women was too far away for Ruby to hear details. It was easy to discern that the McGavins were prominent people in this small town. They were not going to be happy with the will she carried in her purse.

Oh, Cole, she said internally. What kind of a hornet's nest did you send me into? She thought of Cole's ashes, upstairs in her room's spacious closet. Who would want them? His cool, confident mother? His tough, generous aunt? His brothers? Lucas seemed nice, but then she didn't know how he'd react once he found out about Cole's death.

The will in her purse felt like something illicit, drugs or stolen diamonds. Would they just hustle Ruby into some lawyer's office and bribe her to sign away the rights to the family ranch for a token amount of money? Or would they want to get to know her, find out what kind of life Cole had been living all these years? She bet it was the first scenario. Right now, that sounded just fine to her. The less complicated, the less emotions involved, the better. If she let herself, she knew she'd explode with anger at this whole situation. How could Cole do this to her? He'd claimed he loved her more than anyone he'd ever known. So why had he abandoned her? Left her to face his family alone?

This grief was so unpredictable, like a customer who smiles at you and puts you at ease and within minutes turns into an impossible-to-please tyrant, then stiffs you for your tip. Just when she thought she had her emotions under control, some feeling hit her out of the blue. Sometimes she stood in the shower sobbing, crying until the hot water ran out. Sometimes she was so angry at Cole, at this whole horrible, confusing universe, that she felt like she could kill someone herself. With one act Cole had destroyed not only himself, but, in a way, her too. In those few minutes it took for him to press his foot on the truck's accelerator, he threw away the person she'd been with him, the life they'd made, the life she'd longed for and thought she'd finally found.

When Ruby left the lobby, the lodge owner, Birch, was back behind the front desk, her head bent over some paperwork. The top of her white head showed a tiny, vulnerable spot of pink skin. Ruby walked past and silently asked, Will you care that Cole is dead? Or did you and the whole town disown him after he killed his father? Will you at least let him be buried here?

Over at the Chevron station some old guy sat in a torn office chair chewing an unlit cigar and reading a large print *Reader's Digest* magazine.

"Ely's figured out what you need," he said, smiling at her with yellowed teeth. The cigar seemed to wave at her when he talked. "You need a new carburetor for starters. And a new battery—yours is corroded to beat the band—spark plugs, couple of hoses, some electronic stuff. I don't know what else. Flat-out, your car's a mess. We got most of what you need except for the carburetor and some electronic gizmos. The parts guy in the city can get what you need to us by December twenty-sixth if you're willing to pay fifty dollars extra for express shipping. Ground shipping could take three days. Your call." He moved the cigar stub from one side of his mouth to the other.

"How long do you think it will take for Ely to fix it?"

"Once he gets the parts, a day at most. That is, if he don't have fifty other cars he's promised. You'll have to check with him on that one." He gave her a sympathetic smile. "Sorry your Christmas got ruined, miss. Hard time of year for your car to break down."

She returned his smile, not wanting to appear like a complete Scrooge. As for ruining her Christmas, that was a laugh. The holiday hadn't meant much to her for a long time.

The first Christmas after their mother had left, Ruby had tried to make it nice for Nash, who was only seven and didn't quite comprehend that their mother was never coming back. She brought out the aluminum tree and helped him decorate it, tried to bake cookies shaped like bells and reindeer, attempted to make a turkey with corn bread stuffing. But it was too much for her. The turkey turned out dry, the cookies were eaten long before Christmas Day and her father left on Christmas Eve and didn't come home until two a.m. The next morning, after she and Nash opened their few presents to each other and a generic Christmas card with two twenties in each from their father, Nash ended up going to dinner at a friend's house and Joe went out drinking with his newest girlfriend. Ruby ate a turkey sandwich drenched in Miracle Whip, watched *Miracle on 34th Street* and wondered what snow felt like.

Years later, after she was on her own, Christmas became just another workday for her. Because she was a single woman and Nash usually spent it with his foster parents, and eventually at friends' houses, she often agreed to work that day, letting the other waitresses go home to their families. She spent the day serving meals to other lonely people who had nowhere to go. She understood them and tried to make things special—extra butter softened in the microwave so it would spread easily, the freshest tomatoes or a double dollop of whipped cream on their pumpkin pie. Their cups and glasses never wanted for coffee or soda. She liked the alone people, wondered about their lives, not just at Christmas, but the rest of the year, too. She watched them glance over at the tables filled with laughing people, groups that had a rhythm to their talk and laugher, from the easiness of long friendships and close family ties.

The laughing people reminded her of novels she couldn't help reading about groups of women who had been friends since childhood or high school or college. They helped each other through good times and bad, they laughed at, or, if the author was attempting to give them some humanity, pitied the odd people, the ones who weren't like them. She always wondered about that person, the one who didn't fit in, who didn't come from the right kind of family or always know the right things to say or do. That's the person she felt like.

The old man cleared his throat, bringing her back to the present.

She'd already paid for a week at the lodge so she decided on ground shipping. "Thank you for your help. I'll be at the lodge if there's any problem."

She started back down the street heading toward Penney's. Since she was going to be here a week she may as well buy gloves and a scarf. Then she'd kill time in either the bookstore or a library. Would a town this size even have a library? These days, they were closing libraries down in towns ten times the size of Cardinal.

Before she reached Penney's, she sat down on a public bench and, though she didn't know why, decided to call her father. She suddenly felt the urge to connect with someone who shared her history, no matter how awkward their relationship. It was Christmas, darn it. Christmas is supposed to be about being with family or something that approximated family.

Prissy's cigarette-hoarse voicemail answered. "We're obviously busy or driving through a tunnel and can't get your signal. Leave a message or call back."

"Hey, Prissy, Dad," Ruby said. "Just wanted to wish you a Happy Christmas." She paused a moment, then quickly rattled off where she was staying. "I don't know the number, but if you need to get in touch, I'm sure Information has it. I'm not sure how well cell phones connect up here, though obviously I've reached you on mine. Anyway, Happy New Year, too." She hesitated a moment, tempted to add, "I love you." The urge passed and she hung up.

She walked past Holy Grounds, the coffeehouse where she'd talked to Ely last night. Had he told anyone yet who she was? Would they all come at her at once? Obviously Birch and Cassie didn't know yet, or they wouldn't have been so friendly at breakfast. When June McGavin found out, Ruby was sure she'd waste no time in finding her. That was something Ruby dreaded more than anything.

The Novel Experience was right between the movie theater, which was still old-fashioned enough to show a double feature, and the Mountainview Stop 'n' Shop grocery store. A cowbell clanged when she opened the glass-front door. She was surprised to see the man behind the counter counting change was the same man who brought her and Ely muffins last night—Lincoln Holyoke. He looked up briefly, nodded at her, then went back to counting nickels. With tomorrow being Christmas Eve, there were quite a few people shopping. In the background Elvis crooned, "Oh, Holy Night."

Surrounded by books, she felt herself start to relax, relishing the feeling of expectation books always gave her. It reminded her of being a kid. Every two weeks, no matter where they lived, she took a pile of books back to the library and checked out new ones. The thrill of looking at all those unread books, anticipating the joy and comfort lurking between the covers, was the one thing that had never deserted her.

"Good afternoon, Ruby," he said, when she walked by the counter. His sun-bleached, mad scientist hair bounced slightly when he nodded at her. "Make yourself at home. Romance novels on the back wall. Mysteries to the left of 'em, Westerns to the right. Mainstream and literary in front of the store. Let me know if you can't find what you're looking for."

"Thank you," she said, heading toward the section marked "Regional." What better way to understand an area than reading about it? Reading had always been how she'd figured out things. When her mom left, Ruby went to the library and searched for psychology books that might explain why a mother would leave her children. She never found a satisfactory answer, but just being surrounded by books on the subject gave her hope that an answer was possible.

She flipped through a paperback of local oral histories about Tokopah county. It would tell her a little about the area Cole grew up in. As she ran her finger over the titles, she stopped when she came to

one that read *Tokopah Valley Ranch Families—1900 to 1985.* She
pulled it out and turned to the index. Under McGavin there were four
names: Jacob, Kitterage, Carson and Birch. She flipped to the pages
where they were listed and read about the McGavins. Kitterage was
one of the few ranchers, the book said, who didn't sell his water rights
to the Department of Water and Power when they were buying them
up left and right so the California aqueduct could be built. That made
him both admired and hated in the valley, but it also assured his family a special place in the valley because they could still raise cattle and
not have to import their water or alfalfa. Jacob McGavin, obviously
Cole's great-grandfather, bought the land at the turn of the century. Not
much was listed under his name or his only son, Kitterage's, besides
their births and deaths and the births and deaths of their wives.

Under Carson's name there was listed his graduation from Cal Poly,
San Luis Obispo in June 1960 with a degree in agriculture. It was a
long list of affiliations from the Cattlemen's Association to the Rotary
Club to the Farm Bureau to the volunteer fire department to a three-
term stint on the city council. He married June Ann Trowley of Bakersfield, California, on May 11, 1962 and bore three sons, Cole, Derek
and Lucas.

Under Birch's name it listed her graduation from Cal Poly, San Luis
Obispo with a degree in education in June 1961 and her marriage to
Roberto Hernandez on July 1, 1961. No children listed.

Ruby considered buying this book, then decided that it might look
too suspicious. Their prominence in the town intimidated her. How
was she even going to approach this family with the devastating news
about Cole?

"Is there anything in particular you were looking for?" Lincoln
asked, ringing up her one book. "Bestsellers are thirty percent off this
week."

"This'll do. I'm traveling light these days."

He stared over eyebrows bleached as white-yellow as his hair. His
eyes were a bright, clear blue, the rims a pale pink. "Library's over two
blocks, next to Martha Juneau's house. It's the pink and white house
with the American flag flying out front. You can see it from the next

corner. Martha was a local writer, pretty famous back in the thirties. Good friends with Georgia O'Keeffe until they got in a squabble over a horse. Or a man. Or a piece of land. Maybe all three. No one's absolutely certain. I suppose it doesn't make much difference in the long run." He gave a bemused smile. "Whole sordid story is in this book." He tapped the local history book she was buying.

"Sounds intriguing," she said. Reading about someone else's troubled life might be just what she needed to get through these next few days.

He slid her change across the cluttered counter. "Lydia at the library will let you borrow books even if you're just visiting a few days. Just show her your driver's license. But don't think about taking off with one of her babies. She'll track you down like one of her bloodhounds. She has three."

"What kind of person steals a library book?" she said.

"You'd be surprised," he said, then studied her face a second longer. "Then, again, maybe you wouldn't. Work with the public, do you?"

His accuracy surprised Ruby. "How did you know?"

"Watched you perusing the books. When you took something out, you were careful to put it back where you found it. You even reshelved two that others left out. Only people that careful are ones who've worked at jobs picking up after others. That would be retail, housekeeping or food service."

"I was a waitress until three years ago. Now I'm a cook."

He held out her package. "Enjoy the book. To find the library, turn left out the front door, left at the first corner and go two short blocks. You'll see the American flag. Merry Christmas to you."

"Thanks," she answered. "You have a nice holiday, too."

Outside, she followed his instructions and found herself in front of Martha Juneau's house. The small brass historical plaque stated it was an official California state historical landmark. It told about Martha's career of nature writing with an emphasis on California and the Sierra Nevada mountains. It stated she was a contemporary and friend of Georgia O'Keeffe, Mary Austin, another famous local writer, and photographer Ansel Adams.

She stood for a moment looking at the fairy-tale house. What would it be like to be someone like this Martha Juneau, to be a writer, be friends with the famous, have your house turned into an historical landmark? Ruby's mother had lusted after fame like this, even gave up her family to search for it. Did Martha Juneau leave behind any broken relationships?

The library next door was empty except for a middle-aged brunette woman who wore an ecru-colored pullover sweater, a blue denim skirt and navy tights. She looked to be about fifty or so; a few gray hairs at her temple gave her a warm, homespun look.

"Good afternoon," she said in a voice that was soothing enough to be on the radio. Children probably adored her story hours.

"Hello," Ruby said, suddenly feeling awkward for coming here. She should have gone back to her room.

"Are you looking for a particular book?" the librarian asked. "Our selection is small, but we have access to other library collections. It usually takes only three days, but with the holidays it might take longer."

"No, thank you," Ruby said. "I'm just in town over Christmas because my car broke down. The man over at the bookstore said I could check out . . ." She stopped for a moment, realizing that to check out books, she'd have to show her driver's license. The license showed her real name, Ruby McGavin.

"I'd be happy to open a temporary card for you," she said, opening the drawer of her old-fashioned wooden schoolteacher desk. She pulled out a light blue form.

"I think I'll wait," Ruby said abruptly, holding up the package containing the book she'd just bought. "I have something to read right now. I was just checking on the possibility."

"Okay," the librarian said, laying the form down on the desk. "Just let me know when you want to fill it out. Won't take but a minute." She gave her a curious, but friendly look. "Are you on your way to Mammoth? Most people passing through town this time of year are."

"No," Ruby said, taking the form. "Just on my way to see my father in Reno. But, as I said, my car broke down and they can't get the parts to fix it until after Christmas."

"Oh, what a shame!" Her face looked actually stricken.

"It's okay," Ruby assured her, ashamed of her blatant lie. "We'll just celebrate a few days late. May I look at the magazines?" It would kill some time and help her hide for a little while.

"Absolutely," she said, pointing to her left. "They're around the corner in a little room by themselves. You'll have your pick of everything today. Looks like everyone is out doing last-minute shopping."

Inside the magazine room, Ruby settled down in a comfortable tweed chair and perused the racks in front of her. The selection was pretty good for a small town, though almost every magazine was the perky Christmas issue, something she wasn't in the mood to read. She glanced over at a microfilm machine in the corner of the room. Next to it were a couple of gray filing cabinets. She stood up and went over to them. The tiny sign on top of one file cabinet stated: "Please rewind microfilm when finished. Copies are ten cents. Change is available at front desk. Please do not refile microfilm boxes. Leave on top of file cabinet."

Each filing cabinet had a small white card listing the contents and dates. Most were for the *Cardinal Weekly Gazette*. The earliest ones were from the early 1890s. Amazing to think that over a hundred years of this town's history was recorded in three gray file cabinets.

Why hadn't it occurred to her hours ago? The story of what happened with Cole and his father had to be in the papers. A son killing his father in this small town would definitely be front-page news. It was still hard to reconcile the calm, easygoing man she'd married with someone who could kill his own father. In the nine months she'd known Cole, she'd never seen him get angry or even irritated, an incredible feat when one had to drive the Southern California freeway system as much as he did.

Though there were times she remembered now, when he'd fall into a dark, quiet mood for a day or two, where his chameleon eyes would stare at the rugged hills behind their rented house, his mind in another place, seeing something in the shadows that he wouldn't share with Ruby. It was the only moody thing about him, and so small, really, when she remembered her own dad's violent fights with her mother, the yelling, the crying, fists punched through thin apartment walls and Nash cowering under his twin bed. Ruby used to crawl through the dust bunnies to pull him out, afraid he'd suffocate or get bitten by a spider. Mom's leaving had actually brought a kind of sad peace to their house.

No, Cole's quiet, melancholy moods were a small thing in terms of family disturbances. She reasoned that he was thinking about his family, the parents and brothers killed so quickly, so tragically. Now, she realized that the things that made his eyes cloud over, retreat from the life they'd carved out for themselves, were far more complex.

The cabinet holding the microfilm would tell her the facts of his crime, reveal the concrete details that Ely wouldn't tell her. The feelings, the history, the reasons, were something she would have to find out from the family he left behind. His brothers, his mother, his aunt. Who else was he related to in this small town? For all she knew, this woman who was behind the library desk was a cousin.

"What a mess you left behind, Cole McGavin," she murmured to herself, missing him again, in spite of her anger, sorrow like a sharp knife cutting her heart.

She pulled out the cabinet drawer and searched the dates on the small boxes. He'd gone to prison for killing his father. Prison, Ely had said, not the youth authority or reform school or whatever they called it these days. That meant he'd committed the crime when he was an adult. If what Cole had told her about his age was correct, he turned eighteen in March 1981. The same year her mother left. So he either graduated in 1980 or 1981. She glanced over at the door, hoping the librarian wouldn't come in and see what she was doing. She inserted the roll dated January 1980, searching for details of his life.

In the next hour she felt like she was looking at a miniature movie of Cole's life, a life that was as foreign to her as a story on pygmies in *National Geographic*. First string quarterback, homecoming king, champion team sorter—whatever that was—at the Tokopah County Fair, class valedictorian. The McGavin family involved in so much of Cardinal's day-to-day social life. June McGavin served on this committee and that; his father, Carson, had been president of the local Cattlemen's Association a record six times and Cattleman of the Year five times. An article in the paper about Carson when he won Cattleman of the Year that fifth time listed all the accomplishments in the ranch family book and a few others. The front page showed a black-and-white photo of Carson whose good looks shone even through the flat, posed newspaper portrait. He had a strong jaw, dark eyes and an easy smile. She could see Cole in that smile. She wondered if his father shared Cole's thick, straight hair. It couldn't be seen under Carson's white cowboy hat.

She scanned the papers searching for the McGavin name. She read an article about Cole's graduating class of 1981, their class trip to Washington D.C., their prom at a hotel in Mammoth, Senior Ditch day when most of the senior class drove to Huntington Beach to body surf and roast hog dogs.

She and Cole had gone to Huntington Beach the first Fourth of July they'd been married, joining a group of his work buddies and their wives at a beach party to watch fireworks shot off the pier. He'd never let on that he'd been to that same beach as a teenager.

She sped past the rest of the months and years, skipping over stories about entries in county fairs and riding in the Mustang Days parade. She couldn't read any more about the life he'd lead before they met. Though it might interest her someday, right now all it did was hurt in a place so deep inside it felt like a tumor growing. Finally she found what she was looking for in September 1987. The headline told the story in five words.

PROMINENT RANCHER KILLED, SON INDICTED

The photo showed Cole looking a combination of young vulnerability and sullen anger. He was flanked by a sober, dark-haired man in a sheriff's uniform who looked vaguely familiar. After a few seconds she realized it was a younger version of the man who'd intervened last night when Derek tried to pick a fight with Sueann.

She scanned the article, which was surprisingly skimpy with details. The only real information she acquired was that Carson McGavin was killed by a .45 pistol by his oldest son, Cole. It happened on September twenty-fifth at the Circle MG ranch. The only witnesses were his wife, June, and his twenty-year-old son, Derek. She read the next few weeks' follow-up stories written by a reporter named John Henley Jr. who, according to the masthead, appeared not only to be the weekly paper's main reporter, but also related to the publisher. The story stayed on page one of the paper for weeks, though there were few details about what took place. She forwarded through the microfilm until she came to the December fifth headline.

RANCHER'S SON PLEADS GUILTY TO VOLUNTARY MANSLAUGHTER.

That was it. Ruby couldn't read any further. She rewound the film and filed it back where she'd found it. When she came out of the room, blinking her burning eyes, the tiny library was crowded with children. Apparently there was a special Christmas story hour with refreshments. It appeared that every young mother in town had brought her children.

She weaved through the giggling, excited children and opened the library's front door and found herself face-to-face with Santa Claus.

"Oh, excuse me," she exclaimed, stepping aside to let his ample red and white bulk squeeze past her.

"No, pardon *me,* Ruby," he said, chuckling. "Have you been a good girl this year?"

She stepped back, shocked he knew her name until she looked closer under the beard. It was Bobby Hernandez, the man who owned the Tokopah Lodge.

"Oh, hello," she said. "You certainly do get around."

"A multitalented man, that's me," he said. "Don't forget to leave me milk and cookies." He dug into his black velvet bag and pulled out an orange and white candy cane. Handing it to her, he said, "I actually prefer Cheetos, those really hot ones. Don't tell Mrs. Claus."

She took the candy and smiled. "Your secret's safe with me."

Though the short exchange with Bobby Hernandez broke her despairing mood for a moment, it quickly returned when she started walking back toward the lodge. She was confused, hurt and, though she'd never admit it out loud, frightened. This was too much to comprehend, too much to deal with along with Cole's death. Once her car was fixed, she decided, she would leave for Nashville. She'd tear the will up in a hundred pieces and bury it deep in a trash can somewhere along the road.

Just as quickly, she realized that plan was impossible. There was a reason Cole left her his part of the ranch, and she loved him enough to want to see what that was and to make sure his ashes were given to someone who would take care of them. As deceitful as their life together had turned out to be, she needed some kind of closure, an ending to their story. Coming here, she realized now, was as much for her as for him. She knew she'd always wonder and regret that she didn't tie up the loose ends. That was a good reason to stay and see this through, but the biggest reason was that running away would have been too much like her mother.

Walking down the side street toward downtown, she was so deep in thought that she didn't notice the old pickup truck slowly following her.

"Excuse me," the driver called.

She turned to look at him. It was the younger McGavin brother. The mechanic, Ely, had obviously told this man about Cole's death.

"Ms. Ruby . . ." he started, then stopped. His features contorted with some kind of emotion. "Please, we need to talk." He pulled the truck to the side of the road and turned off the engine.

She watched him step out of the rust-eaten truck.

"You *are* Ruby McGavin?" he asked, closing the door behind him.

She nodded, sticking her hands into the pockets of Cole's leather jacket. She watched him walk toward her, taking in his lanky frame, his slightly shaggy blond hair and mobile mouth.

"I'm Lucas McGavin." He paused. "Cole's youngest brother."

"Yes, I know," she said, shivering

"Look, it's freezing out here. Would you like to go somewhere warm to talk?"

She stared at him a minute. "Where?"

He thought for a moment. "How about we just drive? I won't hurt you. I mean, you can . . . trust me."

Trust *you*, she almost blurted out. I couldn't even trust *him*. But, the truth was, at some point she had to talk to one of the McGavins. It had to start somewhere and this brother seemed nice. He'd tried to be the peacemaker the other night.

"Can't we talk here?" she asked. It was ridiculous, of course, to attempt the sort of conversation they needed to have out on the street. But she was reluctant to get into his truck.

He took a step closer. Ruby fought the urge to move backward, not wanting to give him the impression she was afraid. "Unfortunately, there's too many nosy people in this town who'd love to eavesdrop on our conversation. Why don't you come to my saddle shop? We can talk privately without people staring at us. It's three blocks away, right out on Main Street—Cardinal Custom Saddlery. I can give you a ride."

She hesitated. The saddle shop was only slightly safer. Still, it was right downtown, which was busy with shoppers. "Okay, but I'll walk."

He climbed back into his truck and made a U-turn. Though she was tempted to walk the other way, she knew talking to one of the Mc-Gavins was inevitable. This one seemed the least intimidating.

A few minutes later she opened the wooden door of the saddle shop where it was wasn't much warmer than it was outside, but at least she was out of the wind. She stood behind the glass counter looking at an empty room.

"I'll be right out," his voice called from behind a closed door.

She gazed around the shop, inhaling the scents, the thick, buttery smell of leather, combined with the smell of old dust and something that smelled sharp, tangy and a little smoky.

Behind the counter she could see his actual working space. It was filled with dozens of tools, half-made saddles, a couple of wooden stools, and, in the far corner, a beautiful, intricately carved, silver-trimmed saddle.

He came out from a small room she guessed was a bathroom or utility room. "I'm making some coffee. I apologize for how cold it is in here. I didn't get here early enough to start my old heater."

"You make saddles?" she asked, though it was obvious. She felt awkward, not sure of what to say to her husband's brother. She walked over to the counter and ran her hand over the carved leather notebook.

He gestured at her to come around the counter. "Yes, I also do leather repair work of any kind, not to mention checkbook covers, hatbands, holsters, purses, knife sheathes. Shoot, give me a piece of leather and enough money and I'll carved turnips on it if you want." He smiled at her. "Once I even carved a Scottish sporran."

"A what?"

"One of those pouches a man wears in front of his kilt. A kilt has no pockets."

"I guess they don't."

"I do what I can to make ends meet."

"I understand how that is."

They were silent for a moment.

"Tell me what happened," he said, his voice suddenly curt.

She hesitated, alarmed by his abrupt change of tone.

He brought a hand up to his temple, massaging it. "I'm sorry. Too many years arguing in front of a judge. I didn't mean to sound so sharp."

"You're a lawyer too?"

"Was."

She wanted to ask him what made a person go from being a lawyer to making saddles, but that was not why they were here.

"Cole worked for a construction company framing houses," she said, turning away, unable to look at Lucas's face when she spoke of Cole. She studied the saddlemaking tools hung neatly on the Peg-Board above his worktable. "We met when he was working on a job site in San Juan Capistrano. I was a cook at a cafe downtown, next to the mission. For a month straight he ate breakfast and dinner at the cafe where I worked. He always ordered a hot roast beef sandwich for lunch and French toast for dinner. He liked extra hashed brown potatoes with his French toast." She glanced up at him. "He always ordered sour cream for his potatoes."

A smile softened Lucas's face. "Cole loved sour cream."

She looked away again, studying the tools. There were dozens of them, with shiny, smooth wood handles. Did it really take that many tools to make a saddle? She knew next to nothing about horses or saddles. It never occurred to her where saddles came from, that there were actually people who made them. She walked over to the finished, silver-trimmed saddle sitting in the corner. Even to her untrained eye, she could tell the work was exquisite, that of a real artist. She touched a tentative finger to one of the carved flowers decorating a long piece of leather hanging down the side of the saddle.

"Cole made that," Lucas said softly.

Her finger froze on the base of the flower. Tears burned behind her eyes.

"That one and a lot of others in this county and around the country. He was really . . ." Lucas paused, obviously searching for the right word. "He had a gift."

She turned slowly around to face him. "He never told me he could do this."

"I'm sorry," he said. "Cole was my brother and I loved him. But he lived in his own world. A world where he could control things."

"Apparently so," she said, anger drying her tears.

"Please," he said. "I need to know what happened. I need to know about my brother's life." He gestured to the love seat in the lobby. He brought a metal office chair from behind the counter and set it across from her, so he could see her face, but not crowd her on the intimate love seat. It put her at ease, this respect for another's space. It was exactly the sort of thing Cole might have done.

She took a deep breath. "He told our cashier that he wanted to marry the person who made the French toast. She convinced me to come out from the kitchen to meet him. He asked me out to dinner three days later by leaving a note with the cashier. At the restaurant we both ordered the Cajun shrimp and talked about how there were hardly any orange groves left in Orange County. We liked the same movies, the same kind of food and I was . . . and I think he was, lonely. We just felt . . ." She stopped. It was impossible to try to articulate the emotions she felt during those amazing months before they married, the good months afterward. "We fell in love," she finally said. "Nothing spectacular, except to us."

Lucas seemed pained by what she said. Was it because Cole had kept all this a secret, or was Lucas remembering a lost love of his own?

"When did you get married?" he asked.

"We'd known each other three months when we decided to go to

Las Vegas. Not to get married, just for fun." She smiled, remembering. "The Wednesday we arrived there was a midweek special at the Love-Me-Tender wedding chapel. A supposedly three-hundred-dollar wedding for sixty-nine-ninety-five. He kidded that it was hard to pass up a deal like that. Then we were at the mall having lunch and passed by a jewelry store and he turned to me and said 'Why not?' " She looked down at the leather purse in her lap. "We bought plain gold bands and went back to the chapel." She looked up at Lucas, her heart thumping so loud in her chest she was sure it was audible. "The minister kept getting our names wrong, calling us Carl and Judy. It became our private joke. We bought mugs printed with those names at a souvenir shop on the strip. We came back to Orange County and I moved into the house he was renting from his boss. It was one of the last old farmhouses in the county. Freeway in front of us, the hills of San Juan Capistrano behind us." Her voice dropped an octave lower. "We could hear coyotes and squirrels and sometimes saw mountain lions. Cole loved to sit in this old wooden Adirondack chair and watch the hills with a pair of binoculars I bought for him at a pawn shop in Las Vegas. We were happy." She stopped, unable to continue. She couldn't finish her thought—*at least I was.*

"He never spoke of us?" Lucas asked. "Of his life here?"

She didn't want to tell him. "He said his whole family was killed in a car accident. He said it happened when he was twenty-three."

She saw him visibly swallow, his face contorting again. There was a long silence between them. Once she'd started talking, she'd felt strangely comfortable around this man, Lucas. Was it because he looked so much like Cole? Acted so much like him? She wished this was all over, that it was a month from now and she was in Nashville sharing a late-night Waffle House breakfast with her brother with nothing more important than to listen to him gossip and complain about emotional, ambition-crazed singers, cheating managers, cheap club owners and his flaky musician friends.

"How did he die?" Lucas asked.

"His truck went over the side of an embankment on Oretga Highway. The coroner said he was killed instantly." To her own ears, her voice sounded disembodied, unemotional, like she was giving a traffic report. She hadn't intended on telling him more, but her voice kept talking. "Her name, the person from the coroner's office, was Ginger. She kept calling me ma'am. Her voice sounded like she was from the South. My mother is from Tennessee, so I recognized it. She said there were no skid marks." She closed her eyes, the room feeling suddenly warm, her stomach queasy.

"No skid marks." Lucas's voice was flat. "He did it on purpose?"

She leaned forward, resting her forehead on her knees. His tone sounded accusatory to her. Was that what his whole family would think, that she'd somehow driven him to kill himself? Why hadn't she just FedExed his ashes to them? She felt the room start to spin and twinkling lights lit up the darkness of her closed eyes.

"Let me get you some coffee," Lucas said.

He came back a minute later with a brown mug. "Do you take cream and sugar?"

She shook her head and took the mug with both hands. She could tell he wanted to continue talking about Cole, but didn't want to upset her any further. A stab of sympathy caused her to continue. As upset as she was, it had to be harder for him this moment. She'd had a few months to get used to Cole being gone. Lucas hadn't even had twenty-four hours.

"What more do you want to know?" she said softly.

"Do you know about why he left Cardinal?"

"Yes, I think so," she said, wrapping her hands around the thick, brown mug. "I read about it in the library."

"How did you know to do that?"

"Your friend Ely told me a little about Cole's past."

"Yes," he said, his voice suddenly cynical. "My friend."

He looked directly into her eyes, searching for something. The shape of his eyes was so much like Cole's. She felt her throat constrict. Even with all she'd learned about her husband, with all the lies he'd told, she still missed him with a physical ache that was like a disease eating her bones.

She met his gaze, making the decision in a millisecond. "He left me one-fourth of your ranch, but I'll sign it over to you. I just want to give someone his ashes and get on with my life."

He dropped his eyes to stare at the tips of his worn boots. "I'm sorry, Ruby. I am so sorry."

"Will you tell your mother? And your brother?" She continued to hold the mug with both hands, feeling the heat slowly fade away. Outside, a group of people walked by the shop, their cheery laughter an awkward chorus to her and Lucas's conversation.

His eyes were bright and shiny. "My aunt Birch will be devastated."

"What are you going to do?"

He didn't hesitate. "I can't ruin Christmas for her. This is her favorite time of year. She had no children of her own. She raised Cole when he was first born, when our mother couldn't. He was like a son to her."

"All right," she said, leaving it up to him. "How soon after Christmas will you tell her?" She didn't want to say that it really didn't matter if he waited until after Christmas or not. Once she found out, this holiday would never be the same for Birch. Like it never would be again for Ruby.

"The next day, I suppose."

She studied Lucas's face. Did he hold any animosity about Cole killing their father? How close had he and Cole been? He must have been a teenager when Cole was convicted of manslaughter. How much did he know about what happened?

"I've been honest with you," she said. "Now it's your turn. What happened back then, back when . . ." She couldn't say it. *When Cole killed your father.*

His face grew rigid, remembering. She fought the urge to reach across the distance between them and smooth out the frown lines with her thumb like she used to do to Cole.

"Lucas, what happened?" she asked.

He looked directly into her eyes. "That's the trouble. I honestly have no idea. I wish I did."

RUBY

"It was right after school started," Lucas said. "I was sixteen and had come to town to attend a friend's birthday party. I spent the night with my aunt Birch and uncle Bobby. They own the Tokopah Lodge."

She nodded. "Yes, I know. I'm staying there."

"Apparently, there was some kind of confrontation between Dad and Cole, not unusual as Dad was always harping on him about something. Dad wanted Cole to work on the ranch more. Cole loved the ranch, but didn't like working for our parents. Dad was cleaning his favorite pistol. All I was told was Cole and Dad argued and Cole accidentally shot Dad. After it happened, everything was so intense and crazy. Only Cole, my dad, Derek and my mom were there. No one explained anything to me. I guess they considered sixteen years old too young to know the details." His tone was tinged with bitterness. It was obviously still a sore subject for him.

"He was arraigned, but there was never a trial," he continued. "I heard rumors that his court-appointed attorney wanted to try for involuntary manslaughter, but Cole decided to take the district attorney's plea bargain for voluntary manslaughter. They threatened him with second-degree murder. The only thing Cole told me himself years later was he pleaded out to save the family further emotional turmoil. When I was working as a public defender in San Francisco, I tracked down the deputy DA who caught the case. By then, he was in private practice in San Diego. He said there wasn't enough evidence to really win second degree, but he'd wanted to try. He didn't think my family was telling the truth, but that all their stories matched. Too well, is what he said. That's what made him suspicious. He believed that my mom and Derek had been coached by Cole. But, with Cole's clean record, my family's prominence in this county and the fact that the three of them told identical stories, he said he was thrilled to get voluntary manslaughter. He said if it had gone to trial, even a first year public defender probably could have gotten Cole off with involuntary manslaughter, a substantially smaller conviction."

"Then why would Cole plead guilty to voluntary manslaughter?" Ruby asked, sitting forward on the love seat, her head feeling hot and fuzzy.

"*That's* what I don't know, and what no one will tell me."

"Did you ever ask Cole?"

She could tell he was trying not to sound exasperated. "Of course I did. He wouldn't talk about it. Neither would my mother or Derek."

She tried to imagine Cole angry enough to kill someone, to kill his own father. "It doesn't sound like Cole. In the nine months I knew him, I never saw him lose his temper."

Lucas's mouth straightened into a flat line. "He was the calmest person I ever knew. He and Dad argued hundreds of times, but Cole never lost his cool. And we've always had loaded guns around. I think . . . no, I *know*, there's more to what happened. But the only person who might have told me the truth was Cole and . . ." His voice choked. He abruptly stood up, catching his foot on his folding chair. "I'm sorry, we'll have to continue this later." He went into the back room and shut the door with a firm click.

She let herself out of the shop, standing for a minute in front of the brown clapboard building staring at the American flag hanging in the window. What now? If she went back to the lodge, she might run into

Birch and she didn't know if she could carry on a casual conversation with her right now. She looked at her watch. Now seemed as good a time as any to buy gloves. She walked over to JC Penney and took longer than necessary trying on gloves and looking at the colorful scarves. But it killed time and kept her mind occupied with something mundane. The story she'd just heard about her husband was still too new and raw to think about too deeply. It felt like a story about a stranger.

She finally settled on a pair of dark gray wool gloves and a mint green and iron gray scarf. Though she and Lucas didn't discuss any of the legalities of Cole's will, she'd tell him again the next time she saw him that she'd sign her part of the ranch to him. She would give him Cole's ashes and leave this town as soon as she could. Though her brother and father would probably tell her she was foolish for not taking what was legally hers, she didn't want any money resulting from Cole's death or from this family with such a tragic history. They made her disconnected family seem almost normal.

The rest of the day she wandered the streets of Cardinal, not knowing what to do with herself. She waited until six p.m.—dinnertime—to go back to the lodge, judging accurately that Birch and Bobby would not be behind the knotty-pine counter. She spent the evening in her room reading, trying not to think about Lucas telling his family about Cole, about the confrontation she'd eventually have with all of them.

The next day, Christmas Eve, Ruby again did everything she could to avoid Cole's aunt. She was certain something would show on her face, revealing the connection they shared. Birch had been friendlier since the night of the wassail party, but Ruby knew that would change once she found out who Ruby was and heard the devastating news about her nephew.

Ruby read on the guest activity board in the downstairs lobby that hot chocolate, cookies and a reading of the Christmas story and "The Night Before Christmas" would begin at six p.m. The stories would be read by Bobby Hernandez. Ruby decided to stay in town as long as there was a store or a restaurant open, avoiding Birch and Bobby as long as possible. Fortunately the lobby was crowded with excited tourists this morning so Birch was only able to wave at Ruby as she walked out the door.

"Glad to see you're bundled up," she called, smiling. "It's going to be a record-breaking cold. Luckily, I've heard Santa has eight-reindeer-drive."

Ruby smiled and waved back, sick at her deception. Birch was a nice woman, one she wouldn't have minded getting to know. It sounded like she'd really loved Cole. For that, Ruby was grateful. His mother didn't seem as loving. Was it better to have a mother like Ruby's who left, or one like June, who stayed, but made your life miserable? How odd it seemed that Cole knew that they had something so significant in common, yet she didn't. How one-sided their relationship had been. He died knowing much more about her than she knew about him. Smoldering anger mixed with sorrow inside her chest.

She spent most of the day wandering through the local antique and craft stores. She eventually ended back at The Novel Experience discussing books with Lincoln, the owner, who wore another colorful Hawaiian shirt. This one showed palms trees strung with Christmas lights and dolphins bearing wreaths around their necks. At five-fifteen, they were only ones left in the store.

"I'm sorry," she said, embarrassed when he walked to the front of the store and turned the hand-painted sign to Closed. She hadn't realized it was past closing time. "I completely lost track of time. You must want to go home to your family." It was nice, for a moment, to not think about Cole and his family or the fact that she was spending another Christmas alone. If she could, she would have stayed in this warm, comforting bookstore forever.

"No, no, it was my pleasure," he said. "I haven't had a good literary discussion in I don't know how long. Most everyone around here just wants to read Harry Potter or Tom Clancy. That's the first book of short stories I've sold in six months." He pointed at the collection of short stories she'd bought by Tim Gautreaux. "Guy like that probably has to catch and sell nutria to keep up the car payments."

Ruby smiled. "I think one of his characters did just that."

He grinned back. "I know. Just testing you."

"I'd better let you go," she said, picking up her package of books. "Thanks again for the book." Lincoln had given her a copy of this year's *Best American Short Stories* collection.

"No place to go, really," he said over his shoulder as he took the cash register drawer to the back room. "Going to Blue Christmas like I always do, then home. Guess if I didn't show up eventually, Shad might miss me, though he'd probably just move on to one of the widow ladies on my street."

"Shad?"

He came back into the room, pulling a heavy overcoat over his summery shirt. It was already dark and starting to snow. "My one-eyed cat. Named him after Shadrach in the Bible because he was found inside an old house that burned down over near the cemetery. Drug dealers, no doubt. Bob Riley's a local volunteer fireman who comes here once a week to buy his wife her romance novels. He asked me if I'd take the ornery feline and I couldn't say no. Don't even like cats."

She smiled at him, willing to bet that Shad was most likely one spoiled cat. "I'm sure he'd miss you at dinnertime."

He chuckled. "Truer words never spoken. Say, do you have any plans for tonight? If not, Blue Christmas always has room for one more."

"Blue Christmas?"

"Lots of people don't find Christmas to be all that jolly. Maybe they've lost someone, or they're alone or they just flat-out don't like the hullabaloo, so we have a church service where folks are not forced to sing about sleigh bells or joy to the world or about coming home for the holidays. I give a short talk, mostly about how being sad is okay, that Jesus understood sadness and that there's always hope, that is the real message of Christmas. I try not to be bombastic about it. Just try to help others get through the holiday. After the service whoever wants to can come over to the coffeehouse and enjoy whatever they want to eat or drink, my treat." He scratched behind one of his red-tinged ears. "Not trying to convert you or anything, but you being stuck here and all . . ."

"I appreciate the invitation," she said, actually relieved that she'd have somewhere to hide until the festivities at the lodge were over. "I'd love to come." She glanced down at her jeans and beat-up leather loafers.

"Oh, don't worry about what to wear," he said, catching her hesitation. "Trust me, there'll be all versions of clothing from pearls to beach thongs."

"Beach thongs?" she said. "It's freezing."

He tapped his temple with his forefinger. "Not everyone who attends is all there. But we love 'em anyway. *That's* the real meaning of Christmas. I'll give you a lift to the church, if you like."

She waited on the snow-covered sidewalk while Lincoln locked the store's front door. It was a quick drive to the Methodist church next to the high school, too fast for his old Jeep Cherokee's heater to blow more than cold air. The parking lot had more cars than she expected, about twenty or so. Inside the plain green and white clapboard church, the sanctuary was warm and inviting. Though it was decorated for the holidays, it was done quietly and in soothing shades of maroon and deep forest green. A single quilted banner hung down the oak pulpit. It showed a manger holding a sweet-faced baby with a golden halo over his head. The fabric seemed to shimmer even from the middle of the sanctuary where she found a seat. Though she'd not attended church much in her life and felt slightly uncomfortable, it wasn't as bad as she'd anticipated.

There were about thirty-five or forty people in the church. Some, like her, sat alone. A black man with dreadlocks, clad in a tan cowboy shirt, played the piano softly, the tunes recognizable Christmas carols like "Silent Night" and "O, Little Town of Bethlehem." She glanced around and was surprised to see Sueann from the cafe. She sat next to Ely. She saw Ruby, smiled and gave a small wave. Ruby waved back, then concentrated on the program she'd been handed. Why was Sueann here? Why wasn't she attending the festivities at the lodge? Where was her daughter, Cassie?

Lincoln led them in a few songs, then began his talk. She got caught up in his story, was amazed at how personal and open he was.

"Families," he said. "Sometimes you wonder why God even created them. Do you ever wonder if Jesus's sisters and brothers got annoyed with him? A mother often favors her oldest child simply because he or she was the first. But, honestly, think about his brothers and sisters. How do you compete with being the Savior of the world? 'Hey, Ma, look at this picture of a fish I just drew. Oh, never mind, Jesus just *created* a fish.'"

He smiled across the room at the chuckling crowd. "I'm just pulling your leg. I'm sure Jesus's siblings adored him. I like to think of him as being the most perfect, good-natured older brother ever born. He could not only give you awesome piggyback rides." He snapped his fingers. "He could actually zap a pig into existence." Soft laughter again tumbled through the crowd.

"But, seriously," he said, sticking his hands in the pockets of his faded jeans. "This time of year it seems like we just are bombarded with images of perfect families coming together for a joyous holiday created not by God, but by Madison Avenue or wherever it is these days they decide what we should experience with the Christmas holidays. The truth of the matter is, none of us have perfect families. Most of us this time of year probably have mixed feelings about our families, the holidays and who God actually is. And that's okay. God can take our doubts and our sadness. He knows what it's like to be sad, to be disappointed. Though He doesn't always solve each of our problems as quickly or in the way we'd like, I promise you, He is right there with us and He promises to give us peace."

His sun-reddened face grew more serious. "I know what it's like to be estranged from a family. Mine has barely talked to me for twenty years. Why? Because in my family, church was the place you went to on Sunday in order to justify champagne brunch at the country club. I was always a bit of a rebel, but when I dropped out of Yale, hitchhiked to California, became a drunk, then got saved at the L.A. Mission on skid row, that was the last straw for my Philadelphia mainline parents. It was a little too radical. Jesus as an occasional swear word, that's okay. Jesus as a Savior, that's just flat-out embarrassing."

He smiled out at the audience. "I love them, but stopped spending holidays with them a long time ago. It's better for all of us, though I do miss them. And, I like to think, they miss me a little too. They will always be a precious part of my life and I am a part of theirs, despite our differences. And the love I feel for them doesn't even come close to the love God feels for each of us. Whatever you've lost, whomever you've lost, God knows what it feels like and is right there with you. The Bible says nothing can separate us from His love, not death, not life, not angels, not demons. We can be high above the clouds or in the deepest ocean of despair and still His love is there."

After a while, Ruby's attention wandered and she glanced at the people sitting around her, wondering who they had lost or what circumstances compelled them to seek out this service. Lincoln's even, baritone voice soothed her with his assurances though she wasn't sure she believed in this benevolent, Santa Claus God that Lincoln seemed to know so intimately. Still she appreciated his kindness in trying to make this holiday easier for those in the midst of suffering fate's mercurial agonies.

The service concluded with "Amazing Grace," not exactly a traditional Christmas song, Lincoln said, but entirely appropriate in describing what Christmas was all about. All in all, though she had, the few times she'd attended church, found it to be more about asking for money than anything else, she liked Lincoln and his gentle words of hope and encouragement.

"Everyone is welcome back at the coffeehouse for whatever they'd like to eat and drink," Lincoln announced at the end of the service. "We'll stay open until everyone is filled up." His smile told the congregation he meant that both physically and emotionally.

Lincoln drove her over to the coffeehouse where there were already a few people waiting for him to open the door. She already felt like she'd known Lincoln for more than just an afternoon.

"How did you end up here in Cardinal?" she asked, then quickly added, "Oh, I don't mean to pry."

He smiled, but didn't turn to look at her. "Yes, I do seem out of place, don't I? Here's the twelve-ounce version. I moved here five years ago because my wife got a job working for the county. She was a social worker. She grew up in the Sierra Nevada Mountains, up near Bridge-port, and she missed this area, wanted to raise our children here. I agreed to come because I loved her even more than I loved the ocean. I sold some stock I inherited from my grandmother and was living off that while I was deciding exactly what I could do here in Cardinal."

He flexed his fingers on the steering wheel. "Lisa was killed six months after we moved here. She was trying to take some kids out of a home where their daddy had a meth lab. He shot her, took his kids and ran. They caught up with him in Reno. Got life, but killed himself in prison."

"I'm so sorry," Ruby whispered.

"Lisa used to tell me that good comes out of everything, something I didn't agree with. She said sometimes you just have to wait and see what good God is going to do with the situation." He glanced over at Ruby. "Her favorite saying was 'God is good all the time and all the time God is good.' "

Ruby didn't know what to answer to that. It sounded too easy and didn't, for her, explain enough about why bad things happen so often.

"I still didn't agree with her, especially after how she was taken from me." His eyes stared straight ahead, his voice never faltered. "Then Christmas came around. Until she died, I never thought about what sad, and, let's face it, angry, people did at Christmas. I mean, it's such an irritating holiday, when you think about it. The advertisements that start in September, the hype, all those Christmas movies whose plots make you feel like you've eaten a mouthful of sugar. That's when I started Blue Christmas. Lots of people have been helped, so I guess she was right. Good does come from everything."

Ruby murmured a noncommittal sound. Though it all sounded so easy, she wasn't convinced. She still couldn't see what good would come out of Cole dying. It seemed to her that all it did was leave her alone and cause even more agony to his family.

It was much easier for her to enter the coffeehouse with Lincoln. She wasn't sure if she would have gone if she was alone. Lincoln intro-duced her to a few people, then left to talk to others he'd befriended, going from table to table offering cookies, muffins and refilling coffee cups. At the counter were platters of sandwiches on thick white and wheat rolls, cakes, pies, eggnog and bowls of fruit. A small cheer went up in the line of waiting people when Sueann came in carrying a huge pan of brownies.

"Now, don't be Christmas hogs," she called. "I have three more pans in the car."

Lincoln passed by Ruby sitting at a back table and said, "Sueann's chocolate-rum brownies will make you drop to your knees and cry for your mama. Don't go home without tasting one."

"Absolutely," she said, thinking about how ironic his analogy was. She'd not cried for her mother since she was thirteen years old. Though she always swore she wouldn't, as Christmas Day grew closer, Ruby always wondered where her mother was, what she was doing, who she was spending the holiday with. Once when they were in their twenties, she voiced this to Nash.

"Ah, Ruby, who cares?" he'd said. "Do you think she's sitting there wondering about what *we're* doing on Christmas? Don't count on it." She told him he was right and wanted to believe it. Still she wondered. Could a mother who'd abandoned her children really not feel at least a twinge of guilt on Christmas or their birthdays? When she felt herself turning off her emotions, turning away from being involved with people, Ruby thought of her mother and made herself go to a party or on a date even if the guy was boring or irritating. Being selfish or uncaring wasn't set in a person's genetic makeup like the gene for breast cancer or red hair.

Ruby had been joined by two older ladies who were sisters. Both were widowed, without children, and appeared to be in their eighties. One was president of the local historical society, which was housed in a converted train depot outside of Cardinal. She was doing her best to convince Ruby to put down roots here and become a docent at the museum when Sueann pulled up a chair to join them.

"Merry Christmas, Pearl, Emmy," Sueann said to the ladies. Her strawberry-blond hair was out of its two braids and flowed down her shoulders in beautiful ripples. She held out her hand to Ruby. "Sueann Henley from the cafe. Don't know if you remember me."

"Yes, I do," Ruby said, taking her hand. It was slightly rough from repeated washing, a condition common to most longtime waitresses. "It's nice to see you again. I'm Ruby." She glanced around the room. "Where's your daughter?"

Sueann looked down at the piece of apple pie in front of her. "Cassie's celebrating with the upper crust of Cardinal. Her grandma gives a fancy Christmas Eve party every year at the ranch. Unlike me, Cassie's still a McGavin, so she's expected to attend." She shrugged, pretending not to care. "Part of the custody arrangement. I sometimes go to the Tokopah Lodge's Christmas Eve service, but this year I decided to come to Blue Christmas because, well, I'm feeling a little blue."

Ruby nodded in understanding. "Lincoln said I shouldn't miss one of your brownies."

She smiled, her green eyes turning into little slits. "Won first place at the Tokopah County fair five years in a row. They finally asked me to stop entering and made me a judge." She leaned over the table and said in a loud whisper, "It's the *rum*. They're especially appealing to the Baptists."

"Now, Sueann," Pearl said. "There's a few of us Baptists who like a little pinch of the spirit once in a while."

"Pinch?" her sister, Emmy, said. "There's more than a pinch of spirits in Sueann's brownies." Emmy patted her hand. "But all the stuff that makes you tipsy floats away when they're baked. Scientific fact. Isn't that right, Sueann?"

"Yes, ma'am, I've been told it is," Sueann said, winking at Ruby.

By ten p.m. about half the people had left. Lincoln sent each person off with something, a package of ground coffee, a mug, a box of candy, handpainted cards, or a warm knit scarf.

"That's so kind of him," Ruby said, running her hand over the book of old Cardinal postcards he'd given her.

"He's one-of-a-kind," Sueann said. "We have no idea how he keeps this place and the bookstore going when he gives away so much. Fishes and loaves is his answer." She propped her elbows up on the table and rested her small, pointy chin in her palms. "What are you doing tomorrow? I have Christmas dinner down at the cafe. The lodge's dining room isn't open."

"Maybe I'll drop by," Ruby said.

"I started it the year I was no longer welcome at the McGavin festivities. Cassie has breakfast with me and my brother, John, then spends the rest of the day at the ranch. It was my ex-husband's condition—that if he let me have physical custody of her most of the year, he could have her on all the big holidays. It's a terrible arrangement for me, but the alternative would have been her living one week out at the ranch, one week in town. This seemed easier on her."

"How far away is the ranch?" Ruby couldn't help asking even though she knew once Sueann found out who she was she'd look back on this conversation and think Ruby was probing. The fact that this ranch they were discussing was, at this point, one-fourth hers, still didn't seem real.

"About five, six miles," she said, picking up a peppermint cookie from a plate someone placed on the table. "She drives now so it wouldn't be that bad, but I like having her with me, living a life that is halfway normal." She sighed. "I don't know why I'm laying all this on you. Christmas Eve melancholies, I guess. She and I always have our celebration on Christmas night, but she's tired and cranky. It feels like leftovers, you know?"

Ruby nodded, thinking that, at least Sueann had a daughter. Cole left her before they could even have kids, something that was too overwhelming to dwell on at this moment. She was thirty-six years old. The chances of her finding someone to love, marry and start a family with now grew dimmer with each year. And she was old-fashioned enough to want to do it the traditional way. She'd lived with only one parent for half her life, and it wasn't easy.

Then again, would it be so bad if she never had children? Sometimes, when she saw the sadness children brought to many people's lives, she wasn't sure that being a parent was all it was cracked up to be. And Cole's death. If they'd had a child, how would she explain that their dad just didn't want to be around them anymore? Yes, not having children had its good points.

Still, her throat grew tight, thinking about being alone when she grew old. More than anything in the world, more than falling in love again or even having children, she suddenly realized, she wanted a home. She wanted a place where people knew who she was, cared if she was sick, put up with her foibles as she grew older, would attend her funeral when she died, tell stories about her, plant flowers on her grave. *How could you leave me, Cole? Someone who truly loved you. We were starting a life. How could you?*

"Are you okay?" she heard Sueann's voice through her mental fog.

"Yes," Ruby said, her eyes focusing on Sueann's curious face. "Just . . . remembering other Christmas Eves."

Sueann looked sympathetic, not pressing any further. "I understand." She looked at her watch. "Speaking of which, it's over."

"What?"

Sueann pointed to the clock behind Ruby. Ten minutes past twelve. "Merry Christmas," she said.

"You too," Ruby answered.

"I think I'll walk back to the lodge."

"Let me drive you," she said. "It's not that far, but there's muggings even in our little town. Especially when there are so many tourists."

"I came with Lincoln," she said, looking around for him. He was over at the piano, playing the duet "Heart and Soul" with some old guy wearing a camouflage army hat. Along with some other people surrounding the piano, they were laughing at Lincoln's improvised lyrics—"Carp and sole, with butter glazing it, carp and sole, my favorite lunchtime meal . . ."

"Looks like they might have imbibed a little Christmas cheer," Sueann said. "The eggnog in the blue bowl is powered by Bacardi." She stood up. "I'll let Lincoln know I'm taking you home."

"I should go over and thank him," Ruby said.

"No, don't," she said, laying a hand on her forearm. "He really doesn't like to be thanked. Says he does this entirely for himself, so being thanked is being prideful on his part."

Ruby shook her head, perplexed.

Sueann gave a small laugh. "Doesn't make sense to me either, but he's so sweet, we just do what he asks because he truly asks for so little."

On the short drive back to the lodge in Sueann's truck, they didn't speak. Main Street was nearly empty, and the colored Christmas lights reflecting on the white snow and shiny black street gave it a postcard look. What would it have been like to grow up in this town, Ruby wondered, surrounded by people you knew from the moment you could remember faces? Guarded by the majestic Sierra Nevada mountains, smelling the clear, pure air, knowing what your place was in life, knowing you had a home that would always be there?

Except it hadn't been like that for Cole. This picture postcard town had spurned its native son. Granted, killing your father was no small sin, but there was something wrong with the whole scenario, something that didn't fit. Cole was the least violent man she'd ever known. Even when he'd drink, which had been rarely, he'd never become belligerent or combative. If anything, he'd become more quiet than usual. They'd argued, sure, but just typical squabbles—who would take out the overflowing trash, who forgot to write a check in the checkbook, what movie they should see. Not once during the time they'd dated or after they'd married had Cole even yelled at her, something that she'd just started to trust in, tentatively believing that, perhaps, their marriage would be different from her parents. She inhaled deeply, the cold air tasting almost minty.

Maybe if he'd yelled a few times, let our his anger, he wouldn't have felt compelled to push his foot down on that accelerator. What had his last few seconds felt like? When the truck's front tires broke through the barrier and for a moment he was airborne, his fate sealed, did he think about his father, his family, his mistakes in life? Did he think about her? It was more than she could bear contemplating. She was thankful for the short drive to the lodge. Right now, she only wanted to crawl into bed and fall into a deep, unthinking sleep.

"Here you are," Sueann said, pulling up in front of the lodge.

Yes, Ruby thought, here I am.

"See you at the cafe tomorrow?" Sueann asked.

"I'll try." She left it at that, not certain if she'd feel like seeing anyone on Christmas Day.

Sueann nodded, her expression sympathetic. "Anytime during the day is fine. We're open until six p.m. That's when Cassie comes home and she and I have our Christmas."

"Thanks."

"No problem."

Ruby used her flat key to open up the lodge's front door. All the other guests had apparently gone to bed. She stood for a moment in the middle of the room, staring at the dying embers in the fireplace. For the first time, she noticed that there were names on the hand-knit stockings hanging from the mantel. She moved closer to read them. Tears burned her eyes when she read the first one—Cole. Unable to resist, she reached inside Cole's stocking and pulled out a small dark-blue velvet bag. The card attached read: "To Cole with love from Santa."

She opened the bag and pulled out a beautiful silver compass. It was heavy and cold in her palm. She turned it over and in the dim light could barely make out the engraving—*So you can always find your way home.*

LUCAS

Though he had no idea how, Lucas managed to make it through Christmas Day without revealing to his family that Cole was dead. The knowledge that he would never see his brother again made the holiday more miserable than usual. His mother had invited Walt Creston and his two married children, their families and a couple of wealthy newcomers to Cardinal whom Lucas was certain she was courting as possible developers of the Clear Creek property. Leave it to June to turn Christmas into a business deal. That way she'd be able to write off the whole catered meal on her taxes.

There were about thirty people in all, and except for Cassie, Lucas couldn't have cared less about any of them. He and Cassie ended up in the airy, western-decorated den after dinner playing a video game whose purpose procuring some kind of special gold bullets to kill little blue aliens who resembled bug-eyed turtles.

"You really need to learn chess," he said after getting soundly beat for the sixth time. "This game sucks."

"My generation has the best eye-hand coordination of any generation in history," she said.

"That would be impressive if we needed a nation consisting of only fighter pilots and magicians," he replied, finally giving up and pushing back in a brown leather recliner. Through the open double doors they could hear laugher in the formal living room. With each bottle of wine, the voices grew louder, more strident.

"Get with it, Uncle Lucas," she said, smiling at him. "By the way, thanks for the money. And the cashmere scarf. I love it." She was wearing the black and gray scarf that Sueann had helped him pick out.

"The scarf is so you can hide your tattoo from your grandmother."

She giggled and flopped down on the sofa. "You're too much."

"She's not getting a tattoo," Derek said, catching the tail end of their conversation when he walked into the room. He paused under a stuffed elk's head that hung next to an oil portrait of their father. Standing there, wearing a starched pale blue western shirt and holding a crystal highball glass, Lucas was struck by his older brother's resemblance to their father.

"Oh, Dad," Cassie said. "Why do you have to be such a drag?"

"Keeping you from further mutilating your body is not being a drag. It's being a responsible parent." He glanced down at his younger brother. "I'd appreciate a little support from my brother on this."

For the first time, Lucas noticed how tired his older brother looked, how the lines radiating from his tanned face made him look ten years older than his thirty-eight years. Was it living with June that did it? As hard as Lucas's life had been, at least he didn't have to tow the line every day with his mother. He couldn't help feeling a stab of pity for his brother. He turned to Cassie. "I'm not getting involved, okay? This is between you and your parents."

"Thank you," Derek said, his voice weary and a little grateful.

"Coward," Cassie said, frowning.

"Not the first time I've been called that," Lucas said evenly. He stood up. "I think I'll go check on the horses. It's getting kind of warm in here for me."

Cassie jumped up and said, "I want to come. I want to see the new mare."

"Those lousy nags are a waste of good land," Walt said, coming into the room holding an old-fashioned glass half-filled with gold-colored whiskey. His ruddy complexion came as much from the whiskey as it did from the sun. He shook his head at Lucas, his disgust apparent.

"That's what I keep telling him," Derek said, his personality changing once Walt entered the room. "He's been like this ever since he went to Cal State Bezerkley. Next thing you know, he'll be wanting to turn it into a bird sanctuary or trying to deed it to the Nature Conservancy."

"Yes, ski condos would be so much more productive," Lucas said. "Not to mention attractive. Especially for the McGavin bank account."

"*You* don't know anything about the McGavin bank account," Derek said, "because you haven't worked more than a total of a few weeks on this ranch for the last fifteen years. It's not easy keeping it together so we'll have something to pass on to Cassie."

"I don't want it," Cassie said. "It can burn to the ground for all I care."

Derek was across the room in a second, his large hand gripped his daughter's upper arm. "Don't *ever* say that. This is your legacy. It's been in our family for over a hundred years. People have sacrificed a lot so you can inherit this ranch."

"Let go, that hurts!" Tears glittered in her black-lined eyes.

"Derek, you're out of line," Lucas said, moving toward his brother.

"No, *you're* out of line. This is my daughter, not yours. She needs to understand how lucky she is."

"Right, lucky girl, that's me," Cassie said, jerking her arm away.

"C'mon, Derek," Lucas said. "She's just a kid."

"She's *my* kid," he replied, still angry, but his voice a little less belligerent. "I only want what's best for her."

"I know you do," Lucas said, glancing over at Cassie, trying to tell her with his eyes to keep her mouth shut, not to give her father more ammunition to keep this fight going.

Cassie frowned at him, her young face a female mirror of her father's. She'd inherited Derek's quick temper, something that often drove Sueann crazy. But this time, the good sense she inherited from her mother won out and she stayed quiet.

"Is it okay for her to visit the horses with me?" Lucas asked, trying to make his tone as neutral as possible. "I'll drop her off at Sueann's if you like. Save you a trip."

Derek narrowed his eyes, studying his younger brother, trying to figure out if he had any ulterior motives for his offer. Derek had always been a suspicious person, with a short temper that, it seemed to Lucas, would explode sometimes for no rational reason. When he would complain about Derek's unpredictability to Cole, his oldest brother's face would grow still.

"He has his demons, Lucas," Cole would say. "Like we all do. I'm not excusing him, but he's the one who has to deal with June the most. I wouldn't trade places with him for anything in this world."

Lucas knew then that Derek's moodiness had something to do with what had happened the night Cole shot their father. If, Lucas often thought, Cole actually did. He'd wondered more than once whether Cole had taken the fall for Derek.

Then again, how much did he really know about Cole? He'd been barely seventeen when Cole went to prison. The only Cole that Lucas had really known was burnished with a young boy's idealistic viewpoint. Lucas hadn't been that young boy for a long time now. *Cole, you jerk. Why would you kill yourself and never tell me why all this happened?* Now, for the rest of his life, Lucas would be the one left out.

"Tell your mom we're not done discussing that tattoo," Derek said to Cassie. It was his way of conceding and letting the argument go.

"Sure, whatever," Cassie said, wrapping her new scarf twice around her neck.

"You okay?" Lucas asked her while they drove out to Clear Creek.

"It's just the same old crap," she said, turning her head to stare out the truck window at the snow piled alongside the highway. "Dad doesn't really care about me getting a tattoo, you know. He just wants to bug Mom." She said it with a mixture of bitterness and sadness. It made Lucas want to hug her, assure her that she'd survive this family.

They spent the rest of the afternoon with his rescue horses, feeding them carrots and apples. The crisp mountain air cleared Lucas's brain. He sat on the tailgate of his truck and watched Cassie try to seduce the mustang mare, whom she agreed to call Greta. She'd hold out a carrot and the mare would dance within twenty feet, snorting and shaking her head, making Cassie giggle like a little girl. Being out here made Lucas think of Cole and how much he'd loved the Clear Creek section. He and Lucas used to come here to ride when Lucas was eight and Cole fourteen. He tilted his head back and looked up at the white-blue sky. Where was his brother? How could it be that he just wasn't here on this planet anymore? The immensity of that thought overwhelmed him.

He dropped his niece off at the cafe at five-thirty. Inside the warm building, Sueann sat in a booth with Cole's wife, Ruby, eating pumpkin pie. They were laughing about something in that intimate way that women did that always confused and intimidated Lucas. For a moment, it made him angry to see Ruby laughing. What kind of woman was she? Her husband, his brother, was *dead.* He quickly chastised himself, reminded that his brother's death wasn't something new to her. Who was he to begrudge her a few moments of laughter?

"Hey, Lucas," Sueann called, gesturing him over. "Merry Christmas! This is Ruby. She got stuck here in Cardinal over the holiday, but we're trying to make it up to her."

"Nice to meet you, Ruby." He held out his hand feeling guilty for lying to Sueann, one of his only friends in Cardinal. Ruby shook it, playing along with his charade.

"I need to make sure everyone's had enough to eat and force the leftovers on whoever will take them," Sueann said, sliding out of the booth. "You keep Ruby company, Lucas. Tell her scary stories about living in San Francisco."

Once they were alone, Lucas said, "How was your day?"

"As good as it could be," Ruby replied, looking down at her hands. "Sueann's a really nice person."

"I'm sorry about yesterday . . . in my shop . . . I . . ."

She looked up quickly. "Don't be. I understand."

He lowered his voice. "Before I tell my family about Cole, I need to talk to you again. I need more details."

"I told you everything I know." Pain clouded her gray eyes.

"You said you have his . . ." He couldn't say it.

"In my room at the lodge."

"I want to see them. And his death certificate." It had occurred to him last night when he couldn't sleep that, despite how sincere she seemed, how genuinely sad about his brother's death, she might be a con artist. This whole thing might be a ruse to extort money. He almost laughed. He had no money and it'd be less dangerous for her to rob an Oakland bank in midday than try to con money from his mother.

"When?" she asked. "Where?"

"Tomorrow at ten." Where was more difficult. She didn't have a car and he didn't want anyone to see them together until he'd decided how to tell his family. Her coming to his shop yesterday was not a cause for speculation; she could have been a customer. But it was taking a chance meeting there again because his aunt Birch could walk in anytime. They'd have no good explanation why she was there and, eventually, when Ruby made her presence known, Birch would know he'd lied to her.

He didn't like it, but he was going to have to ask Ely for his help. "Ely could pick you up at the lodge and we could meet somewhere out of town. If Birch sees you with him, she wouldn't suspect anything because she knows he's fixing your car. How about ten a.m.?"

"Okay," she said, sliding out of the booth. "Excuse me, but I think Sueann needs help cleaning up. It's the least I can do."

He watched her go behind the counter, pick up a cloth and start wiping it clean. Her reddish brown hair, pulled back in a braid today, left her face open and vulnerable. He studied her as she worked, taking advantage of her concentration and determination not to look at him. Though he fought it, there was something that attracted him to her. Was it just because she'd been his brother's wife? Was he jealous because Cole allowed her to share his life when he wouldn't allow anyone else in? But, in the end, he'd abandoned her too. In the end, she only was given a small piece of him, just like Lucas. Only as much as Cole would allow. Cole controlled everything as he always had.

Who was this Ruby McGavin anyway? What if none of what she claimed was true? He still had a connection in the San Francisco police department. He'd give the detective a call tonight and have him do a quick background check. He knew it was illegal, but right now, all he cared about was verifying that she was who she claimed. He couldn't help hoping that she might be a con artist, perhaps an old girlfriend his brother had pissed off. Maybe Cole was actually alive somewhere.

That night he called his friend, Matt, apologizing for disturbing his Christmas. Matt told him he'd have something by the next morning. Then Lucas called Ely, who agreed to pick Ruby up and bring her out to Clear Creek tomorrow morning to talk to him.

The detective called Lucas at his shop the next morning with his skimpy report.

"Not much to tell," Matt said. "Her story about your brother's death is exactly what the Orange County sheriff's report says. She has no criminal background, not even a bounced check. She worked at the same cafe in San Juan Capistrano for five years. Lived in a series of South California towns before that—La Puente, Azusa, Santa Ana. Has worked as a waitress most of her adult life. Her father and brother are kind of flaky, don't seem to live in one place too long, but they have no criminal records either. Dad's a long-haul trucker. Her brother is a musician. She's as clean as my grandma's kitchen floor. Not even an outstanding library fine. Looks like she's just who she says she is."

"Thanks, Matt," he said, the disappointment more acute than he anticipated.

"No problem," he replied. "I miss you, man. You were the only PD who had any balls or normal clothes. Not to mention the only guy I could beat at squash."

"Haven't played a game since our last one," Lucas said. "Nearest court is five hours away."

"Yeah, but you got trout, man. That's a trade up in my book. Say, you hear about Mitchell Weeks?"

Lucas tensed up. "No, I'm not in touch with anyone from the old days."

"Got the shit beat out of him in San Quentin. Was laid up for months. Serves the baby killer right. Too bad they didn't finish the job. Heard a guard intervened, but not right away. I'd like to buy that guy a six-pack."

Lucas didn't answer. Mrs. Weeks's terrified face flashed through his memory. His temple veins throbbed with the onset of another headache.

"Hey, thanks for the information, Matt. Say hello to Cindy for me. Tell her I miss her Irish stew."

"Sure will, buddy. You keep in touch, okay? And I'm sure sorry about your brother."

"Thanks."

After hanging up the phone, Lucas slipped on the new flannel-lined barn jacket Birch and Cassie had given him for Christmas and started for Maxie's Bavarian Bakery three blocks away. This was definitely a two-donut morning. Maybe three. He walked down Main Street, carefully picking his way through the slushy, gray-tinged snow. The temperature on the bank building read forty-six degrees. The snow was beginning to melt. It never stayed long in Cardinal. Kind of like the kids who grew up here.

Inside the yeasty-smelling bakery, decorated in a cheery, vaguely Swiss-German style, he bought a half dozen donuts and three coffees to go. As usual, it was crawling with tourists. Their shrill, excited voices magnified his irritation with life. Maxie's Bavarian Bakery was the most popular tourist stop in town.

"Got some customers coming in?" Maxie asked, placing his order in a pink bakery box. Her pewter bun was slick and neat, not a strand out of place.

He gave a sort of nod, not wanting to actually lie. "How was your Christmas?"

"Slept in," she said, grinning at him. "All the way to five a.m."

That made him smile. For her, that was sleeping in. Her normal waking hour was two a.m. when she started the day's baking. She was sixty-five years old and she still personally supervised all the shop's baking.

On the drive out to Clear Creek he rehearsed what he was going to say, like he used to his closing arguments. Or tried to anyway. He realized when he arrived at Clear Creek that he didn't have a clue what he wanted to ask Ruby. He had to admit to himself that talking to her again was merely a delaying tactic, a way to avoid doing what he knew had to be done today, telling his family about Cole. Would it be better to have Cole's ashes actually with him to hand to Birch after he told her? Or would that make it more painful? Should he gather everyone together and tell them, or tell Birch and Bobby separately from his mom and Derek? He dug in his jacket pocket for the migraine pills he'd slipped in there. He popped one and took a long gulp of coffee. Maybe that would head it off at the pass. He had no time for a headache today.

Rounding the corner on the dirt road, he saw that Ely and Ruby had already arrived. Ely leaned against the front grill of his red Ford pickup, his arms crossed over his chest. Ruby's back was to Ely, her arms at her side while she gazed out at the horses. The horses, even the mare, were huddled together under the cottonwood tree, trying to keep warm. Ely and Ruby both looked up at the sound of Lucas's truck.

He offered them coffee and donuts. Ely took the coffee. Ruby refused both.

"Okay, we should just get to it," he said, sticking his hands in his pockets. "I need to tell my family today. If you don't mind, I'd like to see Cole's death certificate and take it with me. In case there's some question." He was specifically thinking of June and Derek who would, no doubt, have the most to say about this. It occurred to him as he stood here, that if Ruby sold her part of the ranch to June or Derek, they would have a majority share and could outvote him in the selling of this property.

Without a word, Ruby handed Lucas a manila envelope. Inside was an official death certificate from the State of California. Under cause of death it was stated—blunt trauma to head, vehicular accident. The other papers were his will. The back of Lucas's throat tasted metallic.

LAST WILL AND TESTAMENT OF COLE MCGAVIN

I, Cole McGavin, a resident of the County of Orange, State of California, being over the age of eighteen and being of sound and disposing mind and memory, and not acting under duress, menace, fraud or undue influence of any person whatsoever, or whosoever, do hereby make, publish and declare this to be my last Will and Testament.

Lucas glanced over the numbered provisions. First, revoking other wills, second, declaring Ruby Lee McGavin to be his lawful wedded wife, three, declaring he had no children living or deceased. Provision four was the clincher.

I give all my estate, both real and personal and of whatever kind and whatever situated, including my portion of the Circle MG ranch in Cardinal, California, to my wife, to sell or distribute as she sees appropriate.

He also appointed her executrix of the will. Lucas glanced through the rest of the provisions, all standard, down to the bottom where Cole's bold, strong signature erased any doubt that this was a forgery. Lucas would recognize his brother's signature anywhere.

He looked up at Ruby, who watched him with a wary expression. "Okay if I take this with me?"

She hesitated for a moment, then nodded.

"Was there anything else?" Lucas asked. "Anything that gave a hint about . . ." He stopped, dropped his eyes, unable to stand her sudden expression of pain.

"No," she said, her voice surprisingly strong and unemotional. "Nothing that makes it . . . certain."

He looked up at her and their eyes met. Behind them, the horses whinnied, impatient for treats they now expected every time a human visited.

Ely broke their silence. "You two need to quit avoiding this. Birch needs to know about Cole."

Lucas glanced over at his friend, anger popping like a firecracker inside him. "This isn't something you just dump on people without any thought or planning."

Ely ignored Lucas's sarcastic tone. "There isn't any amount of time or planning that's going to make this easy for Birch. And June will start plotting the minute she hears. If I were you, I'd just get it over with."

"Well, you're not me," Lucas snapped.

Ruby glanced at Lucas in surprise, then over at Ely, obviously confused by the tension between the two men. The horses whinnied again, annoyed at being ignored.

"Dang horses are as spoiled as poodles," Ely remarked.

"I don't want to be there when you tell them," Ruby said.

Lucas looked at her in surprise. He'd not even considered the possibility. This was a private family situation.

"She's his *wife*, Lucas," Ely said, understanding exactly what Lucas was thinking.

Lucas felt his neck grow hot. If Ruby wasn't standing there looking so lost and hurt, he would have shoved Ely and told him where he could take his remark. "Where is he?" he asked her, his voice hoarse.

"There." She pointed at Ely's truck. "Please, Lucas, take good care . . ." She touched her hand to her cheek. "I'm sorry. I know you will."

His anger instantly dissipated and he went to her, instinctively putting his arms around her. He was not normally a demonstrative man, certainly not with someone he didn't know, but Ely was right, this was Cole's *wife*. Cole loved her enough to marry her and leave her everything he owned. For Cole to trust anyone like that said everything Lucas needed to know about her. Cole would not have fallen in love with a con artist. He was too cynical for that.

He felt her tremble in his arms and he thought about the last time he saw Cole, six months ago. August in Las Vegas. They'd joked about eggs frying on the sidewalk. The met at their usual Denny's restaurant on Las Vegas Boulevard. They ate lunch and then spent most of the day and late into the night playing Texas hold 'em at the Golden Nugget and watching baseball games on the casino's big-screen television. They stopped playing cards occasionally to eat a shrimp cocktail or mess around with the quarter slots. Lucas was down a hundred bucks. Cole was up three hundred.

"You were always the lucky one," Lucas had said from behind his tall plastic menu when they stopped gambling at two a.m. to eat breakfast in the hotel's twenty-four-hour cafe. The minute he said the words he regretted them.

Cole's hearty laugh from behind his menu caused Lucas's spine to relax. Though he was a grown man, he still had a boyish desire to please his older brother. "Yeah, lucky Cole, that's me. I'll buy you breakfast. Maybe that'll change your luck."

Lucas lowered his menu. "Hey, I'm sorry, I didn't mean anything by it."

"Forget it," Cole said, his face calm, nonjudgmental. "Though you might not believe it, I do consider myself a lucky man. I like my life. I'm . . ." Cole thought for a moment. "I'm happy."

What life, Lucas wanted to ask. What *is* your life? Why does it make you so happy? Can you clue me in? Lucas was ashamed to tell his brother how, despite all the changes he'd just made in his own life—leaving the law, divorcing his wife, moving back to Cardinal—he was still restless, still unhappy. What was Cole's secret?

It must have been Ruby, he realized now. Ruby who had made his brother so happy. Lucas tenderly held this woman in his arms, feeling an insane combination of sorrow and desire, knowing as he held her, he was touching the last person his brother had loved. Maybe the only person, though he didn't love even her enough to stick around. Maybe Cole wasn't as happy as he'd said he was. Happy men didn't drive their trucks off narrow mountain highways, did they?

She abruptly pulled out of his arms and walked away, her back to Lucas and Ely. She went over to the fence and stared at the timid mare. The horse shook her head and pawed the ground, uncomfortable with Ruby's scrutiny. Ruby turned back around, her face on the verge of tears, but, Lucas could tell, holding back.

"Ely's right. You need to tell your family now, Lucas," she said, her voice so soft it could have been the wind. Standing there, the vast Sierra Nevada peaks behind her, her grieving face like an eighteenth-century painting, he couldn't understand why his brother left.

Cole, he thought, sending a message to wherever he was. You are a fool. He felt his throat tighten. A damn fool.

BIRCH

In the front room of their house, Birch stared at her nephew Lucas, her face white as her cotton shirt. She did not want to believe the words coming from his mouth. She wouldn't accept them. If she didn't accept them, then it couldn't be true. Tears filled her eyes, then flowed silently down her pale cheeks. Bobby moved closer, placing a steady arm around her shoulders.

"No," she said, pushing away her husband's arm. "No!" She backed away from Lucas. Bright pink dots of color highlighted her cheekbones. "It can't be. I would have known. I would have *felt* something. It's a lie. She's lying." If that girl was standing right here, she'd slap her. How dare she come into their lives and tell these lies? Cole was *not* dead. He was alive and someday he was coming home.

"I'm sorry, Aunt Birch," Lucas said, his voice hoarse. "I checked her story out. It's all true."

His aunt let out a wail that was so primal and sad that Lucas winced. "Oh, God," she cried, the moan coming from deep inside her. Her head fell backward, pleading at the ceiling. "Oh, God, why Cole? Why my Cole?"

Lucas started to go to her, but was waved back by Bobby.

"Let me, Lucas," he said, taking Birch by the arm and leading her to the brown nubby sofa. "Sit down, sweetheart. We have to hear the rest."

"There's not much more than I just told you," Lucas said, sticking his hands in his jacket pockets. "Ruby . . . his wife . . . she doesn't even know much. I think she's as much in the dark about his reasons as anyone."

"Ruby?" Her voice was a whisper. "The woman running from her husband?"

"What?" Lucas said, confused.

"She's staying at the lodge," Bobby said.

Lucas nodded. "I know."

"Where is he?" she demanded. "Where did she bury Cole?"

"He was cremated. He's . . ." His voice stumbled. "He was in her room at the lodge. Now he's in my truck."

Birch felt another lurch inside her. Cole had been under her roof for days and she'd never known it. She would never forgive that girl for that. It was the cruelest thing she could imagine a person doing.

"How long were they married?" she asked.

"Since April."

"She should have known something," Birch said. "She should have known him well enough to know he was unhappy."

"Birch," Bobby said, taking her hand. "Don't be making hasty judgments about the girl. You don't know her side yet."

"I will do what I darn well please," Birch said, jerking her hand away. "I'm going to talk to this girl. Get to the bottom of this." She stood up, swaying slightly. She'd find this girl and make her admit this was all a mistake, a cruel, horrible mistake.

"Aunt Birch," Lucas said. "Please trust me, it's all true."

"I'm going for a walk," Birch said. She had to get away, walk and walk until she just walked away from this horrible news.

"Birch," Bobby started, moving in front of the door.

She turned to him, her cheeks shiny, her chest hurting as if someone had shot arrows through it. "I need to be alone, Bobby. Please."

He nodded and stepped aside. "I'll be here or at the lodge. Just . . ." He took her face in his wide hands. "I love you."

She rubbed a wet cheek against his hand. "I know you do. I love you, too."

Cardinal's streets were crowded with tourists dressed in bright-colored sweaters and new hats. Normally she loved the hustle and bustle of the week between Christmas and New Year's. The town celebrated First Night, a family carnival and alcohol-free festival that many tourists came year after year to experience. At the lodge they made huge vats of chili and hot chocolate, selling them for a dollar a cup, the money going to the Cardinal Valley Boys and Girls Club. The town closed off five blocks of Main Street to traffic. People milled about drinking cider and other nonalcoholic drinks, eating popcorn balls and caramel apples and using the noisemakers that were given away by most of the town's businesses. Of all Cardinal's many festivals, Birch had grown to love First Night the best.

But this year would be different. In her heart Birch had always believed that her prayers would be answered and Cole would eventually come home. I suppose, she thought bitterly, my prayers were answered.

She walked down the street barely feeling the cold through her thin sweatshirt. A part of her wanted to find this Ruby, this alleged wife of her beloved nephew, but another part of her dreaded their meeting. What could Birch say that could ever convey to this girl how she'd hurt her? Birch walked until her bones were so chilled she knew she'd better find something warm to drink. Though she was near the Lone Pine cafe, she couldn't go inside. Sueann would take one look at Birch's face and know something terrible had happened. Lucas hadn't told June and the rest of the family yet; he said he would do it after he told Birch and Bobby. From that point on, it would become public knowledge.

There was no place in this town where she didn't know someone well enough that they wouldn't question, with real concern, why she looked so devastated. It was at a time like this when she truly wanted to be alone that she understood the advantage of a big city's anonymity.

She walked past Holy Grounds, the coffee shop where the odd characters in town hung out, then turned around and went back. Here was one place where longtime locals didn't often go. The old-timers like her had a half-dozen other places they met, places that had been around a lot longer than this coffeehouse. She knew the young people liked it here, as did many of the people in town who were what the ladies in the Missionary Guild at church called "marginal." She knew Lincoln Holyoke casually, had met him around the church grounds when she was there for some meeting or another. He used the church recreation room once a week to teach something called "life skills" to the homeless. He provided the refreshments himself and always stayed after to make sure the kitchen was clean and everything locked up. She respected him for that, but they'd never had a conversation longer than two minutes or about anything weightier than where to find the coffee filters or clean dishcloths.

Yes, this odd coffee shop would be a quiet place to sit and gather her thoughts before the town knew about Cole. This whole thing had an eerie feeling of déjà vu about it, reminding her of the days after he shot Carson and how everywhere she walked, she could sense people staring at her.

She ordered plain black coffee and chose a corner table as far from the counter as possible. It was more crowded than she anticipated, mostly with young kids dressed in clothes so full of metal and gewgaws that they appeared to be in costume and tourists wearing their L.L. Bean ski jackets and fuzzy, high-top after-ski boots. She was deep in thought when Lincoln came by with a pot of coffee.

"Happy Boxing Day," he said. "Need a warm-up? It's on the house."

She glanced down at her cup. It was as full as when she'd bought it a half hour ago.

He smiled and set down a fresh cup, poured hot coffee into it. "Noticed you were a bit preoccupied. Is everything okay?"

She looked up at him. His eyes were a deep, bright blue and seemed as soothing as the sea. She surprised herself by blurting out, "I just found out my nephew Cole died. He . . ." She didn't want to say the words, but somehow, knew she had to or she'd never make it through the next few days. "They say he did it on purpose."

He inhaled a quick breath, his eyes narrowing as he swallowed.

"I'm so sorry." He handed the pot to a passing waitress and took the seat across from her. "You loved him very much."

She nodded, grateful to hear someone else say the words.

He pushed the hot cup of coffee toward her. "Just take a sip. Sometimes drinking something hot helps."

She did as he said. The strong coffee burned as it traveled down her throat. Birch felt her eyes start to sting. She didn't want to break down here, but she'd never make it home without crying. It would be worse to walk down the center of Cardinal with tears streaming down her face. Again, she wished at this moment that she lived smack dab in the middle of a huge city where no one knew who she was and no one cared. At least she could mourn alone.

And die alone too, a small voice reminded her. Like Cole.

"I'm sorry, I have to leave," she said, tears flowing unchecked down her cheeks. She stood up, jiggling the table, splashing coffee onto the scarred wood. "Oh, I'm sorry." She frantically dabbed at the dark puddle with her paper napkin.

"Come with me," Lincoln said, gently taking her arm and maneuvering her through the crowd. Humiliation burned in her cheeks. A few of the tourists and kids looked at her curiously, then went back to their own conversations.

He led her to his office, which was decorated with posters from Hawaii, the Fiji islands, Borneo and Alaska's Inside Passage. He cleared stacks of papers off a bright red love seat and helped her sit down. "Stay as long as you like, Mrs. Hernandez. There's tissue on the desk." He pointed to the overflowing desk.

"Thank you," she said. "I just need to not . . ." She couldn't articulate what it was she was trying to say.

"Be yourself for a few hours. I understand. Many people will be needing your strength in the next few weeks. But you can't give strength to others if you are unable to be strong yourself." His face looked as sad as she felt.

She nodded, amazed at how quickly he'd comprehended what she was going through. Then again, he'd lost his wife in such a tragic way.

Things like that either made you more sensitive to others and their troubles or they turned you inward into a selfish puddle of emotion, no good for anyone. "Thank you. I'll be fine in a little while. Well, not fine, but better."

"I never had any doubt about that," he said, closing the door softly behind him.

16

RUBY

L ucas called Ruby's room a little after ten a.m. She'd been lying in bed for hours, staring at the ceiling. "I told my aunt and uncle."

"How are they?" Ruby asked, moving from the bed to the overstuffed leather chair. She wrapped the log cabin quilt around her shoulders like a shawl.

"Bobby took it okay, but Birch is not doing good. She kept saying she didn't believe me, then she took off. We don't know where she is, but she couldn't have gotten far because she was walking. Thought I'd better warn you, she's not very happy with you."

Ruby's spine stiffened. Was it her imagination or was his tone a little accusing? She was normally pretty good at gauging emotions. When you worked with the public any length of time you either perfected that skill or you didn't last long. But this situation was more complex than figuring out whether a person was irritated at her service or just in a hurry. Lucas seemed to be a decent man, but what did she really know about him or any of the McGavins?

"What was I supposed to do, barge in and announce who I was in the middle of the hotel lobby?" She immediately regretted her sarcastic tone.

A tired-sounding sigh came through the receiver. "No, that would have been a disaster."

There was a short silence between them.

"So, what now?" she asked.

"I need to tell my mom and brother. That's a whole other problem."

She waited for him to elaborate. When he didn't, she asked, "Why?"

"My mother, June . . ." His voice faltered a moment. "It'll be complicated. Especially since you now own part of the ranch."

"I'm not here to make any trouble. I told you I'll sign over his part of the ranch. I don't want anything for it." She felt repelled by the prospect of profiting from Cole's death.

"You should receive something," Lucas said. "Cole obviously wanted to provide for you. I think you should honor that."

She couldn't answer over the lump in her throat. When he said things like that, he sounded so much like Cole. Cole had been sweetly chauvinistic about taking care of them. It had bothered him tremendously when he was temporarily unemployed, something that was unavoidable in construction work. She remembered the last discussion they'd had about his job two or three weeks before he died.

"The boss is talking layoffs," he'd said at dinner. "He says only for two months tops until he finalizes that new contract for those homes in Tustin."

"There goes our savings," Ruby said, annoyed. Why did it have to happen just when they were starting to make headway? Cole was almost forty years old and she was thirty-six. It wasn't like they were twenty-one and had all those years to save. She went over to the chipped porcelain kitchen sink and started running hot water for the dinner dishes. They'd never be able to buy their own home if this kept up.

"I'm sorry, Ruby," Cole said, coming up behind her and encircling her shoulders with his solid arms. "I'll pick up some temp jobs. Don't worry. Everything will work out." But his voice sounded tired.

"It's not your fault," she said, nuzzling his hard forearms, sorry she'd sounded irritated. "It's just that it doesn't seem possible for normal people to get ahead these days."

"There's always my life insurance policy," he said, a throaty laugh rumbling from deep in his chest. "That'd make closing costs on a condo in Barstow."

She felt his lips on the back of her head. "Don't tempt me, mister." She laughed, turned around and kissed him on the lips.

How could she have said such a thing, even in jest? Did he know, really know, that she was only kidding? They'd made love that night. She remembered it so clearly. It was unseasonably cold and the farmhouse only had two wall heaters, neither of which reached to the back bedroom. But they hadn't needed a heater that night. She remembered the feel of his corded forearms, braced on each side of her, the heat radiating from them, the outline of his face in the dim room, moonlight filtering through the paper window shades, the smell of him, Old Spice and Zest soap, the sound of his pleasured groans, her own sighs. Everything seemed possible at that moment—a house, children, their lives together. In a warm explosion, she'd pictured them silver-haired, faces sun-creased and happy, sitting on the front porch of a house in the mountains, watching eagles swoop down over a blue, blue lake, laughing and watching their grandchildren build a fort out of fresh pine branches and an old refrigerator box. A life. She imagined their life to the very end. She imagined them dying together, headstones side by side, decorated with red roses and pine boughs by their children and grandchildren. *Forever in love* written on their granite stone.

"I'm leaving for the ranch right now," Lucas said, bringing her back to the present.

She hugged the quilt closer. "I'll be around. In my room or maybe at the bookstore."

"I'll find you. Don't worry. Everything will work out." His voice sounded stronger to Ruby now, more assured.

"Thank you," she said, though she didn't believe him.

After he hung up, she sat in the soft leather chair next to the window. Should she stay here or venture out? What if she ran into Birch? She truly couldn't face Cole's aunt right now. There was nothing she could say to this woman who had obviously loved Cole like a son. For a moment, Ruby daydreamed about what it might have been like had Cole not been estranged from his family and they'd come for Christmas in Cardinal. Would Birch have liked her? Would his mother have approved of her? What about all the people who knew him as a child? How would this Lucas have treated her?

She couldn't help wondering what Cole's father had been like. What kind of man ends up being killed by one of his own children? She'd seen situations like this on nighttime information shows like *20/20* or *Dateline*, but those had always been kids who'd been high on drugs or had a troubled life already or were abused. What was the real story behind that night? Would she be able to let Cole go if she never found out?

Ruby decided to break the ice with Birch by writing a letter. Maybe if Birch read why Ruby felt like she needed to hide her identity, she would understand. This woman had been special to Cole and Ruby wanted Birch to like her . . . or at least not hate her.

She went over to the desk, pulled out the lodge's cream-colored stationery. It was printed across the top in brown ink—*Tokopah Lodge, Cardinal, California.*

> *Dear Birch,*
> *Please forgive me for not telling you who I was when I first arrived in Cardinal. Because I was uncertain what the circumstances were behind Cole keeping his family a secret from me, I was afraid to tell anyone.*

She stopped, wondering if that was exactly what she wanted to say. She hated admitting she was afraid of anything, but she knew if she was going to win Birch over, she would have to be honest. Ruby could tell that Birch was not someone who was easily fooled.

> *I do appreciate your kindness to me. I loved Cole very much, and I am so sorry about what happened. If you want to talk, please do not hesitate to contact me. Sincerely, Ruby Stoddard McGavin*

Ruby signed her maiden name along with her married name to show Birch that she had not been completely lying when she signed the lodge's register. Though when she reread it, it sounded a little distant and cold, and she wasn't sure how she could remedy that. What did they really have to say to each other? They'd both loved Cole. He'd kept secrets from both of them. That was all they really had in common.

She sealed the letter in the envelope. After a quick shower, she dressed and cautiously went downstairs. Though she normally wasn't a procrastinator, she was relieved to see a young Native American man behind the wooden counter wearing a maroon T-shirt that read PAIUTE-SHOSHONE POWER AND LIGHT COMPANY. The shirt depicted the Washington Monument being struck by a huge lightning bolt coming from the mouth of an angry-looking Native American brave.

"Excuse me," she said. "Could you give this to Mrs. Hernandez when she returns?" She held out the cream-colored envelope.

"No problem," he said, looking up from his book. "But Aunt Birch will be back in a little while if you want to talk to her. She never goes very far away from the lodge."

"Thanks," she replied. "I'll watch for her."

Grateful that her meeting with Birch was delayed, Ruby started down Main Street. It was an odd feeling to be walking the same street that Cole had walked so many times in his life. What sort of childhood dreams had he imagined maneuvering these slightly uneven sidewalks? What had his life been like? Where had he eaten, bought his first suit, driven his first car? When she thought they had all the time in the world to build a life, make new memories, what his life had been before they'd met hadn't seemed so important.

She'd always assumed they'd eventually talk about their pasts. In her mind she'd pictured his family as an average one. His father worked and his mother baked cookies and hemmed her growing sons' jeans. Then they died and Cole moved to Orange County and started working in construction. Though she had no reason to, she'd assumed that his father had been some sort of contractor. Didn't sons often follow in their father's footsteps? Except for his love for country-western music, there hadn't been a thing western about Cole. But lots of city-raised people liked country music. She'd never even seen him around a horse or wear cowboy boots. Cole growing up on a ranch was something that would have never occurred to her. And his talent making saddles, that seemed the cruelest thing of all, not knowing that part of him. That saddle in Lucas's shop was beautiful. She had no idea her husband had possessed that kind of talent.

She walked by the county courthouse, six blocks north of the lodge, recognizing the domed building from the newspaper photographs showing Cole's arraignment. She stood on the bottom step and stared up at the glass and wood double doors. What had he felt when he walked through those doors so many years ago? Fear, regret, anger, remorse?

She turned and walked the other way until she came to the Lone Pine Cafe. In the cafe's large parking lot was one of those fancy tourist buses. Swafford Ski Tours was painted on its silver and blue side.

Since she'd slept through breakfast and it was past noon, she decided to eat here. Pandemonium greeted her when she stepped over the threshold. The room was filled with chattering tourists dressed in the neon-colored ski clothes popular this season. Sueann, her face flushed and panicked, glanced up at the sound of the bell. She was balancing six plates of hamburgers and fries, heading toward a corner booth filled with laughing teenagers.

Ruby glanced around, grasping the situation immediately. There was only one person waiting tables, a girl Cassie's age who appeared to be moving as slow as molasses. Except for Sueann, there were no other waitresses.

Ruby weaved her way through the crowd to Sueann. "Need help?"

Sueann's grateful expression was the only reply Ruby needed.

"This busload from Escondido got here about fifteen minutes ago," Sueann said. "Cassie's off somewhere with her boyfriend and not answering her cell. Both of my other waitresses are down with the flu. Britney's new and not fully trained yet. And Carlos, my cook, had to go to the emergency room because his little girl broke her ankle."

Her green eyes flicked over to the counter where Britney was standing in front of the Bunn coffeemaker staring at it with the intensity of a dog waiting for its dinner. "I've shown her how to make coffee three times." Sueann grimaced. "Her mom's out of work and . . ." She didn't finish the sentence.

"I've worked as a waitress for fifteen years and a cook for three," Ruby said. "Which would you rather me do?"

Sueann gave a huge sigh of relief. "Bless you and everyone in your household. If you don't mind, I'll use your cooking talents. I'm a faster waitress than a cook."

"You got it," Ruby said.

As Sueann helped Britney make coffee, Ruby went into the kitchen, glanced around briefly to orient herself to the setup and began filling orders. The Lone Pine Cafe's menu didn't serve anything that she hadn't cooked for Oakglen. For the next two hours she felt in control for the first time in weeks. While she worked, she didn't think once about why she was in Cardinal. By two-thirty, everyone had been fed, the bus loaded back up and on its way to Mammoth.

"You are a lifesaver," Sueann said. Only two local men at the counter eating pie were left in the cafe.

"Can I go now?" Britney asked, walking over to Sueann at the cash register. "I have an appointment to get my nails done."

"Sure," Sueann said. She pulled a handful of bills from her apron pocket. "Here, take my tips as a bonus. Thanks for working so hard. I promise, it's not always this crazy."

"Thanks, Sueann," the girl said. "I'll see you next Sunday."

After she left, Sueann looked through the kitchen pass-through at Ruby who was scraping the grill.

"Hey, girl, are you hungry? I could eat a buffalo."

"What would you like?" Ruby asked.

Sueann groaned and rubbed her neck. "Oh, dear, let me at least make you lunch."

"Sit down," Ruby said, pointing a spatula at the counter. "I'm on a roll and, frankly, it's the first time I've felt useful in two weeks. Cheeseburger and fries?"

Sueann grinned at her and flopped down on a counter stool.

"Honey, you can come by and feel useful whenever Carlos has to leave. Thank you from the bottom of my dog-tired feet. I'd've never made it through the last few hours without you. And whatever it is you do to your hamburgers, people are crazy about them."

"Just a little onion and garlic salt, a dash of Tabasco. You were doing fine before I got here," Ruby said, slapping two patties down on the hot grill. Still, Sueann's praise warmed her.

"Baloney. I was drowning," Sueann said, pushing back a strand of hair pulled loose from her braid. "I'm going to skin the hide off that daughter of mine. I bought her that cell phone for her birthday with the promise that she'd always answer it when I called. Of course, that was B.H."

"What?" Ruby asked.

"Before Hunter. Her new boyfriend. They just started dating, though her generation doesn't call it that. Hooking up." Sueann wrinkled her freckled nose. "Lord, I hate the sound of that. Sounds like something Mr. Spock would do on Star Trek."

"You don't like this Hunter?"

Sueann shook her head and picked at a piece of dried food on the counter. "I hate to sound like a cranky old mother, but he's not a nice boy. I'm sure his mother loves him, but he's trouble on a stick, if you get my drift. And he's way too old for her. But I'm at a loss about what to do. I was sixteen when I married her dad and he was twenty." She shrugged. "Of course, we ended up divorced, but she says she's not me."

Ruby nodded, but didn't answer. When it came to people's children, she'd learned it was always better just to acknowledge what the parent was feeling, but not make a comment either pro or con regarding whatever it was they were complaining about.

"My ex doesn't know it, but this boyfriend is the reason she wants a tattoo and the reason I'm going with her to get one. She originally wanted his name tattooed on her hip. I nixed that, but agreed to let her get one very small tattoo. It's one thing to permanently mark your skin with a heart or a moon, but someone's name? There's nobody's name I'd have etched on my skin except my own." Sueann stood up and went

over to the old green Hamilton Beach Drink Mixer. "How about a couple of chocolate malts to go with those burgers?"

"Perfect," Ruby said.

Over dinner they traded waitressing stories.

"Biggest tip?" Ruby asked.

"That's easy," Sueann replied. "Hundred bucks for a $2.99 break-
fast. The guy had shot a ten-point buck the day before and was still
drunk."

"Wow," Ruby said. "A customer once gave me a hundred twenty
dollars for a twenty dollar meal. She'd just landed a big client for her
interior design business. I had told him about her work for a teahouse
in San Clemente. They both came to the cafe where I worked because
they loved the apple dumpling pie."

"Worst customer," Sueann challenged her.

"Too many to choose from," Ruby said, smiling. "How about the
top twenty."

"I hear you," Sueann said. "Mine was definitely a guy who was on
his way to Mammoth with a group of friends. I think he owned a tire
business of some kind. Anyway, they stopped off here for dinner, ended
up ordering the most expensive steaks on the menu, appetizers, desserts
for everyone. The bill came to a hundred-thirty-four dollars and
change. Know what he tipped me? Five bucks and a coupon for a free
tire rotation."

"No way," Ruby said.

Sueann nodded. "I was so mad I followed him out to the parking
lot, stuck the five dollar bill and the coupon in his shirt pocket and said,
'Here, buddy, you obviously need this worse than me and I just had my
tires rotated.' "

"Good for you," Ruby said.

Once they'd finished their lunch and were lingering over a shared
piece of cherry pie, Ruby started feeling uncomfortable. When would
Sueann find out about Cole? She was starting to feel a sort of kinship
to Sueann. They were—or rather would have been—sisters-in-law.
What were they now? Two women who'd been involved with McGavin
men—one widowed, one divorced. Though maybe it was Lucas's place

to tell her, Ruby didn't want Sueann to be the last to know, to feel left out. Ruby knew what that felt like.

Ruby laid her fork down, the cherry pie suddenly unappetizing. "Sueann, I have something to . . ." She started to say confess, but stopped. That sounded too dramatic. ". . . to tell you."

A puzzled look came over Sueann's freckled face.

"I'm not just a tourist traveling through town. There's a reason I came to Cardinal." Ruby told her about meeting and marrying Cole, his lies about his family and background, how he drove off the steep embankment on Ortega Highway. She spoke in a flat voice, willing herself not to break down.

By the time Ruby was finished, tears were flowing down Sueann's cheeks. She didn't make a sound, but while Ruby talked, had grabbed a handful of paper napkins and held them up to her trembling mouth.

"I'm sorry," Ruby said, not certain why she felt the need to apologize.

"Oh, honey," Sueann said, reaching across the table, but stopping short of taking Ruby's hand. "I'm so sorry you had to go through that. Cole was . . ." Her eyes filled with tears again. "He was a good man. He was a friend to me when I really needed one. Cole deserved a better life than the one he got."

Seeing Ruby's face, she quickly added, "Oh, I didn't mean you. He was obviously lucky to have you. I'm thankful he had some happiness before . . ." Her voice faltered. "I'm sorry, I'm making a mess of this."

"No, it's nice to finally be able to talk about it. I wanted you to know before Lucas told his family." Ruby picked up a napkin and started folding it neatly, making a smaller and smaller square.

Sueann took the soggy wad of napkins in her hand and wiped her wet cheeks. "Lucas knows?"

Ruby nodded, not wanting to go into how Ely had recognized her, his relationship with Cole. She didn't know how much Ely told the people around here about his own history. "It's a long story, but, yes, he does. I told him yesterday. He told Birch and Bobby this morning." She checked her watch. "By now, he's probably already told his mother and brother."

Sueann leaned back in the brown leatherette booth. "I'm glad Birch found out before June. She loves him more than June ever has."

"All of his history here." Ruby looked down at her hands clutching the tiny napkin square. "I didn't know."

"Oh, Cole," Sueann whispered. "All of this must have been such a shock to you."

Ruby nodded, unable to speak.

"I don't know what to tell you," Sueann said. "Each of the Mc-Gavin boys have always been an enigma in their own way. But when you consider how they were raised, how June treated them, like a litter of purebred puppies, it's a wonder any of them turned out halfway normal. Which I don't think Derek is, if you want my two cents." She gave Ruby a self-reproachful smile. "That could just be the divorce talking."

"You and Cole were close?" Ruby asked, both wanting and not wanting to know just how well Sueann knew him.

"He was my first crush, and I wasn't very subtle about adoring him. Even though he was six years older, he never teased me about it. That's the kind of guy he was. When I was thirteen, my dog, Whip, died of cancer. Cole sent me flowers and he helped me bury Whip on their land, even said a prayer over his grave. No one made him do things like that, he just thought of them himself. He was prom king, star quarterback, high school rodeo champion, an incredible saddlemaker."

"I saw the saddle he made in Lucas's shop."

"He was really talented. Trained under Jake Seligman, then went to Cody, Wyoming, for a while, studied under some saddlemakers there. Did Lucas tell you one of Cole's saddles was bought by the King of Spain?"

Ruby shook her head no and tried to wrap her mind around this information. It sounded like Sueann was talking about another person. Except for the kindness. That sounded like the Cole she knew.

"Anyway, Cole was the sweetest man I've ever known. If our town ever had a native son to be proud of, it was Cole McGavin."

Ruby leaned forward. "So how could they turn their back on him? That's what they did, didn't they?"

Sueann tucked a stray strand of hair behind her ear, her nostrils flaring. Behind them, one of the men had put money in the jukebox and "Green, Green Grass of Home" came on. "Yes, they did. I'll never forgive some people in this town for how they treated Cole."

"I read about what happened in the newspaper. What little it told."

"My father was alive then. He owned the newspaper and my older brother was a reporter. He covered that story."

"John . . .?" Ruby couldn't remember his last name.

"Henley. That was my maiden name and it's what I use most of the time. I'd take it back legally, except for Cassie. It was part of the divorce settlement."

"That you keep the McGavin name?" That seemed odd.

Sueann shrugged, acting as if she didn't care. "June's an egomaniac. She hated having me as a daughter-in-law, but hated Derek and me divorcing even more. Tarnishing the family name and all. Apparently, no McGavin had *ever* gotten divorced before us." She rolled her eyes. "My little contribution to the ongoing McGavin saga."

June McGavin sounded more and more like someone Ruby would prefer to avoid. "Did your brother ever tell you the whole story? This may sound weird, but it occurred to me while I was reading the articles that maybe Cole didn't shoot his father, that the real story is different than what people think."

Sueann's eyes darted sideways, then she slid out of the booth. "Does anyone ever know the whole story about anything? What's done is done." She stretched her arms out wide, then shook her hands. "Man, I am tired. I'd better go clean the kitchen. Carlos said he'd be back in time for the dinner rush. Thanks, again, Ruby. You were truly a lifesaver."

"You're welcome," Ruby said to Sueann's back.

Sueann had deliberately squelched any talk about Cole possibly being innocent. Why? Was she protecting her ex-husband? With the little Ruby had seen and heard of Derek, it was not a far-fetched idea that Cole would have covered for his brother. Though she couldn't imagine Cole killing his father, she could imagine him, in his role of older brother, taking the fall for Derek.

She watched Sueann walk through the swinging kitchen door. For a moment, she allowed herself to imagine her and Sueann being friends, going shopping together, sending each other silly cards and gossiping about customers. Like the women in books. She reeled those thoughts back in like a wild trout. She couldn't become emotionally involved with anyone here because she wasn't going to stay.

When she got back to the lodge, she noticed that the cream-colored envelope containing her letter to Birch was no longer in the box marked "Manager." In Ruby's key slot there was a thin piece of paper. Had Birch answered her note?

"I'm in the Dale Evans room," she told the clerk, a girl in her late teens wearing a pale blue ski sweater and large, gold earrings. She had hair as black as licorice and the brightest copper eyes Ruby had ever seen. "Is there a message for me?"

The girl smiled and turned. "Yep, took it myself. About three-thirty this afternoon."

"Thank you," Ruby said, clutching the note to her chest.

At the bottom of the stairs, Ruby couldn't wait any longer and opened the note. It wasn't from Birch, but from her father. Four lines and a phone number.

"Talked to your brother in Nashville. Sounds a little screwier than usual. Maybe you should call. Dad."

17

LUCAS

"Acar accident?" June said. The late afternoon sun shining through the ranch's living room picture window seemed to set her hair on fire.

Lucas stood in front of the stone fireplace, the fire baking the back of his shirt. His stomach felt queasy when he took a step toward his mother. She sat on the black leather sofa, her handsome face as flat and expressionless as a primitive painting.

If someone had asked, he would have said there was no way he could predict how his mother would react to the news. She had always been unfathomable to him. But he couldn't help expecting something more than the cryptic look she exchanged with his older brother. A look that, again, left Lucas feeling excluded. If he had to guess at the emotion on his mother's face, he would have said relief. Was she thinking it would be easier to sell the Clear Creek property now? Was she expecting Cole's portion of the ranch to go to her as his next-of-kin? He hadn't told them about Ruby yet.

She turned back to Lucas. "When did he die?"

Derek sat in their late father's leather wing chair and sipped a bottle of beer.

"October second." He took a guilty pleasure in seeing her mouth part in surprise.

Derek sat forward in his chair, setting his bottle on the mahogany end table. "He's been dead for two months?"

"Why did it take so long to contact us?" June asked. Lucas thought he heard a tremble of emotion in her voice. Then her steel-edged voice returned. "Why didn't the authorities call *me*?" Her voice was annoyed and businesslike, as if Cole's death was nothing more than a late shipment of alfalfa.

His chest bone felt like a chunk of ice. Which bothered her more, that Cole was dead or that she wasn't notified sooner?

He didn't answer, but stared up at the portrait of his father hanging over the massive fireplace. Carson McGavin's eyes were as hidden and dark as a stagnant pond. Lucas was twelve years old when the portrait was painted. He remembered how the artist, a man from Los Angeles, had been frustrated at his inability to capture Carson McGavin's electric persona, the spark that made him so irresistible. Can you paint charisma? Lucas remembered people flocking around his father at rodeos, parties, ropings and Cattlemen's Association barbecues. Neither Lucas nor Derek had inherited Carson's charisma, that unknowable thing that drew people to him, made everyone want to be near him, be his friend, *be* him. It was the one thing he and Cole had in common. Lucas could remember when those two had been in a room together, it was like two suns fighting to shine brighter. When he was a boy, his most carefree moments were when his oldest brother and his father were laughing. His whole world felt right then. He'd often wondered if Derek had ever felt that way. It was something he couldn't imagine the two of them talking about.

He turned back to his mother. She was angry now, in the same way he'd seen her angry when one of her prize bulls had to be put down. Though June had never been a demonstrative mother, Lucas wanted to believe that deep down she cared for her sons even though she'd always treated them much the same way she did her cattle—fed them well, housed them well, and got them the best doctors if they were sick. Yes, her sons and her cattle were given everything they physically needed so they could perform their duties to the best of their abilities.

"There's a complication," he said, feeling again a secret, if childish, pleasure in knowing something before June and Derek.

His mother's powdered face frowned. "What complication?"

"He's . . . he was . . . married."

"What?" Derek said. "As if we don't have enough complications with selling the Clear Creek property."

"Which I haven't agreed to sell," Lucas said.

"You're a fool," Derek answered. "If you don't want the whole ranch to end up developed, then just keep on refusing to sign those papers. We need that money to pay next year's taxes."

"Who is she?" June asked. She stood up and walked over to Lucas, her expensive boots making a soft tapping sound on the polished oak floor. In the large, open-beamed room the pops and snaps from the fire set off little echoes, like voices crying for help.

Lucas turned, picked up a fireplace poker and pushed at one of the flaming logs. "Her name is Ruby. They were only married six months when he died."

"Where did she bury him?"

He faced her, still holding the poker. "He was cremated. Right now, he's at the saddle shop."

His mother's face froze in shock. "Where is *she*?"

"Here. In Cardinal." He paused for a moment. "She inherited his part of the ranch."

Derek stood up, silently walked over to the fire and turned his back to Lucas and June. Whatever it was he was thinking, he kept to himself. Lucas watched his mother's face.

His mother's eyes narrowed slightly. "Who exactly is this woman?"

"She didn't even know he owned anything. He told her we were all dead."

"Unbelievable," Derek said, shaking his head.

"Not really," Lucas said. "Keeping secrets is one of this family's finest talents."

"Not that old crap again," Derek said, turning around. His voice sounded more tired than angry.

Lucas wished he hadn't even brought it up. Twice in the last seventeen years, when he'd come home from San Francisco for Christmas, he'd screwed up the nerve to asked about the night Cole killed their father. Both times ended with Derek leaving the ranch and getting drunk somewhere and his mother making him feel ashamed because he brought up such a painful time in the family's past.

"It's over," she'd said. "Let the past stay there." She never understood how painful it was to be the one member in the family who didn't know what really happened that night. Even Cole wouldn't tell him. In that one thing, he agreed with their mother.

"Sorry," Cole said, when Lucas asked him about it. "I hate admitting it, but she's right this time. Sometimes there's just no good that comes from reliving the past. You're lucky you weren't involved. Let it go."

"Easy for you to say," Lucas had blurted out, then instantly regretted it.

Cole looked down into his coffee. "Nothing about that night was easy."

"Oh, man, I'm sorry, Cole. That was a dumbass remark."

"I'm sorry you feel left out," he said, still staring at his dark reflection. "Trust me, you're better off not knowing."

Lucas wanted to argue with him, but something in his brother's eyes clicked shut and he knew Cole would never speak of it again.

"That's all I know," he said. I've seen the will and it's legitimate. I saw his death certificate. It was an accident."

"How?" she asked.

"His truck went off a country highway in Orange County. He lived a few miles away. He worked in construction."

She nodded, but didn't answer.

"The . . ." He almost told them what the coroner's office said to Ruby, about there being no skid marks. But what good would that do? It was just speculation and Cole's memory was tarnished enough for two lifetimes.

"What?" his mother said.

"That's it." He wasn't going to tell them she said she didn't want anything, deciding that moment to keep that information to himself. He would discuss it later with Ruby. Lucas would make sure she received some money for her inheritance. It was what Cole wanted. This was one last thing he could do for his brother. "I think she'll be fair. She's a nice woman."

Derek shook his head again, giving Lucas a doubtful look. "You know this based on what information?"

Lucas felt his neck grow warm. "My instincts."

Derek chuckled. "The same instincts that told you your wife was banging your next-door neighbor?"

Lucas clenched his fists, resisting the urge to punch his brother. He wished he'd never told his mother that he'd found out about his ex-wife's affair only after the neighbor's wife clued him in. He knew everything he told her was eventually discussed with Derek.

The beginnings of a headache started pounding inside Lucas's left temple. He rubbed the tender spot with two fingers. Please, he thought, let this be over soon. "Derek, I just know she's not out to cheat the family out of our money or our property. I can tell she has a good character."

"You've known this Ruby woman, what, exactly one day? Yeah, that's time enough to know someone's character."

"Screw you, Derek. What would you know about character?"

"More than you. At least I picked a wife who wouldn't take me for everything I had when we split."

Leave it to Derek to spin his disastrous marriage to Sueann in a way that made him look like a decent human being. What had Sueann ever seen in him? Even when Derek was young and less cynical, Lucas couldn't imagine two people less suited to each other. Then again, love, or more likely lust, didn't often make sense. The fact that Cassie was conceived while they were dating, during that surreal time after Carson died, showed they'd felt something for each other. It was June who'd insisted they get married, an action that proved to be regrettable for everyone involved. But their mother would have never allowed her only grandchild to be born without legally wed parents.

"Too bad you were stupid enough to split her lip," Lucas couldn't help replying. "If it hadn't been for Mom buying Sueann off with the cafe, maybe you and Cole would have been cell mates."

"That was an accident," Derek said with a growl. He bolted out of the chair and started across the room. Lucas tightened his fists. This time he wouldn't back down like he did when he was younger.

"That's enough, boys," June said. Her dense, low command caused Derek to stop and look at her face in question, like one of their father's old Labs used to before he gave the command to fetch a downed bird.

"We need to face this as a family," she said, pulling out a carved leather box from a drawer in the mahogany end table. It contained the thin, filtered cigarettes she only smoked when she was nervous. "We need to find out what that woman wants."

"She doesn't want anything," Lucas insisted.

"Don't be absurd," June said coolly, lighting her cigarette. "Of course she wants something. Why else would she have come to Cardinal?"

There were moments he wanted to choke his mother. "What was she supposed to do, UPS Cole's remains?"

"She wants the ranch," Derek said.

"You're paranoid," Lucas replied. "I have to go."

"Wait," his mother said, standing up. She looked worried for the first time since hearing the news. She took a quick puff of her cigarette. "What now, Lucas? I mean, legally?"

Lucas shrugged. "I told you, the will is good. By law, she owns his portion of the ranch. We can offer to buy it from her or . . . we can welcome her into the family."

"She's a stranger," Derek said. His brother's jaw stiffened, his tanned ears flushed with color. Lucas knew that look, it meant he was either afraid or angry or both.

Lucas was surprised at the calm he felt inside. "Like it or not, she's part owner of the Circle MG. She has equal voting rights to you, me and Mom."

"Set up a meeting with the bank," June said, stubbing out the barely smoked cigarette. "We need to make an offer."

Lucas nodded. On the way out of the room, he turned to face them. "We should have a service or something. Cole deserves that much. There are still people here who loved him."

"Call the bank," his mother said, dropping her eyes for the first time since Lucas told her the news. As she did, Lucas thought he saw a shininess in her eyes. Tears? he wondered, walking toward the front door. Or was it just a reflection from the fire?

RUBY

Ruby went straight to her room and called the number written on the note.

"Cafe Oz," a young woman answered, her voice as cheery as a parakeet. "Nashville's favorite yellow brick roadhouse." In the background was a clatter of dishes and the faint twang of a steel guitar.

A restaurant. She wasn't surprised. She hoped he was playing there, but most likely he was bussing tables. Like Ruby, Nash had worked in food service all his adult life when he couldn't find a music gig.

"Is Nash Stoddard available?"

"Just a minute." She called out, "Did Nash come in today?"

Ruby couldn't make out the reply.

The girl came back on the line.

"He called in sick," the girl said. "Fifth time this month, too. The manager's getting kinda pissed. Nash is a good busboy, but kinda not too dependable. He's got some awesome guitar moves, though."

"This is his sister. Do you have his home phone number?" It embarrassed Ruby to have to ask a stranger that question.

"No problem," the girl said. "Hold on just a minute." She came back on the line and rattled off a number. "Tell him he'd better get some antibiotics or something and get back here. Lyle ain't gonna hold his job forever."

"Thank you," Ruby said.

She dialed the number and let it ring seven times, eight times, until a hoarse voice answered. She almost cried when she heard his familiar baritone.

"Nash, is that you? It's Ruby."

"Hey, Ruby," he said, clearing his throat. In the background, she could hear the song "Lyin' Eyes" by the Eagles, Nash's all-time favorite band. "How's tricks?"

It was something their dad used to say when he came in late from a night of drinking and Ruby and Nash were still up watching old movies. Even on school nights he never reprimanded them. Ruby supposed it never occurred to him that staying up past midnight when they had school the next day wasn't the best thing for a child.

"I'm doing okay," she said, sitting down on the firm bed. "It's good to hear your voice."

"You too," he said. "What're you doing in, what did Dad say, Carmine, California? Where's that?"

"You're close. It's Cardinal. Cole grew up here. It's near Mammoth."

"Cool," he said. In the background, she could hear a man's laughter, then a commercial. He must be listening to the radio. "Are you okay, Ruby? I mean, with Cole being . . . gone and all."

Gone, she thought. Yes, he was certainly gone. Somehow, that sounded even sadder than dead. "I'm all right. Just taking care of some business here. He was cremated, you know. I thought his family would like his ashes." She didn't tell him about the will. They could talk about all that when she came to Nashville.

"How are you doing?" She didn't want to tell him that Dad thought he sounded screwy. Ruby wasn't even sure what her father meant by that, but she pressed the phone close to her ear, trying to discern something from Nash's voice. "Did that studio gig work out?"

"Nah," he said, then paused a moment. She thought she heard him take a deep breath. "I'm working at Cafe Oz. It's a cool place, you'd like it. Outstanding Mexican food and on Fridays and Saturdays I sometimes sit in with the band."

"Yes, they gave me your number. Are you making enough to live?"

"I'm doing okay, but I've been sick a few times this last month. Got a cold a while back and it's hung on."

His voice did sound choppy, like he was having a hard time catching his breath. Maybe that's what her father meant. "You should go to a doctor," she said, the advice coming out automatically. "I'm sure Nashville has free clinics. Or I can send you some money—"

"Nah," he interrupted. "I'll get some antibiotics from Rocky. He buys them real cheap in Mexico. Exact same ones the doctors prescribe here."

"That doesn't sound safe," she said, feeling a vague apprehension. Nash had never taken very good care of himself, something she'd learned a long time ago was common among musicians. "When I get done here in Cardinal, I'll come see you. Nothing keeping me here in California."

"That'd be cool," he said. "Like old times. I'll see if I can put in a word for you at Cafe Oz. The swing shift cook's a crackhead. Doubt he'll last long. Hey, it would be awesome if we could work together."

"I shouldn't be here too much longer. I'll call you when I get on the road. Do you have a dependable phone number where I can reach you?"

"Actually, I do. This one." His voice sounded a little sheepish. "I have a girlfriend and I'm kind of staying with her."

"Oh," Ruby said, a little surprised. "How long have you been seeing her?"

"About three months. I just moved in last weekend. Her name is Angela. She's an LVN. That's a Licensed Vocational Nurse. She works at one of those old age homes."

Ruby smiled to herself. "That's great, Nash. I'll look forward to meeting her."

"Yeah, she wants to meet you too. Says she could use a few cooking lessons." He laughed. "She's right."

"I'll show her how to make my stuffed French toast," Ruby said, feeling warmed by the sound of his voice. How she wished that Cole had met her brother. She was sure they would have liked each other. "See you soon."

"If I don't see you sooner," he replied. It was their special way of saying good-bye those years he was still in foster care and she had aged out of the system. Wherever he was living those four years, she would take him to dinner on Sunday nights no matter how far she had to drive to get to him.

After she hung up, she sat in the soft leather chair thinking about Nash. Was he okay? What did her dad mean he sounded screwier than usual? He sounded like . . . well, Nash, to her. Did Nash say something to Dad, tell him something about his circumstances that he was holding back from Ruby? His brother knew she worried about him and his way of showing his love for her was to try to sugarcoat whatever hard times he was going through. She knew she wouldn't feel completely comfortable until she saw him in person. At that moment, she didn't care about Cole's family, his past and whatever happened to cause him to end his life with her without, it seemed, a backward glance. What was done, was done. Ruby had learned that when her mother left and she'd complained to Juana, about the unfairness of it, the selfishness of her mother.

"*El que quiera azul celeste, que le cueste,*" she'd said. "Whoever wants the blue sky, the price they pay is high."

Her answer exasperated Ruby. "What's that supposed to mean?"

Juana shrugged, practical in the way that poverty and prejudice often made a person. "Your mama, she will pay a big cost for leaving her kids. More than you can imagine. Besides, what is done, is done. It is up to you to take care of yourself and *tu hermano*, Nash. That is the job God gave you. Nash, he is one who will always need the care."

All the female wisdom I've acquired, she thought, pulling on her jacket and starting downstairs, was from women who weren't related to me in any way.

There was no sign of Birch in the lobby, a relief to Ruby. She didn't feel capable right then of dealing with Cole's aunt's inevitable questions and grief. She didn't want to be rude or short when they finally talked about Cole face-to-face. Right now, she needed to see what was going on with her car so she could make plans to leave.

Outside, the temperature according to the thermometer on the lodge's front porch was forty-eight degrees. She walked quickly to the Chevron station, her gloved hands cold even in her pockets. The repair bay was open and she could see Ely working on her car. Maybe it was almost finished. That would be the first good news she'd heard since she arrived in Cardinal. The Sleigh bells hooked to the door jingled when she walked into the empty office. Since Bill was nowhere in sight, she went directly into the repair bay. Ely stood next to her car, scrubbing his grease-stained hands with some kind of white cream and a red shop rag.

"You must be psychic," he said, looking up. "Just finished your car about ten minutes ago."

"Great," she said. "How much do I owe you?"

"Parts are one-thirty-five plus tax."

She nodded. "And labor?"

"First time's on the house," he said, smiling. He tossed the rag on a pile of grease-stained rags and pushed up the sleeves of his shirt.

"No, I don't take . . ." She stopped midsentence, remembering how those same words had offended Birch, not wanting to make the same mistake. "I appreciate your help. Please, let me pay you for your time and expertise."

He nodded as if he understood what she meant. "We take cash, credit or personal checks."

"I'll pay with Visa."

"You can wait in the office, if you like. It's warmer in there. I'll get your car ready to roll. Give me five minutes."

"I appreciate it." She walked back into the warm office, thinking about what she was going to do next. First she'd drive by Lucas's shop and see if he was there. If not, she wasn't sure how to reach him except through Birch, someone she didn't really want to see right now. Maybe she should just leave tonight. She could leave a note for both of them. She stared out at the slushy street, her forehead wrinkled in concentration.

"Problem?" Ely said, coming into the office. Behind him, she could hear the beautiful sound of her car idling.

"No, not really."

He raised his black eyebrows, unconvinced. Behind her, the sleigh bells rang.

"Hey," Lucas said. "I was walking by and saw you. How's your car?"

"All done," Ely said. "Just need to take it for a test drive. As brilliant a mechanic as I am, I don't want Ruby to get out on the road and break down. I fixed a few other things while I was poking around."

"What other things?" she asked, alarmed.

"Don't worry, I'm not going to charge you. I just couldn't, in good conscience, let a woman drive off in a car that needed a couple new hoses, new spark plugs, oil filter and other stuff."

"No," she said, insistent. "I have to pay you."

He waved a hand at her. "It's my last good deed for this year."

"It's kind of you, but still, I feel like—"

"Cole was my friend, Ruby," he said softly. "He saved my life. Just let me do this one thing for him."

The sincerity in his face stunned her. She couldn't help looking over at Lucas whose face also looked surprise.

"Why don't you two take it for a ride?" Ely said. "Lucas can tell me if it's fit for your trip, wherever that might be."

Lucas gave her a questioning look. "It's fine by me."

"Actually," she admitted, "I was hoping to talk to you today." She signed the credit card slip that Ely slid across the counter. He handed her the car keys.

"Let me know if something doesn't feel right," Ely said. "I'll be over at Holy Grounds until about nine."

"Thank you," she said. "For everything."

"My pleasure."

It was a little past four o'clock when Ruby and Lucas walked out of the service station. Dusk was already starting to settle into the valley. It seemed to Ruby that it came earlier in Cardinal than other places she'd lived. Maybe it was because the surrounding peaks, the hulking

Sierra Nevada range on their left, the more distant Inyo Mountains on their right, seemed to release the sun later and grab it earlier. The cliffs turned shades of indigo, gray, sienna, and umber. To Ruby, it felt like being held in two giant hands, both comforting and a bit intimidating.

"Do you care if we go out to Clear Creek?" Lucas asked, climbing into the passenger seat. "I need to check the water pump. It's about ten miles, a long enough drive to see how your car is doing."

"Sure," she said.

He was silent until a few miles out of town. "Going to be a full moon tonight."

She nodded, waiting for him to bring up his mother and brother. When, after a few minutes, he didn't, she asked, "How did your family take the news?"

He turned his head to look out the window at the shadowed foothills. They seemed to click by like a newsreel, rows and rows of shadowed creases, looking to Ruby like the skin on those odd-looking Chinese dogs. "It's hard to say."

She thought about his odd response for a moment. "I'm assuming your mom was upset."

He gave a small grunt. "I suppose you could say she was upset."

Ruby didn't quite know how to answer him. It was obvious that Lucas didn't want to talk about it, but he had to know she was curious. "Lucas, what happened?"

"They're not happy with you inheriting part of the ranch," he said with a sigh. "Let's just leave it at that. Don't worry, I can handle them."

She wished his voice sounded a little more confident. "It had to be devastating for your mother."

"Clear Creek Road coming up on your left," he said, making it clear he wasn't going to discuss it anymore.

She grit her teeth in annoyance and drove off the highway onto the small access road. It was almost dark and the moon had risen, lighting up the land like a gold-tinted streetlight. They pulled up to the gate and Lucas hopped out before she turned off the engine.

Still annoyed at his reticence, Ruby climbed out. In a few seconds, her irritation took a backseat to the night sky. She tilted her head back, amazed at the number of stars she could see out here compared to the city. It was hard to believe they were even on the same planet. Above them, on the top of a leafless tree, an owl flew up and perched on a branch that seemed too slight too hold its weight. Its shape was etched, like an ink drawing, against the blue-black sky. The branch bobbed in the breeze, but the owl remained steady. In the distance, she could see the horses pause, raise their heads and appear to be listening.

She turned to Lucas. "Why do you do this? Rescue these horses, I mean?"

Lucas leaned again the car's fender and folded his arms across his chest. In the quiet, Ruby could hear the pings and ticks of her car's cooling engine.

"A psychiatrist would probably give some kind of bullshit about how I relate to their predicament, how I feel abandoned by my father, my mother, my brother . . ."

She cocked her head, surprised by his candor. "You feel . . . felt abandoned by Cole? Why?"

He shook his head. "Too complex to go into."

She almost said, try, but decided maybe he was right. She was not really a part of this family and she was leaving tomorrow. What did it matter to her what his relationship with Cole was?

She turned away and looked back at the darkening pasture. "It's so beautiful here. I can understand why you love your land."

"Don't forget, it's yours too," he said, coming up beside her. "One-fourth of it, anyway."

His words struck a chord deep inside her. She stared at the cottonwood tree, the old barn, the horses. In that moment, the owl took flight and glided over the horses, then was gone.

Hers. Part of this was *hers*. It was beyond her imagining. But she allowed herself to contemplate it for a moment, think about being an owner of any land, *this* land. Being able to come to it whenever she felt like. No one in her family had ever owned anything of substance, certainly not something this breathtaking. How could Cole leave this and never see it again?

In that moment, something took hold of Ruby, some inner, primal being who suddenly understood why wars were fought for the love of land, how brothers could kill brothers for a plot of ground, how a person's whole world could revolve around saving beauty like this, keeping it unspoiled and free. She could imagine defending this land herself, sitting on the front porch of a cabin built with her own hands, a shotgun in her lap.

It was starting to dawn on her, a tiny bud of understanding about why Cole was so desperate, so sad, maybe even why he would choose to leave this world. If he knew he'd never see, never live on this land again, when it was obviously such a huge part of who he was, maybe that was enough, added to his other grief, to make him decide that dying was preferable to even a life with her. Living on their artificial piece of rural property, land that, Cole probably always knew would someday be covered by concrete, was a paltry substitute.

She turned to Lucas. "It's not really mine. Cole should have left it to you. I have no place here."

"I'll be right back," he said. He climbed over the fence and started walking toward the horses, crooning softly. The moonlight lit the pasture like a stage. They came to him slowly, but without hesitation. All except the reddish one. That horse held back even though Lucas pulled some treats from his pockets to feed the others. He walked over to the water trough, fiddled with something for a few minutes, then walked back across the pasture. One of the horses, a whitish, speckled one, followed him like a puppy. The frightened one hovered apart from the others, watching Lucas. Even Ruby could see its readiness to flee at the first sign of danger.

"She's still shy," he said, climbing back over the fence. "Prefers to be alone. Cassie and I named her Greta."

Ruby smiled. "How appropriate. Don't they get cold out here? Will they know to go inside the barn?"

"They're doing fine. They'll seek shelter if it's cold enough."

"I know nothing about horses. Or any animal, really. We never had pets growing up. We lived in apartments."

"I've been around animals most of my life, except when I lived in the city. I prefer working with animals. Easier to figure out than people."

"Do you ever miss being a lawyer?"

"Yes," he said. "And no." He didn't elaborate.

"Tell me about your father." She surprised herself when the words came out of her mouth. But if she was leaving tomorrow, she didn't have time to be diplomatic. She wanted to have some kind of closure, get some kind of last insight into the man she'd married.

His face became blank. "I told you I don't know anything about what happened that night."

"I'm not asking you about that night. I just want to know what Cole's father was like."

He turned his head, avoiding her eyes. "He was big. Physically and psychically. He filled up a room. Everyone loved him . . . or was afraid of him."

"And you?"

"Both, of course." The moonlight on the creek gave the water a ghostly, green patina.

"Why, 'of course?' "

"Isn't that how all men feel about their fathers?"

"Sounds like you're being the psychiatrist now."

"I've certainly known enough of them. I think San Francisco is half lawyers and half psychiatrists. When you go to lunch with shrinks, the conversation always eventually turns to fathers or mothers."

The expression on his face changed slightly. She followed his gaze. Greta had moved closer to the fence and stared at them. Lucas made a soft clicking nose in his throat and the horse dipped its head as if nodding an affirmative. Lucas chuckled softly under his breath.

"Why is she afraid?" Ruby asked. "What happened to her?"

"We don't know," Lucas said. "But she'll come around. She's just playing it safe. Horses know that if they stay inside the center of the herd, they are less likely to be attacked."

"Cole loved this place, didn't he?"

Lucas wiped his hands down his thighs. "When we saw each other once a year, it was mostly what we talked about. He always wanted to know how the creek was doing, how the alfalfa looked this year, how many new heifers we had, which bull calves we were keeping, which were destined to be steers. He even wanted to know what flowers Mom had planted in the ranch house's window boxes. I think he loved the Circle MG more than anything in the world."

Ruby flinched slightly at his words.

He looked at the ground. "Oh, man, that was stupid of me. Open mouth, insert boot. I'm sorry."

She waved her hand, letting him off the hook. "Why do you think Cole kept from you what happened?"

Lucas's voice deepened. "I think he never really saw me as an adult. He wanted to protect me. The closest he came one time was saying he believed that choices were often made for people from the time they were born, that our roles were assigned and it was almost impossible for most people to break away from them."

"Predestination," Ruby said. "I never have bought into that. I think we have more control than that." She hoped so, anyway. She didn't know a lot about religion or God, but, certainly, free will was something she'd always felt in her heart made the most sense. If humans didn't have the ability to make their own choices, what was the point of existing?

He started walking for the car and she fell in beside him. "All I know," Lucas said, his voice tired, "is he said he performed his role adequately. That's the most he ever told me. And I don't know what that means." When they reached her car, he opened the driver's side door. "Your car seems to be running fine, not that I'm any expert. I think Ely just wanted you and me to talk. I know Ely's abilities though. It's in as good of shape as a car could be. He's the best."

After they climbed back into the car, she said. "I'm leaving tomorrow. I need to go see my brother in Nashville."

"What?" The word burst out of him, harsh as a bullet. "Tomorrow? You can't."

The demanding sound of his voice set her bottom lip. "Excuse me, Lucas, but, I can. If you have any papers for me to sign tonight, I will. Otherwise, I'll let you know an address to send them to in Tennessee. I'm not going to fight for anything, so there's no reason for me to even talk to your family. I'm signing Cole's part of the ranch completely over to you. His personal possessions . . . well, I'll go through them and send you whatever I don't keep. To be honest, he didn't own much. They're in a storage unit in Orange County right now, so it won't be anytime soon, but I'll get to it eventually." For the first time in months, Ruby felt calm and in control. This was the right thing to do, she was sure of it.

"What about Birch?" he said. "Aren't you even going to talk to her?"

Ruby gripped the steering wheel, concentrating on the dark road. "What good would that do?" She could sense his eyes watching her.

"It would do *her* a lot of good," he said.

And what about me, Ruby thought. "I'm sorry, I'd really prefer not to. I'll write her another letter once I'm gone. That's the most I can promise."

"So, you don't care what really happened that night? You don't have any curiosity about finding out?"

"Yes, I do care, but I have more important things that need my attention."

"What things?"

"Things that have to do with . . ." She almost said, people who were alive, but caught herself before she did. She had to keep reminding herself that Cole's death was still fresh and raw to Lucas. She'd had a few months to get used to it . . . if you could ever say you ever got used to something so life changing. "*My* family."

"I think you're just running away," he said. "It seems pretty cowardly to me."

His words caused a flame to light up inside her chest, hitting a nerve in her. "How dare you judge me like that? You don't know anything about me. You are nothing but a stranger to me and you don't have any right to make any judgments about what I do or don't do."

"I'm only stating the facts about what I'm observing," he said in a cool, calculated voice she could imagine him using in court.

Angrier than she had felt in years, she felt like striking this man. If her hands weren't occupied driving, she might have. Who did he think he was, a stranger, calling her a coward? What right did he have? What did *he* know about her at all?

She pulled off the highway exit to Cardinal. At the first sign of civilization, a McDonald's on the edge of town, she drove into the parking lot, filled with teenage kids darting from one truck or car to another.

"We're done talking," she said. "Get out."

"No problem," he said, yanking open the door.

She reached over, pulled the passenger door closed. She watched him stride into the brightly lit restaurant, the automatic doors closing behind him, reminding her of the mouth of a dragon she saw in a movie a long time ago.

19

BIRCH

"I'm not going back there," Cassie said. A recent crying spell had caused her black eye makeup to run down her cheeks in thin black rivers. "Mom's totlly freaking out over nothing."

Birch sighed, wishing Bobby had been the person behind the front desk when Cassie burst through the lodge's front door. It was nearly seven p.m. and Birch's day had been almost as bad as the day she lost Emily Robertina. She couldn't believe Cole was gone.

Dead, she corrected herself, always hating euphemisms to describe something that was undeniably what it was. Cole is dead, she thought, you'd best start getting used to it. She'd gone ahead and done some work here at the lodge, despite Bobby insisting she just leave it until tomorrow. But what would she do at home, sit around and cry? She'd cried enough in Lincoln's office. It felt like she'd left all her tears in that small room and, in a way, she was glad. There were things to do now, no time for tears.

The last thing she felt like doing was mediating between Cassie and Sueann, but when Cassie showed up at the lodge a half hour ago, crying to beat the band, Birch didn't have the heart to send her back home. Not until she calmed down a little, anyway. This wasn't the first time she and Sueann had squabbled and it surely wouldn't be the last.

"Oh, sweetie," Birch said, resisting the urge to reach over and wipe Cassie's stained cheeks. "Your mama's just trying to look out for you. She worries about you." She glanced over her great-niece's shoulder in time to see Ruby walk through the lodge's front door. Ruby glanced up, her gray eyes nervous. She nodded and headed for the staircase. Birch wanted to call for her to wait, but Cassie wasn't through complaining about Sueann. In dismay, she watched Ruby disappear up the stairs.

"I know the Dale Evans room is rented, but are you sure you don't have another room I can stay in?" Cassie sniffed and wiped her cheeks with the backs of her hands. It looked a little better now, but what she needed was a good scrubbing with a wet washcloth and a bar of Ivory soap.

"I'm sorry, Cassie, but you know all the rooms are occupied until after New Year's. You can stay with me at the house." She put an arm around her shoulders. "But, only if your mama says it's okay." Birch knew Sueann wouldn't mind, would even welcome the break from Cassie's teenage histrionics.

"I will be so glad when I finally turn eighteen and will not have to ask permission every time I pee," she said. "Can you call Mom and tell her I'm staying with you?"

If Birch wasn't feeling so sad, she might have laughed. The child didn't even understand the irony of her two statements. She wanted so much to be a grownup, yet was still afraid to call her mama. "Yes, I will. You just go on over to the house. Bobby is making sirloin steak chili. It's a new recipe he's testing for the First Night celebration. He's at the grocery store, but he'll be home soon."

Cassie wrinkled her nose. "I'm a vegetarian."

Birch's white eyebrows went up. "Since when?"

"Hunter says meat will kill you."

"I thought you and he had a fight." From what Birch could gather, that was the reason for the tension between Cassie and Sueann. Hunter's band was hired for a gig in Carson City on New Year's Eve and he wanted Cassie to come with them. That meant an overnight trip, which Sueann wouldn't allow. Hunter called Cassie a baby for even asking her mother. Cassie told him to flake off. Then she went home and accused Sueann of trying to ruin her and Hunter's relationship because she was too old to get a man herself.

Oh, dear, Birch thought, when Cassie replayed the conversation word-for-word. Only when you are seventeen can you possibly think of thirty-three as being old. She remembered when Sueann was younger than Cassie, seven months' pregnant and waddling around as plump as a Christmas goose. It had devastated Sueann's father that Sueann and Derek had to get married. Derek was twenty and she was barely sixteen. The pregnancy . . . actually the relationship, had been such a surprise to everyone. Sueann had always carried a torch for Cole, though he'd indulged her like a younger sister. Did she settle for Derek simply because she knew that Cole would never see her in a romantic way? Birch and Sueann had never spoken of it, even now, these many years later.

"I'm telling you, Mom's just jealous and, frankly, I'm sick of it," Cassie said in a haughty tone that sounded eerily like June.

"She's just trying to keep you from making a mistake you'll regret,"

"That's what *she* said. Like I'm a mistake. Thanks a lot."

Birch inhaled deeply, feeling for a minute like taking Cassie by the shoulders and shaking her. Her spark of anger surprised her and made her count to five before answering. "You're not a mistake, Cassie. You're our beloved child. You know that."

Cassie's eyes filled up with tears. "Me and Hunter wouldn't do anything stupid. Why can't Mom see that?"

Because she's been there, Birch wanted to say. And not all that long ago. "Why don't you go on over to the house and ask Bobby to make you some hot cocoa. That's allowed in your vegetarian lifestyle, isn't it?"

She gave a wet sniff. "This is all so bogus. When I turn eighteen, I'm out of here. You just watch and see."

Birch didn't answer, but just hugged Cassie and said a quick prayer. Lord, please call Hunter somewhere else and make it quick, if you don't mind. She turned around, pulled a wad of tissue from a holder behind the counter and dabbed Cassie's cheeks. "You look like one of those little chimney sweeps on Mary Poppins."

Cassie gave a tentative smile and took the tissues from Birch. Mary Poppins was one of her favorite movies as a child. When she smiled like that, Birch saw a hint of the curly-haired girl who used to follow Birch around like a little duckling.

"Once I get my paperwork squared away here, I'll come home and make some chocolate chip Rice Krispie bars."

"Okay," Cassie said, giving Birch a tight hug. "Call Mom for me?"

"I told you I would. But you and she will need to talk sooner or later."

"I vote for later," she said, dancing out of the lobby, her mood buoyant now.

Birch called Sueann and asked her if she minded Cassie staying with her and Bobby tonight.

"She's about to drive me absolutely mad," Sueann said.

"It'll pass," Birch assured her. "Adolescence is a word, not a sentence."

Her joke made Sueann laugh, which made Birch feel better. She wasn't sure if Sueann knew yet about Cole. She'd tried to locate Lucas to ask him who he'd told, but she couldn't find him anywhere. "There's something I need to tell you, Sueann, something that's . . ."

"I know," Sueann said. "About Cole."

"You do? Have you seen Lucas? I've been trying to find him."

"Lucas didn't tell me. Ruby did."

"Oh," Birch said, her throat tightening. She wanted to ask Sueann how that came about, but decided to let it go. She'd find out sooner or later. "Are you okay?"

"No, are you?"

Birch sighed. "No, but I'll survive. We'll get through this."

"Yes," Sueann said softly. "That's what McGavin women do, don't we?"

It was only eight o'clock so she doubted that Ruby had gone to sleep yet. Birch knew it would have been the polite thing to call first, let her know she was coming, but Ruby *did* say in her note that she'd be happy to talk to her whenever she wanted. Well, she hadn't actually used the word *happy*. If Birch remembered correctly, she'd said, "don't hesitate to contact me." Well, that's what she was doing, "contacting" her.

She walked down the long hallway as nervous as if she were going on trial. How in the world would they start this conversation? There were so many things Birch wanted to know. Her heart and throat ached with wanting. How would Cole's wife act when she opened the door and Birch stood there?

Seconds later, they were facing each other. The two women who loved Cole. Behind her Birch was surprised to see Ruby's green suitcase open on the bed, almost packed. Was she leaving? They stared at each other.

Ruby's gray eyes widened, then, without warning, a shudder ran through her body. "Oh, Mrs. Hernandez. I'm sorry." The words came out in a whisper. "I loved him so much."

Birch felt emotion rise up in her chest and without hesitation, she encircled the trembling girl with her arms, and they stood in the drafty hallway of the Tokopah Lodge and cried.

A half hour later, tears still damp on their faces, they sat across from each other in Ruby's room—Birch in the leather overstuffed chair, Ruby on the ladderback desk chair. There was so much Birch wanted to ask her, but now that they were here, her mind went blank.

"I wish I could tell you more. He seemed happy," Ruby said. She tugged at a strand of hair that had escaped the topknot she'd fashioned with one of those fabric pony tail holders. "Honest, Mrs. Hernandez . . ."

"Birch," she corrected.

"Birch," Ruby said carefully, as if testing it out. "I swear he seemed happy. We were talking about taking a vacation to Arizona. To the Grand Canyon. I'd never seen it and he wanted to show it to me."

"We went camping there when he was ten," Birch said. "He took the burro ride down to the bottom of the canyon with Bobby. I stayed in camp with the two younger boys."

"He was going to be laid off, but that had happened before. We weren't being thrown out in the street. I was still working."

Ruby's first sentence sunk in, causing Birch's insides to turn hot and scared. "What do you mean, he seemed happy?" She understood, or thought she did, what Ruby was saying. Why hadn't Lucas told her and Bobby this part? Did he know? She suddenly felt so tired and old. And, the thing that was the saddest, not at all surprised.

Ruby shifted in her chair, suddenly uncomfortable. "Lucas didn't tell you how Cole died?"

"He told me his truck went off some highway there in Orange County. That he died instantly."

Ruby stopped fidgeting and looked Birch directly in the eyes. "What I was told was there were no skid marks."

Birch stood up and walked over to Ruby, who now looked ready to run. She took both of the girl's hands and squeezed them. "This was coming for a long time, Ruby. It wasn't your fault. It wasn't anyone's fault."

Ruby's eyes filled with tears. "Thank you," she whispered. "Oh, Birch, thank you."

"I have so much I want to ask you," Birch said.

"Me too," Ruby replied.

"But, it's late and we're tired. You get a good night's sleep and we'll talk again tomorrow." She looked over at Ruby's open suitcase. "Are you planning on leaving soon?"

Ruby suddenly looked embarrassed. "Actually, I was going to leave tomorrow. I'm going to Nashville. My brother needs me."

Birch didn't speak for a minute. It was obvious now that Ruby was going to leave without speaking to anyone, without speaking to Birch. A part of her was angry, but a bigger part of her understood. If she were in her position and was facing the McGavin clan and their barn-full of sorrows and secrets, she drive out of this town as quickly as she could too.

"I understand why you'd want to hightail it out of Dodge," Birch said, hoping her light remark would set the girl at ease.

It worked. Ruby gave a little smile.

"But I'd appreciate it if you could stay a day or two longer, if your brother isn't in some kind of dire need. It'd help me tremendously to talk to someone who loved Cole."

Her sincere words seemed to touch Ruby, whose eyes filled with tears.

"I can do that," Ruby said. "My brother's not sick or anything. I can stay a few days."

"Thank you," Birch said, reaching over and taking her hand. "I'll see you tomorrow, then."

During the three-block walk to her house, she thought about Ruby's words. No skid marks. Cole had most likely taken his own life. She wished she were surprised, but she'd always suspected that Cole was a far sadder person than people realized. Was it genetic? The thought worried Birch.

For years, it had been unspoken knowledge in the McGavin family that Birch's mother, Emily, had officially, on her death certificate, died of emphysema. The truth was she had swallowed enough pain pills to end her own life. How she managed to hoard them without anyone suspecting was still a mystery. Birch had not known the truth until months after her mother's funeral when she overheard Walt Creston, young then, but just as obnoxious, talking about it to Carson. The fact that her brother knew about it and Birch didn't still hurt. But her father, Kitt, didn't even speak to Birch at Emily's funeral. One thing could be said for Kitt McGavin. Once he swore something, he kept his word.

Oh, Mama, Birch thought, I can't even imagine what kind of pain you were in, but did you have to choose to leave? She always wondered how things would have been different had her mother lived. Would her father have eventually forgiven her for marrying Bobby? Would Mama have been able to convince him to accept Birch's husband?

Birch shook her head. Old questions that will never be answered. So many people gone. Tears filled her eyes. Now Cole. What sort of pain drove him to that desperate measure? Maybe if she and Ruby talked enough, a reason would emerge. Maybe there would be some answers.

When she reached her house, she could see into the brightly lit living room. Standing at the end of the sidewalk, she watched her husband, Bobby, sitting at the piano with Cassie next to him. They were playing some silly tune and laughing. Bobby had always been like the balm of Gilead to her, knowing the right thing to say, the right way to proceed during an emotional crisis. In all the years she'd known him she had only seen him really angry once. It was after Cole shot Carson. They'd posted Cole's bail after his arraignment down at the county courthouse. They put up the lodge for collateral when June couldn't decide if risking the ranch was something Carson would have wanted. To this day, Birch was shocked at her sister-in-law's skewed way of seeing things. She'd always felt there was something desperately off about June's feelings toward her sons. That act cemented that feeling.

June and Derek had already left and Cole walked out with Birch and Bobby. He'd had a small group of supporters there, including Sueann, her father, John Sr., and her brother, John Jr. Most people of the town attended and lurked outside the courthouse more out of curiosity than anything else. Birch learned one important lesson that winter: Incidents like that showed you who your real friends were.

On the way to their truck, Cole had said to her, "Aunt Birch, is it okay if you go home with Sueann and Mr. Henley? I need to talk to Bobby."

Birch admitted that she felt hurt. Why couldn't he tell her whatever it was he told Bobby? But she knew that Cole and Bobby had a special relationship. Bobby had been more of a father to Cole than her brother, Carson, ever was. If he needed to talk to a man, who was she to stand in the way? Still, it had hurt to be excluded.

When she met Bobby at home, his lips were narrowed with anger.

"What is it?" she asked, point-blank.

"He needed to get some things off his chest," Bobby said, pulling her under his arm. "He made me promise not to tell anyone."

"Even me?" Birch said.

"He doesn't want you to hurt any more than you already are."

"That's ridiculous. I am not made of crystal. I can handle whatever it is that happened."

"I'm sorry, Birch." Bobby's deep voice was weary. "I promised."

"Something, Bobby," she remembered saying. "Please, you have to tell me something."

That is when she got the only clue about what happened that night, from the husband who had never before or since kept any secrets from her.

"Your brother is a coward, Birch. That's all I have to say."

LUCAS

He was a complete, low-life jerk. After Ruby dropped him off at McDonald's last night he sat in a corner booth with a cup of coffee trying to figure out at what point things went so wrong. It really wasn't that hard. The minute he spouted off that he thought she was running away, her face completely changed. He called her a coward. What was he thinking? She just lost her husband, obviously had some problem with her brother and wanted to leave Cardinal as soon as she could. How could he blame her? Frankly, if he had any balls at all, he'd find a way to leave too.

He left McDonald's shortly after eight p.m. and walked the two miles back to his apartment. He had to pass the lodge to reach his aunt's house and he couldn't help walking around back and looking for Ruby's car. It was there, parked in a corner slot. At least she made it back okay. A feeling of despair crept over him. He was a failure in helping his late brother's wife, the last thing he could have done for Cole. On top of that, he really liked Ruby. It embarrassed him to think about it, but he was attracted to her. Lord, what was his problem? She's his brother's wife.

Was, a little voice inside him reminded. *Was.*

What should he do now?

When he came to the corner that led to his aunt's street, he kept walking. He only had two real friends in this town, Sueann and Ely. He felt too awkward talking to Sueann about this and though he was still a bit irritated at Ely for hiding his relationship with Cole, he needed to talk to someone. He remembered Ely saying he'd be at the coffeehouse until nine.

Inside Holy Grounds he found Ely sitting at a window table in the busy coffeehouse reading a *National Geographic.*

"Hey," Lucas said, coming up to his table. "Mind if I join you?"

Ely gestured at the free chair across from him. He dog-eared the page he was reading. "The gelada monkeys of Ethiopia can wait. What's up?"

"I screwed up big-time with Ruby and thought you might be able to, with all your vast experience with women, tell me how to fix it." It was an honest and vulnerable request that Lucas felt humiliated asking, yet was desperate enough not to care.

"What'd you do?" Ely asked.

Lucas quickly relayed his conversation with Ruby.

"You called her a coward?" With one finger Ely traced the outline of the word *Africa* on the front of the magazine. "That's pretty raw."

"Thanks for the astute assessment," Lucas said. He ran a cold hand over his face. "Hey, forget I said that. I'm just pissed at myself."

Ely waved away his apology. "My advice, give her a call at the hotel tonight, apologize and tell her you'll have the papers for her to sign before she leaves tomorrow. Have her meet you at your shop and apologize again."

Lucas interrupted. "I can't get legal papers drawn up before tomorrow morning. It'll take a couple of days to get them written, then typed up. I don't belong to some fancy law firm where I can tell an associate and my secretary to take care of it."

"I didn't tell you to have the papers there, I just said to tell her you'll have the papers," Ely said, his voice patient. "It'll give you one more chance to talk to her, make nice before she leaves."

"But I don't want her to leave. That's the whole point."

He laid his hand flat on top of the slick magazine. "That part you have no control over, partner. But you can at least try to allow her to leave with some dignity. You owe that to Cole and frankly, Ruby deserves it."

Feeling stupid that he'd even had to ask how to deal with this, he stood up. "You're right. I'll go call her now. Thanks."

"One other thing may work," Ely said.

"What's that?"

"Tell her you've started looking into what happened that night with Cole and that you need her help. You might be able to persuade her to stay a few days longer." Ely shrugged and took a sip of his coffee. "Worth a try."

"Actually, that's exactly what I want to do."

"Then you'll sound sincere," Ely said.

Lucas stood a moment looking at Ely, tempted to ask, just how much did Cole tell you about that night? But he held off. If Cole did tell Ely anything, it was probably in confidence. Lucas wouldn't push, at least not right now.

"Thanks," he said.

"Let me know how it goes," Ely said, looking back down at his magazine.

Lucas left the coffeehouse and walked quickly to his shop. It was a clear night, no clouds to retain any warmth in the valley. By the time he opened the front door, his hands were freezing. Still, he wanted to call Ruby from here rather than his apartment; he wasn't sure why. Maybe being surrounded by Cole's tools gave him courage. He felt more at home in this tiny shop than anyplace else in Cardinal.

Her room phone rang three times before she answered with a hesitant, "Hello?"

"Ruby?"

"Yes." Her tone grew stronger, more suspicious.

"It's Lucas. Lucas McGavin." Damn it, that sounded stupid. Like she knew any other Lucas here in Cardinal.

"Oh," she said. "Hello."

There was an awkward pause.

"I just wanted to apologize. What I said was out of line and incredibly cruel. I have no excuse except that I'm an asshole. Not all the time, really, but I was tonight. I'm sorry."

"I'm sorry for leaving you to walk home in the cold."

"That's okay. Doc Winters says I need more exercise." He waited for her laugh. When it didn't come, he said, "I made it back fine."

"Look, I know I'm too sensitive and you have a point. It must look like I'm running away. Anyway, things have changed and I'll be staying a few more days. I understand how confused and upset you must be. I've had longer than you have to get used to Cole being . . ." She took a deep breath. "Really, I think I understand."

"I want to find out what happened that night. I'd like for you to help me, but, even if you can't, I'll find out anyway."

He realized as he said the words, they were true. It wasn't just a ruse to keep Ruby here longer. Even if Ruby left and never came back, Lucas knew he needed to find out what happened that night before he could start any kind of life. He had always assumed—counted on—Cole eventually telling him. He'd resigned himself to letting Cole decide when Lucas would be allowed to join this family. Now it was up to him. He'd claim that right and find out himself, with or without Ruby's help.

"If I can help, I will," she said. "Whatever time I have here, I'll do what I can to help you find out."

"Thank you."

"I talked to your aunt."

"How was she?"

"She's . . . she's sad, but I think she's going to be all right. She asked me to stay a few more days and I agreed."

Lucas smiled to himself. Thank you, Aunt Birch. "It's difficult to refuse Birch."

"Yes, it is."

"Can you meet me at the saddle shop tomorrow morning? I have a few ideas about how to find out more." He actually didn't, but he was certain something would come to him tonight.

"Okay. Nine o'clock?"

"I'll bring the coffee and donuts."

After he hung up, he felt lighter than he had in the last year and a half. Maybe finding out the truth would rid him of the empty feeling he'd carried in his chest for as long as he could remember. Maybe Ruby coming to Cardinal, even under the circumstances she did, would turn out to be fortuitous in the long run.

Ruby was waiting for Lucas the next morning. She sat on the wooden bench in front of the saddle shop, her gloved hands shoved deep in her pockets. She stood up when his truck drove up, and when she started to take a step momentarily lost her footing on an icy patch of sidewalk. She fell back down on the bench before Lucas could bound out of his truck.

"Are you okay?" he asked, rushing over to her, then slipping himself on the same patch of ice. He fell forward, grabbing for the bench, but caught her blue-jeaned knee instead. She let out a surprised laugh.

"Oh, man, I'm sorry," he said, jerking his hand back and awkwardly twisting around to sit down next to her. "I shouldn't wear these dang Justins when it's this icy. The leather soles are as slick as . . . well . . . ice."

She laughed again, a puff of white air coming out of her mouth, making it look as if a laugh had physical substance. It was a melodious laugh, low and pleasing to the ear. He could see how Cole would have been attracted to her laugh.

She smiled at him. "Maybe we both should move a little slower."

He was grateful, in a way, for this silly moment. He'd worried this morning while he was shaving about how they'd greet each other after the uncomfortable scene between them last night.

"Let's get out of the cold," he said, pulling his keys out of his coat pocket. "Though, for a while, it won't be much warmer inside. My heater's not working too well these days."

"I think I'm starting to get used to these temperatures," she said, following him into the shop.

"Then you're doing better than me," he replied, turning on the lights. "I've been back a year and a half and I'm still trying to become acclimatized. They say that damp cold is worse, but I'm not sure about that. When I lived right in San Francisco, I was never this cold."

"How long did you live in the Bay area?"

He gestured for her to follow him to the work area behind the counter. "I went to school in Berkeley, then stayed to practice law. In all, I guess I lived there about thirteen, fourteen years."

"Why did you leave?"

He turned away from her. "I'll turn on the space heater and we can sit in front of it until the place warms up." He pulled two stools close to the heater. "I'll start some coffee."

She took the hint and didn't pursue the subject. Silently, he thanked her. While he made coffee, she wandered around the shop, touching things, her face serious and concentrating as if she were trying to memorize what everything looked like. She stood in front of the wide workbench and studied his saddlemaking tools—running her finger across a row of smooth-handled garnishing awls, edging tools, straight knives and pricking irons.

"There are so many tools," she said. "How long did it take you to learn how to use all of them?"

"Apprenticeships for saddlemaking are about six months, less if you work hard. You learn what each tool is for, how to use it. It takes a lot longer to learn to use them well. So I guess my answer is, I'm still learning."

She walked past him to a row of four saddles waiting to be repaired, running her hand down the basket-weave carving on one saddle's fender.

"That's gambler's row," he said.

Her dark eyebrows came together in question.

"They bring them here to be repaired and bet on how long it'll take me to get them done."

She gave a hesitant smile, not certain if he was joking

"I'm not as organized as Cole was." He pointed back at the Peg-Board of tools. "Those are his tools, you know. He gave them to me."

She didn't answer, but went back over to his bench and picked up a stitching awl, holding it in the palm of her hand, then gripping the handle. She held it tightly for a moment, then took the glossy wooden handle and brought it up to her cheek, touching smoothness to smoothness with a look on her face that made Lucas turn away, a little ashamed that he'd witnessed such an intimate moment. He concentrated on the coffee dripping down into the glass carafe.

He heard her place the tool back down on the workbench. He poured a cup of coffee and turned around. "I forgot, cream or sugar?"

"Neither, thank you," she said, reaching for the cup. "Lucas, tell me about him. Tell me about what he was like as a boy and a teenager." She gestured at the Peg-Board of tools. "What was he like when he did this for a living? Tell me about you and him. About Derek. And your mother. Please, help me fill in the empty spaces."

"All right," he said, sitting down on one of the stools. She took the other one and for the next hour Lucas told her what it was like growing up a McGavin in Cardinal Valley, about how much Cole was admired and loved, how he never seemed to make a false step, say the wrong thing, mess up in anything he attempted. He told her again about the night Cole killed their father, how Cole shocked everyone by immediately accepting the deputy district attorney's deal, how Lucas went to the courthouse with his aunt and watched in horror as his brother was led away that last time, his wrists handcuffed behind him.

He didn't tell her that he fled to the courthouse bathroom, locked himself into a stall and tried to drown out the sounds of his crying by flushing the toilet over and over. He couldn't tell her that the sight of his tall, strong brother in handcuffs, the person who had protected him, made him feel safe, the only man besides Bobby he didn't feel embarrassed hugging, broke something inside him. Cole had been his ideal, who he'd measured himself by as a man. If Cole couldn't make it in this world, what chance did Lucas have?

Two times they were interrupted by customers, local men asking about their saddles. They gazed at Ruby with interest, having heard now about Cole's death and Ruby's mission to deliver his ashes. Though none of them mentioned that Cole was dead, Lucas suspected they knew. He didn't bring it up either. He wasn't ready to discuss Cole with any of Cardinal's citizens, many of the same people who probably took a secret pleasure in seeing one of the town's privileged sons taken down more than a few notches.

"Cole is the reason I became a public defender," he said, after the second group of men left. "I was so idealistic. I was going to be the kind of lawyer my brother didn't have."

"But you said he pleaded guilty. That's not the lawyer's fault." She cocked her head, perplexed.

"Adolescent idealism. I got it in my head that if he'd had a really good lawyer, he would have been talked out of pleading guilty. Look at the celebrities who get off these days. Now I think the public defender was just young and didn't know what to make of the situation. He obviously wasn't experienced enough to dig deeper. Maybe he even believed Cole was guilty."

She leaned toward him. "Excuse me if I'm being ignorant or unkind, but with all the money and prestige your family has, why in the world didn't your mother hire a better lawyer?"

Lucas turned his head, his stomach seizing into a fierce not. "That's a good question. I'm afraid only she can answer that. My mother is a mystery I'll never figure out." He looked back at her, gave a half smile, as if laughing at himself. "That's the McGavins. We're a strange bunch."

Ruby looked at him steadily. "I'm a McGavin."

He nodded. "Lucky us."

Her expression looked surprised, a little hurt.

"I meant that as a compliment," he said, holding out his dye-stained hand in apology.

Her face relaxed. "Then, thank you." She opened her mouth to say something else when the door flew open and Walt Creston strolled in. He wore knife-pressed black western dress slacks, a white cowboy shirt and a bolo tie with a chunk of natural turquoise big enough to choke a python.

"Lucas, I need to talk to . . ." He stopped when he saw Ruby. "What in the hell are you doing talking to her? Does your mother know about this?"

Lucas jumped up and started for the door. "Let's talk out front, Walt." He left the older man no choice, but to follow. Walt slammed the door, rattling the window glass.

Out on the icy sidewalk, Walt said, "Are you out of your mind? Your mama was down at the bank this morning begging for money to try to pay this tramp off and you're having a cozy little tea party with her?"

Lucas grit his back teeth. "Don't talk about Cole's wife like that."

"Cole's widow, you mean."

Lucas's fist tightened, itching to smash Walt's florid face. "We were just talking about Cole. We didn't even bring up the will or the ranch."

"Not yet, anyway. That girl in there is not your friend. You'd better get that through your head now. Your mama's in a fix and you need to quit pussyfooting around and help her. The bank refused to loan her any more money so there's nothing to pay this woman off with. Do you have any fancy legal tricks up your sleeve, counselor?" Despite his long romantic relationship with June, it appeared to Lucas that Walt seemed to relish the mess the McGavins were in yet again.

"Why doesn't she just make a withdrawal from the First Bank of Creston?" Lucas couldn't help saying. "Her credit seems to have always been good there. Of course, the interest is a little steep, but that shouldn't bother her too much."

Walt's pale brown eyes turn to slits under his black felt Stetson. "Because she already owes me more than you want to know about. I'm not about to rescue the McGavins one more time. Frankly, I've always wanted that Clear Creek property. Make a great spot for about a hundred time-share condos."

"I'll never sign," Lucas said.

"You might not have to," Walt replied, tipping back the front of his hat. "I might just acquire the whole Circle MG at a bankruptcy sale."

Lucas didn't answer, not knowing if Walt was bluffing. Maybe Derek was right and he should have been more involved with the running of the ranch and its finances. He wondered if that had been Walt's plan all these years, to acquire his best friend's ranch. "What do you want, Walt?"

"Your mama needs you," he repeated. "You'd better wrap up your business with the lady in there and get over to the ranch." He settled his hat snugly on his head and headed in the direction of the Lone Pine Cafe.

Lucas took a few moments to regain his composure, then went back inside the shop. Ruby was standing next to Cole's saddle, running her hands over the carved saddle horn.

"It's yours," Lucas said, coming up behind her.

She whipped around, surprised. "What?"

"The saddle. It's yours. I mean, it was Cole's. I was just keeping it here for him. So, now it's yours."

Her face crumpled and for a moment, he thought she was going to cry. But she regained control and said, "Thank you. I think . . . if you don't mind . . . I'll have to keep it here for the time being. I have no place for it. I don't even have an apartment . . . or a job . . . or . . ." She gave a wry smile. "My car, clothes and books. That's what I'm traveling with these days."

"You can keep it here as long as you like." He hesitated, then added, "Or you can sell it. I got an offer for it the other day, as a matter of fact. He said, he'd give me—or rather you—four thousand dollars for it."

Her eyes widened. "Four thousand dollars?"

"Cash. To be honest, we could probably get more. This guy's loaded and he liked it a lot."

She turned back to the saddle. "It wasn't that man who was just here?"

Lucas gave a cynical laugh. "Walt Creston? No, it was some bazillionaire from Bel Air. Sells plumbing supplies."

She rested her hand on the horn. "I might have to sell it eventually, but I can't yet."

"Despite what you say, I'm going to make sure you receive some money for your part of the ranch," Lucas said. "June will give me grief, but she'll get over it. Apparently, the ranch is hard up for cash money right now."

She turned to look at him. "Was that what that man was here about?"

Lucas nodded.

"I'll be honest with you, Lucas," she said. "I can spare a couple more days to help you find out what happened with Cole. If we don't find out anything fairly soon, I have to leave. There's something going on with my brother in Nashville and I need to find out what."

"Is he okay?"

"I honestly don't know. He sounds fine to me, but he might not tell me if there's anything wrong. My dad, who isn't the most sensitive person in the world, thinks something is wrong. That scares me more than a little." She held up one palm. "He's my baby brother. But, I do want to see this situation here in Cardinal to some kind of conclusion. I'll probably never come back here, so it's now or never."

"I understand," Lucas said, feeling a pang of sadness when she said she might not come back to Cardinal. Was he starting to feel something for this woman or was it just because she had been so close to Cole? There was still so much he wanted to ask her, but that would have to wait.

He walked over to the space heater, the coils glowing red now, finally warming the room. He flipped the Off switch. "The first place I'd suggest we go is the newspaper. John Henley, Sueann's older brother, worked for his dad's paper and was its only reporter when it happened. If anyone has the ability to discern the truth in this mess, it would be him."

21

RUBY

The *Cardinal Weekly Gazette* was located in a small, pink stucco building next door to the Tokopah County Sheriff's department substation. A young receptionist about Cassie's age sat behind the formica-topped front counter. She was dressed in a plaid western shirt and wore her pinkish blonde hair in a curly, rodeo-queen style.

"Hey," she said. "What's up?"

A male voice sounding both irritated and indulgent called from the office behind her, "Josie, try 'Good morning, may I help you?' "

She wrinkled her nose at Ruby and Lucas, then repeated in a singsong voice. "Good morning. Can I help you?"

Lucas gave Ruby a wink. "Yes, may we see John Henley?"

"Do you have an appointment?" she asked primly, touching the side of her salmon pink painted mouth with a matching fingernail.

"Oh, for pete's sakes, Josie," the man's voice called again.

He came out of the office behind her. He was medium height, in his early forties with wavy, strawberry-blond hair and a face liberally sprinkled with freckles. There was no doubt he was related to Sueann. His expression, annoyed when he came over the threshold, brightened when he saw Lucas. "Hey, Lucas. How are things in the saddle business?" He held out a blunt-fingered hand.

"I'm not starving yet," Lucas said. "but, then, Birch and your baby sister would never allow that to happen."

"Without a doubt." He looked at Ruby in interest.

"Sorry, this is Ruby McGavin. Cole's wife."

He shook her offered hand firmly. "Sueann told me you were in town." His face sobered. "She also told me about Cole. I am sure sorry to hear about his passing. He was a good man."

"Thank you," Ruby said.

"We have something we want to talk to you about," Lucas said, gesturing over at John's office. "In private."

"Sure, sure, no problem," John said, ushering them inside his small office. He told Josie to hold his calls.

"Yeah, right," she said, not turning around. "All two of them."

He closed his office door and pointed to two black visitor chairs. "Sorry about that. She's an intern from Cardinal High and I've known her since she was two." He sat down behind the wide, wooden desk and pushed aside a pile of papers. "To quote my lovely intern, 'what's up?' "

"We're looking into my father's death," Lucas said. "We think that . . . well, we're just looking into it. Some things don't seem to add up."

John stared across the expanse of the desk at Lucas. "You know I was the reporter who covered it, don't you?"

Lucas nodded. "That's why we're here. Mostly, I guess we'd like your impression of what happened."

John looked over at Ruby. "I never bought the story that he and Carson got in this huge fight and struggled for the gun. I also don't buy the story that he shot him in cold blood either. It just wasn't in Cole to do that."

Ruby sat forward eagerly. "Yes, that's exactly how I feel."

He leaned back in his wooden chair. A loud squeak caused him to reconsider and sit forward. "It was a crazy time for everyone. It was particularly nuts for me and Sueann. Our mom had cancer and was dying. Dad and I were trying to keep the paper going. Not many people know this, but we were close to bankruptcy at that point, what with all of Mom's medical bills. Sueann was barely sixteen and had gone a little wild, probably out of grief for Mom. Sueann did a lot of the physical care of Mom by herself. Hard on a girl that age."

"Your mom was my Cub Scout leader," Lucas said. "She taught me how to tie ten different types of knots."

John smiled. "Her dad was a sailor. Knots were always easy for her." He looked back at Ruby. "So, when Cole . . . when it happened, Dad told me to just report the bare facts, that the McGavins had enough gossip being spread about them without us adding to it. But there were some weird things about the case, like the pistol being totally wiped clean of fingerprints."

"What?" Lucas said, sitting forward.

John looked surprised. "You didn't know that?"

Lucas shook his head.

"Yeah, that would have come out in the trial, except, as you know, there wasn't one. Cole confessed to it and everyone agreed to a plea of voluntary manslaughter, which left all sorts of questions unanswered." He shrugged. "I wanted to investigate it further. So did Gordon Vieira. He was a new deputy then and the first law enforcement officer on the scene." He gave a wry half-smile. "He's sheriff now and I own the paper. We're the old farts now. Hard to believe." He studied the tops of his hands. "I was told by my dad to let it go, and Gordon was told by the sheriff to do the same. Dad never told me why, not even when he was dying. Gordon and I have discussed it over many lunches during the years. There's something being hidden there. My guess is . . ." He looked up, his face suddenly turning red.

"Go ahead," Lucas said. "I think I know what you're going to say."

But John shook his head and stayed mute.

"He might have covered for either my mom or Derek," Lucas said. "That thought has occurred to me before, though I never had any proof."

"The clean gun is just circumstantial. As the sheriff said to my dad when it happened, it could just as well have been Cole trying to initially cover for himself."

Lucas didn't look convinced. "Then he had an attack of conscience and confessed?"

"I know," John said. "Sounds crazy."

"Were there any records we can read, police reports or whatever?" Ruby asked.

"His arraignment and sentencing is all public record. You can read it yourself."

"How?" she asked.

"It would be at the courthouse in the county records office," Lucas said. "Shouldn't take too long to get one."

"I can speed it up for you," John said. "My ex-secretary works in records and she owes me." He smiled. "I helped her land the job. Paid a lot more than I could pay her here and the benefits are great. I can call now and she'll have them pulled and copied before they close. Don't know if they'll help any. I read them back when it happened and nothing jumped out at me."

"It's not just that," Ruby said, biting her bottom lip. "Court transcripts, they . . . they quote people exactly, don't they?"

He nodded. "Every word."

She didn't know how to say it without sounding strange, but she wanted to see her husband's words. She wanted to hear him—or at least read him—say what happened, whether they discovered something new or not.

"I understand," John said, his voice sympathetic.

"May I ask you something personal?"

He laughed nervously. "We just met, but, sure, go ahead."

She hesitated, suspecting he'd be surprised at what she was going to ask. "Do you think your sister, Sueann, knows what happened?"

His face froze. A flash of anger swept over it, before he composed himself and replaced the emotion with a professional mask. "Why do you ask that?" His voice was crisp, businesslike.

"I'm sorry," she said, though truthfully, she wasn't. She needed to know and John Henley was the person who could most likely tell her. "When I tried to talk to her about it, she shut me down. I think she knows more than she's telling."

John pressed his lips together, then said, surprising all three of them, "Actually, I think you're right. But she's never told me anything so I doubt I can be of any help to you."

Ruby let out the breath she was holding and glanced over at Lucas. He was staring at John in surprise.

"If you find out anything new, I'd appreciate hearing about it," John said, standing up. "Off the record, of course. I have no intention of dredging up old tragedies just to sell papers."

"We will," Lucas said, standing up.

"Thank you," Ruby said. "I appreciate your help."

"You're welcome," he said. "Again, my condolences on your loss."

Outside, Lucas glanced at his watch. "It's almost eleven o'clock. Do you want to give the woman a few hours to get them copied? I could use some lunch."

"Yes, but let's go somewhere other than the Lone Pine." A thread of anxiety knotted her stomach. "Was that cruel of me, asking about Sueann like that? I didn't mean to make things awkward for you. I know Sueann's a friend of yours."

His forehead furrowed. "There's been too many secrets for too long concerning my family. Frankly, I didn't know that about Sueann. I may confront her myself. She's always been aware that I want to know the truth about that night."

"Don't blame her," Ruby said, feeling horrible about causing a rift between two old friends. "If she's hiding something, I'm sure it's for a good reason."

"Yes," he said, nodding. "But you and I still deserve to know why. We deserve the truth."

They ate at the new pizza place in town, which was filled with tourists and teenagers. Not one person recognized either of them. After lunch, they went over to the courthouse. When they stood at the bottom of the domed building's concrete steps, she tried to imagine Cole climbing these same steps. Was he afraid? She turned and looked at Lucas, whose face was stoic. He'd been sixteen years old when he watched his oldest brother plead guilty to killing their father. What does that do to a boy?

"If you want, I can go in and get them," she said.

"I'm fine," he said, not looking at her.

They walked through the busy lobby toward the department of records. When they reached the glass door, she touched Lucas's sleeve. "I'll get them."

"Okay," he agreed. "I'll wait out here in the hallway."

On the other side of the door was a small counter. Behind it were three desks, the tops covered with files, papers and coffee cups. A thirtyish petite lady wearing tiny Ben Franklin eyeglasses walked up and Ruby gave her name.

"Oh, yes, John called," the woman said. "I have them all copied for you." She walked over to one of the desks and picked up a sealed manila envelope. Two other women were in the office, working at computer terminals. They both paused to stare at Ruby.

When Ruby tried to pay for the copies, the woman refused. "Don't worry about it. This county owes John a lot more than a few photocopies." She tilted her head and looked at Ruby over her glasses. "I remember when this happened. I was teenager. It shocked everyone in the county. I'm sure sorry to hear Cole's gone."

Ruby nodded. Cole's death and her arrival were now probably general knowledge in Cardinal. "Thank you for doing this so quickly."

"You're welcome."

In the corridor, Ruby found Lucas leaning against the wall next to the stained porcelain water fountain. "That was fast."

"She had them copied already. She said she remembered when it happened, that she was a teenager." Ruby clutched the envelope to her chest. "She said it shocked everyone in the county."

"It did," Lucas said, pushing away from the wall. "Let's go. You need to go someplace quiet and read those transcripts and I need to start work on Bernie Gorman's saddle."

BIRCH

It was three p.m. and Birch hadn't seen Ruby all day. She'd obviously left before Birch arrived at the lodge this morning. Though she had no reason to worry about her, she just couldn't help it. In her heart, the girl felt like family. She wished she could have seen her and Cole together. She was certain Ruby had made him happy. She realigned the guest register and gold pen on the counter. Obviously, being happy wasn't enough. What had Cole been feeling those last minutes before he drove off that highway? Didn't he know how much he was loved? Why hadn't that been enough?

Where was that girl? Birch looked out the window to the almost empty street, now slushy with melting snow. After their talk yesterday, Birch had looked forward to seeing her again, talking more about Cole. Was she deliberately avoiding Birch, embarrassed that she'd revealed so much? Birch didn't want her to feel that way. When she'd held the sobbing girl in her arms, it was as close as she would ever come to holding Cole again.

She walked into the office behind the counter where Bobby was behind the desk eating a baked potato covered with sour cream and cheddar cheese. "I'm telling Doc Winters on you," she commented, sitting down on the office chair next to the desk.

"You said you weren't cooking tonight," he replied.

"Yes, but there's healthy things for you to eat, even if I don't cook." She nagged him halfheartedly, more out of habit.

"What's wrong?" he asked, putting down his fork and holding out his hand.

She reached across the desk and took it, feeling warmed, as she always did, by his calm spirit. "I haven't seen Ruby all day."

He squeezed her hand and went back to eating his potato. "Give her time, Birch. She probably needed to escape for a bit from all this emotion. Now that she's staying a few days, she'll most likely have a run-in with June. She'll need all her strength to get through that. She'll turn up."

"You're probably right. I just hope she's not avoiding me. I think I made a bit of a fool of myself last night, getting all weepy and sentimental."

"You're no fool," Bobby said, taking a bite of cheese-ladened potato. "You just loved Cole. He was special to you. To everyone." He stared at the office wall across from him.

Birch followed his gaze. There were pictures of every niece and nephew on both sides of their families—twenty-two of them. But Cole had been the first. And he had practically lived with them full-time that first year when June had had a hard time settling down to be a mother. Yes, she'd never admit it out loud to any of her other nieces or nephews, but Cole *had* been special.

Birch stood up and stretched, then reached for her denim barn coat hanging on a metal hook behind the door. "I'm going to walk down to the Lone Pine to talk to Sueann about Cassie, let her know she can stay with us as long as Sueann likes."

Bobby laughed, poked at his potato. "She'll be here until she graduates then. Maybe you should drive. It's pretty cold out there."

"I need the exercise, and I wouldn't mind if Cassie stayed forever." She pulled some red gloves from her jacket pocket.

"Oh, she'd start to get on your nerves after a week, mess up your routine. She'll be pining for her mama after a day or two. Mark my words, she'll be back in her own bed before New Year's."

"I don't know," Birch said doubtfully. "This thing with Hunter is pretty serious. At any rate, I'm going to make good and sure Sueann's okay with Cassie staying here. She has enough grief in her life without me making it worse by interfering with her parenting."

Bobby came around the desk and took a wool scarf from the door hook, wrapped it tenderly around Birch's neck, tucked the ends inside her buttoned jacket. "She loves your interfering. I think both of them just need a time-out."

She stood on tiptoe and kissed his warm lips. "Sometimes I think the whole world needs a time-out."

He laughed. "There are times I imagine God thinks so, too."

After two blocks, Birch was beginning to regret walking. The temperature, according to the bank sign, was forty degrees. This winter had to be the coldest one on record. Well, it was only two more blocks to the Lone Pine. She'd ask someone to drive her back after she'd talked to Sueann. She hadn't taken time to eat lunch. A nice big bowl of Sueann's clam chowder sounded really good right now.

When she passed by Holy Grounds, she glanced into the front window and spotted Ruby sitting at a round table, a cup of tea and an uneaten scone in front of her. She was deep in concentration, reading some papers. Remembering Bobby's words, Birch almost passed by, then decided to go inside.

"Hello, Miss Birch," Lincoln called across the almost empty coffeehouse when she walked through the door. There went any chance of quietly approaching Ruby.

"Hello, Lincoln," she called back.

Ruby looked up when Lincoln greeted Birch. The immediate smile on her face relieved Birch. She walked over to her table.

"What can I get for you?" Lincoln asked, coming over, wiping his hands on the towel tucked inside his jeans.

"Some chamomile tea would be nice. Thank you."

"Coming right up. How about a marionberry scone? Nothing like a good marionberry to brighten a chilly Tuesday afternoon."

She smiled at him. "Okay, you talked me into it."

"Join me?" Ruby said, pointing to a chair.

"I'd love to. I was on my way down to the Lone Pine for some soup." She gave a small grimace and unwrapped her scarf, hanging it over the back of the chair. "And to assure Sueann that Cassie was doing fine."

Ruby laid down the papers in her hands. Her face wrinkled in concern. "Is something wrong with Cassie?"

Birch waved a hand. "Nothing but the normal spittin' and hollerin' between a teenage girl and her mama. You know how that goes."

Ruby's face became thoughtful. "Actually, I don't. My mother left when I was thirteen."

"Oh," Birch said. "I'm sorry to hear that." She wondered what exactly Ruby meant by 'left.' Was that her emotional code for die, or had her mother really walked out on the family?

Ruby seemed to read her mind. "She walked out on my brother, Nash, and me. And my dad, of course. He married lots of times after that, but it wasn't the same."

Birch nodded. "I guess it couldn't be." She wanted to ask where her mother was now, but didn't. She waited, but Ruby didn't volunteer the information.

After Lincoln brought Birch her tea and scone, she looked over at Ruby's papers with interest, hoping the curious look on her face would prompt Ruby to reveal what she was reading.

Ruby hesitated when she saw Birch glance at the papers, then said, "These are Cole's court transcripts. I got them from the county courthouse today."

Birch inhaled sharply, not expecting those words. "May I see them?"

"Of course," Rudy said, pushing them across the table.

Birch's hand gave an involuntary tremble when she picked up the first page.

SUPERIOR COURT OF THE STATE OF CALIFORNIA
IN AND FOR THE COUNTY OF TOKOPAH
BEFORE THE HONORABLE KAREN S. GRAY, JUDGE

THE PEOPLE OF THE STATE OF CALIFORNIA,
PLAINTIFF
VS.
COLE ANDREW MCGAVIN,
DEFENDANT.

Appearances of Counsel:
For the Plaintiff:
Sarah D. Harper
District Attorney
County Government Center
Room 50
Cardinal, CA

For the Defendant:
Lance Atkinson
Attorney at Law
112 Main St.
Independence, CA

Birch set the paper down. It brought back too many memories. "Why are you reading this?"

Ruby fiddled with her used tea bag, pressing it between her fingers. "At first, I thought I could find out something new, maybe find out he didn't do it." She gave a self-deprecating smile. "Like on a television cop show. But even though the gun was wiped clean of fingerprints, something that's puzzling, he confessed. His mother and Derek told the exact same story." She set down the paper and picked up her teacup. "But you know all that. It's weird, reading Cole's words. They don't really capture who he was. At least, not the Cole I knew." She stared at the pages in front of Birch.

Birch picked up another page. She'd never seen the transcripts, never saw in black-and-white what she'd experienced in person. That day in court seemed like it happened yesterday. While she grieved for her brother's death, it tore her up more to see Cole so young and vulnerable standing next to his public defender, a boy who looked barely old enough to drive, much less save her Cole from prison. She remembered arguing with June about hiring a good attorney.

"He's confessing," June had said, her voice so cold and practical. It was hard to believe she'd just lost her husband. "No use throwing away money on an attorney if he's confessing, is there? We already pay for a public defender with our taxes." Had her unemotional attitude been an act? Birch couldn't tell. She'd found out later that June continued carrying on with Walt Creston even through all that. For the life of her, she didn't understand one single thing about that woman.

She looked down at the page, remembering the words when they were spoken so many years ago.

> *Cole Andrew McGavin, called as a witness, was duly sworn and testifies as follows:*
>
> *The clerk: You do solemnly swear the testimony you are about to give in the matter now pending before this court shall be the truth, the whole truth, and nothing but the truth, so help you God?*
>
> *The witness: I do.*
>
> *The clerk: Please be seated in the witness stand. Please state your full name.*
>
> *The witness: Cole Andrew McGavin.*
>
> *The court: Thank you.*
>
> <u>*Direct Examination*</u> *by Ms. Harper*
> *Q: What is your occupation, sir?*
> *A: I'm a saddlemaker.*
> *Q: How long have you been so employed?*
> *A: Since I was sixteen. Well, that's actually when I started apprenticing. I guess, six years.*

Q: State your place of residence.
A: The Circle MG ranch.
Q: State for the record where the ranch is located.
A: Cardinal, California.

Birch looked up, unable to read any further. She remembered the sound of Cole's voice when he'd said these words—soft, but unhesitant, resigned, as if he'd known this moment was coming his whole life.

"I understand why you want to read this," Birch said, placing the sheet back on the thick pile of papers. "But I've found as I've gotten older that sometimes the past is best left alone."

"Do you know what happened that night?" Ruby asked, her voice as unemotional as the court clerk asking Cole to state his name and place of residence.

Birch shook her head. "Only what Cole told in court."

"Did you ever ask him about it?"

Birch felt herself start to become annoyed. "No. If Cole had wanted to talk about it to me, he would have. We were close, but it was a painful subject." She tried to quell her irritation. After all, Ruby was only asking questions because she loved Cole. Still, it wouldn't bring him back, so why drive over that same bumpy old road? "What's done is done, Ruby. We can't change the past."

Ruby set down her teacup abruptly. It hit the porcelain saucer with a loud rattle. "What about finding out the truth?"

At that moment, Lincoln walked up with another pot of tea. " 'Surely you desire truth in the inner parts; you teach me wisdom in the inmost place.' That's Psalm 51:6. Desiring truth is a uniquely human trait. More tea, ladies?"

Ruby gave, what looked like to Birch, a triumphant look.

"Knowing what's true or not is not that easy," Birch insisted, irritated now at both Ruby and Lincoln. Neither had lived through this particular situation, neither had seen or felt the agony her family had gone through.

"Recognizing truth is not always easy," Lincoln agreed amicably. "But truth itself is black or white. Something is either true or it isn't.

We might not agree with what truth is, but something can't both be and not be. Simple rule of logic."

"So," Ruby said. "Do you think that guilt is black and white also? You don't believe there are levels of guilt?"

"Guilt isn't like truth," Lincoln said, warming up to the subject. "There are degrees of guilt, like when a soldier kills in the line of duty. He is guilty of killing, but, ultimately, the people who started the war, off in some distant office somewhere, are *more* guilty. At least, in my humble opinion." He smiled at the women.

"What I'm saying," Birch said, "is things are often better left in the past. It doesn't help to go over and over things that can't be any different than what they are." Trust me, she wanted to tell Ruby, I've done that with too many things in my life, talked them into the ground wishing for a different outcome. And not a one of them changed.

" 'Who of you by worrying can add a single hour to his life?' Matthew 6:27," Lincoln said. "Good advice to us all."

"Amen to that," Birch agreed.

After Lincoln left, she said to Ruby, "I need to talk to Sueann right now. Can we get together later?"

Ruby nodded, her face thoughtful. Would she keep probing until her curiosity was satisfied? Maybe that was to be expected. Even though the thought of all that being stirred back up caused Birch's stomach to feel uneasy, maybe things *had* been secret for too long. But still Birch worried. What if the secrets surrounding Carson's death were better left in the grave?

"I'm leaving, too," Ruby said, standing up, gathering up the papers. "I want to get back to the lodge before it gets much colder."

At the Lone Pine, it was also slow, so Sueann joined Birch for an early supper. After assuring Birch that she didn't mind, even appreciated, Cassie staying over there, Birch told her about the conversation over at the coffeehouse.

"Ruby has copies of Cole's court transcripts?" Sueann asked, her face surprised. "What for?"

Birch shrugged and crumbled a soda cracker into her clam chowder. "I suppose she wants to know the details. They were only married six months and he lied to her about his past. Maybe knowing a little more will make it easier for her to let him go."

"Look, I'm as sympathetic as anyone else about her situation, but how does dredging up all that old crap help? It sure wouldn't help me grieve." She stabbed at her grilled chicken salad, her fork making angry punctuation marks to her words.

Her vehement reaction surprised Birch. "I think she can't help herself. She probably doesn't know what else to do."

Sueann looked up at Birch, her expression miserable and a little lost. "I suppose you're right, but I'm afraid."

Again, Birch was surprised. Sueann was tough, a born and bred western woman raised in this high desert country, a desolate, hard land that had never been kind to women. Even the night she showed up at Birch's door with a bleeding lip, toting nothing but her car keys, Cassie and a pitifully inadequate diaper bag, telling Birch she couldn't live with Derek one more minute, she didn't admit she was afraid.

"What are you afraid of, sweetie?" she asked, reaching over and taking Sueann's cold hand.

"That it's all going to change. That . . ." She faltered. "Oh, I don't know. This thing with Cassie and Hunter has me all upset. And Ruby showing up making us think about Cole again. Lucas and her . . ."

"What about Lucas and Ruby?" Birch was confused.

"They're both determined to find out what is the supposed truth of the night Cole killed Carson. Why can't they accept it just was what it was?"

Sueann's voice sounded desperate to Birch. Did she know more than she'd let on all these years? Had Derek, in a moment of vulnerability, told her what happened that night?

"Lucas and Ruby might just have to eventually realize that," Birch replied evenly. And so will I, she thought. A part of her would have given her left arm to find out it was Derek or June who shot Carson, though if that were true, their whole family would be in for rough times again. And it still wouldn't bring Cole back.

Sueann stood up, picking up her half-eaten salad. "It's so slow I may as well catch up on setups. Busy is hard, slow is harder."

"I know what you mean."

Sueann reached into her apron pocket, pulled out a fortune cookie and laid it next to Birch's bowl.

"It's Tuesday, not Wednesday," Birch said.

"I know, but a little unexpected fortune might be good for the soul."

Birch watched Sueann go through the swinging doors of the kitchen. She opened the cellophane wrapper and broke the cookie in half. The tiny piece of paper read, *The smart thing to do is prepare for the unexpected.*

That, Birch thought, could be the motto for my life.

23

RUBY

Later that evening, Birch called Ruby's room. "How are you doing?" she asked.

Her voice sounded subdued to Ruby and she felt a stab of pity for the older woman. This had to be incredibly hard for her, finding out about Cole's death and now trying to deal with Ruby looking into it.

"I'm fine," she replied. "How about you?"

"Not so good," Birch said, surprising Ruby with her candor. "I know I said we should talk tonight, but I don't think I'm up to it."

"I understand," Ruby said. "How about tomorrow?"

Birch sighed. "I'm short of staff tomorrow. All Bobby's nieces and nephews are going to Mammoth to ski so I'll be busy all morning, but I'll be free by lunch. We can drive somewhere out of town, have some privacy."

"I'd like that," Ruby said. "I'll come by the desk about noon. One last thing. I have a question."

"Yes?"

"Do you think I should contact Cole's mother? Or should I wait for her to get in touch with me?"

The long silence from Birch told Ruby this wasn't an easy question.

"I don't know what to tell you," she eventually said. "I think it's really up to you. The only advice I can give to you concerning June is that she can be intimidating, but she's a human being just like you and me. Her hurts are deep and they have always, since I've known her, been expressed with anger rather than sadness. Don't let her run you over."

"I'll keep that in mind," Ruby said.

The next day, while taking a walk before breakfast, Ruby came upon Cardinal High School, closed now for the holidays. It was one of those huge, concrete and brick buildings where all the classrooms came off inside corridors, not like the Southern California high schools she attended where the sprawling campuses had doors that open directly to trees and grass and outside corridors.

She climbed the steep steps and peered through the glass double doors trying to read the engraving on the trophies displayed in a wood and glass case. Was Cole's name on any of them? The floors were a shiny, dark linoleum, like the floors at the courthouse. An artificial silver Christmas tree stood next to the trophy case. It was covered with red and black decorations, the school colors, she remembered from a newspaper article.

She stood at the top of the stairs and looked out over the long front walk, lined by pine trees, where snow patches dotted the huge lawn. She imagined Cole sitting on this lawn, walking this sidewalk, worrying about algebra tests, his afternoon job and teenage girls. She turned back to take one more look, when she saw a bronze plaque on the left wall next to the glass entry doors. Even from where she stood, the man's face in relief, looked familiar. When she came closer, she could see why.

"By order of the mayor of Cardinal and the unanimous vote of the town council, this building is hereby dedicated to the memory of Carson McGavin, rancher, businessman and city council member, whose generous donation provided earthquake retrofitting thereby making this building safer for Cardinal's young people."

There was no date, which Ruby found odd. Was this done before or after Carson was killed? She supposed it didn't matter. It showed what the town thought of him or, at least, what the leadership of the town thought of him. Though she knew that things like this were mostly political, he obviously cared enough about the town and the children of the town to make sure where they went to school was safe. Earthquake retrofitting often cost millions of dollars, she knew. Was that why the McGavins were so cash poor now?

She decided to avoid the crowded lodge dining room and grab a quick breakfast at Holy Grounds. It was also the only place she knew for certain Cole had never been. This coffeehouse, like her, had such a short history with Cardinal, it was someplace where she could sit and not feel compelled to think about Cole once coming here. She was becoming weary of this heightened state of emotional turmoil she'd been in since coming to Cardinal. Nashville was looking better, like a calm port after a stormy sea. She just wanted to go somewhere where no one knew her past, where she could begin to forget about this last year.

She was sipping a cup of chai tea when Derek came through the coffeehouse door. He removed his dark cowboy hat and walked over to her table.

"Can we talk?" he asked, his voice subdued. Though she'd only seen him a few times, at each encounter he'd been agitated and loud. This quiet, restrained man before her seemed at odds with her initial impression. Like with Lucas, his physical resemblance to Cole was so strong, a part of her just wanted to sit and study his features. Had Cole ever dressed like this?

"Certainly," she said, wondering if he'd been sent by June.

He pulled out a chair, setting his hat, brim up, on the table. She watched him warily, stirring her tea to occupy her nervous hands. The coffeehouse was half full, but she'd feel a lot better if Lucas were here, or if this conversation were taking place under a lawyer's watchful eye.

"Would you like something to drink?" she asked, then felt like snatching the words back. Her waitress persona had momentarily taken over. It put her, she knew, at a disadvantage now, made her the subservient one.

"No, thanks," he said, picking up his hat and running his finger along the rim. He refused to look at her. Not a good sign.

"You know, we've never officially met," she said, deciding to take charge, to make up for her lapse into the serving role. "I'm Ruby." She held out her hand.

"Yes," he said, taking it. "I'm Derek. Number two McGavin boy."

She tilted her head. "That's an interesting way of identifying yourself."

He shrugged. "It's the truth."

She blatantly studied his face for a moment. Though Lucas had a bit of the essence of Cole in his mannerisms and his personality, and actually looked like a younger Cole, Derek looked like the Cole she'd known. Had being a shadow version of his adored older brother been a burden growing up? It reminded her of Lincoln's sermon on Christmas Eve, his joke about Jesus' siblings. At least that was something that kept Nash and her from having any animosity against the other. Neither of them was particularly successful.

She sipped her tea and watched him, waiting for him to continue the conversation. He just kept rubbing the edge of his hat, not looking at her, not saying anything.

"Is there something you want to ask me?" she prodded gently.

He looked up, pushed his hat aside and placed both of his scarred, dirt-stained hands on the wooden table. "It's gotten around town that you're looking into my father's death. I'd like you to stop. It's going to cause a great deal of pain to my mother and . . ." He paused, as if his words were a script and he'd forgotten the next line.

"That was fast," Ruby said, wondering how he'd heard about it. The woman at county records, most likely. She was certain John Henley or Sueann wouldn't say anything. "I just want to know what happened that night. I would stop right now if someone would tell me the truth."

He stared at her, unblinking.

She didn't sense any hostility so she decided to keep talking. "I can't let Cole rest until I know the truth about what happened, Derek. Lucas feels the same way. He's felt left out for years." She braced herself for his angry tirade.

But he just sat there, not saying a word. After a minute or so, he stood up, put his hat on and carefully pushed the chair back under the table.

"I'm sorry he feels that way," Derek said. The lines deepened on his suntanned face, reminding her of the foothills that surrounded this town. "You want to know the truth? The truth is, Lucas is the lucky one. It's better not knowing."

"He doesn't feel that way," she answered. It flashed through her head in that moment what an odd position she was in, explaining one of her husband's brothers to the other. "He doesn't feel like he's ever been part of the McGavin family."

Derek gave her one of the saddest looks she'd ever seen. "Please, I'll give you money for your part of the ranch. I don't know how I'll get it or how much, but, please, just leave Cardinal." With that, he turned and walked out of the coffeehouse.

She stared at her teacup for a minute. What had just happened? She stirred her cold tea, replaying their short conversation in her head, when Lincoln walked up with a pot of hot water.

"More tea?" he asked. He held a plastic box of tea bags under his arm. He set it down in front of her.

"I think chamomile," she said, choosing a pale yellow package. "I could use a little serenity right now."

"Don't worry, I was keeping an eye on him," Lincoln said, pouring hot water in her cup. "I've never formally been introduced to Derek McGavin. Don't think he's been in here before, but his reputation precedes him."

She unwrapped the tea bag and stuck it in the water. "He was actually pretty nice."

"Like most families, I imagine the McGavin family has its prescribed saints and sinners. That doesn't necessarily mean that deep inside he's everything that his role demands him to be."

She stared at her hand, dipping the tea bag in and out of the water. "Still, don't you think our true selves are eventually revealed?"

"Depends on how good our acting skills are. Or how strong our conscience."

"You're probably right."

He shifted the pot of water from one hand to the other. "Who knows? I'm sure even Judas had his kind moments. But that didn't change what he ultimately did."

She thought about the implication of what he was saying. "Do you really think one act truly defines our life?"

He paused to consider her words. Behind him, a young man in a black ski jacket started picking out "A Hard Day's Night" on the piano. "A single act doesn't always define the whole of our life, but it often affects what people think of us. Think about the times we've watched a public figure's reputation change in a heartbeat with an affair or a revelation of some other impropriety. Unfortunately, that is what we remember, not the good things he did."

"I think we should look at everything a person did in his life, not just one thing." It tore at her heart to think that Cole would be forever judged by so many people by that one horrible moment when he shot his father. She understood now why he hadn't wanted her to know about his past. With her, he could pretend to be a new person. She couldn't judge the whole of who he was by one single incident.

The piano player switched midsong to "It's a Small World After All." A couple of groans from the coffeehouse patrons caused him to segue into "Summertime."

Lincoln turned to look at the piano player, his face amused. Then he turned back to Ruby. "I agree, but it also depends on what they did. Sometimes it's just a momentary lapse of judgment. Sometimes it's not just an incident, but the revelation of a huge character flaw."

She took a deep breath. "Like the difference between killing someone in the heat of anger and a serial killer."

He looked her from under his white-blond eyebrows, his lake blue eyes kind. "Something like that."

"Do you know about my husband? What he did?"

He nodded. "Actually, ever since you arrived I've been wanting to talk to you about him."

She carefully set her cup in its saucer, not taking her eyes off his face. An odd, electric current of fear ran through her. "What do you mean?"

"I was waiting for the right moment to tell you. Cole and I met in Los Angeles, right after he was released from prison."

She tried not to look shocked. "Were you in prison too?"

He shook his head. "We met at an AA meeting. I was his sponsor."

24

RUBY

It was one more piece of Cole's life she hadn't known about. He rarely drank alcohol when they were dating or married. When they'd watch his friends and coworkers drink to excess at company picnics or weddings, he'd always comment wryly to her that getting drunk was a young man's indulgence.

"If I'm going to pack on a gut," he'd say, patting his flat stomach, "it's going to be because of your banana cream pie not malt liquor."

His abstinence was a relief to her. She'd grown up surrounded by alcohol, hating the fights it had ignited between her mismatched, unhappy parents.

"I apologize for being deceitful." Lincoln dropped his head, his voice quiet with regret. "I've struggled with how to bring it up since I discovered who you were."

She pushed her teacup aside, her stomach too upset for even chamomile tea. "No one could ever accuse you of being deceitful, Lincoln. You and Cole didn't stay in touch?"

"Only occasionally. Last time we talked was a few months after Lisa was killed . . ." He turned his head to stare at a folk art quilt of a blue turtle flying above a mission-style plaza. "After what happened to her, my faith failed me. I jumped right back into the arms of Jack Daniels." He turned back to Ruby, his eyes somber. "My faith failed; God didn't. One morning after a long night of drinking, something in my foggy mind thought of Cole and I wondered how he was doing. I remembered he'd moved to Orange County and the name of the construction company he worked for. When I was sober enough, I felt compelled to find the company and leave a message with the office assistant. To this day, I believe it was God's doing. A few days later Cole called me back. We talked a long time. It was humbling to have to confess to someone you sponsored that you had fallen off the wagon, but Cole was never judgmental. As a matter of fact, I think he saved my life."

His words struck a chord in Ruby. Those were the exact words Ely had used describing his relationship with Cole, though he never told her what he meant. "What do you mean?"

"He told me to find a meeting and start going. Then he said to find someone who knew about God to answer my spiritual questions. He told me that I should stay in Cardinal, that it was a nice town, that most of the people of Cardinal were good, caring folks. He said to take whatever money I had left and buy a business here." He smiled. "I did all four things. I stayed here, found a meeting, found Father Joe at the Catholic church who was—and is—willing to listen to all my questions and try to answer them. I bought the bookstore and the coffeehouse. The town's old-timers haven't exactly embraced me yet, but they're coming around. Most important, I've found a home. This place . . ." He looked past her through the front window of his coffeehouse. "It's grown tentacles around my heart. That's the only way I can put it."

Ruby felt tears start behind her eyes. It gave her hope that if someone who had experienced the sadness Lincoln had could find a place he felt at home, maybe she could too. Maybe not here, but somewhere.

"Thank you," she said. "You've given me another piece of my husband's past."

He squeezed her hand. "Someday, this'll all be clear to us. We will not be peering through a glass darkly."

"That sounds so right. Life is sometimes like peering through a dark tinted window"

He rubbed his chin, his eyes narrowing with humor. "Can't take credit for the observation. It was the apostle Paul in his letter to the Corinthian church. Now there's a group of folks who makes this town look like a bunch of amateur sinners." He stood up. "I'd better see if my customers need anything. Let me know if I can help you in any way, okay?"

"I will," she promised.

Back at the lodge, Birch handed Ruby a sealed envelope from her room key box. "This was here when I got in this morning."

The message was written on thick, off-white paper and went straight to the point. *Please come to the offices of Wagner and Smith, 157 Second Street, at 1:00 p.m. on Monday, January 3, to discuss the will of my son Cole McGavin. Sincerely, June McGavin*

"Another message from your brother?" Birch asked.

"No," Ruby said. "It's from June." She held the note out to Birch.

She read the note, then handed it back to Ruby. "Well, that solves your dilemma."

"Not exactly. I was planning on leaving before then."

"Maybe it's best," Birch said. "Driving during the holidays can be dangerous."

It appeared to Ruby that Birch looked relieved. Ruby knew that Birch wanted her to stay longer. But Ruby suspected that it had to do more with Birch's desire to capture some lost essence of Cole, that as long as Ruby was here, a part of Cole was also.

Ruby wasn't sure she would be able to give Birch what it was she needed, at least not in the time she planned on being here in Cardinal. Still, Birch was right, traveling during the holidays could be troublesome and, besides, it gave Ruby a few more days to find out what she could about Carson's death. But, no matter what, right after her meeting with June McGavin on Monday, Ruby would leave town.

"Derek came by Holy Grounds when I was there," Ruby said, wanting to change the subject of her eventual departure.

"Oh, Lord," Birch said. "What did that boy do?"

"He was actually pretty nice. Sort of sad, really. Said he thought Lucas was the luckiest of the three boys."

Birch fiddled with the stapler on the top of the front desk, her face thoughtful. "He might be right, though, like I told you, I don't know any details. Derek was a nervy child and a cocky adolescent, took wilder chances than either Cole or Lucas."

"Middle child trying to stand out?" Ruby said.

"Maybe so," Birch said. "But, as obnoxious as he could sometimes be, he also had a way about him, a drollness that made you laugh at his attempts to be dangerous."

"Derek droll?" Ruby said, unable to imagine it.

Birch's expression sobered. "The night Carson died changed him. After that he had an anger inside that never seemed to go away. A lot of the anger spilled over on Lucas probably because Derek had nowhere else to put it. Any sensible person would have seen that her children might need professional help to get through a trauma like that. Not June, though."

"That night changed a lot of people," Ruby said softly.

Birch reached across the desk and took one of Ruby's hands. "You and I should talk again. You know, there's a lot of happy things I can share with you about Cole's life."

"I'm sure there are," she said. Birch's hand was cold and dry.

"Even though you have to leave to see to your brother, I hope you'll be coming back."

Ruby didn't answer. What could she tell Birch, who was only trying to be kind? That unlike Lincoln, she didn't think she could just move here and plug right into this community. She truly wished she could. She liked Birch, but she was afraid there were too many memories, too many reminders of what might have been. This had been Cole's town, but she couldn't imagine how it could ever be hers. Right at this moment, the person she most longed to see was her brother. She wanted to sit across from him at a roadside cafe that still played Bob Wills songs on the jukebox and eat hickory-smoked bacon, scrambled eggs and a huge mound of buttermilk pancakes. She wanted to talk about her mother to someone who understood and feel the comfortable easiness she only experienced with Nash. Now that Cole was dead, Nash was the only constant—or semi-constant—person in her life.

With the prospect of staying until after New Year's in front of her, she tried to decide what she should do with that time. She didn't have any idea about how to look further into Carson's death and she wasn't even sure there was a point to it. It had seemed a good idea until she read the court transcripts. Now she wondered if Birch was right, that it was better to leave some things firmly in the past.

What could she do the next few days? Where could she go? Next to Birch, the only people in Cardinal she'd become friendly with were Lucas, Sueann and Lincoln. She felt uncomfortable around Sueann now, and she'd already spent so much time hanging around the coffee-house and bookstore that she was embarrassed to go to either place again. Maybe she should drive someplace out of town. She'd seen an advertisement for outlet stores up near Mammoth, except shopping was the last thing that appealed to her right now.

Lucas, a little voice inside her said. She hadn't seen him since yesterday when they'd parted outside the courthouse. She'd not told him about her conversation with Derek or about Lincoln once being Cole's AA sponsor. Did Lucas know that Cole had a drinking problem or that it was his suggestion that Lincoln settle down in Cardinal? She wanted him to know everything she found out. He deserved that much.

"Be with you in a minute," he called, when she opened the saddle shop door. He sat on a stool, his head bent over a piece of leather, picking at it with one of his smooth-handled tools. A small stereo in back of him played "Ring of Fire" by Johnny Cash.

"No hurry," Ruby said.

At the sound of her voice, his head popped up. A smile replaced the look of concentration. "Ruby! I was wondering what had happened to you." He set the tool down on the workbench, wiped his hands down the sides of his jeans. "You're the perfect excuse for me to put off picking stitches."

"Picking stitches?"

"Worst kind of grunt work in saddlemaking. People bring in their old saddles and want them restitched. You have to pick out the old stitches before you can do it. It's dependable money for a saddlemaker, but not too creative."

She laughed. "I'm glad I could be of some help."

He walked around the glass counter, his face concerned. "I was worried when I didn't hear from you yesterday, but I was trying to be sensitive and give you some space. What's going on?"

She felt the sudden urge to reach up and touch his cheek, reassure him that everything would be okay, like she had so often done with Cole. The tender feeling caught her by surprise. She'd not intended to become emotionally involved with any of Cole's family, but here she was wanting to comfort Lucas, feeling pity for Derek and wishing she didn't have to say good-bye to his aunt Birch.

"I'm fine," she said, busying her hand by unwrapping her new scarf and setting it on the counter. "I read the transcripts from beginning to end, but they didn't really shed any new light. I don't know if there's any way to find out what happened that night short of torturing it out of your mother or brother." She brushed a stray piece of hair from her eyes. "Who, by the way, stopped by the coffeehouse and talked to me yesterday when I was reading the transcripts."

"My mother talked to you?"

"No, I meant Derek."

Lucas frowned and shoved hands deep into his pockets as if to keep them from striking something. "What did he want?"

This time she did give in to her urge. She reached out and placed a hand on his forearm. It was warm to her touch and she could feel the tense corded muscles under the wiry hair. A strong physical memory of Cole shot through her, causing her to pull her hand back. "Lucas, he was okay, even polite. He didn't even lose his temper."

"A first," Lucas said, his tone bitter.

"He did ask me to stop looking into your father's death. He . . ." She hesitated before continuing, not wanting to further irritate Lucas.

He pulled his hands out of his pockets and stepped closer to her. She could smell the sharp icy scent of his aftershave.

"What?" he asked.

"He offered me money to leave."

He swore softly under his breath. "That's so typical of him. He was probably sent by June."

"Maybe not," Ruby said. "She left me a note at the lodge asking me to meet her at her lawyer's offices next Monday to discuss Cole's will." She tilted her head. "Did you tell her I was going to sign Cole's part of the ranch over to you?"

He shook his head.

"Why not?"

He looked away, his face coloring slightly. "I guess I was procrastinating. Something I'm good at."

She inhaled deeply, wishing this were all over. "I'll tell her on Monday, but I'd like for you to be there."

"I agree with Derek about one thing, you should receive some money, though I'm not talking about bribing you to stop asking questions about Dad's death."

"I don't care. I'm leaving Monday afternoon, no matter what. I need to see my brother."

"You've given up trying to find out what happened?" he asked, his tone disappointed.

"I guess I don't have the stomach to be a private detective. I don't think we'll find out anything anyway. Only two people know what happened that night, and I'm sure neither Derek nor your mother will tell. And even if they did, how would we know it's the truth? Our only chance for that died when Cole did." She regretted her words the minute she said them. Lucas's face seemed to deflate, making him appear to age years before her eyes. "I'm sorry, Lucas. I didn't mean for that to come out so harshly."

"That's okay," he said. "Look, it's lunchtime. How about I go over to the Lone Pine, get us a couple of burgers and we can talk a little more?"

Though she was tired of talking, she couldn't turn him down. He had not had the time she had to get used to Cole being gone. Like with Birch, his feelings about Cole probably were mixed up with Ruby's role as Cole's wife. Hopefully, long after Ruby was gone, he and Birch could figure out a way to comfort each other.

"All right. I'll have a cheeseburger. And an iced tea."

"Coming right up," he said. "Please, don't sneak away."

"I won't," she promised.

He was gone only five minutes when the cowbell on the door jangled. Ruby was sitting on the love seat flipping through a copy of *Leather Crafters and Saddlers Journal*. Her stomach lurched when she saw June McGavin standing in the doorway.

"You," June said, stepping into the lobby. Frigid air blew in around her. She wore black tailored slacks and a bright teal blue sweater. Her eyes, a dense coffee brown, were shiny as beetles.

Ruby didn't respond. What could she answer to that one word?

"Where's Lucas?" June asked.

"He went to buy lunch," Ruby said, using her best *keep the agitated customer calm* voice. "He'll be back shortly."

They stared at each other a long moment. Ruby decided to break the standoff. "Mrs. McGavin, I'm so sorry about Cole. I know you must miss him. I want you to know I loved him very much."

June didn't answer immediately, but continued to study Ruby, her dark eyes and pale complexion revealing nothing. Ruby held the woman's gaze, certain that she'd eventually give some sort of indication of emotion. No matter what had happened between Cole and his mother, the fact remained, he was her son. She had to feel something about his death.

"Lucas said he did it on purpose," June finally said. "Is that true?"

Ruby inhaled a ragged breath. "That's what the assistant coroner indicated. She said there were no skid marks."

Ruby thought she saw June's bottom lip tremble, then stiffen. Or was it just her imagination?

"Did you receive my note?" June asked.

"Yes, I did."

"You'll be there?"

She nodded. "I want to tell you—" Before she could tell her what she planned on doing with Cole's part of the ranch, Lucas opened the shop door.

"Mom," he said, his voice flat. He walked around her and set the two white bags down on the glass counter. "What are you doing here?"

"I came by to tell you the family has a meeting at the lawyer's office at one o'clock on Monday. But, I suppose you already know that now. The family is meeting a half hour earlier. Please be there at twelve-thirty." She left without saying one more word to Ruby.

"What did she say to you?" he asked.

"She was only here a few minutes," Ruby said. "I told her I was sorry about Cole and that I was sure she missed him."

Lucas snorted. "That's doubtful."

"She asked me if I received her note. I started to tell her I was signing Cole's part of the ranch to you when you walked in."

"Saved by the saddlemaker," he said. "It's probably better she doesn't know that before Monday."

"Why not?"

"I've just found it's better, if at all possible, to be one step ahead of my mother. It gives her less time to find ways to undermine you." He opened up one of the bags. "I bought you a side salad too. Sueann says hi, by the way."

Ruby walked over to the counter. "She's still speaking to me?"

"Why wouldn't she be?" He pulled out two wrapped hamburgers and two clear containers of macaroni salad.

"Like I told you and John, she was not happy I was looking into Carson's death."

He unwrapped his hamburger and sat down on one of the stools. "Sueann doesn't like change. Never has. Frankly, she stayed with Derek longer than she should have just for that reason." He took a bite out of his hamburger. "If she knew something, I'm sure she would have told me."

Ruby didn't answer, busying herself by stirring her salad. She wouldn't argue the point with Lucas, but she didn't think he was right. Sueann knew something, Ruby was certain of it.

"So," she said, trying to stay away from the subject of Cole, his mother and his father's death. "Why did you decide to stop being a lawyer and go into saddlemaking?"

He took another bite of his hamburger, his expression intentionally vague. "I'd rather not talk about it right now."

"I'm sorry," she said, surprised. "I was just making conversation. I didn't mean to pry."

He continued eating, his face blank.

They silently finished their lunch. After they were done, while she helped clean up their lunch debris, she said, "I have a question."

"Shoot," Lucas said, then grimaced at his choice of words.

"Where is Cole?"

"In there." Lucas pointed to a large oak cabinet. A calendar advertising leather tools hung on the door.

"I want to have a service or something. Can we do that? I want to see him settled before I leave. Maybe you and me, Birch and Bobby, your mom and Derek if they want to come. We can ask Lincoln to say a prayer or read something appropriate."

Lucas nodded, unable to speak.

"Okay, then," she said, picking up her scarf. "I'd better get going." She carefully wrapped the long scarf once, then twice around her neck. "Even though Sueann's a little annoyed at me, I think she'd like to come to any service we had. I'm okay with that. I think, in another life, maybe she and I could have been friends."

LUCAS

After Ruby left, Lucas decided to go back to the Lone Pine and talk to Sueann, make it clear that it was as much him as Ruby looking into Carson's death. Frankly, he couldn't understand why it mattered to her. Maybe Ruby was right and Sueann did know something. She had been married to Derek for five years. Lucas knew that many confidences were spilled during unguarded bedroom talk. He had too often, after sex, revealed more to women about himself than he intended.

Sueann and Derek together. Even after all these years, even with Cassie as proof, he couldn't imagine whatever caused those two to get together. Sueann, in his opinion, deserved much better than Derek. What in the world ever drew her to him?

Of course, it was probably an accurate statement that he couldn't see his brother in the same light a woman would. The truth was, many women, before and after Sueann, had been attracted to his older brother. Derek McGavin had a self-assured manner and enough prestige even when he was a teenager to appeal to the needy girl Sueann had obviously been at sixteen when she became pregnant with Cassie. Sixteen and pregnant. Lucas couldn't imagine being a parent now at thirty-four, much less be faced with it at sixteen.

The cafe was only half full when he walked in. He glanced up at the clock above the cash register. Two p.m. The lunch rush was over and dinner was still hours away. Maybe Sueann would have time to take a break. Cassie, her hair now a merlot red, stood next to a couple of ketchup bottles watching them drain into each other, a bored expression on her face.

"Hey, Cassie, your mom around?"

She shrugged. "I suppose."

He smiled at her. "That's not much help. I like your hair. Maroon is so much more soothing to the eye."

She didn't take her eyes off the draining bottles. "I think she's in the storeroom."

"Are we going to work the chili booth again this year at First Night?"

Lucas thought the town's New Year's celebration was one of the best things that the town council had ever come up with. Gordon Vieira told him drunk driving arrests were down 50 percent since they started the family oriented, alcohol-free celebration that culminated at midnight with a professional fireworks display set off by the local volunteer fire department. The police blocked off a good portion of Main Street and the street fair usually lasted until two a.m. Different businesses around town had food booths whose profits paid for both the fireworks show and their favorite local charity.

Cassie made a disgusted noise deep in her throat. "Not if I can find something better to do. Who wants to start out the new year by working?"

He gave a hesitant laugh. Last year she'd thought it was a blast. "Who put the king-size burr under your saddle?"

She turned to look at him, her dark eyes reminding him so much of his mother's. Her maroon hair looked definitely less garish than that weird electric blue, but Lucas missed the pretty reddish-blond hair she inherited from her mom. "I'm just pissed, okay? Is a person allowed to be pissed or do they have to, like, explain themselves to the world for every little emotion?"

He held up his hands in surrender. "Sorry to interrupt your bad mood. I'll just trot on back and see your mom."

She frowned and went back to watching the ketchup bottles.

Back in the storeroom, he found Sueann unpacking boxes of canned goods and condiments. "Hi, Sueann, got a minute?"

"For you, my friend," she said, holding a bright yellow squeeze bottle of mustard in each hand, "I might have two." She lined the bottles next to similar ones on a metal shelf that held a variety of condiments. "What do you need?"

"First, what's with Cassie? She turned vampire on me when I spoke to her."

Sueann leaned against the metal shelves, folding her arms over her chest. The air was warm and a little damp, causing wisps of fine hair to escape her braid and curl around her freckled neck.

"She's got a stick up her butt because I refuse to let her spend New Year's Eve in some skanky motel with that Frankenstein boyfriend of hers."

"She asked you if she could spend the night in a motel with her boyfriend?" Lucas shook his head. What planet had he been living on for the last few years? When did daughters start asking mothers permission to do things like that? What ever happened to good, old-fashioned sneaking around?

Sueann picked up another bottle of mustard and tried to smooth out the creased label. "Not in so many words. Apparently, he and his band have a job on New Year's Eve in Carson City and she wanted to go with them. They'll be playing until two a.m. She knows I don't want her on the road that late so her suggestion was to spend the night."

"Cassie actually thought you'd give that plan any serious consideration?"

Sueann nodded, put the bottle of mustard on the shelf into a domino line of lemon-colored bottles. "Hard to believe, huh? So now she is mad at the world in general and me in particular. She'll get over it."

"Guess so," Lucas said. He shifted from foot to foot, not quite sure how to bring up Ruby.

"What can I do for you? I'm sure you didn't come back here just to tell me Cassie was being a brat."

"No, I want to talk to you about something."

He hesitated, again unsure about how to start. Tension between women was something foreign to him, not only because he was raised in an almost exclusively male household, but also because his mother was not like other women. The whispered joke among the other ranchers and the people she'd dealt with in Cardinal was that she had bigger balls than her husband or any of her sons.

"Just spit it out, Lucas," Sueann said, taking the empty box that held the mustard bottles and started breaking it down with a box cutter.

"Maybe not while you're holding that knife," he said.

She stopped cutting and tilted her head. "What's got into you? Since when have you ever had any trouble talking to me? It's Sueann, your old buddy. What's up?"

"It's about you and Ruby."

A troubled expression narrowed her features. She carefully laid the cutter on the wood counter. "What about us?"

He kept his voice unemotional, pretending he was trying a case. "I wanted you to know it's not just her looking into my dad's death. It's me, too. She said you had some problems with it—with her—delving into it. She was his wife, Sueann. She has a right to know about whatever happened in Cole's life that might have had repercussions later."

She lifted her hands, her expression frustrated now. "What good will it do? It had nothing to do with her marriage to Cole. It's old business best left in the past." Her green eyes took on a desperate gleam.

Her reaction verified that Ruby was right. Sueann knew what happened that night. It pained him to think that all these years his childhood friend had kept something this important from him. Since he'd come back home, the only people he'd felt were true friends were Sueann and Ely. Both were proving to be relationships based on false pretenses. A childish feeling of devastation washed over him. Then it was replaced by anger.

"Just how long have you known what happened with my father?"

"It's more complicated than you think," she said, lowering her voice. "There are people who could get hurt."

"How long?"

She shook her head mutely, her green eyes filling with tears, unable or unwilling to answer.

"I have a right to know." He clenched his fists and took a step toward her, his anger like a ferocious animal that a part of him didn't want to control. *All these years she knew and I didn't.*

When Sueann flinched and dropped her head, his anger turned immediately to an overwhelming shame. Oh, Lord, what was wrong with him? Was he any different from Derek or his dad? Or for that matter, Mitchell Weeks? Was it really this simple, the escalating violence that started with angry words, progressed to splitting a woman's lip, and ended with her lying in a pool of blood, her three children dead at her feet?

"Sueann," he said, unclenching his fists and holding out his palms. "I'm sorry. I didn't mean to scare you. I don't know what . . ." A headache started like a hammer behind his eyes. "I'm sorry."

Silent tears flowed down her cheeks. He turned and strode out of the warm, steamy room, as ashamed of himself as he'd been the day Mitchell Weeks had been taken away in chains. He was in the court-room when the judge agreed with the jury's recommendation of life without parole. If he'd had a gun that moment, Lucas suspected he would have shot Mitchell Weeks himself.

But, coward that he was, he merely watched the guilty man be lead away and remained in the courtroom until the last person left. Then he went to a bar across the street called The Advocate and drank shot after shot of Jim Beam until the bartender called a cab to take him home.

BIRCH

"Mind how much cayenne you add," Birch said, peering into the giant silver pot Bobby stirred. It was noon on New Year's Eve and they were making chili for the First Night celebration, which started in four hours. "Have you seen Ruby today? I swear, the last two days I've only caught glimpses of her. I hope she's okay."

"You keep your feminine wiles out of my chili," Bobby said. "This is a man's chili." He dumped another teaspoon of flakes into the reddish-brown mixture.

"Then we'd better stock a lot of manly mint-flavored Mylanta for all the men who are going to have aching tummies tomorrow morning," she replied, going back to her own simmering ten-gallon pot.

Most of the chili and other food—baking powder biscuits, macaroni salad and cinnamon-sugar donuts—was ready for tonight's festivities. Even though Sueann and her staff at the Lone Pine were also making chili as well as chicken noodle soup, after some debate with Bobby, Birch had decided they need ten more gallons of chili.

"Whatever we don't use, we can freeze," she said. "Have it next Friday with spaghetti."

"Are the goodie bags done?" he asked.

The Tokopah gave out New Year's goodie bags to each guest containing a fortune cookie, a colorful noisemaker, a silly hat and a candy bar.

She dipped a dinner spoon into her chili and tasted it. "Perfect. Just spicy enough."

He rolled his eyes at her and added another tablespoon of red pepper to his batch.

"The bags are almost done," she answered him. "You know the Miller girls, the twins with the curly hair and pretty brown eyes? They didn't feel like skiing today so I told their parents to go on to the slopes, that I'd watch them. They're helping me with the bags."

"We're providing babysitting service now?"

She wrinkled her nose at him. "That would be the royal we. They're thirteen, so I don't really think of it as babysitting and they've been a big help. They're decorating the bags right now." She sighed and stirred her chili. "I remember when Cassie was that age and loved helping with things like that. She and Sueann ran into each other this morning and had another big argument in the dining room right in front of the whole world."

"The Tokopah Lodge proudly presents for your breakfast entertainment, the incredible battling McGavins," he said.

"Oh, you," she said, laughing in spite of the fact that Sueann and Cassie at odds with each other truly bothered her. "It wasn't *that* loud, though a few guests received an earful. Cassie is still angling to go with her boyfriend to that overnight gig in Carson City tonight and Sueann is still putting the kibosh on it."

"Good for her," Bobby said. "That young fellow shouldn't be hanging around with someone Cassie's age anyway. It's downright criminal."

Birch laughed. "Apparently, that's exactly what Sueann told him."

"Sueann has never been one to mince words."

The kitchen door swung open and Ruby walked in.

"Hello, Ruby," Bobby said. "Were your ears burning? Birch was wondering where you've been hiding."

Birch elbowed him, her face blushing pink. "Quit making me sound like I'm keeping tabs on her. She's a grown woman."

Ruby, dressed in brown cords and a pale green sweater, smiled hesitantly. She looked over at Birch. "I've come to offer my services. I offered to help Carolyn and Janice decorate the goodies bags, but they said they didn't need my help, that it would take too long to train me."

"The girls have a *vision*," Birch said, winking at Ruby.

"A what?" Bobby said.

"Their mother is an interior decorator," Birch said. "She's striving to be the next Martha Stewart. They picked up a little of her lingo, I think."

"You think?" Bobby said. He gestured at Ruby. "Hey, I've got something you can do. Watch this chili while I make sure the front walk is not too slippery. Don't need any lawsuits."

"Glad to," she said.

"Don't let it burn," he said, handing her the wooden spoon.

"What difference would it make?" Birch said. "People's tongues will be so burnt from the cayenne pepper they won't be able to taste it."

"Can't hear you," he called over his shoulder.

"So, what were you saying about me?" Ruby asked, stirring the chili.

Birch could tell by her rigid posture that it bothered Ruby to hear they'd been talking about her. Obviously Ruby hadn't gotten used to Bobby's teasing or his candid way of speaking. She would someday. Then she chided herself. Ruby had already made it clear she was leaving after Monday. A pang of sadness ran through Birch. There was something about this girl that made her think of the daughter she and Bobby had lost so many years ago. Emily Robertina would have turned forty this year. Birch tried to imagine what she might have been like. It wouldn't have bothered Birch if she would have been a lot like Ruby.

"We were actually discussing Cassie and Sueann's little spat this morning. Did you hear it?"

Ruby nodded and continued stirring the chili. "I felt so bad for both of them. Even thought I've only seen him a few times, that

Hunter's bad news. My brother is a musician and I'm not saying they are all like this, but I wouldn't want my daughter dating one like Hunter. Especially when she was as young as Cassie." She glanced over at Birch. "I wish I could tell Cassie that she's darn lucky she has a mom who cares about what happens to her."

"That's exactly what she *doesn't* want to hear right now," Birch said.

"That's why I won't do it." She tapped the wooden spoon on the side of the pot. "People are going to love this."

"Have you ever been to a First Night celebration?" Birch asked.

Ruby shook her head. "I usually work on New Year's Eve. Tips are pretty good and for so many years I didn't have anywhere to go anyway."

Birch set her spoon on a spoon rest next to the chili and turned down the heat under both pots. "I think we can let these simmer awhile." The oven bell rang. She walked over to the large commercial oven and pulled out a batch of caramel-colored biscuits. "Perfect, as always." She set the pan down on a large iron trivet. "It's my mother's biscuit recipe. She used to make them for the ranch hands when we had roundups."

"I've never been to a roundup," Ruby said. "Is it like in books? Riding horses and roping cows and branding irons?"

"Pretty much," Birch said. "Back then it was. Today, the Circle MG still does it the old-fashioned way, more for tradition than efficiency. It would actually be more economical to hire a crew and have them bring their own lunches in a paper sack. But it's fun getting together with the other ranchers, the few of us left here in Cardinal Valley. The old men especially like it. A chance to relive old glories. The kids used to love it. When he was a boy, Cole used to get so excited the night before a roundup that he couldn't sleep. I'd sit up with him and we'd watch old Westerns until he fell asleep with his head in my lap." Using a bent spatula, Birch started lifting off biscuits and placing them on a cooling rack.

Ruby leaned against the wooden butcher block in the center of the kitchen. "It still feels strange to me, hearing about the life Cole had here in Cardinal. It's like we're talking about two entirely different people."

Birch didn't know what to answer. Maybe they *were* talking about two different people. The Cole before and the Cole after. Before and after. We all had pivotal moments in our lives, places where we'd always look back and think, *Right there, right then, that's when the change happened. That's when my life took a detour, that's when ever afterward, nothing was the same.*

"Is there anything else I can do to help?" Ruby asked. "I feel useless standing here watching you work."

Birch pointed her spatula at a platter of cooled biscuits. "You could wrap each of those individually in plastic wrap. They stay fresher that way and it's a little more sanitary."

Ruby smiled. "Sanitary is good. Where's the plastic wrap?"

Birch pointed to the drawer next to the sink. She watched Ruby dig through the drawer looking for the wrap and allowed herself a few seconds of daydreaming, pretending that Ruby had come here with Cole, that he'd brought her home to Cardinal to settle down, make a life, have some babies. Birch had such a longing to hold a baby in her arms. She remembered how Cole smelled as a newborn, milky and sweet, like some kind of exotic flower she'd never smelled before. It seemed like only a few years ago when June used to drop Cole off at the lodge for Birch to watch. Those were the happiest months of Birch's life. She would pretend Cole was hers, and losing Emily Robertina stopped hurting for the time that Birch rocked and fed her nephew. Before he turned two, without any warning, June stopped bringing Cole to Birch. Had she seen how much pleasure it brought Birch? Was it when Cole started becoming confused and calling Birch "Mama"? Or maybe it was Kitt McGavin's doing, something Birch wouldn't put past his malevolent heart. At any rate, June hired a Mexican girl to watch Cole out at the ranch, the one place she knew Birch couldn't go, not as long at Kitt was alive.

Birch sighed. This girl, Ruby, and her beloved Cole, what pretty babies they would have made. Lord, she thought, if there's a purpose in these kids suffering, I sure don't see it. I don't see it at all.

Ruby turned to Birch, her face questioning. "Did you say something?"

Birch felt her cheeks turn warm. She'd obviously been murmuring out loud, a habit she'd just recently caught herself doing. "Don't mind me. I've taken to talking out loud to myself lately. Symptom of old age, I guess."

"If that's a sign of old age, I'm in big trouble," Ruby said, laughing.

"It's good to hear I'm not alone," Birch said. "So, what are your plans? Long-term, I mean."

Ruby turned back to wrapping biscuits. "I don't know. It depends on what is going on with my brother. Maybe, if I like it, I'll settle down in Nashville. Then again, my brother ups and moves at the drop of a guitar string, so I'm not sure that's a great idea. Luckily, I can get a job anywhere. There's restaurants everywhere and they always need cooks."

"Maybe Sueann could use another one at the Lone Pine." Birch's voice was teasing.

Ruby kept her back to Birch, unaware of Birch's serious expression. "I doubt that will happen. Sueann's not too happy with me right now. She agrees with you, that the past should remain in the past."

"I've changed my mind," Birch said.

Ruby turned to look at her, her lips parting slightly in surprise. "You have? Why?"

Birch was tempted to tell Ruby that she knew what it felt like to be left out, that her own husband had excluded her from the truth all these years, something for which Birch had never quite forgiven him.

"I've had some time to think about it," she said instead. "I've decided that you have a perfect right to find out about your husband's past even if it means exposing the family to public scrutiny again."

Ruby's eyes widened in surprise. "You do?"

Birch nodded wondering if her words might come back to haunt her. "Frankly, that whole mess has been a secret too long. I think we all need to know what happened that night. And, in my opinion, the sooner, the better."

27

RUBY

After Ruby finished helping Birch in the kitchen, she wandered into the crowded hotel lobby to watch the preparations for First Night through the front window. The front door opened and Cassie walked in carrying a basket of corn bread muffins propped against her hip. She wore baggy army-green pants, a cocoa-colored sweatshirt that read VOTE FOR PEDRO and silver hoop earrings the diameter of a small apple. Her once blue hair had been dyed a sort of maroonish-black.

"Hi," Ruby said, going over to her. "Need help with those?"

"Nah," Cassie said. "I'm dropping them off with Aunt Birch to go with the chili."

"She made biscuits, too," Ruby said.

"Good, her biscuits are the bomb."

Ruby nodded over at the noisy crowd. "This First Night celebration looks like it's really something. It seems like there are more people here than at Christmas."

"Yeah, the lodge is always packed at New Year's now and the town just goes crazy." She shifted the basket of muffins to the other hip. "Well, as crazy as this lame town gets. We've only been doing First

Night since I was ten, but it's, like, totally famous now. This year there's three bands. One is an old-fart band, but the other two are pretty awesome."

"Who's Pedro?" Ruby asked, pointing to Cassie's sweatshirt.

"Haven't you seen *Napoleon Dynamite*?"

"No, is it a television show?"

Cassie shook her head, obviously amazed at Ruby's ignorance. "It's basically the coolest movie ever made. It's totally famous. You should rent it. Pedro is a character in the movie. He's running for class president."

"Oh," Ruby said, feeling a hundred years old. "So, what are you doing at First Night?"

Cassie made a face. "Working either the cafe or the lodge's booth like I've done since forever. Mom has me working a full shift today, too. Give me a break, where's a union when you need one? I think she's trying to keep me busy so I can't see my boyfriend. Like that's going to stop me."

Ruby didn't answer. She would have loved to tell Cassie just exactly what kind of guy she thought Hunter was, but this wasn't her battle.

"He's going to Carson City for a gig at a casino tonight," Cassie continued. "I'm so pissed off that my mom won't let me go. Like I'm a child or something."

"It might not be that much fun for you if you did go," Ruby said. "Hunter would be working the whole time and being under twenty-one in a casino limits a lot of things."

"Oh, that wasn't going to be a problem," she said flippantly. "Hunter got me a fake ID." She put a hand over her mouth. "Promise you won't tell my mom."

Oh, dear, Ruby thought. That was a promise she didn't want to make. Before Ruby had to try and finagle her way out of it, Hunter came through the front door. He stood in the doorway and searched the noisy crowd for Cassie. He wore baggy army pants identical to Cassie's and a black long-sleeve T-shirt depicting a leering Charles Manson. Ruby was glad Sueann wasn't here right now. The T-shirt alone would make any mom come unglued.

"Hey, babe," he said, coming over and putting his hand on her neck. She tilted her head back so he could kiss her.

"Hey," she said back. "You leaving already?"

"Yeah, we want to get to the club and check the sound system. Just wanted you to know we'll be staying at the Lucky Horseshoe Motel on Fifth Street. Paula and Terry are driving up later. Maybe you can catch a ride with them if the dragon lady changes her mind."

"Fat chance," Cassie said, her tone miserable. "You guys are having all the fun and I'm going to be serving chili."

"That'll be a gas," he said, laughing at his own joke. Cassie rolled her eyes at Ruby.

They were still laughing when Sueann walked in. The expression on her face caused Hunter to comment under his breath, "Shit. Dragon lady approaching runway . . ."

Sueann marched over to where they stood She didn't acknowledge either Ruby or Hunter. "Cassie, you were supposed to deliver those biscuits and come right back to the cafe."

"Chill out, Mom," Cassie said. "I'm, like, taking my break."

"You haven't worked long enough to earn a break," Sueann snapped. "It's a madhouse over at the cafe. We need you."

"I said I'm taking a break." She glanced over at Hunter and smirked. "It's the law, you know."

Sueann grabbed her upper arm. "Young lady, I've had about enough of your attitude."

"Leave me alone," Cassie hissed, jerking away.

"Yeah, leave her alone," Hunter added. "She's almost eighteen."

Bad move, young man, Ruby thought, bracing herself for the explosion.

Sueann slowly turned to face Hunter, her face white with anger. Her words were low and measured and reminded Ruby of a dog's low growl right before it bit. "If you don't walk out of here right this minute and leave my daughter alone, I will have you arrested for statutory rape. I've already looked into it and the charges would stick. Don't forget, her uncle Lucas is a lawyer and, though I doubt it's possible, he likes you even less than I do. Take a long, hard look at her, young man. Is she worth going to prison for?"

Hunter stared at Sueann, his mouth half open in shock. Then, without looking at Cassie, he lifted both hands in surrender. "Hey, man, I don't want any trouble." He walked out of the lodge without a backward glance.

Cassie whipped around to face her mother, her eyes bulging with fury. "I can't believe you did that! Who do you think you are?"

Sueann looked at her grimly. "Your mother."

Cassie's voice went shrill with hysteria. "I love him! How could you say that to him!"

"You don't have a clue what love is."

Cassie voice came out with a hiss. "I know one thing. I don't love *you*."

If her words hurt Sueann, her expression didn't show it. All those years of being a waitress, Ruby thought. All the obnoxious patrons with their demands for hotter French fries, rarer steaks, fresher bread, colder water, more butter, more butter, *more butter*. You learned to never let anyone see what you really felt. You learned never to let anyone see you hurt.

"Get back to work," Sueann said, her voice weary. "We have customers waiting." Then, still not acknowledging Ruby, she turned and walked out the front door.

Cassie stared after her mother. When a tear dripped down her cheek causing a black mascara rivulet, Ruby dug into her pocket and held out a clean tissue. Cassie took it, swiped it across her cheek and stuck it in the pocket of her baggy pants.

"She's going to be sorry she did that," Cassie said.

Ruby couldn't help defending Sueann. "She loves you. It's probably hard for her to realize you're growing up. You're all she has."

A look of fixed sullenness came over Cassie's face. "She needs to get a life." She gave her cheek another wipe with the back of her nail-chewed hand. "See you later."

"Okay," Ruby said, watching Cassie leave. Though she often longed for a child, especially when she saw young mothers and their babies, this part of parenting was not something she desired to experience. Then again, did anyone? Did any parent ever anticipate that the gurgling infant in their arms would ever be capable of explosive adolescent anger, sullen rudeness, being hooked on drugs, sleeping around or ever saying the words "I don't love you"? Did any mother ever anticipate having to stand in a courtroom and watch her son be charged with murder? Much less, the murder of his own father?

She sighed. All of this speculation wasn't doing her any good. Keeping herself busy over the next few days would be the best thing. Though she didn't particularly want to attend First Night it was preferable to brooding alone in her room. She'd offer to help at the lodge's food booth. That would make this evening go by faster. Then only two more nights here in Cardinal and she could leave.

She went upstairs and started packing her clothes in anticipation for leaving Monday afternoon. Afterward, she sat in the leather chair and stared at the phone, debating whether she should call Nash again. No, that would just cause her to worry more and make the next three days seem longer. If anything really bad was happening with him, surely his girlfriend, Angela, would call her.

Cardinal's First Night celebration officially started with the ringing of the old Methodist church bell. A large section of Main Street was closed off and was already curb-to-curb people. There were mimes and clowns making balloon animals and a one-man band who seemed to only know three songs. The Girl Scouts sold caramel apples, the Tokopah County 4-H Club sold corn dogs and the Cardinal Pauite-Shoshone Tribe had a booth selling their native crafts, beaded earrings and coiled baskets. Ruby stopped at the booth and fingered a pair of delicate, beaded earrings depicting galloping red horses.

"Would you like to try them on?" a young Native American girl asked. She was dressed in blue jeans and a blue, puffy down jacket. Three grayish-white feathers were stuck in her long, black hair.

"Okay," Ruby said. She put them on and looked in the hand mirror the girl held.

"They look great," she said.

"I'll take them," Ruby said, even though they were not close to being something she'd ever wear. But they were made in Cardinal and she had a sudden desire to take something with her from Cole's hometown. It struck her in that moment that when she left on Monday, Cole would be staying here. The devastating sorrow that flooded her caught her by surprise. Though she knew the ashes in the wooden box weren't actually him, they were all she had left. She pushed the feeling aside to think about later.

The chilly winter air seemed to promise snow before the night was over, but for now was scented with roasting corn-on-the-cob, hot apple cider and spicy barbecued meat. The local Cattlemen's Club was selling dinners of beef ribs and pinto beans, the money earned being split between the fireworks fund and rodeo scholarships. After a quick trip through the festival, she went back to the lodge's booth where Birch accepted her offer to help serve.

"Can you watch the booth alone for a minute?" Birch asked. "I need to fetch more biscuits."

"Absolutely," Ruby said.

A few minutes later, Cassie walked up, her expression as sulky as when she left the lodge hours ago. She wore some kind of hair ornaments that blinked red and green, reminding Ruby of traffic lights.

"Hey, Cassie," Ruby said, handing two bowls of chili to a couple wearing matching red and black argyle sweaters.

"Hey," Cassie replied unenthusiastically.

Birch came down the lodge steps carrying more wrapped biscuits. "Hello, sweetie," she said to Cassie. Then she said to Ruby, "Did you manage to see the rest of the booths?"

"Yes, ma'am," she said. "This is quite a celebration."

"It's lame," Cassie said. "Everything in this town is. It's totally manufactured fun. Totally fake."

Birch raised her eyebrows and didn't answer, handing her greatniece the basket of wrapped biscuits. "Lay these out for me, okay?" She turned to Ruby. "We do love our festivals here in Cardinal. This one started about ten years ago. Too many kids—and adults, if you want the truth—were spending New Year's Eve drinking and driving and shooting off guns. We figured this was a good, family alternative. Gordon down at the sheriff's office says it has actually lowered the drinking and driving statistics. It can be cold, but that's half the fun. And most folks can walk to the festivities and walk home, no motor vehicles involved."

"I think it's great," Ruby said.

Cassie snorted and continued stacking biscuits. "I still think Mom's being totally paranoid about Hunter."

"By this time next year you'll be eighteen," Birch pointed out. "You'll be able to do whatever you want on New Year's Eve."

"For sure," Cassie said. "And I will, too."

"And be liable as an adult," Birch added. "That means when you do something bad, it's big people's jail, not the Youth Authority."

Cassie flashed her a withering look. "I *know* that, Aunt Birch. For the record, I don't plan on doing anything where I'll end up in jail."

"I know," she said, patting her niece's arm. "Just wanted to remind you."

Ely came by to grab bowls of chili for himself and Lucas, who was hiding out in Bill's Barbershop "He's trying to avoid Maxie's oldest granddaughter."

"Melinda?" Birch said. "She's fifteen years his junior. What's he afraid of?"

Ely winked at Birch. "She's got a Mount Whitney–size crush on him and is determined to be in his vicinity the minute midnight hits."

Birch laughed. "That's what he gets for being such a handsome and eligible bachelor."

"There's a handsome, eligible bachelor in Cardinal?" Sueann said, walking up in time to catch the tail end of Birch's sentence. "Where?"

"Lucas is hiding from Melinda, the baker's granddaughter," Ruby said lightly, hoping that Sueann would call a truce. Though she knew it shouldn't matter, for some reason Ruby didn't want to leave Cardinal with Sueann angry at her.

Sueann didn't answer, but looked at Ely in question.

"She wants his body," Ely said, grinning.

"She's a child. A promiscuous one, but a child, nevertheless."

"Look who's talking," Cassie muttered loud enough for everyone to hear.

"What did you say?" her mother said, whipping around quick as a cat.

Cassie's voice was hard and clear. "Just how old were *you* when you and Dad screwed around? Aren't you the pot calling the kettle black?"

"You know, grasshopper," Ely said. "Technically, that is a racist remark."

Cassie and Sueann ignored him and continued glaring at each other.

"Looks like you need a break," Birch said to Cassie. "Why don't you go have a caramel apple? My treat." She pulled a five dollar bill from her pocket and pressed it into Cassie's hand. Cassie stuck the money in her pocket, gave her mother one more angry look and walked away.

"The proper response would be *thank you*," Sueann called after her. Cassie didn't even turn around.

"I'm sorry," Sueann said to Birch. She looked closer to losing control than Ruby had ever seen her.

"Try not to worry," Birch said, putting her arm around Sueann's shoulders. "She's being seventeen. That's a curable disease, believe it or not." She ran her fingers through her white hair. "Lord, I must look a wreck. I feel like we've been working for days. My dogs are barking for some relief." She glanced down at her high-top snow boots.

"Why don't you take a break and I'll watch the booth?" Ruby said.

"How about coming with us to pick up the fireworks?" Sueann asked. "Bobby, Lincoln and I are driving down to Ridgecrest to get them."

"What're they doing in Ridgecrest?" Birch asked.

"We combined our order in with theirs so we could save on the delivery cost. They were supposed to be there hours ago, but the delivery truck blew a tire and had to be towed into town."

Birch hesitated. "I don't want to leave Ruby alone at the booth for too long. You know how busy it can get. We don't know when Cassie will come back."

"More like *if* she'll come back," Sueann said, frowning. "Honestly,

I'm so angry at her. After going to bat for her about that tattoo, this is the thanks I get."

"I can stay and help after I take this chili to Lucas," Ely said.

"Really, I'd be fine alone," Ruby said.

Birch glanced out over the crowd, where a group of ladies across the street wearing neon-colored top hats waved to her. "Actually, there's my knitting group. I would love to go over and see what's going on with them. I am so busy this time of year that I missed our Christmas brunch." She turned to Sueann. "You go on without me. The front of Bobby's truck really only seats three comfortably. I'd feel better staying here and working the booth."

"Okay," Sueann said, still not looking at Ruby. "We'll see you in a little while."

"Be careful," Birch said. "The roads are icy and you know how crazy tourists drive this time of year."

"What time of year *don't* they drive crazy?" Sueann said.

"I'll be back shortly," Birch told Ruby.

"I'll stay until you get back," Ely said. "Lucas can wait for his chili."

"Take your time," Ruby said to Birch, sitting down on one of the canvas director's chair printed with the lodge's name and triple pine tree logo. "Ely and I can handle things here."

Ruby leaned back and watched the crowd wandering around visiting and waiting for the fireworks planned for midnight. She wanted to absorb every little bit of Cardinal to reflect on later, when she was far away from this town.

She let Ely help the next few customers, leaning her head back and closing her eyes, letting the ocean sound of the crowd wash over her when it was interrupted by June McGavin's gruff, no-nonsense voice.

"Don't get too comfortable, Miss Stoddard," June said. "This will be your last First Night in Cardinal."

Ruby stood up and walked over to Cole's mother who was dressed tonight in sharply creased jeans, a black silk cowboy shirt and an expensive-looking rust and black Pendleton jacket. Walt Creston stood next to June, his arm draped across her shoulders in a proprietary way.

"I'll be leaving after our meeting," Ruby said.

"Good," June said, giving Ruby a level look. "I appreciate that you see how inappropriate it is for you to remain in Cardinal. It's good for people to know their place."

Ruby felt heat start to burn in her chest. "What do you mean by that?"

June's expression stayed even. "Let's be honest, if life had worked out how I planned, my son would not have had to marry someone like you."

A million responses sped through Ruby's mind, but all she could see was Cole's face in his mother's. Tears burned the back of her eyes. She felt Ely move around her, blocking June from Ruby's view.

"That was uncalled for, Mrs. McGavin," Ely said.

"Ely, this is none of your business," Walt said. "Back off."

Ely didn't move an inch. Ruby pushed her way around him, angry now. "He has as much business in this as anyone."

"How is that?" Walt asked.

Ruby hesitated, not certain it was her place to divulge Ely's relationship with Cole.

"Cole and I were friends," Ely said.

June narrowed her eyes. "What do you mean?"

"Cole was my friend and my sponsor. He overcame a lot of demons in his life and he helped a lot of people overcome their own."

Ruby looked at Ely in surprise. So that was what he meant when he said Cole had saved his life. Cole's relationships with so many people in this town were weaved together in a warp and woof tapestry that continued to amaze her. Like his father, he'd made his mark, but with people, not things.

June's nostrils flared. "Are you saying that my son was an alcoholic? Was he drinking the night he drove his truck off that highway?"

Ely's face looked pained. "I hope not."

Ruby felt her chest tighten. "No, he wasn't. It said so in the coroner's report."

June surprised Ruby by turning around and walking away.

Ely put a hand on Ruby's shoulder. "Are you okay?"

She nodded. "Thank you for defending me. I just wish it was next Tuesday and this place was nothing but a memory." She grabbed her purse and hitched it over her shoulder. "I don't think I'm in the mood for any more celebrating tonight."

She walked away without looking back. She was so tired of this town, this family, even, God forgive her, of Cole. She was angrier at him than she'd ever been. How could he do this to her? Leave and thrust her into this mess? It was the most cowardly thing she could imagine. The moment the thought flashed through her mind, she regretted it.

"I'm sorry," she whispered out loud.

She walked toward the lodge, leaving the First Night revelers behind her. More than anything she wanted to be alone. After Monday, everything would be finished, and she could leave and start to put her life back together.

RUBY

She fell asleep in the leather chair in her room, awakening at seven p.m., her stomach growling with hunger. Though she'd served hundreds of bowls of chili, she hadn't eaten any dinner herself. Outside her window, the First Night celebration was still going strong. In the distance, she could hear a band playing "I Heard It Through the Grapevine."

She sat there a minute, contemplating her hunger. Though she was in no mood for a joyous New Year's celebration, there was no reason to start out the year being hungry. Not with all the food booths right in front of the lodge. She'd run downstairs and grab something to eat at one of the booths, then come back to her room.

She bought a chicken burrito at the VFW booth and was walking by Lucas's saddle shop when he burst out of the door, his face rubbery with panic.

"Ruby?"

"What's wrong?"

"There's been an accident. Bobby, Sueann and Lincoln."

Her insides turned to ash. "Where?"

His forehead wrinkled in pain.

"Are you okay?" she asked.

"Yes," he said. "I mean, no." He put a hand over his eyes. "I've got a migraine." He took a deep breath and dropped his hand. "Louise is the admittance clerk at the hospital. We went to school together. She said I need to get there fast. They're flying my uncle to Reno."

"What about Sueann and Lincoln?"

His face contorted in agony. "She said Sueann was hurt, but is going to be okay. She didn't say anything about Lincoln."

"Where's the hospital?" she asked.

"Edge of town. About a mile. I was inside trying to work on that saddle, the one for Bernie Gorman . . ."

"I can drive us to the hospital," she said, holding out her hand for his truck keys. "Give me directions."

Within ten minutes they were pulling into the parking lot of the small, Tokopah County Hospital. Though she'd never been religious, she found herself asking God or whoever was up there to please spare these three people. Each of them had been kind to her at a time when she really needed it. They don't deserve this, she pleaded. Please, they don't deserve this.

Lucas was out of the car and running for the emergency room doors before she turned off the ignition. She hurried after him through the cold night. Above her, she could hear the soft, distant chopping sound of a helicopter.

It was busy inside the small emergency room with the typical injuries that happened during a public festival—cuts, scrapes, a vomiting child, a teenager whose pierced ear had been torn. Lucas was already at the reception desk talking to the admittance clerk. "Where are they?"

"Go right on back, Lucas," the woman said. "Birch is here already. Your mom and Derek are on their way. But, I'm warning you, it's pretty bad. They were hit head-on by a van. Bunch of drunk kids on their way back from Mammoth."

Lucas stopped, frozen in place. "Sueann? Bobby?"

"Sueann's the least injured," the woman said. "Some broken bones. Bobby has internal injuries. The medivac helicopter just arrived. Like I told you on the phone, they're taking him to Reno." Her face grew still, her eyes darted away from Lucas.

"What? What is it? Louise, tell me." Lucas placed both his palms on the counter and leaned toward her.

Ruby lightly touched his jacket sleeve, wanting to comfort him, but not really knowing where her place in all this was.

The clerk, Louise, looked over at Ruby, then back at Lucas. "Two kids in the van were killed."

"Oh, no," Ruby whispered.

"And Mr. Holyoke . . ." The clerk swallowed, the skin around her eyes turning pale.

"Lincoln?" Lucas said. "What happened to Lincoln?"

"I'm sorry," Louise said. "But he died at the scene."

BIRCH

It was the phone call everyone dreads and no one ever really expects to receive.

"You'd better get here quick, Mrs. Hernandez," said Louise, the emergency room clerk. "There's been a car accident."

"Who?" Birch managed to ask. She'd come inside the lodge to use the bathroom and was walking by the front desk when the phone rang.

"Bobby, Sueann and Lincoln," Louise said, her voice soft, but clear. Louise had been a student of Birch's. If Birch had to hear this kind of news from anyone, she would have chosen Louise. She had always been a calm girl; nothing ruffled her easygoing manner, perfect for her job. "Right outside of Independence. The ambulances just arrived."

"How are . . ." Birch couldn't finish her sentence.

"There's a call in for a helicopter for Bobby. They're taking him to Reno."

Birch's head grew fuzzy. A medivac helicopter to Reno meant surgery. Surgery that was too difficult for their little hospital.

"Don't let them leave without me," she said. Then added, "Unless they need to. I'll get there some other way." Maybe there was someone at the airport who could fly her. The thought of flying over all those mountains scared her to the depths of her soul, but not as much as not being there when Bobby woke up from his surgery. And he *would* wake up. Please, Lord. Please. *Please.* It was the only prayer she could think of right now.

"Do you have someone to drive you to the hospital?" she asked.

"No, but don't worry. I'm able to drive." She took a deep breath. "How's Sueann? And Lincoln?"

"Sueann's didn't look too bad. She's in X-ray. They didn't order a helicopter for her." Louise paused a moment. "Mr. Holyoke . . ."

Birch put a trembling hand over her face. "He didn't make it?"

"No," Louise whispered. "He was driving. He got the worst of it."

Birch wiped her wet hand on the side of her blouse. No time for tears right now. The family had to be told. "Louise, sweetie, could you call Lucas at his saddle shop? If he's not there, he might be at Bill's Barbershop or at his apartment. Darn, I wish I had me one of those cell phones right now."

She'd always laughed at them, not understanding why people, especially young people, were connected to each with those things, like long, electronic umbilical cords. Though 9/11 had somewhat changed her mind about them—she was glad for those who had been able to speak one last time to their loved ones—most of the time she found them to be an irritation.

"I'm going to get me one," she murmured to herself as she ran out the back door of the lodge.

On the drive to the hospital, Cassie came to mind. "We need to find her before someone else tells her about it," she said out loud.

At the hospital, Louise told her that Bobby was in room one, but he wasn't conscious. The helicopter was due any minute. Sueann was in X-ray, but it looked like she would be okay. She had a broken leg, arm and some ribs.

"Oh, no," Birch said, her legs feeling unsteady. "Bobby . . ."

"Here's Dr. Mapson," Louise said.

A young woman in green surgical pants and top, someone who hadn't grown up here, strolled toward Birch. "Mrs. Hernandez?"

"Yes," she said, straightening her spine. She needed to be strong for

Bobby. She patted Louise's hand, thanking her for the momentary support.

"The helicopter will be here soon. Mr. Hernandez has sustained considerable internal damage. He also has a bad break in his collarbone and his left leg. We just don't have the facilities to operate here."

"I understand," she said. "Can I go with him?"

"Certainly. Is there anyone you'd like us to call?"

"Louise is taking care of that, but thank you. May I see him?"

The doctor nodded. "He's pretty heavily sedated."

"How's Sueann?" she asked, following the doctor.

"Mrs. McGavin should be fine," the young doctor said. "She'll be uncomfortable for a while, but she's healthy. Her bones should heal quickly."

Birch didn't ask about Lincoln. She knew it was something she'd have to face eventually, but right now all she could concentrate on was Bobby. A thought flashed briefly through her mind. Where was Lincoln's family? Did he have any? Who would know? She knew when Lucas arrived, he'd take care of that, find out who to notify.

When she walked into the brightly lit room and saw Bobby lying on the bed, attached to all sorts of quietly beeping equipment, she felt light-headed. Blackness started creeping in around the edges of her eyesight. A foot away from him, she froze, unable to walk any closer.

"Mrs. Hernandez, are you all right?" Dr. Mapson asked quietly.

She nodded, inhaling deeply. "May I touch him?"

"Certainly," she said. "Just be careful." She turned to Louise. "Could you please find Mrs. Hernandez a chair?" She fingered the stethoscope around her slender neck as if it were still something unfamiliar. "I'll check back on you in a few minutes."

Birch nodded her thanks, then sat down next to Bobby, pulling the chair as close as possible. She stroked the top of his large, brown hand. It was cool to her touch. Was that good or not?

A nurse, another person unfamiliar to Birch, came in and checked the beeping machines. "Medivac should be here pretty soon, Mrs. Hernandez. Is there anything I can get for you? Some water or coffee?"

"No, thank you," Birch said.

She sat with him, stroking his hand, willing him to survive. "Don't you even think about leaving me, chief," she whispered. "We still have things to do."

Just before they came to load him into the helicopter, his eyes opened.

"Bobby!" she cried, feeling as if her insides would melt. "I love you. I'm right here."

The whites of his eyes were red as apples. "Birch," he whispered. "It . . . what . . ."

"Don't talk," she said, touching a finger on his lips. "You're going to be okay. Just concentrate on that."

"Tell . . . tell . . ." His voice grew soft, almost inaudible.

She leaned closer. "What, sweetheart? Tell what?"

"Sueann . . ." His lips struggled to form words.

"She's fine," Birch said, stroking his cheek. "A few broken bones. She'll be fine." She prayed he wouldn't ask about Lincoln.

"Tell Sueann . . . it's time . . . to tell . . ." His eyes closed, exhausted from the effort.

"Tell what?" Birch asked.

His eyes opened slowly. "Birch . . . love you."

Before she could answer, the medivac personnel came into the room.

"It's time to go, Mrs. Hernandez," the young man in the blue uniform said. "Could you please step aside for a few minutes while we get him ready?"

She did as she was told, watching these young people, entrusting the person she loved the most in the world to kids who seemed to her barely old enough to drive, much less care for a broken human body.

"Be careful," she whispered. Then she closed her eyes briefly, picturing the simple walnut cross that hung above the altar at church. "Help us, Lord," she prayed. "I believe you're in control and I trust you. But, please, help us."

RUBY

They were wheeling Bobby down the hallway toward the emergency room double doors when Lucas and Ruby met them. His aunt Birch followed behind, talking to a young, curly-headed woman who appeared to be the doctor.

"How is he?" Lucas asked, rushing up to his aunt. Ruby stayed back, giving them privacy.

"We're going to Reno," Birch said, her normally strong voice subdued. "He has internal damage." Lucas put his arm around her shoulders, resting his cheek on the top of her snowy hair.

"He'll be okay," Lucas said. Ruby knew those were empty words, but sometimes, you didn't want to hear the truth. Sometimes you wanted nothing but assurances no matter how false they were.

"What can I do?" he asked. The emergency room's flickering florescent lights shadowed his face and sharpened his cheekbones.

Birch pulled away. Her cheeks shined with tears. "He asked for something. Something from Sueann."

"Sueann?"

A uniformed paramedic came through the room's automatic doors. "Mrs. Hernandez? We need to go now."

She kissed Lucas's cheek. "He wanted Sueann to know he thought it was time to tell. That's all he said. I'll call you from Reno." She hurried out of the double doors, calling over her shoulder. "Call his family, Lucas. And find Cassie. And Lincoln's family. Someone needs to tell his family. Oh, those poor people. I love you." The doors slid shut before he could answer.

He turned to Ruby. "What did she just say?"

"That there was something that Sueann needed to tell."

"What in the world did he . . ." Then it dawned on him. "What happened with my father. Do you think . . .?"

"The only way to know is to ask," Ruby said. "Let's find Sueann."

Louise informed them she'd already been checked into a room. She was alone when they walked in, groggy from pain medication. Her left arm and leg were both in casts.

"Sueann," Lucas said, walking over to her.

"Lucas?" Her voice was an agonized cry. "What happened? Where's Bobby and Lincoln?" Tears started flowing down her face. She was so pale that her freckles stood out like tiny drops of copper rain. "Where's my baby? I want to see Cassie. They've tried calling her cell phone, but she doesn't answer."

He turned to Ruby, a question on his face.

"I'll see if I can find her," Ruby said, though she had no clue how to go about doing that.

She walked out of the room into the hallway. Maybe she'd head downtown and just start asking teenagers. In a town this size, they all knew each other so surely one of them would know where to find her or at least give Ruby a hint about where to look. A nervous feeling came over her. This night had that same surreal feeling as the early morning the coroner had called her, the feeling that this was happening to someone else. Though she hadn't known Lincoln long, she felt his loss with a sharp pang. Someone that vital, that alive, and then he was just gone, like an amputated limb, leaving behind only a phantom pain.

When the emergency room door opened, she ran into Ely. He caught her by her shoulders, keeping them from colliding.

"I heard . . ."

"There was an accident when Lincoln, Bobby and Sueann were picking up the fireworks," she said, her words tumbling over each other in an avalanche. "A head-on collision with some kids. Bobby's being flown to Reno. Sueann's okay except for a broken leg and arm, some ribs too, I think. She wants Cassie, but Cassie won't answer her cell phone."

"Lincoln?"

She choked. "Oh, Ely, Lincoln died."

Ely put his arm around Ruby and led her outside where the snow was gently falling.

She looked up and said, "Will the helicopter be okay flying in this weather?"

"They know what they're doing," Ely said calmly. "Don't worry about that right now." He pulled a cell phone out of his denim jacket and punched some numbers. "She's probably screening her mom's calls and doesn't recognize the hospital phone number."

He waited a few minutes, then said, "Cassie, get your butt over to the hospital. Your mom's been in an accident." He listened a minute. "No, she's okay, but she's got a broken leg and arm." He looked over at Ruby. "What room?"

"Five," she answered.

He told Cassie the room number and repeated that she needed to get here quickly. When he got off, he asked, "Does Lucas know?"

"Yes, he's in with Sueann right now."

"Let's go tell them Cassie's on her way."

Just as they were about to go back inside, a shiny black Cadillac pulled up next to the emergency room exit. They watched it swing into a handicapped parking space. June and Derek McGavin stepped out.

"What are you doing here?" June said to Ruby.

Before Ruby could answer, Ely said, "Bobby's on his way to Reno for surgery. Birch is with him. Sueann has a broken arm and leg." He took Ruby's arm and started walking back into the hospital. "Sueann's in room five. We're going there now."

"Who does he think he is?" Ruby heard June say behind them. "He's not a part of this family."

Sueann's eyes widened when June and Derek walked into the room. "Where's Cassie?" she whispered.

"I got in touch with her," Ely said. "She's on her way. She's at her friend Meg's house."

Sueann struggled to sit up. "I have to do it, Lucas. Bobby asked me to."

"You can do it later," he said. "When you feel better."

"No," she said, her voice firm. "Now. We don't know . . ." A sob escaped from deep inside her. She looked past Ely and Ruby directly at her former mother-in-law. "What Bobby was trying to tell me is I need to tell the truth. He's right. It's been too long. Lucas and Ruby deserve to know about Carson."

"No!" June said, marching over to Sueann's bed. "It's none of their business."

Lucas turned to his mother, his face furious. "None of *my* business? Damn it, he was my *father*! You know, Derek knows, Cole knew, Sueann and Bobby know. I've spent my whole life in the dark about what happened that night and I'm not leaving this room until I'm told the truth." He turned and pointed at Ruby. "She was thrust into this mess of a family without any idea of what we were. The least we can do is give her an explanation."

June's face stiffened with anger. "Lucas, you have no idea what you're saying."

He turned his back to her. "Sueann, tell us what happened that night. Bobby is right. It's time."

Sueann's normally mobile mouth went rigid with pain. "Your father . . ." Her voice faltered.

"No!" Derek cried, taking a step forward.

Ely moved from Ruby's side to stop him.

"Fine," June said, putting a hand on Derek's arm. "Just go ahead and wreck our family, Sueann. Frankly, you ruined it eighteen years ago."

"He raped me," Sueann said, her voice emotionless. "That's what started everything, Lucas. Your father raped me."

31

LUCAS

Lucas stared at Sueann, trying to take in what he'd just heard.

"No," his mother said, her voice fierce.

Lucas turned to his mother, shocked, both at Sueann's words and his mother's reaction. He glanced at Derek, who stared at the shiny, tiled floor and Ruby, whose face was so white she looked ready to pass out. Ely stood next to the door, his dark face expressionless.

Sueann's cheeks were wet with tears. "Poor Cole. He suffered the most. I was hurt . . . but Cole . . . he bore the brunt of it all. I, at least, got Cassie."

Lucas froze for a moment, trying to piece together what she was saying. "Cassie?" He turned to his mother and said. "What does Cassie have to do with it?" What Sueann implied made him feel like vomiting.

June's face struggled to hide her emotion. "I am not going to be a party to this. Take me home, Derek."

Derek looked up, his own face ravaged with pain. "We can't keep it a secret any longer."

"I'm leaving with or without you," she said.

He looked over at Sueann, his voice tender. "I'll tell them what happened that night. You've been through enough. I am so sorry, Suzie. Really, I am."

"Thank you," she whispered.

"Derek!" His mother's voice snapped like a firecracker.

He turned to look at his mother, his shoulders slumped under his navy cowboy shirt, his expression tired with defeat. "I'm sorry, Mom. I can't do this any longer."

"Coward," she hissed at her middle son. He flinched as if she'd hit him. Then she was gone.

Everyone in the room waited, watching Derek. When he started talking, he dropped his head, muffling his voice. "You know how women loved Dad. They could never stay away from him, not even . . ." He swallowed hard, unable to finish his sentence.

Lucas couldn't help looking at Sueann who had laid her head back on the pillow and closed her eyes. Her mouth was pressed closed as if she were a young child refusing a bitter-tasting medicine.

"It was in September. Remember that year, Lucas? When Dad got that automatic skeet shooter?"

Lucas nodded, remembering the barbecue clearly. He never got to use it that weekend because so many of Dad's friends wanted to try it out. There weren't many kids his age at the party, which had made him mad. There'd been a party at a friend's house, but June wouldn't let him go. He spent most of the evening up in his room eating beef jerky and watching old movies on television.

"Sueann and I had just started dating," Derek said.

Sueann interrupted, her voice wavering. "I was so sad about my mother dying and the rum made me feel warm and happy."

"There were so many people there," Derek said. "No one noticed that Sueann and I were putting rum in our Cokes." He inhaled deeply. "We got into a fight. I don't even remember about what."

Sueann opened her eyes. "You wanted to date other girls. You wanted to go out with Jodi Wilson. She worked at the drugstore."

Derek looked embarrassed. Lucas couldn't tell if it was because of what they argued about or because he didn't remember. "She left town right after that."

"Derek and I didn't ever get along," Sueann said. "We always argued. Cole walked in on us fighting in the barn. He intervened, calmed us down. Said we should stay away from each other for a while, before we said things we'd regret." She shifted in bed, moved the cast on her broken arm, grimacing in pain.

Derek moved over to the window, turning his back to everyone in the room. "Yeah, Cole jumped right in and made everything better. Good old King Cole, always there to lend a helping hand."

Lucas hadn't heard Derek call Cole that since they were kids. He used to tease him with the nickname, mocking his position in the family.

"He cared about us," Sueann said.

Derek turned to look at her. The pain in his face shocked Lucas, and he realized that Derek had loved Sueann and, perhaps, still did. "He cared about you."

Her answer was a whisper. "That's not true."

"And it was always him you loved, not me."

Sueann turned her face on her pillow and didn't answer.

Lucas looked over at Ruby who stood still as a fawn. Her face seemed ready to shatter.

Derek's face became grim. "It doesn't matter now. The truth is you were drunk and mad and not thinking straight and Dad took advantage of that."

There was a long silence. Finally, Lucas couldn't stand it. "What happened?"

Derek started to speak, but Sueann turned her head back to look at them. "It's my story, Derek. I need to tell it."

He gave a quick nod in agreement.

She took a shallow, shuttery breath. "I was in the barn looking at the horses, trying to stop crying, to calm down. Carson came in and started talking to me, teasing me. You know how funny he could be when he wanted. He told me I was pretty, that I was going to be a beautiful woman. It sounds dumb, I know. But I was sixteen and insecure and no man had ever talked to me like that. He said he had something to show me in his office, pictures of a new horse he was thinking about buying. You know how horse crazy I was. We were there and I was so tipsy and he was so . . . you know your father . . . it was hard to say no . . . before I knew it he was . . ." She broke down, unable to go on.

Lucas felt his stomach lurch, wanting not to imagine the scene. Cole had been right all along, it was better not knowing.

"You ran to Cole," Derek said. He moved toward her, his hand gripping his cowboy hat. "You ran to him, not me."

"You would have blamed me," she cried. "You *did* blame me. All those years we were married. You blamed *me*."

He blew an angry breath through his nose. "You could have said no. You could have fought him off."

"I was sixteen years old and drunk! I was stupid, but, I was *sixteen*." Sueann started to softly sob. "It was my first time. I barely knew what was happening."

Ruby moved silently across the room to Sueann's side. She sat carefully down on the bed and took Sueann's free hand. She didn't say a word, but just held her hand.

Lucas shook his head, trying to readjust his father's image. He'd been a strong, often intimidating man, but Lucas would have never guessed he was a sexual predator. As a public defender, he'd worked around people like that for years, had even been assigned to defend them in court. Why was he so surprised? He knew they never looked like the scary monsters people wanted them to look like. They almost always resembled your easygoing neighbor who loans you his hedge clippers, the funny guy who worked in the cubicle or at the worktable next to you, the woman who teaches your children or your own father.

"What did Cole do?" Lucas asked.

Derek shrugged. "What could he do? He confronted Dad the next day after Dad was sober, and he denied it, of course. When Cole screwed up enough guts to go to Mom, she just said that Dad had always had a "problem" with young girls. That Sueann wasn't the first and probably wouldn't be the last. That they had a special fund set up for his little messes." He cleared his throat harshly as if it contained some disgusting bit of food. "His little messes. Who knows how many little messes he's caused in this town."

Sueann looked directly at Ruby, as if telling only her the rest of the story. "Three months later, I found out I was pregnant. I hadn't told anyone about it, but my father eventually figured it out and pried the story out of me. He confronted Carson. Carson told him he'd pay for the abortion, but then just laughed and said my father should keep a closer eye on me. My dad said he would have killed him if it hadn't been for Mom being so close to dying. If he had gone to prison, John and I would have ended up in foster homes. Dad was never the same after that night. I think it's what eventually killed him."

"Your brother never knew the truth," Lucas said.

Sueann shook her head. "No, that was the whole reason for the wedding. Me and Derek . . ."

"Yes," Derek said. "I did my duty and Cole did his." His voice was flat, unemotional. "That's the thing about us McGavin boys. We always step up to the plate."

"What happened after Mr. Henley went to Dad?" Lucas asked.

"That same night Dad and Mom had a huge fight. You were in town. Cole and I were there and overheard them. Mom said he had to stop all his screwing around, but especially with girls under eighteen, that it was eventually going to bring the family down." Derek's face contorted in memory. "He said he doubted that was going to happen and that in some cultures, girls the age of Sueann were married with babies already. Mom started crying . . ."

"Mom?" Lucas said.

"Cole, ever the white knight, rushed into the den and told Dad exactly what he thought of him. That he needed to stop, that he needed psychiatric help."

Lucas could imagine his father's reaction. "He obviously didn't agree."

Derek gave a cynical laugh. "To say the least. He said he wasn't hurting anyone, that every woman he'd ever screwed gave her consent. He called Cole the crazy one. And he said that, someday, Cole would know what he was experiencing, that he had the same genetics. Dad said, chances were, all of us boys would turn out just like him. He said he hoped we would. It would give us something to talk about."

Blood throbbed in Lucas's temple. What kind of father wishes that on his sons? "Then what?"

"Cole called him a disgusting son of a bitch. He said he didn't deserve to have the life he did."

"And I bet Dad laughed," Lucas said bitterly.

Derek cocked his head. Behind him, Lucas could hear people in the hallway, laughing and singing some song. "Actually, he didn't. He picked up the .45 he'd just cleaned, loaded it and then handed it to Cole."

"What?"

"Cole took the gun and pointed it at Dad. He was so mad that I could see the gun tremble. Dad told him to go ahead and shoot, that was the only way he would stop. He said Cole might be the only one of us with balls enough to do it. *Then* he laughed."

Derek grew glassy. "Cole fired once. That was it. It sounds weird, but I swear Dad looked almost . . . glad. That was it. Cole only did what Dad told him to do." Derek looked back down at the ground. "And I did my part and married Sueann, let everyone think that Cassie was mine. Like I've always said, Lucas." His face looked ravaged and raw. "You were the lucky one. You got to have a life."

"Cassie is . . ." Lucas started to say, but was interrupted by a small moan coming from the doorway.

"A freak," Cassie said.

RUBY

Cassie turned and ran back into the hospital corridor.

"Someone go after her," Sueann cried, trying to sit up.

"I'll go," Lucas said.

"Yes," she said, her eyes bright red and almost swollen shut. "Cassie will listen to you."

"I'll stay with Sueann," Ely said.

Ruby released Sueann's hand. "Would you like me to go with Lucas? Maybe I can help."

"Thank you," Sueann said.

"We'll call you as soon as we talk to her," Lucas promised.

In the hallway, Lucas said, "Let's try the lobby first, then the cafeteria. Maybe she hasn't left the building."

They found her huddled outside the front entrance sobbing and talking to someone on her cell phone.

"Cassie," Lucas said, his voice gentle. "We need to talk."

Cassie disconnected and said, "Tell them I'm fine, but I don't want to talk about this, not tonight. I'll be at Julie's house."

Lucas placed a hand on his niece's shoulder. "Would like us to drive you?"

She wouldn't look at Lucas. "She's picking me up here."

"We'll wait, then," Lucas said.

"Whatever," she replied.

The fifteen-minute wait was excruciating for all of them. Ruby wanted to step in and tell Cassie that she should go be with her mother, that no matter what had happened in the past, this was her *family*. That meant something. She wanted to tell her that her mother was suffering in ways that Cassie could not understand.

But she kept quiet. Because to a hurt and betrayed seventeen-year-old the only thing that mattered was her feelings. Sueann and Cassie would work this out eventually.

While they waited, Lucas told Cassie about Bobby. "He's on his way to Reno now. Aunt Birch is with him. He has internal damage and they need to operate."

She stared silently past him at the dark mountains, flipping the lid of her cell phone open and closed.

Lucas gave Ruby a frustrated look. What should I do now? his expression seemed to say. Ruby shrugged. To be honest, she didn't have a clue what to say or do with Cassie.

When Cassie's friend drove up, Cassie opened the passenger door of the bright blue Volkswagen bug without a backward glance.

"We'll call you and let you know about Uncle Bobby," Lucas called after her. "If you even care."

His comment caused her to turn slowly around. She blinked her eyes rapidly in the harsh light of the hospital parking lot. "Is he going to die?" Her voice rose on the first word, then faltered on the last.

"I don't know," Lucas said, bluntly. "Keep your cell phone on and answer it every time we call."

"Okay," she said.

Back in Sueann's room, Sueann was relieved when they told her that Julie had picked up Cassie.

"Julie's house is the best place she could be right now," Sueann said. "She's the most sensible of all Cassie's friends. And I'm sure Lynda and Wade will be home all night."

"Is there anything I can do for you?" Ruby asked.

"No, thank you," Sueann said, leaning back against the pillow. "All I want is for Bobby to be all right and Cassie to . . ." She choked on her words. Ely took her hand and squeezed it.

"I'll leave then," Ruby said. "You need to get some rest."

Lucas nodded and dug into his coat pocket for his keys. "My head is killing me. I'm going to go back home and wait to hear about Bobby there. I'll take Ruby back to the lodge."

Ruby drove slowly through the icy streets until they reached the Tokopah. On the street in front of the lodge, the First Night celebration was still going strong.

"What can I do to help?" Ruby asked.

He shook his head. "Nothing. I have medicine at home. It helps a little, but mostly I just have to ride it out, preferably lying down in the dark."

She reached over and lightly touched his cheek. "You'll get through this."

He froze under her touch, causing her to pull her hand back.

"No," he said, stepping closer. "I . . ."

"It's been a long night, Lucas," she said, embarrassed by her spontaneous gesture. What was she thinking? "Call me the minute you hear about Bobby. You have my cell phone, right?"

He nodded, then turned and left without another word. Through the front window, she watched him walk across the frosty lawn, his head bent down. Maybe she should have offered to wait with him over at Birch and Bobby's house. No, she thought, that might not have been smart. She had no idea why she touched him in such an intimate way.

She watched the First Night revelers through the big picture window. The night felt so surreal. To everyone on the street, it was just a normal New Year's Eve. It seemed odd to her that all these people would be laughing, talking and eating when such monumental secrets were unraveling in the McGavin family. And what about Lincoln? How many would care about the gentle man who was a friend to so many, who bravely stood up to grief only to be taken in this unfair way?

It reminded her of her first day back at work after Cole died. She stayed out a week, but the cafe manager had begun calling. The schedule was getting more difficult to fill, would she be back? She worked a double shift that day, lunch and dinner, glad for the activity, but slightly amazed that life went on so normally for everyone else when her own life had changed in such an immense way. Grief and loss were both universal and particular, she learned that moment. It was something she supposed she always knew from the time her mother left, but it took root inside her that day. The truth was, when you were hurting, very few people were affected. She began understanding why people turned to God. At least you had the assurance that maybe there was a bigger picture, some worthwhile reason that you didn't yet know as to why this life-shattering event happened to you rather than someone else. She remembered thinking it would be nice to have the faith that someone, *something*, greater than you, was actually in control of this crazy world. It was something she would have liked to talk about right then. She felt tears roll down her cheeks. The person she'd have liked to discuss it with was Lincoln. Now he knew, she thought. He knew the answers to all the things the rest of them were seeking.

She glanced at the clock above the fireplace. It was only ten-thirty. Not even midnight and so much had happened. The lobby coffeepot was empty so she made a fresh pot, more for something to do than anything else. The cold, lonely room upstairs was the last place she wanted to be right now. She sat with a cup of coffee in an easy chair in front of the fire. Who made this fire tonight? It was usually Bobby's job. A few minutes later a twentysomething young man wearing a pale blue sweater and his black hair in braids came out from the back office and sat behind the front desk. He opened up a book and started reading. One of Bobby's nephews?

Bobby. How was he? Please, she prayed again to this God who Lincoln had talked about with such familiarity. You have Lincoln. Please, let us keep Bobby.

Us, she thought, the minute she made the silent request. When did she start thinking of herself as being part of this community? That was dangerous ground for her to be walking. Now that she knew what really happened on the night Cole killed his father, she had no reason to stay. She had Nash, her own family, to take care of.

She sat by the fire until midnight, when the sound of the crowd behind her grew louder. In the distance, she heard the *rat-tat-tat* of gunshots, causing her to rise and peer out the picture window. The scent of the Christmas tree next to her was sharp and pungent. Outside, under the bright streetlights, she could see people embracing, kissing, throwing confetti in the air. Little children, neon balloons tied to their wrists, jumped up and down and screamed with the hysterical joy of staying up so late. She watched a young father pick up his daughter and swing her up on his shoulders so she could see above the crowd. The girl wore a balloon hat shaped like a crown. It was snowing again. Ruby touched the cold glass, leaving a damp fingerprint. Where would she be next year at this time? She couldn't even begin to imagine.

She turned away from the happy crowd and went back to the easy chair where she watched the flames jump and change color—orange, yellow, blue. She didn't even realize she'd dozed off until she felt a hand gently shaking her shoulder.

"Ruby," Lucas said, his voice a low rumble. "I need your help."

"What time is it?" She bolted up, instantly awake, aware of him standing over her. "What's wrong? Is it Bobby?" Behind them, a group of tired guests murmured, slowly making their way upstairs.

"No, he's still in surgery. I just talked to Birch. It's about twelve-thirty. I need to drive somewhere and my head . . . I still can't see too well."

"I'll drive," she said, without hesitation. She stood up, rubbed her eyes. "Where are we going?" She grabbed her jacket and purse from under the chair where she'd been dozing.

He filled two disposable cups with coffee and snapped on lids. "Black, right?" he said over his shoulder.

"Yes," Ruby said, pulling on her gloves.

Walking to his truck in the street, he told her what he knew. "When Julie took Cassie back to her house, Cassie was there for only a few minutes. Julie's parents were downtown at First Night. Some of Cassie's friends were going to see Hunter and Cassie caught a ride with them. She told Julie she'd be back the next morning before anyone knew she was gone, that she needed to talk to Hunter."

They reached the truck and he opened the driver's side. "Apparently, when Cassie got to Carson City, she discovered that Hunter was checked into the motel all right but . . ."

"But he wasn't alone," Ruby finished, stomping her feet in an attempt to keep warm. It was such an old, tired story.

"Cassie called Julie and was so hysterical that Julie became frightened. She was afraid to call her mom and didn't want to bother Sueann in the hospital, so she called me." He frowned. "Can you believe Cassie told Julie that Hunter was the only one who'd care about what she was feeling?"

"Yes, she's seventeen," Ruby said. "Poor kid, guess she found out how wrong that was." The first time you are deceived in love is always so hard.

She climbed into the driver's seat and waited until he was inside the truck. "Sueann doesn't know?"

"No one knows, but you, me and Julie. I promised I wouldn't snitch on Julie to her mother. I figure we can drive to Carson City, pick up Cassie and be back before Sueann has breakfast. It's about a four and a half hour drive." He handed her the keys.

She adjusted the seat and mirrors, then started the truck, letting the rough-sounding engine warm up. "Do you know where Cassie is?"

"The Lucky Horseshoe Motel just outside Carson City." He closed his eyes and leaned his head back against the seat, his face rigid with pain. "The manager there sounded like a nice woman. She is letting Cassie stay with her until someone can pick her up."

"Does Cassie know we're coming?"

He opened one eye. "She thinks Julie is picking her up."

"Oh," Ruby said, thinking, this will be fun. She gave an involuntary shiver.

Lucas turned the heat on high. Cold air blew on her feet.

"Maybe we should take my car," she said.

"It'll warm up soon. We might need the snow tires on the truck. We don't know what kind of weather we'll hit going up 395." He gestured at her to pull out onto the icy, almost empty street. He looked down at the dashboard where a clock read twelve forty-five.

She concentrated on the slick highway, gripping the cold steering wheel as if it were a life preserver. It was black as coal water outside, especially once they started up the mountain. There were a surprising number of cars on the road, their headlights flickering in the darkness. Then again, it was New Year's Eve. Or, actually, New Year's Day. The start of a new year. This was certainly not the way Ruby had expected to start this year.

Lucas turned the radio to a weather channel, which predicted snow flurries through midday. It was falling fast and thick, the road slushy and every once in a while they'd hit a slippery patch and slide a little.

"Easy now," Lucas said as if she were one of his horses. "Easy."

She smiled, keeping her eyes on the road. "If I were a more sensitive woman, I'd take offense at that."

"What?"

She glanced at him. "It's what you say to your horses."

"I do?" His face turned red. "I'm sorry, I didn't mean anything derogatory by it."

"I know."

She stole another glance at his profile. His expression was a combination of worry and fatigue. His cheeks were dusky with a day's stubble, giving him a slightly sinister look. It was strange, but the longer she knew Lucas, the less he reminded her of Cole. It seemed to her it should be the other way around.

The truck eventually warmed up and, despite her fear at driving in these weather conditions, she felt herself start to drift off. She hated disturbing him, but also didn't want to kill them. She reached over and shook his knee. "Lucas, I'm falling asleep. Talk to me. Tell me about what it was like growing up in Cardinal."

His eyes popped open and he sat up in the seat. "You mean, what was Cole like as a kid?"

"No, tell me what it was like for you."

She could sense more than see his hesitation. Had no one ever asked him that question before?

"My life was different from Cole's."

"How?" she asked.

"I was a shy kid, not very macho. Hated hunting, didn't even really like fishing, though I would do it. Didn't mind working cattle, but found roping and branding them unnecessary when there are easier and less traumatic ways to accomplish the same task. Needless to say, my father did not take to my personality traits very kindly. And my mother *always* agreed with my father."

"Being the youngest, is it difficult?" It made her think of Nash and she wondered what he was doing right this minute.

"I used to watch Cole and Derek bumming around school, girls flocking around them like magpies, at the football games, at dances, at the Dairy Queen. I remember them competing at steer wrestling at the Cardinal County Fair rodeo, and both lettered in football and baseball."

"Hard acts to follow," she said sympathetically.

He shrugged. "It was just the way it was."

"It didn't bother you?"

"Not particularly." He turned his head to look out the side window.

She didn't buy that. "It would be natural to be jealous."

He leaned his head back on the seat and closed his eyes. Did that mean he didn't want to talk anymore? They were alone on the twisting road now. Ruby felt almost disembodied, like they were in a swirling cloud or a gentle purgatory.

They didn't talk for a long time. Ruby's mind kept drifting from person to person and she pictured their faces—Cole, Sueann, Bobby, Birch, Ely, Lucas, Cassie, Lincoln. For each of them she wished and hoped for better times to come. *Please,* she asked, not quite sure to whom she was speaking. It was a sort of prayer, she supposed. Maybe it was time for her to start thinking about things like that, start thinking about exactly what she believed about God. She could imagine Lincoln's genuinely happy smile if she'd told him that.

The snow began falling faster, thicker. She was having trouble maneuvering the truck on the narrow highway.

"My head is clearer now," Lucas said, rubbing his knuckles across his cheek. "Let me take over the driving. I'm used to this weather."

She gladly switched places with him, feeling her own head start to ache with the strain of keeping the truck on the road.

They settled back into silence and Ruby felt herself start to drift off again. When her temple touched the cold glass window, she jolted awake.

"Sorry," she said. "I should stay awake."

His face was lit by the lights on the dashboard, giving a craggy vulnerability to his features. "Take a little nap, if you like. I'll get us to Carson City in one piece."

"I'll be fine." She picked up her cup of coffee, took a sip and made a face. "Cold."

"It's caffeine," he said.

"Yes, it is." She drained the cup and willed her eyes to stay open. "So, when did you leave Cardinal?"

He flexed his fingers on the steering wheel. "I went to college at Berkeley right after high school. I went to law school. Then I worked as a not-very-good defense attorney."

He'd sidestepped the subject before, but she wanted to know what it was that brought him back to Cardinal, what made him switch from carrying a briefcase to carving flowers on a rich man's saddle. "Why do you say you weren't a very good attorney?"

He shifted the truck into low gear and turned on the brights. He hesitated a moment, then started talking. She had to strain to hear over the truck's engine.

"My mother had the money to hire a stable of lawyers to defend Cole, but she didn't. I see now that Cole probably wouldn't let her. Still, I felt then he'd been cheated of a fair trial. So, when I decided to study law, I became particularly fascinated by the defense rather than the prosecution. Liked the idea of being an advocate to those who didn't have one. Doesn't take a brilliant psychiatrist to see my motivations. At the time, prosecutors seemed like the bad guys to me. They were the ones who offered Cole the deal."

"Do you think it happened like Derek said it did?" This was the first time she and Lucas had spoken of what Derek revealed in the hospital room.

They'd reached a stretch of road where they hadn't passed a car for ten or fifteen minutes. If they broke down would their cell phones work?

Lucas shifted his weight, settling deeper into the seat. "He'd have no reason to lie. I think in that split second, Cole just lost control. Who knows, maybe it was all those years of having to be perfect, the town's crown jewel, the golden boy, that finally made him crack. And he had this innate morality, you know? Some people have to struggle to be good. It just came natural to him. So I'm not surprised his way of cracking would be something he did because he thought he was defending those who couldn't defend themselves." He took one hand off the steering wheel and ran it over his face. "And who knows? Maybe he did save countless girls from going through what Sueann did. Maybe what he did was a moral act of some kind."

Ruby didn't know what to say to that. She hadn't thought long enough about what Cole did, how or if it changed the way she felt about him. There was plenty of time to do that for the rest of her life.

"So that explains why you became a lawyer. Why did you leave?"

In the pale glow from the dashboard lights she could see his lips straighten. "Because I didn't deserve to be a lawyer. Not after what I did."

Once he started, the words rushed out like rocks tumbling down a hillside. "Her words haunt me at night when I can't sleep. I sometimes see her face in my dreams."

"Who?" Ruby said softly.

"Madeline Weeks." He shifted the truck back into first gear. They were on a more level road now and the snow had stopped falling. "It was another routine domestic battery case. Mitchell Weeks was a regular-looking guy. An insurance salesman who sometimes drank too much and occasionally slapped his wife around. When he went too far one night and broke her nose, their seven-year-old daughter called nine-one-one. The police officer talked Mrs. Weeks into filing charges. Mr. Weeks's file was dropped off on my desk along with two other similar cases. I'd just pleaded out three other cases that month that were almost duplicates of his."

He moved his head from side to side, remembering. "This guy was actually easier than the others. I didn't have to clean him up, finagle some nice clothes for him, tell him to lose the attitude in front of the judge. He just seemed like a nice guy who lost his cool one time."

"Like Cole?"

"No," he said vehemently. "*Not* like Cole." He shifted into a lower gear as they went up a hill. "What a cocky, naive son-of-a-gun I was. Out to save the world. Going to be the kind of defense attorney that Cole didn't have."

"You were young," Ruby said. "Idealism is allowed when you're young."

"Arguing bail for Mr. Weeks was a snap, though the prosecuting attorney tried to convince the judge that he was a threat to his wife. It was just the game attorneys played. Each of us had our part. Mrs. Weeks tried to talk to me outside the courtroom. She asked me to reconsider, that she was afraid of her husband." His face contorted in memory. "I told her that she shouldn't be talking to me, that I was her husband's attorney. I told her that it was the judge's decision, not mine. When she tried to plead with me, I . . ." He stopped, then after a few seconds, forced himself to finish the sentence. "I pushed her aside."

He looked over at Ruby, his shame like a physical essence in the cab. "I did feel some sympathy for her, but I'd seen too many cases like hers through the years. Odds were she'd drop the charges, take the jerk back and waste everyone's time."

He turned his eyes back to the road. The sign for Carson City limits flashed by on their right. "Two days later a deputy district attorney stormed into my office and slapped four eight-by-ten photographs on my desk, one by one. She didn't say a word. They were of Mrs. Weeks and her three children. Mitchell Weeks shot them all in the head."

"Oh, Lucas," Ruby said. "I'm so sorry."

"That afternoon I went back to my apartment, finished a half bottle of cognac and passed out. The next day I turned in my resignation. I lived off my savings while waiting for his trial. I felt like I had to watch every moment, hear every detail, see him get sentenced. I guess it was a sort of penance. Once it was over and he received life without parole, I went across the street and drank until the bartender poured me into a cab. The next day I loaded up this truck with the few possessions I had left after my divorce and drove back to Cardinal. I apprenticed under a local saddlemaker, the same guy who taught Cole. I rented the space for the saddle shop with the last of my savings, got Cole's tools out of Aunt Birch's attic and started my business."

He pulled into a no-name gas station–mini-mart and switched off the ignition. Dawn was still an hour away, but there was a dusky-pink hint of morning in the darkness. "We need gas and I need some more coffee. Would you like some?"

Before he opened the door, she put a hand on his forearm. "Lucas, everyone makes mistakes."

"There's no excuse for what I did. I should have helped her." He looked angry, like he wanted to hit something.

She wished she could somehow convince this good man to not torture himself over something he probably couldn't have prevented. "I'm sorry you've had to see so much of the bad side of human nature. I've dated cops, so I've heard the stories. You just get tired. You stop believing in the goodness of people and then you make a mistake. That's all I'm trying to say. You're human, Lucas. Just like Cole was."

"Cole would have helped her." He leaned his forehead against the steering wheel. "I wanted to tell Cole. Somehow, I thought if I told him, I'd feel better."

"No," she said. "You wouldn't have. But he would have still loved you. That wouldn't change."

"I know." He sat up straight, his voice tired. He got out of the truck before she could say anything else.

He filled both gas tanks and after verifying with the mini-mart clerk the motel manager's directions to Lucky's Horseshoe Motel, they drove through the sleepy streets of Carson City. Unlike Reno, which was probably still lively with New Year's revelers, Carson City's celebrations were over. It was almost five a.m. and the first day of the new year. They pulled in front of the old fifties motel, the parking lot crowded with cars. They rang the office bell and stood on the small, concrete step, stomping their feet to keep warm. In a few minutes, a lady who looked to be in her eighties came to the glass door and pointed to the Closed sign.

"We're here for Cassie," Lucas called through the door.

The lady, dressed in a bright green and gold Oriental housecoat, her orange hair up in sponge curlers, smiled and nodded her head. She quickly unlatched the door and waved them in.

"Come in, come in. She's on my sofa fast asleep, poor little lamb. She's had quite a night, she has." The woman's whispered voice was rough as a corn cob with a hint of an Irish accent. An aroma of corned beef and talcum powder enveloped Ruby and Lucas when they walked into the foyer.

"Is she okay?" Ruby asked, trying to see around the woman through the office door that lead to her living quarters.

"She's fine," the woman said, holding out a red-nailed hand. "I'm Ruby."

Startled, Ruby stared at her a minute, then looked at Lucas and laughed. He grinned back at her.

"What?" the old Ruby said, a frown deepening her wrinkled face.

"I'm sorry," Ruby said, taking the woman's hand. It was as cold as chipped ice. "We don't mean to be rude. It's just that my name is Ruby, too."

The woman's face stretched into a smile. "I don't meet many other Rubys." She lowered her voice, as if telling a secret. "My real name's Rubella, like the disease."

"Oh, my," Ruby said. "I'm just Ruby."

"She's in here, just Ruby," the old woman said, crooking her finger.

They followed her into a living room so full of china knickknacks that it had to be some sort of obsessive-compulsive disorder. Upon closer inspection, Ruby noticed they were all monkey and giraffe figurines.

"She's exhausted," the old Ruby said. She pointed at an over-stuffed, orange corduroy sectional sofa where at one end lay a sleeping Cassie, covered up to her chin by a red, white and blue flag motif afghan. She looked twelve years old. Ruby hated waking her, but they needed to get back to Cardinal.

"Cassie, honey," old Ruby said, taking it upon herself to awaken her.

"What?" Cassie said, her voice cranky. Then she bolted up, suddenly remembering where she was. "Where am I . . . Who . . . ?" Then she saw Ruby. "What are you doing here? Julie was supposed to pick me up."

"I came with your uncle." Ruby pointed at him.

Lucas walked up to Cassie, his hands in his jacket pockets. "Hey, kiddo."

She sat up, clutching the afghan around her like a child. Her black and green eye makeup stained her cheeks like pop-art bruises. Tears turned her eyes shiny. "Hunter is a jerk and I'm a freak."

"Oh, sweetheart," he said, sitting down next to her. She put her head against his shoulder and started sobbing. "You're not a freak."

"Let me make some tea," the old Ruby said, shaking her orange hair, causing one sponge roller to drop on the ground. An overweight calico cat came from under the sofa and started batting at it. "Scooter, leave that be."

Cassie's voice was muffled against Lucas's flannel shirt. "Yeah, right. My dad is not really my dad, he's, like, my half-brother and my grandfather is really my father, which totally confuses me about who June is. It's so perve I want to die. It sounds like some kind of creepy TV movie."

"Look," Lucas said. "I'm not going to bullshit you. It is strange. Shoot, the whole McGavin clan is certifiable. But, we're the only family you have and we love you. We can figure this out, Cassie. You, me, your mom, your dad . . ."

"My dad is dead," she said flatly.

Lucas hugged her. "No matter how irritating Derek can be, he's tried to be a good dad. This hasn't been easy for him either. Derek was just trying to do the right thing, to *be* a good son. And Cole . . ."

Ruby held her breath. Don't, she wanted to cry.

"Your uncle Cole did his best under horrible circumstances," Lucas said, his voice gentle.

"A lot of good that did him. He still ended up killing himself," Cassie whispered.

"Yes, he did."

She thought for a moment. "I think I understand why. Sometimes, you just feel so bad that seems like the only good idea there is." She inhaled, a deep shudder rattling through her body.

"I don't know if anyone can truly understand what another person is going through," Lucas said, "but we can come close. You and I have talked about that, about how really good books can make you feel things, *get* things, you never thought possible."

Cassie's eyes filled with tears. She made a fist and rubbed one eye like a little girl. "Uncle Lucas, I can't go back to that town, have people find out who my father really is, who *I* am."

"Who you are, Cassandra McGavin, is a wonderful girl who is loved by a whole lot of people. You're smart and young and have your whole life ahead of you."

"I'm the product of a rape," she said bitterly. "My grandfather . . ." She made a face. "My *father,* was a pervert."

"So what?" he said so bluntly it startled Cassie and Ruby both. "You have the choice to let the circumstances of your birth screw you up or you can take what you've been given and do something with it."

"I can't." Cassie clutched the afghan to her cheek.

"Yes, you can. Your mother needs you and you are grown up enough now to step up to the plate."

"People will laugh at me. They'll be disgusted."

Lucas's face hardened. "Then screw 'em. Be like Nancy Sinatra, wipe them off the bottom of your boots and keep walking."

"Nancy who?" Cassie's face looked genuinely confused.

A small smile tugged at Lucas's lips. He glanced over at Ruby.

"Hey, Gramps," Ruby said, smiling. "What can I say? We're getting old."

Lucas grabbed Cassie's bare foot sticking out from under the afghan and shook it. "We gotta go, Cassie. I know this has been a bad night for you, but it's a long drive home. And, frankly, the sooner we see Carson City in our rearview mirror, the better I'll feel."

"Who wants tea?" the old Ruby called out, carrying in a tray of cups, tea bags and a beautiful blue and white teapot.

"That sounds good," Lucas said. He turned to Cassie. "Why don't you wash your face and have some tea while I call and see how Bobby is doing?"

While Lucas called the hospital in Reno, trying to track down Birch, they drank peppermint tea and nibbled on the Oreo cookies the old Ruby served on a platter covered with purple monkeys.

"What about Lincoln?" Cassie asked, picking up a cookie and opening it to lick the white frosting. "No one told me what happened to Lincoln."

Ruby looked down into her half-empty tea cup. "I'm sorry, Cassie. He didn't make it."

A small "Oh" escaped from Cassie. "He was, like, the nicest guy," Cassie said, setting her cookie down, her face crestfallen. "He used to give me free mochas. He was just good, you know? That's so cracked, him dying."

Yes, Ruby thought. Cracked describes it perfectly. It made her think of broken pottery, dropped mirrors, trucks that ran off the road on desolate highways leaving people who loved them behind. This whole darn world was just so cracked.

"Is my mom okay?" Cassie asked. "I feel like such a jerk running out of there without asking."

"Physically, she's going to be fine," Ruby said. "And, I'm guessing, now that all of this is out in the open, maybe things will start to heal."

"Is she really okay?" Cassie asked. "Because I'm not a baby, you know. I can handle it if she isn't."

"I wouldn't lie to you about that," Ruby said.

Cassie gave a half-smile. "So, what would you lie to me about?"

Ruby couldn't help smiling back. There were times Cassie sounded so much like Sueann. "Maybe your blue hair. I really prefer this new maroon shade to your old toilet-bowl azure."

Cassie picked up her cookie and popped it in her mouth. "Sometimes you are just too funny, Ruby."

"Have some more tea," the old Ruby said. "It's a long way back to Cardinal."

"That sounds like the name of a song," Cassie said.

Ruby cocked her head. "Or a book."

"It's a long road to Tipperary," the old Ruby sang.

"Where's Tipper-whatever?" Cassie asked.

"A place in Ireland," Ruby said.

Lucas walked back into the room, a huge smile on his face. "Bobby's out of surgery and they're pretty sure he's going to be fine. There'll be some physical therapy and he'll be sore inside for a while, but he's going to be okay."

"That's wonderful news," Ruby said, standing up. "How far away are we from the hospital in Reno? Should we go see if Birch needs us?"

"It's probably another hour. I talked to Birch. She has plenty of support. Bobby's three nephews, two nieces and their families are all at the hospital. A lot of Bobby's family lives in the Reno area. She said that we should go home. Cassie needs to see her mama." He looked over at Cassie. "Birch sends her love and says she'll see you soon." He stuck his cell phone in the front pocket of his jeans. "So, finish up your tea, ladies, and we'll get going. It's a long way back to Cardinal."

"Not to mention Temporary, Ireland," Cassie said.

Ruby and old Ruby burst into laughter.

"What's so funny?" he asked.

LUCAS

"We don't have to do this today," Lucas said to Ruby. It was Tuesday morning, the fourth day after the accident, and they were in his saddle shop, waiting to walk over to the office of Wagner and Smith, attorneys at law. Though Ruby could sign the papers without June being there, his mother insisted she would meet them there at one p.m. "I can call my mom and tell her you aren't ready yet."

He figured the longer they put it off, the longer Ruby would stay in town. The thought of her leaving Cardinal left a hollowness inside him that he suspected had part to do with the feeling of losing Cole again and part to do with other feelings he didn't want to think too deeply about right now.

"We've already postponed it one day. I want to get this legal stuff out of the way," Ruby said. "The sooner your mother knows I'm not taking part of the Circle MG, the sooner she can feel at peace. I have no desire to make her suffer."

"Trust me, she wouldn't do the same for you," Lucas couldn't help saying.

She touched the fender of Cole's saddle, running her hand over the intricate carving. "I brought Cole home. That was the only thing I intended to so. Still, I can't help but think, if he'd only told me about all this, I could have helped him through it."

"Cole had a hard time asking for help," Lucas said, picking up a skinning knife, touching the blade with his fingertip. It needed sharpening. "All McGavins do."

Ruby rested her hand on the saddle's unused seat. "Maybe that's some of the attraction Cole and I had for each other. I wonder if we really knew each other at all, if what we had was just a big charade."

"Not a charade," Lucas said, setting down the knife. "I think it was what it was. Two people who loved each other at a certain time of their lives."

She took her hand off the saddle and touched the front of her neck. "And now that time is over." She turned to look at him. "I talked to Nash last night."

"How's he doing?"

"Not good. I finally pried out of him what was wrong." Her eyes closed for a moment, then opened again. The tremble in her voice was audible. "He went to a free clinic and they did a test. He has hepatitis C."

"Oh, man, Ruby, I'm sorry," Lucas said. "Is there anything I can do?"

She shook her head. "I just need to wrap things up here and get to Nashville as soon as I can."

"Have you talked to your father?"

"I left him three messages. He finally called back this morning. He and Prissy are in North Dakota. They have jobs lined up for the next three months. He says he can't really afford to take the time to go to Nashville."

Lucas could tell by her expression that she was disappointed.

"I'm sorry," Lucas said, going over to her. "Is there someone who can help him until you get there?"

Her expression softened. "He actually has a girlfriend who sounds responsible." She gave a wry smile. "A first for him. Anyway, he's staying with her and she's an LVN, so he'll be okay until I get there. I want to stay for Lincoln's funeral tomorrow and Cole's on Wednesday. Have you talked to Birch?"

Lucas went over to the coat rack and grabbed her jacket. "This morning. She says Bobby's making amazing progress, but he probably won't be released for at least two more week. A friend of mine is flying her here for Lincoln's funeral and Cole's memorial service. Then he'll take her back to Reno."

"I'm glad I'll get to see Birch again, be able to say good-bye. But I'm sorry I'll miss Bobby's homecoming. I'll probably leave right after Cole's service on Wednesday."

He helped her on with her jacket. "You should fly back to Nashville. It would be faster."

They stepped outside into the bright afternoon. The temperature had risen today to the low fifties, melting most of the snow. It felt good on his face and in his soul. Spring would be here in a few months. He was more than ready for it.

"Yes, it would be faster," she said, stepping carefully on the wet pavement. "But it's also more expensive. I don't know what treatment Nash is going to need so I need to conserve my money. He doesn't have health insurance."

He cupped her elbow with his hand when they crossed the street. A warm scent of oranges came from her and he felt a physical longing as strong as a teenage boy's. "I've arranged for you to receive some money for your part of the land. It's only twenty thousand dollars because the ranch doesn't have a lot of liquid assets, but . . ."

"That's a lot of money!" she exclaimed, pulling herself from his grasp and gaping at him. "I told you I didn't want to profit from Cole's death."

He held up his hand for her to stop. "Ruby, it was Cole's last wish for you to be taken care of properly. That's why he left you his part of the ranch. I can understand why you wouldn't want to be affiliated in any way with the McGavins, but you need this money, for your brother and for yourself. And, to be blunt, I don't think it's right for you to ignore Cole's last wishes."

He could see her eyes tear up. "You're right."

He held her gaze. "No matter how it ended, Ruby, I know my brother was happy that last year. He told me he was. Whatever happened to him that last day, I know it had nothing to do with how he felt about you."

She didn't answer for a moment, then whispered, "Thank you, Lucas."

Lucas glanced at his watch. "We should get going. Mom despises tardiness."

While they walked the three blocks to the lawyer's office, she said, "I'm so glad Clear Creek will be okay."

They had driven out there yesterday morning with Cassie to feed the horses. Ruby and Lucas had sat on the wooden fence and softly cheered when Cassie finally convinced Greta to take a chunk of apple from her hand. It had made all three of them laugh, lightened their hearts just a little.

For Lucas, it had been a perfect day, cold and clear, the sky such a deep blue that the beauty of it hurt your eyes if you stared at it too long. The Sierra Nevada peaks were frosted a brilliant white, like cream cheese frosting, and looked close enough to dip a finger in and taste. On days like this he never regretted moving back home.

He turned to Ruby. "Derek and I have agreed to sell part of the ranch to cover my mother's debts and pay off her loans to Walt Creston and the bank."

"Not Clear Creek?" Ruby had asked.

"No, we have another section that is actually closer to the Mammoth airport. No creek, but it's has some beautiful views. It's good grazing land so it's a shame that condos will be built over it, but it's a compromise. Clear Creek is saved for now."

She'd turned to look at him, her dark hair blowing in the cold breeze. He'd caught a whiff of her perfume, a light, citrusy scent. It seemed out of place here in this sage and grass-scented pasture.

"But not forever," she'd said, grabbing a handful of hair and holding it away from her face.

He'd shrugged and turned his eyes back to Cassie who was crooning softly to Greta and stroking her neck. "No storybook ending. Just another compromise. Cardinal history . . . shoot, Western history, is full of them. I've learned the only thing we can do with any real certainty is enjoy what we have today."

Inside the lawyer's office, June gave Lucas a cursory nod and completely ignored Ruby. To June, this was all business, as if this were merely the ownership transfer of a car or a horse. Lucas felt like shaking his mother.

Ruby signed in every place the Will Wagner Sr. pointed to, without making eye contact with anyone. Lucas could tell she wanted to get out of this stuffy office and away from June as quickly as she could.

"That should do it," Will Sr. said, after the last paper was signed.

"Here's your check, Mrs. McGavin." He pushed a cream-colored envelope across his wide shiny desk.

Lucas took a secret pleasure in watching his mother flinch when Ruby was called by her legal name.

Ruby hesitated before reaching for the envelope. Lucas could tell she was having second thoughts.

He leaned close to her ear and whispered, "Nash needs it, Ruby."

Her expression tightened and she nodded. In seconds, the envelope was inside her purse.

June stood up and straightened her black silky jacket. "That's that. I'll see you at the memorial service tomorrow, Lucas."

"Yes, Mom," he said wearily. "And Ruby too."

She glanced over at Ruby, who stood tall and looked her husband's mother straight in the eyes. "Yes, of course." She left the office without saying good-bye to either of them.

"I'm glad that's over," Lucas said, walking back out in the sunshine.

"Me, too," Ruby said.

They passed by Cardinal Valley Travel Agency and he grabbed her arm to stop her. "You could buy your ticket now."

"Oh, Lucas, you weren't serious, were you?" She laughed, a low, easy kind of laugh that Lucas had heard only once before. This was, he was certain, the laugh his brother heard when she came out from the kitchen to meet the man who loved her special French toast. This was the laugh his brother fell in love with. Lucas was absolutely certain that, before the despair and guilt swallowed him, his brother had moments of pure joy, listening to this woman's laugh.

"I'm completely serious," he said, pulling her toward the door. "You want to get back there quickly, don't you? You have plenty of money now."

"In case you've forgotten, I also have a car. A car full of my worldly goods."

He let go of her arm. "I could drive it back for you."

"What?"

"It won't take me long. I don't need much sleep and Motel Six does me fine. I can fly home afterward." He didn't say how long afterward. He intended on staying long enough to convince her to come back to Cardinal, maybe bring her brother with her. It was crazy, but he couldn't just let her disappear. Birch was going to be proud as punch and his mother would want to kill him.

She laughed again. "Lucas, are you insane? You have a business here. You have saddles to make."

"Build," he said.

"What?"

"Build. You build saddles, not make them."

She shook her head, her face looking, he thought, a little relieved. "You're nuts."

"I'm a McGavin."

"I can't let you do this."

He smiled at her and opened the door to the travel agency. "Actually, you can't do a thing to stop me."

RUBY

She had no idea how many people's lives Lincoln Holyoke touched until his funeral the next day. It was held in the high school gymnasium because none of the town's churches were big enough to hold the number of people who wanted to attend.

"I hear they printed five hundred programs and they've run out," Lucas said. He caught sight of Ely waving at them to join him and Cassie in the third row of folded chairs.

"Hey, Cassie," Ruby said, giving the girl a hug. "How are you doing?"

"I'm fine," she said. "Hunter tried to call me last night and make up. I hung up on him. What a creep. Like I'd want him now. I am so over him. Isn't it awesome how many people have come for Lincoln's funeral?"

"He was loved by a lot of people," Ruby said. "I didn't know him long, but he touched me too." She looked at the front row, a place usually reserved for family. It was filled with some of the people she'd seen in the coffeehouse.

"His family sent flowers," Ely said, pointing over to a large standing spray of white roses. "When they learned he requested to be buried here in Cardinal next to his wife, they all found excuses not to attend."

"That is so sad," Ruby said.

"Ely's his executor," Cassie said. "That's, like, the person who's in charge of all his stuff."

The service was short, as per Lincoln's request. The minister of Cardinal Valley First Baptist, a good friend of Lincoln's, told the story of Lincoln's life, then gave a quick explanation of who Jesus was and what he meant to Lincoln. He ended with a quote from one of Lincoln's favorite philosophers.

"Blaise Pascal said, 'In faith there is enough light for those who want to believe, and enough shadow to blind those who don't.' What we know for sure about Lincoln Holyoke is that he believed, and that now he is with his Savior and in shadow no longer.' "

Afterward, Ely opened Holy Grounds and served free coffee and food until he was completely out of everything. Ruby pitched in and helped Ely, Lucas and Cassie serve Lincoln's friends.

At eight p.m. they closed the doors and started cleaning up.

"What's going to happen to this place now?" Ruby asked, wiping down the slick counter.

Ely looked a little embarrassed. "Well, he left it to me. I guess I'll keep it open if I can find someone to run it."

"How about me?" Cassie piped up, carrying a plastic tub of dirty cups and plates to the back where Lucas and Lincoln's two dishwashers were cleaning the kitchen.

"Maybe after you're out of college, grasshopper," Ely said. "Besides, for the next few months, your mama's really going to need your help at the cafe."

"How's Sueann doing today?" Ruby asked. "I meant to call her this morning, but I got busy packing and then it was time for Lincoln's service."

"She's coming home tomorrow," Ely said. "But she'll be off her feet for another six weeks. Carlos's sister and sister-in-law are working at the cafe, so it should be okay. It's driving Sueann crazy, though. She hates to lay around and do nothing."

"Frankly," Ruby said. "A few weeks with nothing to do but read or watch television sounds pretty good to me."

"So," he said, pushing chairs underneath tables. "When do you leave?"

"Thursday morning. Lucas is driving us to Los Angeles and I'll catch a late flight to Nashville."

"I've check your car over again. It should make the trip fine, but it is old and you can never tell. I'm glad Lucas is driving it back, not you. A woman driving that far alone is a frightening thing these days."

Ruby gave him a shy smile. It was nice to have people concerned about her welfare. Lincoln was right, this town did have a way of growing tentacles around your heart. "I can't thank you enough. You all have been so kind."

"Hope you'll come back and see us sometime," he said, picking up a stray napkin off the floor. "I'd like that and I'd venture to say some other people would too."

"I don't know," Ruby said. "It's . . . hard."

He tossed the paper napkin in the trash and flipped the open sign in the window around. "Life is hard, Ruby. But it's easier when you live it around people who care about you. Lincoln taught me that. He told me that if I wanted people to care, I had to stay in one spot long enough for them to get to know me."

"And it was Cole who told Lincoln to stay in Cardinal to live."

"See," Ely said, holding up a palm. "It's all connected. Somehow, I think Cardinal hasn't seen the last of Ruby McGavin."

She laughed. "You never know."

"Just remember, if you decide to come back home to Cardinal, you have a job here at Holy Grounds."

Back home to Cardinal. For some reason, those words made her want to cry.

"I'll keep that in mind," she said and started wiping off another table.

35

BIRCH

On Wednesday, before the family arrived at Cole's private memorial service at the Cardinal Cemetery, Birch came early to put yellow tulips on Emily Robertina's grave. Lucas's friend had picked her up early this morning in Reno and they'd flown through thick, pillowy clouds tinted pink by the morning sun. Normally, she would have been afraid of the bumps and jolts of the small Cessna, but ever since the accident, she'd been so thankful that God had spared Bobby, that nothing scared her.

From where she stood right now, she could see the McGavin section in the middle of old windswept cemetery. She knew the names and dates on the elaborately carved gravestones by heart—her mother and father, her grandparents, her great-grandparents, her brother, a great-aunt who'd died in infancy. She stared at the section, next to the biggest oak tree in the cemetery, the place where she and Robert would not be buried. When Emily Robertina died, they'd bought two plots here on both sides of their daughter. Her little headstone looked so lonely.

"Thank you," she prayed when she laid the yellow tulips on Emily Robertina's grave. She bent down and brushed off the dead winter grass. "Thank you, Father, for Emily and for the years I had with Cole.

Take care of them until I get there. Tell them I miss them. Say hello to Lincoln for me. I bet he's already organized a potluck." She kissed her fingertips and touched the top of Emily's tiny gravestone. "And thank you for letting me keep Bobby for a little longer."

When she stood up, she saw June's black Cadillac enter the cemetery gates. It was still an hour before the service. Birch couldn't imagine why June would come early. She watched her step out of her car and walk slowly over to the McGavin section, her head down. In her hand she carried a white rose. She walked over to her husband's tall, granite headstone and laid the flower on top. She stood there for a moment, the cold wind blowing her navy jacket open.

The air was so clear that the sound traveled across the cemetery's dried yellow grass. Birch could hear the soft sound of crying. And the sound of a name. Cole.

Birch walked quickly across the yellowed grass toward her sister-in-law. At that moment, she didn't think about all the years of problems between them; she only heard the mourning of another mother who'd lost her child. The sound of her feet on the dry grass and old pine needles caused June to turn around, her face soaked with grief.

"He loved you," Birch said, her arms coming up to embrace June.

June stared at Birch, her painted mouth slightly open. "Go away," she said, her voice hoarse and angry.

Birch stood for a moment, shocked. What had she expected? For June and her to suddenly bond, become friends? Even the death of a child, a *beloved* child, can't, in a split second, change everything that had happened in the past. Birch turned and started walking back toward the cemetery's entrance. She would wait in her car until the rest of the family arrived.

"You," June called out. "It was always you he loved best. You stole that from me when he was a baby."

Birch turned slowly around. "No," she said, her voice surprising in its calmness. "I didn't steal his love, June. You gave it away. And, no matter how he felt about me, you were always his mother. You were always the one, deep in his heart, he wanted to please. He did it all for you, June. All to please you."

She turned around and walked toward her car, ignoring her sister-in-law's sobs. For the first time since she'd met the thin, pretty girl from Bakersfield who her brother had brought home to marry, she wasn't envious.

She was waiting at the cemetery entrance when the others arrived, Sueann and Cassie, Derek, Ely. Derek helped Sueann out of the car, holding her crutches for her as she got herself situated. The truth about Carson's death had changed something in Derek. He seemed calmer, less angry. Though she knew that he and Sueann would never get back together—Sueann had stated that without any room for doubt—it was obvious that they'd come to an understanding, a willingness to coexist peacefully. That would only make things easier for Cassie.

Lucas and Ruby were the last to arrive. Ruby, clad in a simple navy dress and low-heeled pumps stepped out of Lucas's truck, carefully holding the wooden box containing Cole's ashes. She lay her cheek on the smooth top for a moment, before handing it to Lucas. Birch knew the grief that girl held inside her and she wished she could take some of it from her. But, there was nothing she could do except walk over and hold out her arms.

Without hesitation, Ruby walked straight into them and they stood there for a moment, arms around each other like they had that night in the lodge, the two women who'd loved Cole the most.

The ceremony was short and no one spoke other than the minister, who gave the same funeral sermon Birch had heard too many times in her life.

. . .Jesus said, 'Do not let your hearts be troubled. Trust in God; trust also in me. In my Father's house are many rooms; if it were not so, I would have told you. I am going there to prepare a place for you. And if I go and prepare a place for you, I will come back and take you to be with me that you also may be where I am. You know the way to the place where I am going . . . In this world, you will have much tribulation, but, fear not, I have overcome the world . . . I will not leave you as orphans; I will come to you . . . I am the way, the truth and the light . . . Holy Father, protect them by the power of your name . . .'

While the minister talked, Birch stood on one side of Ruby, Lucas on the other. When Ruby started trembling, Birch put an arm around her shoulders. Ruby leaned into it and Birch felt her heart settle. We were part of her family, Birch thought, though Ruby didn't know it yet. She'd told Birch this morning about leaving this week for Nashville to help her sick brother and to, perhaps, start a new life.

"Of course you must go," Birch said. "Stay as long as you need. But you have to come back. Cardinal is your home."

Ruby had been silent for a long time. Birch wondered if she'd hurt the girl's feelings.

Ruby's voice was hesitant. "I want to believe that."

"Just think on it while you're gone, sweetie," Birch said, reaching over to touch her cheek. "The heart is a funny thing. If you really listen to it, you'll know the right thing to do. I believe that's often how God talks to us, you know. But it takes a special ear to hear."

Ruby gave a gentle, skeptical laugh. "I doubt I have the right ears."

"You do," Birch had said. "Otherwise, you wouldn't have come to Cardinal to begin with."

After Cole's service, they went to the cafe for a special lunch Sueann had her employees prepare. June didn't come, something that made Birch a little sad. Would she ever change? It saddened her to think of her sister-in-law alone at the ranch, grieving by herself.

Derek showed up, looking more relaxed than she'd ever seen him. At her request, he'd gone by the lodge and picked up a dish Birch prepared this morning—ambrosia. It was a sweet fruit and marshmallow creme salad that had been one of Cole's favorite. Birch made it with pecans instead of walnuts, just how Cole had liked it.

"Ambrosia!" Ruby cried when she saw it. "With pecans!" She turned to Birch and laughed. "Cole loved this."

For a moment, Birch almost felt like Cole was there, his spirit hovering over their meal, flowing between them as they told each other all the things they'd loved about him, all the times he'd made them laugh, made them proud.

Lucas leaned over and whispered something in Ruby's ear. Birch watched them, seeing something starting to bloom there that she was not certain they saw yet. She wasn't a bit surprised when Ruby told her he was driving Ruby's car to Nashville.

"It'll be good for him," she said. "Maybe he can convince you to come back to Cardinal. Bring that brother of yours. We'll get him well."

"I'll see," Ruby said, smiling. Birch could see in her face that is was a real possibility. Cardinal had gotten to her, that was a fact.

Ruby stood up at the small table and cleared her throat. "Can I say something?"

The chattering gradually quieted.

"When I came here three weeks ago, I knew that my life would change. I had no idea . . ." She stopped a moment. "I had no idea it would be for the better. I will never forget my time in Cardinal." She touched her chest. "I will always carry you in my heart." She sat down quickly, looking down at her plate, her face blushing a soft pink. Lucas slipped his arm across the back of Ruby's seat, the tips of his fingers grazing her shoulder.

She'll be back, Birch thought. And sooner than she thinks. She settled back into the familiar booth and listened to everyone laugh and talk and tell stories, not even trying to join in, but listening and remembering as much as she could so tomorrow she could tell Bobby every little detail.